PARKER BILAL is the pseudonym of Jamal Mahjoub. *City of Jackals* is his fifth Makana Investigation. Born in London, Mahjoub has passed through Sudan, Egypt, Denmark and Britain, before settling in Barcelona.

CITY OF JACKALS

PARKER BILAL

BLOOMSBURY
LONDON · OXFORD · NEW YORK · NEW DELHI · SYDNEY

Bloomsbury Paperbacks
An imprint of Bloomsbury Publishing Plc

50 Bedford Square   1385 Broadway
London   New York
WC1B 3DP   NY 10018
UK   USA

www.bloomsbury.com

BLOOMSBURY and the Diana logo are trademarks of Bloomsbury Publishing Plc

First published in Great Britain 2016

British Library Cataloguing-in-Publication Data
A catalogue record for this book is available from the British Library.

ISBN: PB: 978-1-4088-6448-7
ePub: 978-1-4088-6449-4

2 4 6 8 10 9 7 5 3 1

Typeset by Integra Software Services Pvt. Ltd.
Printed and bound in Great Britain by CPI Group (UK) Ltd, Croydon CR0 4YY

To find out more about our authors and books visit www.bloomsbury.com.
Here you will find extracts, author interviews, details of forthcoming
events and the option to sign up for our newsletters.

Anubis's heart is happy
over the work of his hands and the heart
of the Lord of the Divine Hall is thrilled
when he beholds this good god,
Master of those that have been and
Ruler over those that are to come.

Coffin Texts no. 197

Prologue

She opens her eyes to find the nightmare is not over. It's still very real. It takes her a moment to recognise the face leaning over her. Her brother seems to have aged a lifetime, no longer the soft young boy she has always known.

'Jonah!'

'Shhh.' He puts out a hand to silence her roughly. She can smell his fear.

The room is close, gloomy and hot, the air thick with the smell of oil and dust. Dark, even though she can hear what sounds like a street in full swing. Daytime, but it's hard to see. The details come back to her slowly, torn fragments floating by like moths in the air. Their dreams so close. It pained her to think of that now, of everything that had lain ahead of them and was now gone. Tears well up inside her chest again and she sucks desperately at the hot air of the sealed room, trying to breathe.

'Where are we?' she repeats, over and over, unable to get beyond this simple question.

Jonah sinks down beside her and puts his arm around her shoulders. They are slumped on the hard floor, their backs to the wall.

'Listen to me,' he says. 'We don't have much time.'

'Why are they keeping us here?'

She can't bring herself to look at him. She knows he has no answers, that for all his bravery he is as scared as she is. Beatrice feels exhausted, too tired to even stand. She feels as though she has been running all her life.

'I'm not going back to that place,' Jonah says. Beatrice starts to sob quietly to herself again. 'I'm not,' he repeats. 'You know what will happen.'

'Then what? What can we do?'

'We must escape from here.'

'But how?'

There is no way out. The room is small. There is one door and no windows. She can hear the sound of a television from somewhere above them, an advertisement for some kind of snack. A silly, childish jingle. It seems to come from another world.

They had almost made it. Then everything seemed to slip away.

'Why did they do it?' The image of Jonah leaning over her came back to her. The fear. The blood on his T-shirt. 'I don't understand,' she cries.

Her brother silences her with a finger to his lips. Now he has his head pressed against the door. She moves closer and they stay like that. Outside there is the sound of a car. The engine stops. A door opens and closes. Voices whisper. She cannot take her eyes away from Jonah.

He is all she has, all she has ever had for as long as she can remember.

This is not the first time they have faced danger together. She still remembers when they were children and the soldiers came. That day their mother took them to the edge of the village and told them to run and never look back. Smoke was already rising in thick black plumes from the huts. An uncle ran towards them, his clothes burning. She saw a soldier step out and shoot him. As easily as if he were a dog. From their hiding place they watched their mother being dragged away by a group of men in uniform. They were grinning and laughing. Jonah wanted to go back and rescue her, but it was Beatrice who knew that would be the last thing they ever did. So they turned and ran and now, after all of this, all these years, they were running again.

Everything had been going so well. It pained her to think that her dreams were over.

Beatrice recalls falling asleep. Something in the drink they had been given. When she woke up it was like waking up inside a nightmare. She thought she was going to die, but then Jonah had saved her, had saved them. He fought. She watched him, too terrified to move. He was strong and fast. He had learned to fight on the streets when he was a child.

Somehow he got them out of there. Then they were running along the road in the dark, through the oncoming cars. She was terrified. Cars beeped their horns, drivers leaned out of their windows and yelled curses. Luckily the cars weren't moving fast. Men shouted insults, called her dirty names. She was aware that she had lost most of her clothes. It was hard to run, her legs seemed to be asleep. So many cars, so hard to know which way to go. They walked for hours, keeping to the sidestreets, away from the light. Jonah said he knew a place, somewhere they would be taken care of. When they came in sight of the square she saw what he meant. The camp. There in the lights on the square, she saw people who would help them. She could have cried.

They almost made it. Then a car came out of nowhere, cutting across their path and knocking Jonah to the ground. He was hurt, bleeding. He tried to get up. Two men jumped out and grabbed him. They kicked him and threw him in the boot of the car. Then they came for her.

Beatrice screamed and called for help. A woman watched from a balcony but then simply turned away and disappeared inside. The men tied her hands and threw her in the back of the car. She could hear Jonah crying in rage from the boot.

She listens at the door, straining to hear the voices. In the distance, the sound of a muezzin calling people to prayer, the lazy honk of car horns, the rumble of traffic. They are in a basement, that much she knows, but why, why are they holding them here? She feels despair wash over her again. Jonah rests a hand on her shoulder. He points upwards towards a small metal hatch set high on the wall.

'It's the only way.'

'But we don't know what's on the other side.'

'Whatever it is, it's better than dying in here.'

Beatrice shakes her head. 'It's hopeless. We can never reach that.'

'If you get onto my shoulders you can reach it.'

'Then what? How do you get up?'

Jonah doesn't answer. He places his hands flat against the wall and she climbs up onto his shoulders. It's not easy – she is weak from the ordeal, lack of sustenance, fear. The sound of voices draws close, silencing them. Two men. A third behind them, an older man. When someone rattles the padlock Beatrice gives a shriek. There's a moment's silence. One of them thumps the door with something heavy, followed by laughter.

'Can you reach it?'

They can hear the screech of metal being dragged along the doorframe very slowly.

'I can't reach it.'

'Yes, you can. You can do it,' Jonah urges.

5

She stretches up slowly, her fingertips scraping over the cement. At full stretch she can only reach it with the tips of her fingers. The bolt is old and rusty. She struggles to pull it back.

'I can't do it.'

'You must. It's our only chance.' She feels him trembling beneath her and knows that he can't hold her up for much longer. With a grunt, she tries again, ignoring the pain in her fingertips. Finally, with all that remains of her strength she manages. The bolt flies loose and the metal hatch swings open. Taking hold, she pulls herself up until the floor inside the hatch is level with her eyes.

'What can you see?'

'A room. Very dark, but I can feel the wind. I think we can get out.'

'Then go.'

'No,' Beatrice cries. She feels herself grow weak and slides back down, almost falling. 'I'm not leaving you.'

'You have to go. I can't hold you for much longer.'

So finally she launches herself upwards, grasping the edge and pulling herself into the narrow space. She rolls over, reaches down for his hand.

'Now you.'

The door flies open with a crash. The two men stand in the doorway. One of them holds an axe. There is another, older man behind them.

'Jonah!' she screams.

'Go,' he shouts. 'Run.'

She rolls away and crawls through the narrow space, feeling her way with her hands. All around her is blackness. Ahead of her she can feel air. There is a way out. She just has to believe she will find it.

Chapter One

Makana's body ached as if he was coming down with a fever. He hadn't slept well, in fact he'd spent most of the night sitting in the big wooden chair on the upper deck watching for the sky to grow light.

It was December. The end of the year was just over a week away, but this winter seemed harder than any he could remember, which made him wonder if time was beginning to take its toll. Perhaps he was starting to feel his age. The awama, the houseboat he'd come to know as home, felt as squalid and damp as a sunken wreck. Thin wisps of morning mist drifted over the surface of the river. A fisherman balanced on the bow of his small boat as he struggled to untangle his nets. Makana wrapped the blanket more tightly around his shoulders. The electric radiator at his feet generated about as much heat as a candle. Cold air whipped around him in vicious draughts that found every little crack in the lopsided structure, window shutters, roofing sheets and doorframes. This was the last year, he promised himself. He had to move out. Find somewhere on dry land with proper walls around it. He couldn't go on like this.

He considered lighting a cigarette, but the last one had triggered an attack of coughing so violent it had left him wheezing like a geriatric on his last legs. Beside his chair was the stack of books that he relied on to get him through the bouts of insomnia that seemed to come more and more often these days. Mainly it served as a stand for his packet of Cleopatras and his lighter. Reaching now for a cigarette, Makana noticed that the top of the stack was occupied by a volume on ancient Egyptian medicine. It was curious, he reflected, how one could draw comfort from knowledge that served absolutely no practical purpose. As he smoked, he fixed his eyes on the flickering orange lamp on the radiator switch in the hope that it would convey some warmth. In a while the sun would break through the mist and the day would warm up. He could call Aziza to make him some tea. The breeze rustled the newspapers stuffed into the cracks in the window frames.

The previous night he had visited the Verdi Gardens, a respectable Italian restaurant in Zamalek, its dark and somewhat gloomy interior crowded with fake neoclassical pillars wrapped in plastic vines. The effect was complemented by a number of oil paintings in heavy frames that adorned the walls. They depicted scenes from Rome – the Colosseum, the Spanish Steps, a touch of class from times gone by. The rest of the wall space was strewn with cheap prints in tacky frames – sunset over the Bridge of Sighs, the leaning Tower of Pisa, the kind of décor that might come your way from a cousin who happened to be in the tourist business. The Verdi Gardens had been in the Hafiz family for three generations. The current owner was Hossam Hafiz, grandson of the original Hafiz who, many years ago, had once visited Italy and decided there was a sacred bond between Italian cuisine and his own country. The embodiment of this connection was the composer Giuseppe Verdi, who, rumour had it, was commissioned by the Khedive to write the opera Aïda for the opening of the Cairo Opera House in 1871. The story had passed into legend and, like so many tales about this country, it was overshadowed by doubt.

In its heyday, the Verdi Gardens had been an exclusive place, frequented by film stars and their mistresses. Now it looked a touch old-fashioned and neglected. In a country that was so fond of its own cuisine there was little motivation to explore foreign fare. The Verdi Gardens' appeal rested on its prestigious reputation, a style that recalled another age, one in which the finer aspects of European culture were appreciated in this country.

By the looks of the people dining last night, it wasn't just the place that was getting on. The clientele of loyal patrons were also beginning to show their age. Young people went elsewhere. Those with money preferred to spend it in new venues: the lavish, open-air restaurants along the Nile that made you think you'd stepped into a movie. They modelled themselves on the French Riviera, or Los Angeles. It didn't much matter which. Times had moved on, leaving Mr and Mrs Hafiz in possession of a gloomy place where elderly couples tucked into creamy pasta dishes that didn't strain their dentures.

Still, the Hafiz family were managing. They had few worries in the world other than maintaining standards and keeping up appearances. That is, until their son Mourad went missing. They had heard nothing from him in nearly three weeks, but when he failed to attend the little party that had been arranged to celebrate his mother's birthday they began to suspect that something was wrong. They went through the usual routine – called his mobile repeatedly, went to visit his hostel room at the university, talked to his friends. All that remained after that was to check the hospitals, and finally they did what they had been hoping to avoid and went to the police, which resulted in a series of interviews with a parade of different officers, the filling out of a variety of forms and, finally, absolutely no result. It was their lawyer Munir Abaza who advised them to find an independent investigator to look for their son, which is where Makana came in. Abaza was a colleague of his old friend Amir Medani, and so the world turns.

Mr and Mrs Hafiz were in their early fifties. Both had that weary, lived-in look of a couple weighed down by years of good eating and now by concern about their only son. They seemed oddly out of place, as if trying to live up to the standards of another age, like marble busts or leather-bound books. Also present at the meeting was their daughter Sahar, in her twenties. She listened attentively to everything that was said, but contributed little. Makana had the impression she disapproved of their choice of investigator, or else she was holding something back, or perhaps had some sort of grudge against her brother. In any case she kept her mouth shut and her head down most of the time. She tended to avoid Makana's gaze when he looked in her direction.

They sat at a big round mahogany table in the centre of the dining room usually reserved for large parties. Mr Hafiz did most of the talking. He was small in stature and fleshy, with a dusting of flour in his thick hair, his hands clasped together on the table in front of him and his head bowed.

'Mourad is headstrong. When he gets an idea into his head he sticks with it.'

'He gets that from you,' declared Mrs Hafiz, turning to Makana. 'They are alike, father and son, perhaps too much so. My husband and son argue often, sometimes fiercely. But when it is over, it is forgotten.'

'We never bear a grudge. We never let things drag out. We just . . . carry on.'

Makana glanced at the daughter to see if she had anything to add. If she did she was keeping it to herself.

'Mourad is at university.'

'Ain Shams. Studying engineering.'

'Is that something you approved of?' asked Makana. Hossam Hafiz smiled.

'Nowadays it makes little difference what the parents want. Whether I approved or not he would do what he wanted. I understand that. I was like him when I was young, but I had responsibilities. Young people today don't know the meaning of the word.'

'Baba . . .' began the daughter. Her father silenced her with a dismissive wave before continuing.

'I was expected to take over the business from my father. That is the idea of a family business, the next generation takes up the burden and carries on.'

'But Mourad didn't want that?'

'He had ideas of his own. I decided, fine, let him follow his dreams. Let him study to become an engineer. One day he may wake up and decide that he wants to come back and take over the business.'

'But he gave no indication that this was his plan?'

'Not at all.' Mr Hafiz shook his head. 'He takes his studies very seriously.'

'We hardly see him.' Mrs Hafiz decided she would not remain silent any longer. 'Even though he's here in the same town. Other mothers see their sons more often than we do. They come home to eat. Some of them even live at home. Not Mourad. He wanted to live in the hostel, to be independent. Independent of what? That's

14

what I'd like to know. What did we ever do to make him feel that he was not free?'

'*Yallah*, Medihah, don't excite yourself.' Hossam Hafiz put out a hand to cover his wife's. 'As you can see, Mr Makana, we are rather upset by this whole business. We can't understand where he could be, and we fear the worst.'

'Baba . . .' The daughter again implored, and again her father lifted a hand to calm her.

'It's okay. We must be prepared.' Hafiz addressed Makana. 'Do you think you can find him?'

'It depends. You understand that if your son doesn't want to be found there's a good chance he won't be. Is there a possibility he might have left the country?'

'I don't think he has a passport.' Mr Hafiz frowned at his wife, who looked at the table.

'He's never been abroad,' said the daughter, addressing Makana for the first time. 'He's always dreamed of it, but he's never been.'

'He's a boy. Twenty-two years old. He doesn't know the world.' Mrs Hafiz held out a photograph. Mourad Hafiz was smiling at the camera in that clear-eyed way of young people who have nothing to fear.

Mr Hafiz grasped Makana's hand. 'Just find him,' he pleaded. 'I don't care what it costs. Please, just find him.'

A ray of sunlight was edging its way along the floor-boards. Makana unclamped his fingers from the blanket.

He tried to think of the reasons why a young man who had no troubles would go missing. It wasn't a question he was ever going to answer sitting here, but maybe it was a good reason to try and make a start to the day. The sound of footsteps came from the stairs leading up from the lower deck. Makana knew the sound of Aziza's tread anywhere and already he felt his mood lifting. Over the years he had found in his landlady's daughter a kindred spirit. He had watched Aziza grow. Seventeen, she was quick-witted and funny. Perhaps it wasn't so strange, considering the fact of his own absent daughter. He was about to open his mouth to ask for tea when he saw the look on her face and knew that today, for some reason, tea was going to take a while.

Chapter Two

Aziza led the way along the riverbank with the sure-footed tread of a child who had spent her entire life running up and down these muddy parts. Makana followed more cautiously. His body felt stiff and out of sorts and he wished he had had time for at least one glass of tea, but he trusted Aziza, and if she said he was needed urgently then there was no point in delaying.

'How is school these days?' he asked, partly to get her to slow down.

'School?' She turned to him. 'I'm thinking of dropping out next year.'

'Why? I thought you liked it.'

'What's the point of spending years learning stuff I don't need when I could be earning money?'

He detected the note of sarcasm in her voice.

'You're a smart girl, you shouldn't let it go to waste.'

'Tell that to the birds.'

It sounded like her mother talking. Umm Ali was pragmatic to a fault, and to her it was as clear as the sun that sending a girl to school wouldn't get you anywhere. She herself had been married by the time she was sixteen, and raising a family not long after that.

'You can do more with your life than sell vegetables in the market.'

'Who's going to pay me, you?'

Before Makana could think of an answer, he noticed a crowd had gathered up ahead. A stream of new arrivals was trickling steadily down the riverbank from the road. The bank was shallower here and the land open, with only the rubble of a collapsed wall to bar the way. Here and there heaps of broken bricks and the odd rubber tyre poked out of the long grass. More people stood on the roadside gawking as they waited for transport to materialise. It was still early and there was some blessing in that, because the number of onlookers was still low.

Makana was impressed by the authority Aziza wielded. Dressed in a shapeless, ragged dress that trailed around her ankles, there was still something of the tomboy about her. She was quick and lithe, and having grown up along here she saw the riverbank as her own private domain.

'Clear the way! Come on, let the *mualim* through.'

The crowd parted to reveal a small fishing boat beached in the shallows. Makana wondered if it was the same one

he had seen not so long ago from his window. The fisherman was a small man with bandy legs and grey bristles
around his gills. The boat was old, the wood worn away
where ropes and nets had cut deep in the course of time. A
frayed blue and orange nylon net was heaped in the bottom
of the hull. Resting on this was a sack. He looked up at
Makana as he approached with the sceptical eye of a man
who had seen enough miracles in his life to know trouble
when he saw it.

'Who's he?'

'What do you care? He's an expert. He works with the
police.' Aziza dispatched him with such ease that Makana
almost felt sorry for the fisherman, as if an apology might
be in order. Instead he found himself pressed in closer as
everyone else crowded in behind him.

'Give him room! Move back there!' Aziza jumped up on
the bow of the small boat and began issuing orders like a
seasoned admiral. The sack rolled to one side. It was ragged
and waterlogged and the size of a football.

'Did you find this? Where was it?'

'Out there in the water, I snagged it with my net. It must
have been lodged on a tree branch under the surface.'

'Did you look inside?'

The fisherman's eyes held Makana's. Silently, he jerked
his chin downwards. Makana leaned over and hefted it to
find it weighed more than he had imagined. Carefully he
pulled back the edges. As he did so, something inside gave
a kick. Instinctively, he pulled back, bringing a snort of

derision from the fisherman and laughter from somewhere in the crowd. Makana held the sack open and peered inside. He saw a grey seething mass.

'Are you sure about this?'

The fisherman shook his head in disgust. Makana stuck a hand inside and was rewarded with a sharp electric shock that shot up his arm. He dropped the sack and stepped back.

'Some expert,' muttered the fisherman.

Makana threw him a weary look and returned his attention to the contents of the sack. His fingers were slightly numb, but he managed to grasp whatever it was that had stung him and pull it out. The crowd reared back as the catfish hit the ground. With a grunt the fisherman stepped over it and with a hand on either side he flipped it out into the water. The crowd murmured their approval. Makana held open the sack and peered inside again. Brushing as best he could at the flies that had surged in around him, he ventured to take another look, the fisherman peering over his shoulder.

'Looks blacker than the devil himself.'

'Aziza,' said Makana, over his shoulder. 'Run back to the awama and fetch my telephone, would you, please?'

She leapt off the bow of the boat and sprinted away. The crowd turned to watch her go. This was a lot more entertaining than watching the traffic go by.

'You're going to have to move back up to the road now,' Makana told them. 'Before the police get here. You stay where you are,' he added to the fisherman, who had started edging away the moment he heard the word police. 'They're going to want to talk to you.'

Okasha took half an hour to arrive, by which time much of the crowd had dispersed, leaving only a few young men with nothing better to do with their time except lean on each other and stare. In his black woollen uniform and accompanied by dozens of officers, the broad-shouldered Okasha made an impressive entrance. People fell back to make room. Looking back, Makana caught sight of a familiar figure.

'I thought it made sense to bring her along. From what you said, this is a forensic matter.'

Makana watched Doctora Siham making her way carefully down the incline from the road, followed by two assistants hauling a large grey trunk full of her equipment. The Chief Forensic Officer had a formidable enough reputation to make most of the policemen who knew her straighten up and focus on carrying out their duties properly. Where Okasha had to yell to have them behave she managed it without raising her voice, at times without having to speak. Even the crowd lining the route seemed to sense her authority and pulled themselves back. One cheeky youth made some derogatory comment and was silenced at once by his friends.

'Where is it?'

Makana indicated the sack, still resting on the fishing net. Okasha stepped forward and cursed as the water lapped around his boots. Makana was wearing plastic sandals and hadn't noticed his feet were wet.

'Better leave it till she gets here.'

'My thoughts exactly,' muttered Makana.

They waited while Doctora Siham prepared herself, pulling on gloves and a face mask. She glanced at Makana.

'This is your doing, I take it? Getting us down here so early in the morning?'

'The river is very special at this time of day. I thought you'd appreciate it.'

She said nothing, turning and stepping in to lean over the boat.

'Did you have a look?'

Makana raised his eyebrows. It was almost a frivolous remark, coming from her. Surely she didn't expect him to have taken the fisherman's word for it before calling her? She went back to peeling the sacking carefully away. 'Can we get something up to shield us from all those curious eyes?' Her assistants immediately produced a large tarpaulin which they held up to prevent onlookers from seeing what she was doing. Flies began to buzz furiously as the sacking came away to reveal the head. It was sitting upright, somehow balanced on the fishing net. The skin was blackened and streaked with grey. A web of eager flies swarmed in excitedly. Around the jaw the flesh had started to come away.

'Something has been feeding on it.'

'There was a catfish in the sack with it.'

'Another reason not to eat fish in this town.'

Okasha and Makana exchanged glances but said nothing. They watched as Doctora Siham carefully cleaned off extraneous debris and collected it in sample bags before preparing to put the head into a sterilised container for transport back to her laboratory.

'Any idea how long he's been dead?' Makana asked.

'Sure, and as soon as I get him back to the lab I'll be able to tell you what he had for supper and what his favourite music is.' She gave Makana a withering look, as if to say she expected better of him. 'One thing I can say, but you must have worked that out for yourself.'

'What are you talking about?' demanded Okasha.

'The same reason he knew this was a he.' Doctora Siham pointed to the strange pattern of lines drawn across the victim's forehead. 'He's one of your fellow countrymen.'

Chapter Three

After the pathologist had left them, Okasha gave orders for boats and chains to drag the water up and downstream from their spot in the hope they might find the rest of the body. The fisherman was taken away for questioning. He objected at first. 'I have work to do, a family to feed,' he protested as he was led away. Okasha and Makana left them to it and made their way back to the awama, where Aziza was quick to produce the tea she had prepared for them. Okasha looked around the place.

'Doesn't it get cold at night?'

'It gets cold all the time. Every year seems colder than the last one.'

'That's because you don't have a good woman to take care of you,' Okasha said, brushing a speck off the brass stars on his shoulder. 'I tell you, I don't think I could live like you, all alone like this. I would go mad if I didn't have a family to go home to.' Makana looked at him but said nothing. Okasha returned the look. 'What? I'm not supposed to say anything? Who else is going to tell you? You have to get over it. You have to move on.'

'If you're suggesting I meet one of your wife's friends again you know how that ended.'

'You don't have to remind me. I'm still apologising on your behalf.'

It had been one of the most awkward events in the many years the two had known each other. Okasha's wife's idea, or so he claimed. An excruciating experience. They went to the Galaxy Cinema in El Manial. The film was a dreary melodrama that seemed to only involve people yelling at one another and breaking things. Makana hated every minute of it while his companion of the evening found it adorable. What to say? The golden age of Egyptian cinema lay groaning in its vault. In the end he had sneaked out for a cigarette and never gone back inside.

'All I'm saying is that you should get out. I mean, just open a window or something!'

As Okasha headed for the stairs Makana called him back.

'What's going to happen?'

'To our friend from the river? Who knows. We'll see what the good doctor comes up with, but without a body and no identification, there's not much we can do.'

'You mean because he's from South Sudan?'

'We don't know that for certain yet,' sighed Okasha. 'But yes, if that's the case then I don't see people getting too excited about getting to the bottom of this.'

'More a case of one less problem?'

'You said it, not me.' Okasha examined Makana. 'You're not taking this personally, are you? Come on, even if he is from South Sudan, you're at war, right? North and South?'

'Someone has to take an interest.'

'Well, don't hold your breath, right now the Sudanese are not exactly popular in this town.'

He was referring to the protesters who had been occupying a maidan in Mohandiseen since late September. The square, a park the size of a postage stamp, was opposite the Mustafa Mahmoud mosque and more significantly, right around the corner from the United Nations High Commissioner for Refugees. The protesters were mainly Southern Sudanese who were demanding the right to claim asylum status in Egypt and thereby gain access to services such as public schools and hospitals. It would mean an end to a twilight existence where, because they were not officially recognised as refugees because of an open-border agreement, they didn't qualify for help. It was safe to say that the Sudanese generally were enjoying a moment of acute unpopularity among their Nile Valley brethren, blamed for everything from moral degeneracy, drunkenness, prostitution and crime to posing a threat to national security. The president still hadn't forgiven them for the Sudanese involvement in the assassination attempt

26

on his life in Addis Ababa ten years ago. Makana understood what Okasha was telling him. Nobody was going to
care too much about a dead body, or even part of one, that
had just been fished out of the river.

'I'm just asking you to let me know if there are any
developments.'

'Sure,' nodded Okasha, unconvincingly. 'Don't you have
other things to worry about?'

Makana did, of course, have matters of his own to see to.
He took a taxi across the river to Ain Shams University.
The main building was a former palace of the Khedive
Ismail, lovingly modelled on Versailles. An air of decay and
decadence lingered in the drained ornamental pool
and dry fountain. The Vice-President for Education and
Student Affairs was at least willing to meet him, which was
always something. The appointment had been set up by
Munir Abaza, the Hafiz family lawyer. Makana found
himself sitting across the table from a slovenly man wearing
a shirt like last week's menu, spattered with food stains. He
gave the impression he had more important things to do
with his time than discuss missing students.

'Students are under a lot of pressure, you understand,'
he said, picking his nose when he thought Makana wasn't
looking. 'Most of them don't come here because they love
studying. They come because they think it will help them to
get a better job. They want to please their parents. They
want to impress the girls. Most of all they don't want to

27

grow up. They want to put off starting out in real life for as long as possible.'

'What can you tell me about Mourad?'

'I can't claim to know all the students personally, you understand? I spoke to the parents. I understand their concern.' He examined something on the end of his finger before wiping it on the underside of the desk. 'He wouldn't be the only one to lose his way. There's a lot of pressure on young people nowadays. Sometimes the future of their families depends on them. Naturally, there are many who cannot cope. They become disheartened. They lose their way.'

'Are you suggesting that's what happened to Mourad?'

'Not in so many words. I mean don't go running back to them with all this. I'm just trying to show you that these situations can be complicated.'

'Does that happen often, I mean a student dropping out without a word and disappearing?'

'I wouldn't say often, but it happens.' The vice-president nodded to himself. 'These are difficult times. The classes are oversubscribed and crowded, and there are no guarantees that any of them are going to find work once they leave here.' He leaned back in his chair and waved a hand vaguely. 'And there are temptations.'

'Temptations?'

'Girls, alcohol, drugs. Many young students find themselves brought face to face with a whole new world with which they are not familiar.'

'Do you think he fell in with the wrong crowd, was led astray somehow?'

'Now you are reading too much into my words.' The director seemed pleased with himself for no apparent reason.

'His parents are worried, which is why I'm here.'

'We're approaching the end-of-term exams. Students often feel they are under more pressure at this time of year. And then the cold weather.' He shivered and tried to smile, revealing a set of uneven yellow teeth. 'Inshallah, he will return to the family safe and sound, when he has had his fun.' He rested his hands on the table. The interview was over.

A porter in a shabby lab coat pockmarked with burn holes shuffled along beside Makana to take him to the student hostel. His eyes could barely settle on the steps in front of him, distracted as he was by the female students hurrying by. He didn't say much, and when they finally arrived at Mourad's room in a modern cement building with all the charm of a mausoleum, he grunted and stood aside, hands in pockets, and stared at the ceiling.

Mourad shared a room with another student. There wasn't much to see. There were two beds, one on either side of the narrow space. Each student had a desk and a wardrobe. Jeans and T-shirts were heaped with no apparent order on the different shelves. Makana, aware that the porter was there to keep an eye on him as much as anything else, wandered loosely around.

29

'He's not here,' said the porter helpfully, as if Makana might expect Mourad to be hiding under the bed. Taped to the wall over the desk was a map of the world. Heaps of folders and textbooks cluttered the desk. When he slid open one of the drawers the porter gave a cough from the doorway. A shelf over the bed yielded a handful of novels. Makana read the names García Márquez and Sonallah Ibrahim. There were flyers and leaflets, a mix of university administrative material, concerts, a demonstration in support of Palestine, another for something called Kefaya. On the bedside table was an old-fashioned alarm clock with bells on it and an image of Goofy on the front. On the wall above the bed was a black and white poster of Malcolm X and alongside it a poem in English by Langston Hughes: 'Lord, I been a'waitin for the Freedom Train.'

On the other half of the room the wall was bare but for a calendar pinned up with a nail displaying a picture of the Kaaba in Mecca lit up at night by garish green lights. There was also a single photograph stuck to the wall of a young man with the wispy beginnings of a beard around his chin and a distant look in his eye, dressed in a pilgrim's white robes. This would be Mourad's roommate. Portrait of a pious person, thought Makana.

'What about the man who shares the room, any idea where he is?'

The porter shrugged. He might have been on another planet at the end of the universe for all he cared. Makana took a last look round. Hanging on a hook on the back of the door was an American-style cap, red with a logo emblazoned across the front that read *Westies*.

'I'd like to speak to him, the roommate.'

'Abdelhadi Wahab.' The porter ran a gnarled finger across the name taped to the wall. 'You might find him in the cafeteria.'

It didn't sound encouraging. As the porter turned towards the door Makana leaned over to pluck the photograph off the wall and tucked it into his back pocket. The porter led the way down the stairs. Hands in the pockets of his worn-down coat, he strolled along with the confidence of a proprietor. A superior smirk rarely left his face. He owned this place, with its palace walks and fountains. In his eyes the students were just passing through.

The cafeteria was cavernous and noisy even though it was almost empty. A group of students at the far end were squealing and jumping up and down.

'Exams are coming,' said the porter. 'Most people are studying.'

'Is he here, Mourad's roommate?'

'They all look the same to me from here.' There was a note of irritation in his voice. 'I think I've seen him with that group.' He gestured halfheartedly across the room. Clearly he had lost interest in Makana's cause and was beginning to think whatever tip was coming his way wasn't going to be enough compensation for his precious time. He produced a half-smoked cigarette from his pocket and asked for a light. Makana studied the narrow features as the man bent over the flame. He had the quick, furtive eye movements of a dog that expects to be set upon at any moment. The confidence was a role he pulled on, like the grubby coat.

'You must hear a lot of things in your job.'

'I mind my own business.' He straightened up, smoke leaking from his nostrils like despair. One sincere hand rested flat against his chest. 'On my honour, I do my job. You see the number of students here. Of course there are problems. You can't have that many people in one place without problems.' His gaze settled on Makana. 'You come here asking about one student. Who can remember one face out of a thousand?'

Who indeed? Makana watched him saunter off and approached the group of students.

'How's the food?'

They laughed. 'You don't want to know,' said one of the boys, rocking back precariously on the rear legs of his chair. A man who liked to live dangerously. It succeeded in drawing the attention of the girls who no doubt were waiting for him to fall flat on his back. In the meantime they fiddled with their headscarves and regarded Makana warily.

'Mourad Hafiz, any idea where I can find him?'

'Why, is his mother worried about him again?'

The laughter felt uncomfortable and gave Makana a chance to reassess the group.

'You haven't seen him then?'

'What is that accent?' He was enjoying his moment. 'Another Sudanese? Is that all his parents could afford?'

One of the girls murmured something, cautioning him, but the young man was not going to miss an opportunity.

'We should make you pay to get into this country. Then we'd see how many of you stayed around. No, listen, we pay taxes to keep this country going, and people like this just think they can walk in and help themselves.'

'You pay taxes, really? That's interesting.'

The young man scrabbled around for an answer. 'I don't mean me personally. I'm a student. I mean, in general. The people in general.' The others were laughing now. The chair dropped back to the floor with a thump that drew more attention to his plight. He left the room, dragging a couple of boys with him. Of the two girls who had remained, one was a slight, pale girl with acne, wearing a cheap black scarf covering her hair, the other was darker in complexion and her gaze was steadier.

'Do you study with Mourad? Are you friends of his?'

'He doesn't have many friends,' the second one said. She spoke flatly, sure of her facts. The other one looked on.

'Why is that?'

'Because he's different.' She held a blue folder decorated with puppies and pop stars clutched to her chest like a shield. Her eyes glanced in the direction of the porter who stood by the door smoking. Talking to strange men was perhaps not to be undertaken lightly. 'He's dropping out.'

'He said that?'

'He doesn't believe in it anymore.'

'In what?'

'This.' She gestured at the institution they were standing in, as if it was obvious. 'Education. The future. Everything.'

The second girl nudged her, as if to caution her.

Makana nodded at the counter. 'Can I get you something? A drink, snacks, a sandwich?'

The second girl's eyes lit up, but her smile faded as her more conservative friend put her foot down.

'We have to get back to the library. We're studying you know.'

'I know. I'd just like to hear more.'

'What is your interest in Mourad, anyway?'

'His parents are worried about him. They've asked me to try and find him.'

'We don't know where he is.'

'Well, maybe you know other things.'

'Like what?' Her eyes narrowed, suspecting a trap.

'Tell me about this thing you're studying, civil engineering, is it?'

'It's not what you think. It's about urban planning, social divisions. The way we use walls to separate the wealthy from the poor.' She talked quickly, as if sure it was of no real interest to him.

'Why do you think Mourad wanted to study that?'

The girl's jaw dropped for a moment. It was an unexpected question. She seemed surprised that anyone would be interested in hearing her opinion.

'He wants to change the world.'

'Change the world how?'

'Who knows? He's a bit of a dreamer.'

Perhaps it was the surroundings, or maybe the tone of the conversation, but something had brought back memories of Makana's brief time at university, a long time ago and far away. He had dropped out after only a year of history and politics, convinced that nobody could ever learn anything of value in such an environment. He had gone through it all simply to please his father, but the truth was that his heart wasn't in it. In the huge, hot, over-stuffed auditoriums professors sleepwalked their way through lectures they had delivered a thousand times, while students lolled half-consciously on their benches. They jotted down notes they did not understand. It wasn't about expanding your mind or changing the world, it was about the perpetuation of a myth. His father was a subscriber to that myth, having never had the benefit of a university education himself. A schoolteacher who fervently believed that qualifications were the key to prosperity.

'What can you tell me about his roommate?'

The girls looked at one another and rolled their eyes.

'He'll be in the library swotting away, or sucking up to the professor or something.'

Makana showed them the photograph he'd plucked from the wall of the dorm room. 'Is that him?' This elicited more giggling. 'Have you seen him recently?'

The two were shaking their heads as they began to edge away. Makana managed to hand them his card, which was something at least.

'You've been very helpful. I'd like to talk again, about Mourad. If you feel like it. Perhaps you could give me a call?' Asking for their numbers would be out of the question.

The porter had sidled up with his now familiar hangdog expression. Makana offered him a cigarette, which seemed to cheer him up. They walked over to the library and looked for the roommate, but without luck. As they came back outside the porter grew philosophical.

'Not a bad life, eh? They hang around chatting and there's a cushy job waiting for them at the end of it. Makes you wonder what makes them so special, doesn't it?'

Makana couldn't think of an answer to that. He found some money and pressed it into the porter's hand. He didn't expect him to be satisfied with it, but then some people never are.

Chapter Four

Makana dropped by the vice-president's office on his way out to see if they had an address for Mourad's roommate in Mohandiseen, which by some stroke of luck they did. Abdelhadi's aunt was down as his next of kin. It seemed like a good omen, so Makana caught a taxi and went straight over there. As they drove up the broad avenue of Sharia al-Dowal al-Arabiya he noticed the maidan in front of the Mustafa Mahmoud mosque. Normally it was an unremarkable patch of scruffy grass hedged in by an ankle-high fence. Now it was covered with makeshift shelters, tents, blue and red tarpaulins draped over ropes strung between light poles. Cardboard boxes transformed into huts, walls, rooftops for precarious lean-tos.

'It's going to end badly,' muttered the driver, a young man muffled up to the eyeballs inside a brown scarf.

It wasn't the first time Makana had seen the camp. It had been there for months, but it was growing. A small island of displaced people in the middle of a six-lane river of moving metal.

'Maybe they think they don't have a choice.'

'So what? Aren't they in our country as guests? People have enough problems of their own.'

You couldn't argue with that. There was an air of desperation over the squalid camp. Not so much the end of the line as a medieval siege. They were trying to get into the visible world and become real people, with rights. It wasn't a wish that would be lightly granted. Makana craned his neck to look back. As they swung away from the round-about, his eye caught a flash of a brightly coloured chicken on wheels. Bouncy red and yellow letters spelled out the name Westies. He had just enough time to read an address near the Hunting Club before the billboard was gone.

The image of the rotting, waterlogged head in the sack came to him. Dismembering a body required a lot of hard work. It wasn't something you took on lightly. Bone, cartilage, sinews, tendons. So why go to all that trouble? The way things stood right now you could probably have dumped the body in the middle of Tahrir Square and no one would have been in any hurry to investigate.

Abdelhadi's aunt lived on the fifth floor of an unremark-able yellow apartment building on Sharia Ramiz. Makana took one look at the state of the lift and decided to walk. When he leaned on the doorbell he heard it chirping away but nobody answered. Somewhere in the building Umm Kalthoum was wailing at full blast. The sound echoed down the stairwell as he descended again. He stood in the entrance and looked up and down the street, wondering what he was doing here.

Amir Medani's office looked as though it had been recently ransacked. There was nothing unusual about that, though it was hard to fathom how anyone could operate in the midst of such chaos. Somehow he managed to run a highly efficient legal service. The international awards scattered about the room, holding down piles of folders or propping up shelves of books, testified to his success as a human rights lawyer. Amir Medani himself had the appearance of a nocturnal creature unused to daylight. His eyes blinked behind the small round frames of his spectacles as he gazed up from his desk.

'I have a heart condition. My doctors prohibit anyone from sneaking up on me.'

'I thought you would be expecting me.'

Amir Medani threw down his pen. 'Months I don't hear from you and then suddenly you appear without warning.'

'Didn't you give my name to Munir Abaza?'

'Oh, yes, sorry about that. He said he was looking for a reliable investigator for one of his clients who had a problem. He hasn't given you any trouble, I hope?'

'Not yet.'

'That's good. I mean, he's a useful person to know, has a hand in all kinds of pots. He moves with the high and mighty.'

'So why the concern?'

'Because he's only truly loyal to one person and one person alone. Himself. Stay on the right side of him and you'll be fine.' The lawyer sat back and reached for a half-smoked cigar that rested in an ashtray. He examined it for a moment before snapping open a fancy silver lighter. In his early sixties, there was something about Amir Medani's style that was elegantly outdated. Like the well-tailored suits he always wore, the fruit of another age, before he was exiled. They had not known each other in the old days. Unlike Makana, the lawyer had been active politically, organising rallies and secret meetings. He was accused of plotting to stage a *coup d'état* and leaving was the only way of avoiding the hangman's noose. He looked at his watch.

'You think it's too early for lunch? I look at you and I think I haven't eaten for a week.' Without waiting for an answer he got up and led the way, slowing down only long enough to inform his staff, 'We're going for lunch.' He waved. 'Don't contact me unless it's a national emergency.' The three women exchanged looks of concern.

'I like to leave them alone from time to time. They need to learn to think for themselves. The education system in this country doesn't encourage that.'

They went down the stairs and out into the street. Amir Medani led the way in a meandering fashion that involved stepping out into the moving traffic without warning, causing all manner of mayhem. He was oblivious. Makana followed him down a sidestreet to a secluded restaurant wedged between a perfume merchant and a mobile telephone dealer. If you didn't know it was there you would never find it, which explained why the interior was almost deserted. Behind latticed wooden screens it lay like a hidden enclave of calm. A waiter detached himself from the shadows to greet them discreetly and lead the way to a table at the back.

'They do very good fish, brought in from the Red Sea every morning.'

Makana thought about his experience that morning but decided not to make a fuss. Who knew what fish fed on normally? The Red Sea part sounded promising. He nodded his assent. Within seconds a glass of pomegranate juice had appeared in front of Amir Medani.

'Good for the blood pressure, I'm told, and since I don't have a problem I shall carry on drinking the stuff daily.' Makana watched him drain the glass in one go. 'They want to give me another award. I have become a symbol of the struggle for human rights in the Middle East. Strange to think of oneself as an icon. I feel like a hostage to a lost cause. Anyway, they want me to come to The Hague to receive it and the government is naturally trying to block it. They take us all for fools, but they know we can do little about it. And with all this refugee business going on they are making life difficult for all of us.'

'I saw the camp.'

'Don't get too close. One of these days they're going to clear it, and it's not going to be a pretty sight.' The waiter appeared bearing a tray of starters. Amir Medani carried on talking as the small plates were set out on the table. 'It's perverse. To punish the government in Khartoum the Egyptians are hurting those who have fled persecution in Sudan. They are getting it from both sides. The public has already turned against the protesters. Brotherhood between nations is fine, so long as we all remember our place.'

'It's not something I've given much thought to.'

'That's because you like to think you're above it all. One of these days you're going to wake up and realise that everything is political.'

'This sounds like a speech I've heard before.'

'Well, get used to it, because it's coming again. You and I survive because we're lucky enough to be making a living of sorts, but many are struggling, especially if they have families.'

'Something turned up on the riverbank this morning,' said Makana. He described the severed head. 'There's not much to go on. It's hard to even tell if it's a man or a woman, but the ritual markings suggest it is likely to be a Southern male.'

'Why go to all the trouble of separating the head from the body?'

'To make it easier to dispose of usually. If the killer doesn't want to draw attention to themselves, or simply for practical purposes, getting rid of the pieces is easier than a heavy body.'

'Sounds like you've given this some thought.'

'It's not every day I have heads washing up on my doorstep.'

'There's some irony to it, though. Don't you think?'

'A severed head? In what sense?'

'Well, our country has been at war with itself, North and South, for almost fifty years, ever since independence. Now, here we are concerned about one another.'

'I'm not at war with anyone.'

'Presumably this doesn't interfere with the work you're doing for Munir Abaza?'

'Not so far, and besides, if I don't take an interest, who will?'

'Good point. Let's eat.'

The fish had arrived, grilled to perfection. Makana's qualms faded into the background.

Since no conversation with Amir Medani was ever light-hearted, the talk turned inevitably to the crisis in Darfur. Estimates of casualties ranged from two hundred thousand to almost a million.

'In America, where they know about these things, the people are donating millions. Actors from Hollywood are lending their name to the cause. It's being described as a genocide.' He rolled his eyes. 'Very few people could even find Darfur on a map a year ago, and now suddenly they want to save them all. Out of Iraq and into Darfur is the current slogan.'

'We're not important enough to warrant an invasion.'

'Well, exactly.' Amir Medani wiped his mouth with a paper napkin. 'You know they are trying to indict our president? They want him to stand trial for war crimes.'

'Is that why they invited you to The Hague?'

'The thought did occur to me. Of course, it would never come to court, even if they did manage to apprehend him.' Amir Medani sighed, then produced the remains of his cigar from his pocket and lit it thoughtfully. 'I must be getting old. I don't think anyone really believes in the law any more. Like everything else, this is all about doing things for appearances. I can't turn down the award, but I do feel like I'm being used.'

'I can't imagine a more unlikely candidate.'

'In the meantime those people in the camp are trapped between two governments that don't care for them. The United Nations has seventeen thousand cases in their backlog. It's not even their job. Technically, responsibility falls on the government.' Amir Medani puffed away like an engine building up steam.

'Where would I go if I was interested in finding out more about the Southerners?'

'One of the churches. I would try Our Lady Josephine in Arbaa-wa-Nus.'

'I don't even know where that is.'

'It's in the name, four and a half, as in kilometres, in this case from the road to Suez. It used to be known as Ezbet al-Haggana, but don't expect a warm welcome.' Amir Medani's smile was that of a man who liked secrets. 'To them, you and I are the enemy.'

Chapter Five

I t was almost sunset when Makana climbed out of another taxi close to the Hunting Club. It wasn't hard to locate Westies. An enormous hoarding climbed up one side of the building facing the street. It covered at least four floors and was in need of freshening up. At least a decade of dust, rain and sunshine had left traces of their passing. Barbecued chicken with our special tasty sauce, it proudly proclaimed. The restaurant's logo was painted in blue and red letters and accompanied by the same image Makana had seen on the cap hanging on the back of Mourad's door: a chicken on roller skates holding high a box that no doubt contained some of his less fortunate fellows now roasted and basted in special sauce. *Westies . . . mmmhhh!* Now that he looked at it Makana could actually recall eating something from here once. Ali Shibaker's studio and car repair shop were not far away. They delivered food not on roller skates but in small vans and motor scooters.

The interior was dreary the way only a place that tries to look cheerful can be. The colours had faded. It seemed like an idea that had had its day, a franchise that had outlived its usefulness. Backlit signs over the counter gaped like missing teeth where neon strips had expired. At the far end of the counter a youth leaning wearily on a cash register radiated all the joy of a condemned man awaiting a reprieve. A wide hatch behind him afforded a view of the kitchen area where an argument was taking place.

'How do I get one of those?'

'One of these?' The man straightened up and touched a hand to his cap. He seemed uncertain of himself, as if there was some trick to the question he couldn't make out. 'You have to work here,' he frowned, as if the idea was patently absurd.

A swingdoor flew open and a short, sturdily built woman in her twenties strode out of the kitchen, still shouting at someone behind her. The language of fast food seemed to demand a certain amount of English, or American. They might have been speaking Mandarin as far as Makana was concerned.

'Is that the manager?' Makana nodded at the young woman giving orders.

'Ruby,' he nodded. 'You don't want to order anything?'

'Let me think about it.' Makana nodded in the direction of the manager. Reluctantly, the young man left his post and returned a moment later with the young woman. In case there was any doubt, the name Ruby was printed in English on the tag pinned awkwardly to her chest.

'I wondered if I could speak to you for a moment.'

'Is there something wrong?' She frowned, immediately assuming a defensive position.

'Are you the only manager here?'

'No, there are two of us. But we work different shifts.' She pushed her glasses back up her nose. She was not too tall, which accentuated her weight. Heavy with the kind of food they served in here. Already the sickly sweet smell was beginning to nauseate him. She indicated a Formica-covered table halfway down the room.

'Ruby, is that your real name?' Makana gestured at the yellow plastic plaque.

'Look, if this is about the non-Egyptians we have working here . . .' She lowered her voice. 'All of that has been taken care of.'

'I'm glad to hear that.'

'I mean, I can't pay you, if that's what you're here for.'

'It's not about that.'

'Then I don't understand.'

Curious faces had gathered in the wide kitchen hatch to peer in their direction. Concern about his presence had obviously overcome whatever problems they were having in there. Makana reached into his pocket and placed the photograph Mrs Hafiz had given him flat on the table.

'Do you know him?'

Ruby's gaze barely brushed over the photograph before returning to Makana.

'Is he in some kind of trouble?'

'He's been missing for a couple of weeks. His parents haven't heard from him and they are worried.'

Her eyes returned to the picture and this time they lingered. 'He did work here. Officially, I suppose he still does. But he hasn't shown up for a while.'

'Isn't that unusual?'

Ruby shrugged. 'People find other things. Nobody works in a place like this unless they have to.'

Underneath the hard shell Makana detected some measure of concern.

'You said he hasn't been here for a while, can you tell me how long exactly?'

'A couple of weeks maybe. I can't tell without looking at the records.'

'Could you do that?'

There was a moment's hesitation, as if she was still unsure whether to trust him.

'I need a minute.'

She disappeared back through the swingdoors into the kitchen. More voices could be heard and then silence. Makana looked around him. A slim dark girl was wheeling a metal bucket between the tables as she mopped the floor. He knew at once that she was a Southerner. Her back bowed with fatigue, she didn't once raise her head.

'It's less than two weeks,' Ruby announced as she returned holding up a worksheet.

'Can you tell me exactly when he was last here?'

'Sure.' She ran a finger down the paper she held. 'It was the thirteenth of December, so that's . . .' She counted on her fingers.

'Nine days.'

'Right.'

'And how long had he been working here before that?'

'Oh, I'd say about six months. Since the summer.'

'What can you tell me about him?'

'About Mourad?' She put a hand to her hair a little self-consciously. 'A hard worker. I used to tease him that if he put his mind to it he would have my job soon. He's the kind that can do anything they set their mind to.'

'Did he want your job?'

'That's just it. His heart wasn't in it.'

'Do you know why he was working here?'

'Why does anyone work in a place like this?' She rolled her eyes. 'He needed the money.'

'Did you know his parents have a restaurant of their own?'

'I knew he had some experience, which in a place like this makes you a freak, but he didn't talk about it.'

'The work doesn't require kitchen skills?'

'It's automated. There's no difference between working here and running a garage. A trained monkey could do it. In fact, monkeys would be easier to deal with than this lot.'

'Did Mourad ever talk about going away?'

'No, not really. But he did disappear a couple of times, now that I think about it.'

'How do you mean, disappear?'

'I mean he just didn't come in. No explanation, just said he was out of town for a couple of days. He didn't say why.'

'You weren't curious?'

'I just figured it was his own business. I mean, he got told off, but he was a hard worker. Dedicated. You only had to ask him to do something once, not like some people I could name.' She glanced towards the kitchen hatch, where faces would appear for a time, watching them furtively before disappearing again. Work didn't seem to be pressing. Behind him Makana could hear the slap of the mop and the squeak of the bucket drawing closer.

'So you must have been surprised when he stopped coming to work?'

'Well, like I said, people come and go.'

'So, that was it? I get the feeling you knew him better than most.'

'We talked.' She gave an awkward shrug, slightly embarrassed. 'Is he in some kind of trouble?'

'I don't know,' said Makana. 'At this point it's impossible to say.'

'But there must be some indication. I mean, people don't just disappear, do they?'

'If you don't mind my asking, how did you wind up here?'

Ruby gave him a long look. 'My father had a stroke. He can't work. He needs constant help, which means my mother has to take care of him. I have four younger siblings, three of them are still in school. One is at university. Somebody has to support them. I took the first job I could find.'

'And now you're managing the place.'

'Well, this is as far as I can go, unless I win a million dollars and can buy the place and start building my own empire. Right now there doesn't seem much chance of that happening, so I'll just stick around and take it out on the rest of these poor losers.' Out of the corner of her eye she saw the swingdoors open and jumped to her feet. The new arrival had a round face set with a fierce frown. He wore a blue shirt and red clip-on tie. A pencil-thin moustache added an odd touch of vanity. He waved her explanation aside.

'I don't care. We are trying to run a business here. Any inquiries should be addressed to our head office in writing. You know that, right?'

'Mr Khalil?' She indicated that they should step away. Makana watched her speaking in a low voice. Whatever she was saying seemed to have an effect. Mr Khalil fingered his tie, which had the chicken logo on it. After a moment he turned and walked away. The swingdoors flapped behind him.

'What did you tell him?'

'That you were a government inspector and that if he didn't let me deal with you my way then we might be closed down.'

'And he accepted that?'

Ruby sighed. 'He's a man. He likes to think he's in charge, but knows that he could never manage without me.'

Chapter Six

Makana decided to walk back to the awama. It took him the best part of an hour. He was in no hurry and it gave him a chance to think. So far he had learned that Mourad had decided to find work in a fast-food place rather than to help out in his parents' restaurant. According to them he had been missing for some three weeks, but for twelve of those days he had been well enough to come to work at Westies even though he had not been in touch with his parents. None of this was all that unusual. For a young man in search of independence, perhaps it was only natural that he should want to distance himself from his family. Nine days ago something had happened to change that, but what exactly? Nobody had seen him. The fact that he had gone missing with the end-of-term exams coming up so soon suggested that if he had gone missing of his own free will, and so far there was nothing to indicate otherwise, then Mourad's disappearance might mean he had simply lost interest in becoming an engineer, that he saw his fate lay elsewhere. Even young idealists who dreamed of changing the world sometimes had moments of doubt.

Makana paused to stare out over the river, leaning on the railings to smoke a cigarette. At this time of the day, as the sun vanished and the shadows emerged to swallow it, this city was at its most enigmatic. Across the river white bars of neon flickered awake, casting their garish web over the world. Cars trundled across the bridge like soft thoughts sliding into oblivion.

Could it be a case of Mourad having had a breakdown of sorts? He wouldn't be the first student to do so. Had he dropped out, gone to seek a better life elsewhere? If so, where? Curiosity led Makana on past the awama to where the fisherman had come ashore with his macabre catch. The riverside was muddy and scuffed from the traffic that had traipsed through there that morning. A torn plastic strip fluttered in the breeze; here and there lay other debris left behind by the police in their haste to be away from this place. He reminded himself to give Okasha a call to make sure they hadn't decided to make life difficult for the fisherman. Sometimes the police felt a need to stamp on someone, just to remind everyone who was in charge.

Climbing the steps to the upper deck, Makana recalled the fatigue he had felt that morning. Now he was tired, but hopeful. Halfway up the stairs he heard the sound of someone coughing and stepped onto the upper deck to find that his place had been taken over by Sami Barakat. The journalist was curled up on the divan with a blanket around his shoulders, his unruly curly hair and face illuminated by the glow from his laptop.

His spectacles glinted as he looked up. 'Aziza let me in, I thought you wouldn't mind.'

'Have you ever known me to refuse you anything?'

'I never really thought of it like that, but you're right. What are friends for?'

'I'm not complaining, but what does your wife think of your decision to move in with me?'

'Ahh.' Sami gave what could only be described as a philosophical wave.

'I'm not sure what that means. Don't tell me you're going through one of your phases?'

'I don't know.' Sami removed his glasses and rubbed his eyes. 'I mean, it's as if I'm not good enough the way I am. She wants to turn me into something else.'

'Maybe she sees something in you that the rest of us don't?'

'That's always possible.' Sami set aside the computer and struggled to sit up.

Makana crossed to the corner where a small kerosene stove stood, and began making coffee.

Over the years, the upper deck had gradually become his living quarters. The awama was simply too big for him.

The damp lower deck was now converted into storerooms. Up here he had the essentials. His books, folders and the stacks of newspapers that comprised his archives. There was a bathroom and toilet below and a kitchen which he rarely used. There was an airy sensation up here. He had never been able to sleep down below. It felt enclosed and claustrophobic, too close to the water. Up here he was not so much flying, but at least still floating, which was always something.

'Did you never have that feeling that perhaps you were not suited? Never any doubts?'

Makana thought for a moment. It was a long time ago that he had been married. More than fourteen years had passed since Muna had died and not a day had gone by since then that he had not thought about her. He spooned coffee into the small brass pot.

'Never.'

He pumped the lever a few times and struck a match. The lithe blue flame flickered around the edges of the burner. He set the coffee to boil and lit a cigarette.

'If you want my advice you would be a fool to lose Rania,' he said, blowing out the match.

'I thought you would be understanding.'

'You wouldn't thank me for not being truthful.'

'I wouldn't be too sure of that.'

'Whatever it is that's bothering you, it's not her fault.'

'Have you talked to her about this?' Sami looked alarmed.

'How long have we known each other?'

'This is not the first time for you to see me this way, is that what you mean?'

'So what is it?' Makana asked. 'The thing that's bothering you.'

'Oh, the usual.' Sami sighed as he lay back, hands behind his head, to look up at the ceiling. A man contemplating his future and seeing only problems. 'This country. The mess we're in.' As usual with Sami, it wasn't possible to separate his own life from the state of the world. 'People have a right to know what is being done in our name. I still believe that, but the more I see around me the more that's becoming impossible. We are living a lie. Our politicians are only concerned with lining their pockets. The president and his friends live on another planet, smiling for the cameras while they sell off everything they can lay their hands on.' He raised his head to check Makana was still listening. 'Did you know that we are selling off our natural gas reserves to Israel for a fraction of market value? What happens when it's all gone? What do we do then? And why are we doing this? For political reasons? For stability in the region? No, because somebody saw a way of making a quick profit and screwing us into the bargain. You know what's really amazing? If I write about this I can go to prison for treason because it's deemed a security issue. Pretty funny, huh?'

'You shouldn't be here. You should be on holiday.'

'Where would I go? Is there somewhere I can stop thinking about all of this? A drug, perhaps? Maybe that's the answer. Rania is my wife and I love her, but it's like we have fundamentally different views of the future. She's optimistic. Imagine!'

Makana had a sense of where this was leading, but before he could say anything the coffee came to the boil. He let it reach the rim of the pot before lowering the heat, then brought it up again. Three times was the rule. He stirred in some sugar and then poured it into two small cups.

'Anyway, enough of my problems,' said Sami. The coffee seemed to revive him. 'Aziza tells me you had some drama here this morning.'

Makana told him about the morning's excitement.

'Only a head? No sign of the rest of him?'

'The police dragged that section of the river but they found nothing more.'

'Sure, I can see them breaking their backs over that. One less to worry about.'

In another age a head emerging from the water would have been taken as an omen, a sign of the gods' displeasure, perhaps. Now it was a nuisance, a distraction from the business of ridding the city of unwanted intruders. Makana had no idea why he felt some personal obligation. He couldn't explain it. Perhaps it was simply the sadness of anyone having to wind up that way. The feeling that under other circumstances it might have been him washing up on the riverbank. And then there was the memory of that night years ago when his wife and daughter had plunged into this very same river. Did he see some twisted form of resolution in all of this?

Why was the past so hard to put behind? They were bound together, North and South, by a history of discrimination. The Southerners carried the memory of having once been slaves, while the Northerners had the burden of their slave-trading forefathers. Makana had had little to do with Southerners here. Culturally and racially they were different, chained together by a common history, by the borderlines that fate had dealt them. He saw them on the streets sometimes, selling things in the market or just going by, but they didn't move in the same circles. That seemed like an almost shameful omission on his part.

Makana's phone interrupted his thoughts. It was Sahar Hafiz, Mourad's sister.

'I was hoping we could talk,' she said.

'Would it be possible to meet in person?' He wondered if perhaps she might be more forthcoming in the absence of her parents.

'Yes, that would be better. Should we say tomorrow?'

They agreed to meet at a fashionable bookshop in Zamalek, around the corner from the Verdi Gardens. When the call was over Makana found Sami staring at him.

'Mysterious appointments with women? This is a new development.'

'How did you know it was a woman?'

'Your tone of voice changes when you speak to women.'

This was news to Makana. He suspected Sami was guessing, but felt obliged to explain about Mourad Hafiz.

'Why should it be a mystery? He simply decided that studying was a waste of time. You can't blame him for that. Congratulate him on coming to his senses. Wish him good luck.'

A certain delirium seemed to have come over Sami. Makana suspected this might have something to do with his marriage crisis.

'He's a dreamer, apparently. Wants to save the world.'

'Save the world how?'

'I'm not sure.' Makana lit a cigarette, felt the reassuring burn of tobacco hitting his throat.

'Rania has a cousin who's a researcher at Ain Shams, doing something connected to urban planning. Maybe it would help to talk to him.'

While Sami tried to locate the cousin without going through Rania, Makana made a call of his own. Sindbad sounded glad to hear from him, as he always did after a long layoff. He didn't actually work for Makana, but there was an unwritten collaboration between them, an agreement that when his services were required he would make himself available. And in return . . . Makana did his best to make it worth his while, although clearly money was not Sindbad's only incentive to drive for him. He was off as soon as he heard Makana's voice, describing the dreary reality of ordinary life as a taxi driver.

'One whole week, *ya bash-muhandis*, driving Americans around, not just to the Museum and Giza. Oh, no, up and down, to Sakkara and Dashour and Memphis even. The truth is they put us to shame, these foreigners. They know more about our country than we do, I swear. We visited pyramids I've never even heard of. Also, they paid me exactly what we agreed on, no haggling at the last minute to try and cut the cost.'

'It's good to hear that there are still honest people in the world.'

They agreed a time and place. When he hung up Makana turned to find Sami holding out his telephone. Rania's cousin did know Mourad Hafiz and was willing to talk.

'We ran a workshop for them, about three months ago. I remember him. Smart, but like a lot of young people nowadays he lacked focus.'

'I'm trying to get an idea of the kind of person he is, the sort of things that interest him.'

'The same thing all kids of that age are interested in, at least those with a modicum of intelligence. He sees the world as unfair. The division of wealth. That was very much the focus of our workshop. Urban decay, the kinds of communities who live scattered about the city. He was quite shocked, I think, to realise how bad things are for people.'

'You mean, what, the poorer quarters of town?'

'Refugees. Sudanese, mostly, but also Eritreans, Ethiopians, Africans generally. They have the worst of it.'

61

'This would have been after the camp started outside the mosque in Mohandiseen?'

'It would have been around that time, yes.'

When he had finished talking Makana thanked him and turned around to hand back the phone. He found Sami busy unpacking a rucksack.

'You don't mind, do you?'

'Why would I mind?' Makana pointed at the bag. 'Looks like you're thinking of staying for a while.'

'Well, just until this blows over. Who knows how long that might take.'

'Who knows,' echoed Makana.

Sami grinned. 'Still, what are friends for, eh? Maybe you can order something for supper while I take a shower?'

Chapter Seven

The church of Our Lady Josephine was protected by a wall of grey breeze blocks. Fists of cement like petrified tears leaked from cracks here and there, like an everyday miracle. The pinnacle of the church roof could just be glimpsed over the top: sheets of rusted corrugated iron cut and bent into a rough spire. The improvised construction seemed to say something about the dedication and humility of the congregation, as if their faith had been shaped and beaten out of remnants discarded by the city. The gate to the church compound was made of the same material. It reverberated like a drum when Makana rapped on the door. A face appeared framed in a little window cut into the metal at around waist level.

'Yes?'

Makana bent to address the speaker. 'I'd like to speak to a priest, or someone in charge.'

The man eyed him warily. 'What is your business here?'

'I'm not going to discuss that out here. Just get the person in charge please.'

'You have no business here.'

'Are you the priest?'

'No, but I am telling you.'

There was something hard and stony about him that went beyond mere distrust. The door wouldn't be opened by threats nor, Makana suspected, by money.

'Look, I'm not looking for problems. Just let me speak to whoever is charge.'

'Cornelius! Let the man inside, please.'

There was a delay as the doorman fumbled with a set of keys to unlock the padlock and draw the heavy chain through. The task was not made easier by the fact that the man's left arm ended in an ugly stump where his hand should have been.

The door swung open to reveal a corpulent man in a white soutane. Beside a solitary palm tree planted in the middle of the bare yard, a short, round figure stood with his hands clasped behind his back. The tree barely matched his diminutive height. His name, he said, was Father Saturnius.

'Anyone who comes here in peace is welcome.' The priest's smile revealed a wide gap between two prominent front teeth.

The compound was dominated by the church, a simple structure made of more of the same grey breeze blocks as the outer wall. A large wooden cross rose above the vaulted roof from a roughly fashioned spire of iron sheets. Along one side of the compound a row of simple rooms was connected by a low veranda held up by green wooden posts. A string of coloured lights were draped around a makeshift wooden manger to mark the forthcoming nativity celebrations. Father Saturnius tilted his head to one side as Makana explained his visit. When he mentioned that Amir Medani had recommended he visit the church, the priest grew warmer.

'Amir is a great friend. He has represented us in court several times, always contributing his expertise for free. A great and noble man.'

As he led the way along, Father Saturnius indicated the buildings and their purpose. Makana, it seemed, was to be treated to the full tour.

'A schoolroom for teaching the young ones. A dining hall allows us to provide meals for the needy. Our resources are limited but people are struggling. We try to do the best we can.'

The wall was decorated with naïvist paintings depicting scenes from the Bible: Moses in the desert accompanied by a burning bush; the exodus from Egypt; the Ten Commandments wafting down from heaven on feathered wings; Jesus entering Jerusalem; Noah ushering animals onto his ark, two by two. There was something about the

65

style that struck Makana as vaguely familiar. At the end of the montage he found the answer he was looking for: the name Fantômas was scrawled low down. Father Saturnius was delighted to hear that he also knew the artist.

'He works with a friend of mine. They share a studio.'

'One of our most dedicated supporters. He came and offered his services. He runs workshops for the children. It is a great thing to share one's God-given gifts.'

'I'm sure you're right,' said Makana. They had drawn up to a mural dedicated to Josephine Bakhita, after whom the church was named.

'I was particularly happy about the way this turned out.'

The panel was an illustrated account of the saint's life. Born in Darfur in the nineteenth century, she was taken captive by slavers who scarred and beat her. Salvation came in the form of an Italian family into whose hands she was mercifully sold. When the Mahdi's Islamist revolt swept across Sudan in the 1880s, they decided to bring her with them to Italy for her own safety.

'There she was revered. She once said that if she ever met those who had kidnapped and enslaved her she would fall to her knees and thank them, because it was through them that she had discovered Christ.' The rotund priest was positively aglow. 'There could be no better example of the values we try to pass on to our young people.'

Two rooms were reserved for a small dispensary and clinic. A row of people sat on a bench waiting, several of them with children. A slim white woman with short blonde hair appeared in the doorway. She wore a lab coat and had a stethoscope draped around her neck.

'And this is our medical officer.' Father Saturnius's broad face split in a grin. He introduced the woman as an American doctor, Liz Corbis. 'Alas, she is with us for too short a time.'

Makana would have put her age at around the mid-forties, but there was something unworldly about her, as if uncomfortable with the attention. She studied him when she thought he wasn't looking at her.

'Miss Corbis and her brother the Reverend Preston have been a great help to us in our time of need,' the priest explained. 'We receive no help from our own government or from this one. We depend on the Lord's help, and the kindness of a few strangers. How many years have you been coming back to us, Doctor Corbis?'

'Oh, this is our fifth year.'

'Every year we are blessed with their assistance for a few short weeks. We shall leave you to see to your patients, Doctor.'

With a brief farewell Doctor Corbis retreated inside her clinic. Makana still hadn't got to the matter he had come here for, but that didn't seem to matter so much right now. Gaining the priest's trust was his first priority.

'Shall I tell you what the hardest thing is? It is preaching to the young, telling them that they must not meet hate with hate.'

Father Saturnius's office was at the far end. Here too there was a bench set outside for people to wait, in this case a young man. The room was sparsely furnished. A simple table acted as a desk. A low cupboard against one wall had chipped paint and one leg supported by a rough block of wood. On the wall behind the desk hung a crucifix with a vividly painted and bleeding clay figure of Christ suspended on the cross. On the other side a series of newspaper clippings and photographs had been fixed to a noticeboard on the wall. Father Saturnius settled his bulk into the creaking chair.

'How do you teach a generation who have grown up knowing only war and exclusion not to meet violence with violence? This is a question I struggle with every day. The young man sitting out there has a problem with drugs. It is common among the young. They sniff glue, petrol, anything they can get their hands on. All I have to offer them are the teachings of Christ, the belief that we must learn to turn the other cheek.'

'Sounds like you have your hands full.'

Father Saturnius lifted his hands in a gesture of resignation. 'I wish I could say that I believe it is working. Now, please tell me why you are here.'

Makana described the human remains that the fisherman had pulled out of the water the previous morning. Father Saturnius heaved a sigh.

'A tragic story, but I do not see how this is of your concern.'

68

'It isn't, not really.'

The priest raised his eyebrows. 'This is what you do, take up the causes of injustice?'

'I wouldn't put it quite like that. People come to me for help and sometimes I can do so. In return they pay me a fee for my time. It's not much of a living, but it's what I do best.'

'Forgive me for prying, but I get the impression that you have worked previously with the security services?'

'I was a policeman before I came to this country. I fell foul of the regime, which explains how I wound up here.'

'Your situation is not so different from ours then.' A sly smile crossed the priest's face. 'Forgive me for being so inquisitive, but I still do not fully understand. Unless I am mistaken nobody has asked for your assistance in this case.'

'That is correct.'

Father Saturnius folded his hands together on the desk. He was silent for a moment. 'I think I understand.'

'I'm not sure I fully understand myself, Father.'

'You are here because you feel that an injustice has been done. Not by yourself, of course, but by your fellow Northerners.' He lifted his hands almost in a gesture of prayer. 'Do you really believe that centuries of Northern oppression can be put right single-handedly?'

Makana glanced out of the window to his left. 'I grew up in a country that is very different from what it is today. There used to be a belief that if we could only overcome our differences, if we could see beyond race, religion and tribe, we could truly become a nation.'

'The evidence suggests that we failed that test, wouldn't you agree?'

'Perhaps, but surely that doesn't mean the idea was wrong.'

'Mr Makana, please don't take this the wrong way. I understand what you are saying, but there is nothing you can do.' The priest smiled. 'My advice is that you forget this unfortunate incident. Go on with your life. Leave us to heal our own.'

'With all due respect, Father, this is not about you or me. A crime was committed. Someone murdered that young man and cut the body into pieces to try and cover up the crime. If the killing was racially motivated the killers may strike again.'

'We can take care of our own.'

'You can believe that if you want to, but I'm telling you that you're on your own. The police are not going to take an interest. Nobody is coming here to help you. I'm all you've got.'

Father Saturnius was silent for a moment. He shifted in his chair. 'Tell me, Mr Makana, are you familiar with the Christian saints? No matter. Jude the Apostle is known as the patron saint of hopeless causes. It would seem that you are something of a modern equivalent.'

'I didn't come here for a reward, Father, spiritual or otherwise. I came because I think I can help. Maybe I was

70

wrong.' Makana started to get to his feet. The priest held up a hand to stop him. He gave a loud sigh.

'I suppose I am as guilty as anyone. I wish I could put the war behind me, but I can't. I too have lost family. I too have experienced prejudice at the hands of Northerners and I have little optimism in the idea of our continued coexistence.'

'The war is over, Father. North and South are at peace.'

'And I hope that it lasts, but there's very little trust left between us, too many agreements dishonoured.'

'If we cannot come together over an issue as grave as this then the bigots will have won the day. What does your faith say about that?'

'Christmas is almost upon us. A time of celebration. It is a season for generosity.' Father Saturnius allowed himself a smile. 'I believe you are a good man, Mr Makana, that your heart is in the right place. Your gesture is appreciated. I can assure you that you can count on my support and the assistance of our volunteers. As for the rest of the congregation, I can ask them to cooperate but I cannot promise they will comply. Distrust runs deep, and a Northerner coming to help us will be viewed with some suspicion, I'm afraid.'

'I understand.'

They both got to their feet and moved towards the door.

'You are a persuasive man, Mr Makana. I am old enough to admit that I allowed my prejudice to momentarily blind me.'

'Whoever killed that young man may have been driven by the very same prejudices you speak of.'

'A hate crime? Yes, of course, it is possible.' Father Saturnius nodded. 'I wish I could say I am shocked, but my years here have hardened me to the cruelty man is capable of. It goes without saying that you can rely on my help in any way.'

'Thank you, Father.'

'Do you have any idea who the victim is, or was?'

'There isn't much to identify him I'm afraid. The water and the fish have done their work, so his face is not what it was. The rest of the body has not been located. The head is with the Chief Forensic Officer right now, undergoing tests.' Makana described the lines on the man's head, drawing them with his finger on the desk. Father Saturnius nodded before he was finished.

'Mundari. It is a very distinctive pattern and that might help us, because it is a relatively small community compared with others.'

'It's possible that this man, whoever he is, was mixed up in some kind of criminal activity. The fact that he was cut into pieces suggests his killers could be very dangerous people.'

'It is the tragedy of a generation. The younger ones feel alienated. We try to give them a sense of belonging. They grew up in refugee camps without fathers. They look for leaders, older boys sometimes lead them into bad ways. There are limits to what the church can achieve, I'm afraid.'

Makana handed him a card with his telephone number.

'Give me a call if you hear anything. Anything at all. No matter how small, it might help.'

As they strolled back along the veranda Father Saturnius indicated the building at the centre of the compound.

'The church is a rock we must cling to. Our people have been in danger for centuries. We have lost our land, our families. Many dream of homes that no longer exist. They dream of making a new life abroad. The truth is that most of them must accept that this is where we have to make our home. Watch it!'

Makana had to swerve to avoid colliding with a girl coming out of the kitchen carrying a large plastic tub full of gleaming enamel plates. Around her neck she wore a distinctive silver cross.

'Sorry, Father,' she sang out as she went around them.

'Watch where you are going, Estrella,' Father Saturnius scolded before turning back to Makana. 'A special meal is being prepared for the Christmas celebrations. Everyone is a little overexcited, I'm afraid.'

'I think I understand your position, Father,' said Makana as they continued.

The priest's sharp eyes examined him carefully. 'Maybe you do, and maybe you don't. Take Cornelius for example. It is easy to comprehend his distrust.' Ahead of them the gatekeeper perched on a lopsided stool, staring morosely at Makana with a malevolent look.

'When Cornelius was a boy he was caught in the market in Khartoum stealing a mango. The judge ordered that his hand be removed, as prescribed by Islamic law. This despite the fact that the boy was not a Muslim. To him you will always represent the North, the Arab slaver, the fanatics who took away his hand.'

'Maybe we all have to learn how to trust each other.'

'I couldn't agree more.' Father Saturnius indicated the small trees and aloe vera bushes planted in split oil drums that dotted the wall. 'The neighbours don't like us here. This was a desolate patch of wasteland when we came here. Still, they call the police, claim drugs are being sold, that prostitution and gambling are taking place. They come out. We argue. They go away. All it takes is a spark and one day it will all go up in flames . . .'

Makana shook hands with the priest and approached the exit where Cornelius got reluctantly to his feet to open the gate for him. He had the sense someone was watching him. When he glanced back towards the row of buildings he saw the girl standing in the kitchen doorway and he remembered where he had seen her before.

Chapter Eight

Outside Makana found Sindbad in a heated discussion with two ugly men standing next to a battered Mazda the colour of a rotten banana. It wasn't clear what was going on. Sindbad was nose to nose with the larger of the two. Both men wore cheap leather jackets. The smaller one stood to one side, looking idly on, smoking a cigarette.

'Is there a law against parking here?' Sindbad stepped forward, almost butting heads with the other man, who was obliged to step back. Despite his bulk, the big man was light on his feet, a legacy of his years in the boxing ring before he started driving for a living. 'That's all I'm asking. If there's a law then show it to me.'

'One of these days someone is going to teach you some manners.'

'Sure, but you'd better bring your mother along to help you.'

Makana pushed Sindbad off to one side and led him away. He took it badly.

'What are you doing, *ya basha*? I can take care of both of them.'

'I'm in no doubt that you can. I just don't think it's a particularly good idea.'

He pushed Sindbad towards the battered black and white Datsun taxi and turned back to face the two men. They had the stamp of the *Dakhliya* all over them and clearly hailed from some branch of the security services.

'What's going on here?'

'He's a little hot-headed, your man there,' said the second man, pushing off the Mazda to come forward. 'We're just doing our job.'

The two men were physically opposites. The first tall, this one short, with skin like a lizard and a thin moustache. The tall one had a bent ear.

'What job would that be?'

'What do you think?' asked the moustache. 'What makes it your business, anyway?'

'This man was waiting for me. We're not breaking any laws. The car is perfectly fine where it is. So, if you have an official complaint, I'd like to hear it.'

'I don't answer to you. I asked you your business, and I'm asking again. What are you doing inside that church?'

'Like I said, we're not breaking any laws. And unless you have evidence that says otherwise I don't see that has anything to do with you.'

'How about we begin with not cooperating with officers of the state?'

'You're police officers?'

'That's right.' Moustache grinned as he flipped up a grubby warrant card that identified him as Detective Sergeant Hakim of Giza prefecture. 'This is my colleague Karim,' Hakim said, nodding at Bent Ear.

'You're a long way from home.'

'I could say the same about you,' Hakim replied. 'So what is your business here?'

'A social call. How about yourselves?'

Hakim grinned. 'You're a funny guy. What kind of social call? You're not Christians, are you?'

'I don't think there's a law against being a Christian in this country. Not yet, at least.'

'You have some kind of ID on you?'

Makana produced the battered card that identified him. Hakim studied it for a moment before handing it to the tall one who had sauntered over.

'Makana. Funny name. Rings a bell though.' Karim tapped the card against his hand before flipping it back.

'Go on now. And make sure you keep King Kong over there chained up next time.'

Makana watched the two detectives head back to their car and wondered what their interest in the church

77

might be. Rare to see such dedication these days, and somehow they didn't strike him as the conscientious type.

The delay was made worse by the traffic, so that Makana arrived at the Diwan bookshop twenty minutes after the appointed time to meet Mourad's sister. Not seeing Sahar in the café he assumed that she had given up and left, but decided to wander through the bookshop anyway, where he found her browsing through a stack of the latest novels, most of which Makana had never heard of.

'Mourad and I often used to come here together. He's more drawn to the factual stuff, biographies of politicians, history, stories about wars. I'm always trying to get him to read novels, but he thinks they are a waste of time. I suppose that's what you expect from an engineer.'

'Is that how he thinks of himself, as an engineer?' It seemed to contradict the picture Makana was beginning to form of a dreamer who lacked focus and had possibly dropped out of university just before the end-of-term exams.

'It's an interesting question. Sometimes I think he is less realistic than I am. I suppose with him it's this idea that there is so much to learn.'

They made their way back through to the café, where two well dressed ladies, fresh from the hairdresser by the look of them, were debating what a caffè latte actually was. The waiter, a young man with a nervous smile, was sweating under the pressure. Sahar asked for cappuccino. Makana ordered the same, if only to simplify matters.

'I was hoping that you would be able to tell me that you were making progress,' she began. 'My parents are more worried than they like to admit. They don't say it, but they think something terrible has happened to him.'

'And you, what do you think?'

'I don't know what to think, really.' She stared at the table. 'The idea of losing him seems too awful to bear.' Her eyes lifted to meet his. 'I can't believe he would go off without saying something.'

'If he disappeared of his own free will it's possible that he had a reason, perhaps something or someone he was afraid of. Did he ever mention anything like that?'

'Never.' Sahar shook her head.

'Did you know he was working in a fast-food place?'

'No. Why would he do something like that?' She frowned. 'What kind of fast-food place?'

Makana told her what he knew. Sahar was taken aback at first and then surprise gave way to anger.

'He must have known how much that would hurt my parents. They did all they could to help him, and he knows we're not rich. The restaurant doesn't make as much as we like to think it does.' Her eyes glistened and she dabbed at her tears with a paper napkin. 'I can't believe he would do something like that. Why not come and help us?'

'Perhaps he didn't want to be a burden. He thought he could make some money on the side. Is that so strange?'

'We're a small family, Mr Makana. We're very close. He knows how much the restaurant means to them, especially my father.'

'Then maybe this was his way of breaking free?'

Sahar looked at him for a moment. 'You mean taking a job just to spite them?'

'Not necessarily. He's a young man. He needs to make his way in the world. This job gave him independence, a chance to prove he could do things his own way. It made him less dependent on your parents for money that is in short supply.'

'But why keep it a secret?

'Perhaps he knew it would upset them.'

'I suppose you might have a point.' Sahar stared down at the folded napkin in her hands. 'He knew the sacrifices that were being made to allow him to study.'

'Did he resent that in some way, being dependent?'

'I don't know. I know that he almost refused to go to university. My parents insisted. They wanted their son to have what they never did.'

'What about you?'

'Me?' The question seemed to take Sahar by surprise. She allowed herself a half-smile. It was a tense, awkward effort.

'You seem to bear more than your fair share of the weight.'

'How do you mean?'

'I mean, there's Mourad off pursuing a career, which leaves you at home, literally in the kitchen helping your parents. It doesn't give you a lot of time to be yourself.'

'I don't really think about it all that much.'

The coffee arrived and she began to stir patterns in the layer of frothy milk on top. Makana studied his cup. Things had changed, he decided, if this was what a cup of coffee was nowadays. He reached for the sugar bowl the way a drowning man might clutch at a twig.

'I've always been more closely connected to the restaurant,' Sahar continued. 'There are a few things I would change.'

'You mean, to modernise the place?' A scattering of sugar grains seemed to help calm the effervescent milk.

'We need to get young people to come in. My parents think differently. They see themselves as upholding a tradition, which means serving exactly the same dishes that my grandfather did.'

'But you don't?'

'I think we need to move with the times.'

'How does Mourad feel about it?' The milk had finally subsided to the point where Makana dared to take a sip. Underneath the frothy façade the coffee was watery and faint. A cigarette might have improved matters, but he suspected this wasn't that sort of place.

'Oh . . .' Sahar put a hand to her forehead as if to think. 'He's always seen himself as rather special. You know how it is. The boy in the family . . .' Her voice tailed off, as if reading his mind, hearing the touch of resentment in her voice. Looking out towards the street she tried to correct herself. 'I mean, he's always seen himself as different, as if he had some important purpose in life.'

'How do you mean?'

'When he was a kid he was always getting crazy ideas. He would run away and we would all have to go out and search for him. Once he's got his heart set on something he never gives up. He won't stop until he gets it. That's why he and my father were always arguing.'

'What did they argue about?'

'The same things fathers and sons always argue about,' she shrugged. 'The way things are done. Nothing serious.'

'What about politics? Does he take an interest in that?'

'Not really. He thinks it's all quite hopeless.' She sipped her coffee quickly. 'I mean, everything is such a mess. The economy. He says we're all part of a great big game. Democracy is a farce. We don't even have a country any more.'

'What did he mean by that?'

'Just that it's been hijacked by those in power. He says we have no values any more. All we believe in is money and getting by.'

'Sounds like quite the idealist.'

'I never took any of that too seriously. A lot of hot air. He would never do anything about it. It's all pie in the sky. Now he's studying engineering. Before that it was agriculture. He wanted to end famine, find a way to grow enough food for the world. One day Africa will feed the world, he used to say. I would laugh at him.'

*

In Makana's view, idealists, like fanatics, should never be underestimated. He had already pulled his Cleopatras from his pocket when the waiter caught his eye. With the exaggerated gestures of a professional mime, he indicated the sign on the wall behind Makana. He still had the perpetual smile of an idiot who has been kicked in the head by a horse, but had cheered up somewhat. The two ladies were comparing the flavour of their coffee, their cups now adorned with traces of lipstick.

'His interests changed all the time. When he was a teenager he wanted to run away and join the Palestinian freedom fighters. He would get upset and launch into these long tirades at anyone who would listen.'

'What about this Abdelhadi he shared a room with?'

'A strange one. He took things. Mourad asked for another room. Nothing happened. I think he's quite religious. Mourad hates people who take their religion too seriously.'

'You say he took things. What kind of things?'

'Just things. Books, pens. Mourad even caught him trying on his clothes once,' Sahar giggled.

'How about girls?'

'No, he never had time for that kind of thing.'

'You mean he isn't interested in girls?'

'Oh, no, I don't mean to imply . . .' She was momentarily embarrassed. 'He likes girls. It's just that most of them at university, that's all they think of. He thought it was all a bit shallow.'

'Can I get you anything else?' The beaming waiter interposed himself, picking up Makana's barely touched cup. Makana gave him a look which sent him away.

'Please go on.'

'Well, the way he saw it, politics was hopeless. People spend all their lives dreaming about making money. They don't think about changing their environment. We're stuck together like chickens in a cage, he would say. Urban planning would give him a chance to make this city a better place to live.' The idea made her smile. 'We need air to breathe.'

'If it's so important to him, why disappear now, just before the end-of-term exams?'

'I don't know. That's what worries me.'

Sahar gave him the names of a couple of people who might talk to him.

'He doesn't make friends easily. Those that he does have tend to be like him, people who keep to themselves.'

'What does he spend his money on?'

'He doesn't, not really. He's not interested in fashion, or clothes. He did buy a computer. I was surprised at that.'

'Is that unusual?'

'Well, it was an Apple PowerBook. You know how expensive they are.' Makana would have hazarded a guess but didn't want to make an issue of it. 'Anyway, he wanted to keep it a secret. I understand that. Our parents wouldn't understand spending money on something like that.'

'Where is this computer now?'

'I don't know. It should be in his room.'

Makana sat back. He avoided her gaze. Sahar seemed to be waiting for something that he couldn't supply. Answers, when all he really had was more questions.

'My parents are not young, Mr Makana. This matter is affecting their health.'

'If Mourad had wanted to disappear, where would he go? Is there some favourite place he might have in mind? Somewhere you went as children?'

'Nowhere that I can think of. And why would he run away without telling us, his family?'

'People run away for all sorts of reasons. He could simply need some time to himself.'

'I'm afraid for him,' Sahar said as she got to her feet. 'I was really hoping I could tell my parents that you were making progress.'

'Soon. These things take time.'

He remained where he was long after she'd left, until he noticed the waiter on the other side of the room still smiling at him, and decided he'd had enough of the place.

Chapter Nine

There were a thousand reasons why a young man might disappear for a few weeks. The proximity of the exams might have put pressure on Mourad, spurring him to get away from it all, to lose himself in the anonymity of unfamiliar territory. He might have fallen in love, lost his head to a whirlwind passion and be hidden in some secret corner of the world, oblivious of the concern he was causing at home. To a young man worry was something you didn't need to concern yourself with just yet. Its time would come, and when it did there would be plenty of it – his parents were proof of that. Up to a point, Makana had no cause to worry about Mourad's well-being. He believed there were enough benign possibilities to explain his absence. In all likelihood the young man would turn up, unharmed and no worse off, stricken by a guilty conscience possibly, but secretly glad that he had had the courage to follow his dreams. At the back of his mind, however, there was a stirring that upset this picture, a loose thread in this story, something that wouldn't shake itself out into a real worry but remained a concern. Until it emerged, Makana decided he might just as well pursue the case that fate had delivered to his doorstep. The severed head preoccupied him in a way that he could not quite explain. It had something to do with his past, with unresolved issues that lingered out there on the edge of his mind. It left him restless and unsettled.

He found Doctora Siham buried in the unforgiving basement of the Institute of Pathology, deep in thought. So much so that she barely registered the heavy door opening and closing behind him with a hiss of rubber flanges, but raised her head slightly before bowing down to the task in hand. Doctora Siham was the chief forensic officer and leading pathologist at the institute. She wasn't the director because, naturally, the director was expected to be a man, but she was undoubtedly the best. The institute was affiliated with the Forensic Medicine Authority, which came under the Ministry of Justice. This peripheral status meant, effectively, that Doctora Siham could pick and choose the cases she took on. She had to balance work with her teaching obligations, and this suited her just fine. It also meant that she didn't have ministry officials breathing down her neck like awkward suitors.

The downside was that the department received very little funding and was essentially expected to make do with what was available. That they could function at all was in large part due to Doctora Siham's resourcefulness. They were economic with the lighting, with electricity in general, with storage tanks and specimen jars, with chemicals used in analysis, which limited the tests they could perform. All of this found perfect expression in the damp, dark basement; stifling in summer and shivering in winter. Even as a regular visitor over the years, Makana had never really grasped how anyone could spend so many hours down there in the gloom, in the company of the recently departed. The smell of the place would stay with you for days on end, returning in slight gasps, like an overdose of garlic. Doctora Siham's reputation as a hard-headed, no-nonsense woman preceded her wherever she went. Men tended to be intimidated by a woman who not only answered back, but was invariably correct when she did so. Physically she was striking, even in the harsh white light of the neon strips overhead. Tall and austere, square-shouldered, with a finely honed face, she tended to dress down, actively making herself look plainer and older than her years. How old she really was remained a mystery. He would have put her in her mid-forties, still handsome for her age.

Her office was a gloomy corner fenced off behind a screen of shelves crammed with old-fashioned specimen jars, bulky glass cylinders in which various human organs and deformed fetuses were suspended in jaundiced fluids.

A bizarre wall dedicated to our frail physical purchase on life. The office itself was cluttered with odd pieces of furniture like unwanted skeletons, ugly grey filing cabinets and cupboards that spoke of centuries of obscure research. Rows of obsolete instruments were ranged along counters like milestones on the road towards eternity.

Most of the time she was to be found in the examination room, perched on a high stool by the counter that ran along the far wall, poring over reports in cool silence. Makana had somehow managed to keep on the right side of her over the years, despite her reputation. On good days he was almost capable of imagining there existed a form of mutual respect between them.

'I was wondering when you would show up,' she said, stubbing out her cigarette as she slid off the stool. There was a strict no-smoking policy here, but it was rarely enforced, especially by Doctora Siham, and no one as yet had plucked up the courage to try. Pushing her hands into the pockets of her white lab coat, she tilted her head towards the steel examination table nearest to them. 'I'm thinking of calling him Yorick, or maybe Hussein would be more appropriate. Why rely on Shakespeare when we have our own tradition of venerating fallen heads?'

'Has anyone else taken an interest?'

'You've been around long enough to know that nobody in the police department goes looking for problems to solve. Around here forensics is an afterthought. A sprinkling of pistachios on the pastry. First they find the guilty party, then they beat a confession out of him and then, and only then, does it occur to them that perhaps they could use something to fatten up the report.'

She seemed to be in fighting form this morning. Makana lit a cigarette and hung back, sensing it was wise at this instant to give her space. She whipped back the sheet covering a deep stainless-steel tray. The battered, grizzled skull looked even more forlorn in this setting. It resembled the remnants of a bizarre ritual. Having been cleaned up it was now missing strips of tissue cut away for tests, the skin pulled back like a mask to reveal the bone structure underneath.

'I've only completed a preliminary examination, a few tissue samples and so forth. A detached head poses its own challenges. On the one hand you don't have much to go on. On the other it forces you to focus your attention carefully.'

The room hummed quietly to itself. Makana studied the empty eye socket that seemed to be aimed straight at him as the good doctor moved around the subject.

'I'm growing fond of this one, which means that I'd dearly like to find out why he was so abused.' She gave Makana a long look. 'So, what can I tell you about him? Well, first of all he is young, no more than sixteen or seventeen – a child really. He has fairly good teeth, which suggests a good diet until recently. There are signs of tooth decay developing. I don't think he has ever visited a dentist in his life, but he would have had to do so soon if he'd carried on like this.' She glanced back up at Makana. 'You know what's wrong with most forensic dentistry studies? Most of them were done somewhere like Sweden in the 1960s. Everyone has dental records and there's a high degree of social homogeneity. In the real world nobody can afford to see a dentist and there are no records.'

'You're saying you can't identify him by his teeth.' Makana leaned in over the tray. 'Any idea how his head got separated from his body?'

'I'm getting to that,' snapped Doctora Siham. Makana straightened up quickly. She caught his eye and relented. 'If you don't let me do this at my own pace I shall miss something.'

'I'm sorry. Please ignore me.' Makana stepped back. She studied him for a moment before returning to her work.

'I found fragments of cotton.'

'Cotton?'

'Loose, open-weave cotton to be exact.' Doctora Siham used a wooden spatula to indicate the corner of the mouth. 'It looks like the kind of material you find in a bandage.'

'He was in hospital?'

She gave him what might have been a look of exasperation. Makana decided to keep quiet for a while.

'Abrasions around the corners of his mouth suggest that he was gagged, at least for a time.'

'So this was not an accident?'

91

Doctora Siham shook her head. 'The trauma to the head is consistent with a heavy blow, administered here, at the base of the neck, with an instrument sharp and heavy enough to eventually pierce the spinal cord.'

'He was alive when his head was chopped off?'

'Not only alive, but the damage to the base of the neck suggests that a fairly small axe was used and that several blows were required. Whoever did this was no expert. He basically hacked away until it came free.'

Makana looked at the skull with renewed respect, and some revulsion. The boy, whoever he was, had been executed, brutally decapitated.

'So is that why he was gagged?'

'I leave that to you,' Doctora Siham said. She smiled. It was an unexpected gesture that took him by surprise. On her it seemed positively frivolous. It took a moment to focus on her words again.

'The skin tissue shows post-mortem cell decay consistent with a long period of immersion.'

'How long?'

'A week, perhaps a little more.'

'What about these wounds here?' Makana indicated what looked like deep cuts in the side of the neck and ear.

'Yes, interesting you should have noticed that.' She leaned closer for another look. 'At first, like you, I assumed they were caused by contact with a moving object, perhaps the propeller of a boat. That seemed the most likely explanation for the severing of the head.' Doctora

Siham straightened up and looked at him. 'These were not made by a piece of machinery.'

'What then?'

'For one thing they are too deep and also too narrow, fine. These were made by a series of sharp instruments that were used in a tearing movement.'

'You mean, like fishhooks or something?'

'Similar, but no, from the pattern I would say more like a claw.'

'A claw?' Makana echoed. 'You mean an animal did this?'

'A dog possibly. I've taken tissue samples, but with that amount of immersion I think it unlikely we will get a more accurate analysis.'

Makana reached for his cigarettes. From a single head the pathologist seemed to have extracted far more than he had imagined possible. He struck a match and breathed the smoke deeply into his lungs, replacing one chemical assault with another.

'But why remove the head?' He was thinking out loud, his eyes following the doctor as she retrieved her cigarettes from the counter and lit one. It was impossible not to smoke in here. The walls were slick with damp and the air impregnated with a stifling combination of harsh disinfectant, formaldehyde and the putrid sweetness of human decay. Compared with that the flavour of tobacco came up pure and clean. Doctora Siham studied the end of her cigarette.

'A ritual of some kind?'

'Are there rituals which involve removing the head?'

'I think the Incas and the Mayas did something like that. Also, in Nigeria there are tribes that practise sacrifices which involve removing the head.'

'You think that's what we're dealing with here?'

'I took the liberty of consulting Professor Asfour, who is head of the Department of Social Anthropology, and a friend.'

'I see.'

His comment drew an inquisitive look before her gaze returned to the head on the examination table.

'Professor Asfour said that the markings on his forehead suggest our young man is of Mundari ethnicity. As far as he knows they have no tradition of human sacrifice or decapitation.'

'So it could be something else. Some kind of tribal revenge?'

'Perhaps you'd like to talk to him yourself.'

Makana nodded, his eyes on the head resting in the steel tub. The more he learned about this young man's fate the more keenly he felt his pain. Somewhere there was a mother and father, a family that probably had no idea what had happened to their boy. It was beginning to feel personal.

'Like I said,' shrugged Doctora Siham as she stubbed out her cigarette, 'we'll know more when the lab reports come back.'

Chapter Ten

On the ride back across town Makana was lost in thought, though vaguely aware that Sindbad was still eager to share his new-found understanding of Ancient Egyptian traditions, thanks to his clients.

'Did you know they could remove the brain without breaking open the head? Shall I tell you how they did that?' The big man gestured with one hand while wheeling the Datsun around a cart whose donkey had decided to come to an abrupt standstill in the middle of the road. Cars hooted and weaved around the obstacle, which remained in place, stubbornly refusing to budge despite the knotted whip being lashed at its raw hind quarters. There was something noble and doomed about this protest, aimed not so much at the animal's cruel master as at the madness of modern life.

'They went in through the nose. Can you imagine?' Sindbad's face was a picture of wonder. 'They knew so many things. I swear, the doctors who are treating my poor mother could learn a thing or two.'

Makana refused to be drawn. He knew from past experience the dangers of encouraging Sindbad to talk while driving, especially on the subject of his mother's health, a bottomless well of stories.

'Then there are the artists. Have you heard of this Amen-something or other? He got rid of the priests and made himself god.' Sindbad was grinning now. 'We should do the same thing ourselves.'

'Get rid of the priests?'

'No, all those imams who keep telling us how to live our lives.' He held up a finger, growing solemn again. 'Actually, it made me realise how things never change in this country.'

Reaching for his phone, Makana marvelled at how there was a little philosopher in everyone. Ali Shibaker wasn't answering his phone, so he asked Sindbad to take a detour up to his studio. Ali was an old friend, an artist who ran a garage on the side. This time it was neither his artistic nor his mechanical talents Makana was after. It was already dark when they reached Sharia al-Sudan, and the poorly illuminated stairwell seemed to be overrun by a family of cats that scattered like smoke as he approached, scraping by him in a rush of fur. Cats made Makana's hair stand on end. Superstition, he knew, but cats had something other-worldly about them. He didn't like disturbing them, or causing them offence.

When he leaned on the bell it stuttered through a high-pitched chirp that eventually wound down. The door was opened by a young woman he had never set eyes on, one of the constantly evolving procession of 'assistants' Ali seemed to find. The man himself was in his studio hard at work on an engraving. He threw down his tools when he saw Makana and led him across to the other side of the apartment. The office faced onto the street, and down below it was possible to see the little workshop that Ali ran on the side, his boys still hard at it despite the late hour. He called out for coffee and sat down heavily behind the desk to light a cigarette.

'You still haven't given up on that old Datsun?'

Ali had been trying to persuade Makana to invest in a new vehicle for Sindbad. The last thing he had offered them was an enormous ship of an American car.

'I think Sindbad is planning to be buried in that car when he goes. That or build a pyramid and stick it on top.' Makana explained that he had been hoping to talk to Fantômas, the young artist who shared the studio with Ali.

'You're out of luck. He's caught up in this crazy protest. What in Allah's name do they hope to achieve? I ask you.' Getting to his feet, Ali strode across the room to begin rifling through a stack of canvases resting against the wall. 'Spend more time painting, I tell him. An artist can't allow himself to become distracted by politics. He's talented, but talent only gets you so far.'

While Ali carried on grumbling Makana studied the oil paintings. He was reminded of what he had seen at the church. These pictures all seemed to be steeped in anger and frustration, not sentiments he would have associated with the easygoing Fantômas. He wondered why he had not noticed this before. Perhaps he hadn't wanted to see the anguish. Ghostly figures. Dislocated faces floating in a void. Bathed in dark colours, blacks and blues, they had an ominous air about them. They spoke of loss and pain. It seemed extraordinary that anyone could produce something so complete out of the chaos of everyday.

On the way back down Sharia al-Dowal al-Arabiya, Makana thought about the paintings at the church. He remembered the girl he had seen in the doorway of the kitchen, the way she had been watching him. It was definitely the same girl he had seen mopping the floor in Westies. Estrella was the name, but who was she? Was there a connection between her and Mourad, he wondered.

The camp looked even more ramshackle than before. Scraps of cloth and colourful acrylic blankets were draped over lengths of washing line strung between lamp-posts. Sheets of cardboard were bent and shaped into walls and shelters bound together with blue nylon twine. It all seemed random and improvised. The inhabitants moved in a daze. Some sat around in groups, others lay patiently as if waiting for a solution to present itself. Incongruous objects like hard-shell suitcases and large televisions were dotted about, stacked here and there. Somewhere a radio was playing, elsewhere a lute, improvised from a tin can and a strip of electric wire, was being softly strummed. An air of despair hung over it all, as if some unnameable catastrophe had struck, leaving this community high and dry on their little concrete island in the midst of a city that no longer cared to see them.

Through the forest of tall dark men and women, Makana spotted the slight figure of the American doctor he had met at the church. Under her white coat Liz Corbis wore plain trousers and flat, sensible shoes.

'Your duties never end, Doctor.' She stared blankly back at him, momentarily at a loss. 'Father Saturnius introduced us,' he reminded her gently.

'Oh, yes, of course. Mr . . .?'

'Makana.'

She broke off to issue orders to two young men covered in a sheen of sweat who were busy unloading boxes of bottled water from a heavily overloaded pickup.

'There's really not much for me to do. It takes care of itself and Preston manages the rest.'

'Preston?'

'My brother, Preston.' She pointed out a man dressed in black shirt and trousers. The white band of his collar stood out in the half-light. With his hands on his hips he addressed a group of men who were speaking earnestly to him.

'I'm sure you provide invaluable assistance, and are much appreciated.'

Liz Corbis took a moment to study him. The evening breeze disturbed her hair. As she put up a hand to push it aside Makana saw the uncertainty in her eyes. To be expected perhaps, in a devout Christian woman who finds herself in a foreign country surrounded by Muslims. She saw in him what she saw in most of what was around her: potential threat. It explained her affinity with the church: the Southerners being Christians made them more welcoming hosts, not to say grateful recipients of their charity.

'You must know this country well by now,' he offered, trying to put her at ease.

'It's hard to believe, but ten years ago I would have had trouble picking out Sudan on a map. Now I know the Dinka from the Nuer. I even speak a few words of their language.'

'Progress,' he said, finding a smile.

'Yes, I suppose you could say that. And what brings you here?'

'I was looking for information, about a young man who has gone missing.' As he spoke the words Makana marvelled at the irony. Which young man was he looking for, Mourad Hafiz or the nameless head lying on the examination table in the pathology lab?

'Correct me if I'm wrong, but you're a Northerner, are you not?'

'That's right.'

'And a Muslim? No offence, it's just that we don't see many Northerners here.'

'None taken.'

'Is this man bothering you, Sister?'

The newcomer was a young man with a lean, hard face criss-crossed by scars. He wore the staple uniform of his generation, outsize blue jeans that threatened to fall about his ankles. Over this a khaki vest and white tracksuit top with red, gold and green stripes down the arms. Around his neck a handful of chains and necklaces, strings of leather amulets to ward off evil. Behind him trailed a small entourage of similarly dressed young men. Doctor Corbis took the intrusion in her stride.

'No, Aljuka, he's not bothering me in any way.' Her smile was a mixture of annoyance and amusement.

'Policeman? Spy?' he said with scorn, looking Makana up and down. 'What brings you here?'

'You're mistaken,' Makana said, surveying the crowd.

'A brother from Khartoum.' His accent gave him away, the smile as lean and mocking as a razor blade. 'You have no business here.'

'Are you running all this?' Makana gestured at the disarray surrounding them.

Aljuka ignored the question. 'Don't think you are safe here. Khartoum kills our people, burns our villages, murders our women and children.' Behind him the men bristled, eager to get at Makana. They clenched their fists and spat on the ground. A raised hand held them uneasily at bay.

'Then your fight is with Khartoum, not with me.'

101

'My brother!' Out of the crowd a loping, dreadlocked figure. Fantômas was older than Aljuka and more heavily built. Age commanded its own respect, or perhaps the artist had a reputation among the young men.

'You know this man?'

'He's one of us.' Fantômas patted Makana on the shoulder.

Aljuka frowned. 'What are you saying? He's one of them.'

'This time you are mistaken. He's one of us.' Fantômas carried himself with calm confidence. Already the tension was seeping away.

Aljuka shook his head. He stuck a finger in Makana's face. 'I'm watching you.' With that he turned on his heel and marched off, his men falling in behind. They cut a swathe through the camp as people stepped out of their path.

'Oh, my,' said Liz Corbis a little breathlessly. 'He is rather intense.'

'Aljuka is an orphan of war,' Fantômas said, as they watched the gang vanish into the crowd. 'He lost his family during government attacks in the Nuba Mountains in the 1990s. Since then he has moved from camp to camp.'

'Just when I think I understand a little about your country I discover that I don't.' Liz Corbis smiled. 'Where did he get that name anyway?'

'It's a kind of playing card. You know, a figure with a funny hat, who can do anything?'

'You mean a joker?' Doctor Corbis shook her head at the absurdity of it.

Fantômas explained, 'He and his men are always up to all kinds of tricks, money-making schemes. People respect him because he's so generous. He helps those in need.'

'Oh, you mean a kind of Robin Hood?' the doctor asked.

Unfamiliar with the name, Fantômas frowned. She waved her own suggestion aside, and excused herself, saying she had work to do.

'Actually, it's you I came to see.' Makana turned to Fantômas. 'What are you doing here?'

'Trying to do what I can to help in this crazy mess.' They turned to survey the scene before them. 'This is a bad time. People are suffering with this closed-file business.'

'Closed file, what's that?' Makana asked.

'If the UN rejects your application for political asylum, then the case is closed. You have no chance of being allowed to stay legally. It makes your situation worse. Better to be a grey area than to be identified as a reject. That's why many prefer to have nothing to do with the authorities.'

'Why do they get turned down? I mean, aren't they here because of war and persecution of one sort or another?'

'Sure, but try and prove that.' Fantômas brushed his dreadlocks back. 'Your case is different. You're a former officer of the law. You were arrested and imprisoned.'

Makana was well aware of the precarious nature of his presence in this country. He had no dependants but he was making a living of sorts. In many ways he knew that his

103

situation could change in the blink of an eye. He had found himself on the wrong side of the security services more than once and the threat of expulsion was never absent.

'Most arrive here without documents of any kind. To seek political asylum you need refugee status, and that's their first mistake. They've been betrayed by their own government. They don't trust anyone, not even the UN. They've heard enough stories about others being turned down, so they make stuff up. Of course in the interview it all falls apart.'

'What happens when they're turned down?'

'They have to start all over again. Two years more of waiting.'

They surveyed the camp in silence for a moment.

'You know what they call this place?' Fantômas asked. 'Jackal City.'

'Where does that come from?'

'Well, traditionally, the jackal used to inhabit cemeteries, and this is a graveyard of sorts.'

The astonishing thing wasn't the protest, but why it had taken so long to happen. Makana turned to Fantômas again.

'I saw some of your artwork this morning, at the Church of Josephine Bakhita.'

'What took you all the way out there?' Fantômas rubbed his chin. Makana told him about the severed head. 'The early forensic investigations suggest the victim was a young man, a Southerner. A Mundari, to be exact.'

'Mundari? There aren't many of those around.'

'You're smiling,' said Makana. 'I know what you're thinking.'

'Northern guilt. You can't put centuries right. You know that, don't you?'

'So people keep telling me.'

'You can't take it all back. People like Aljuka will still hate you.'

'Let me ask you, what makes you decide to paint one thing and not another?'

'I don't know.' Fantômas shrugged. 'You see it, the moment seizes you. Something like that.'

'Well, maybe that's what this is,' said Makana.

'Somebody came to you for your help on this?'

'There are always exceptions.'

'You're all right, Makana.' Fantômas laughed. 'A little strange sometimes, maybe. So tell me how I can help you.'

'There's someone working at the church I want to talk to, and it might help if I have a little backup.'

'You mean you need me to lend you some street credibility?'

'It's just that I get the feeling I'm not too popular over there right now.'

'You're Nubian, not Arab anyway. That practically makes you one of us.'

'When did it all turn tribal again?'

'It never stopped. You just weren't paying attention.'

'What do you know about those two?' Makana nodded off towards Liz Corbis, who was wandering through the crowd, pausing here and there to speak to someone, offer advice or dispense medicines from a trunk being carried around by a young man who followed behind her. Now she was joined by her brother.

'What can I tell you? Missionaries. It seems there are plenty of good people in America who are willing to give money to help us. They are here a couple of times a year. They run a clinic at the church and they have a programme to help young people to get to America.'

'Everyone needs something to believe in.'

On his way back to the car, Makana's phone began to vibrate. It was Okasha.

'I need you to get into that thing you call a car and drive out on the Cairo–Ismailia highway. Just before 10th Ramadan City you turn to the right.'

'What am I looking for?'

'You'll know when you see it.'

Chapter Eleven

The fire was visible from the main highway, some way off to the east. They missed the turning for the curiously named Geneva Road and had to double back to find themselves on a narrow strip of tarmac running through open ground. An angry orange glow spiked the black horizon, ringed by a nervous flurry of red and blue lights. A roadblock had been set up to control the traffic and Makana leaned out of the window to speak to the first police officer they reached.

'Inspector Okasha?'

They were flagged on from one officer to the next until they reached the firefighters still spraying gouts of white foam which, from time to time, released the flare of a hot blue flame. Black smoke billowed up from beneath the gutted chassis of what appeared to have been a petrol tanker.

A succession of uniformed men blocked their progress, armed soldiers who peered inside the Datsun before waving them on. An officer was shouting into a hand-held radio set, apparently to no avail. Ambulance crews stood around waiting to be told what to do. Nobody appeared to be in need of urgent medical attention. The victims were all beyond that. They finally located Okasha standing off to one side surrounded by a group of officers. The location of the accident had clearly drawn various police forces in. When he caught sight of Makana he waved him to wait to one side. Eventually, he made his way over.

'A little off your usual beat, aren't you?'

Without a word, Okasha beckoned for Makana to follow him. The air left a smoky, singed feeling in his mouth, like steel and ashes. The sand was covered by a hard crust that crunched underfoot like glass crystals. The tanker was sprawled half on its side, sunk down onto its frame, the tyres melted into the scorched sand, a blackened, burnt-out wreck. The driver, or what was left of him, looked small behind the wheel, as if the heat had shrunk the body into a charred wooden icon, a doll whittled out of carbon and toasted to a crisp. It bore only a bizarre resemblance to a human being. Wisps of smoke rose from the curled shoulders. Okasha was pointing to the tracks in the sand curving from the lip of the roadside.

'He was trapped when the vehicle tipped over as it came off the road. He's young, perhaps fifteen. No doubt he was driving too fast and very probably without a licence. He wouldn't have stood a chance. He'd be cooked alive.'

The driver's mouth was locked wide in a never-ending scream that would never be heard. The faintly sweetish smell in the air was that of roasted meat. Not a nice way to go. Okasha was already moving towards the second vehicle, a small Mitsubishi minivan with panelled sides that was some thirty metres away. It had no markings on it. The front end was completely crushed. Three firemen were busy trying to cut what was left of the occupant out of the mangled remains of the driver's cab.

'It didn't catch fire?'

Okasha shook his head. 'It's so light it must have bounced on impact and rolled away, but the occupants were badly crushed.'

'What is the army doing here?'

'Anti-terrorist squad. The tanker was almost full. The explosion was big enough to make people think it was a bomb.'

'So they were the first on the scene?'

'That's right.' Okasha beckoned Makana over. He crouched down and pointed into the cab. 'We haven't identified the driver yet, but we think there was a second man in the car. There's blood on the dashboard and door.'

'Where did he go?' Makana looked up and down the road, following the tracks made in the sand, trying to work out how the accident might have happened.

'We don't know. Maybe he was concussed or something.'

It could happen. A head wound might cause all kinds of confusion. 'The van was coming from Cairo, and the tanker?'

'The other way. There's a refinery about ten kilometres away.'

On the main highway the traffic streams were separated by a wide gap and a concrete barrier, but here it narrowed to a thin strip of tarmac that ran in both directions.

'So you have a road-traffic accident. Very interesting, but I don't see how this is connected to me, or to you for that matter.'

Okasha tilted his head and they moved round towards the back of the van. The rear door had been popped open. The interior was scattered with small bottles and packets. At the far end, up against the driver's cab, a long metal locker had been welded in place. It was the size and shape of a coffin. The interior was lined with some kind of foam cushion. There were stencilled hazard signs on the side of it.

'The van is registered to a medical supply company in Cairo. Shaddad Pharmacies. They distribute pharmaceut-icals around the city.'

'Why the locker?'

'To keep valuable or dangerous items secure. It was locked. We opened it to make sure it was safe, and this is what we found.' Okasha led the way around the side. Laid out on the ground was a body, small, dark-skinned and

110

wearing ragged trousers and a torn shirt. His feet were bare. A young man in his teens.

'For someone who was in a car crash he looks surprisingly unharmed.'

'The locker would have protected him to some extent. My feeling is that he was dead before they put him in there. We'll have to wait for Doctora Siham to tell us how he died.'

'Why did you call me?'

Okasha grinned. 'Call me impulsive, but wouldn't you say he was from South Sudan?'

'It's possible.'

'More than possible I'd say. You know what I think? I think you've started something with your head in the river.'

'Careful, you sound almost concerned.'

'You know how it is. If I report this the Major is going to tell me to get on with some serious work.'

'So you're handing it to me?'

'Whatever this is, we both know there's something wrong here, but I have my hands tied. Resources are scarce. We're being asked to cut back on all sides. I hate it, but you know how it is, nowadays policing is getting more like politics.' Okasha glanced over his shoulder to see if anyone was listening in. 'I can give you any help you need, and full access to the forensics reports.' He noted the look on Makana's face. 'I know, it's not a lot, but I'm telling you, this thing is going to be forgotten in a hurry.'

'Where were they taking him?' Makana wondered, looking off into the darkness. In the distance he caught a glimpse of what looked like a glowing coal, a smudge of smoke and the pinpricks of lights picking out chimney stacks.

'It's some kind of industrial complex. Steel, I think.'

Makana reached for his cigarettes. Okasha, still eager to farm out the case, pointed back up the road.

'So, as I see it, the boy lost control of the lorry. Perhaps he fell asleep. Some of these kids drive for hours without a break. He wakes up as the lorry is coming off the road and manages to twist the wheel, which turns it over. As it goes it knocks the van aside, just a glancing blow but enough to send the lighter vehicle flying off the road. The tanker caught fire instantly. One spark is all it takes. There are enough fumes coming off these things for it to explode. That's why they hire kids. They're too young to have any fear.'

Makana walked up the road a way, looking for tyre marks. Okasha followed along. Something didn't quite fit.

'What's the matter?' Okasha asked.

'The way the vehicles are arranged it could almost be the other way around.'

'How do you mean?'

'Could the van driver have lost control and veered across the tanker's path?'

Okasha shrugged. Makana went back to the wreck of the van.

'It's the boy in the back that I don't understand. I mean, what was he doing in that locker?'

'They were taking him somewhere.'

'If he was dead, as you say, then where were they taking him?'

Okasha looked up and followed Makana's gaze into the distance.

Chapter Twelve

The head office of Shaddad Pharmacies was on Sharia Shihab in Mohandiseen. Okasha suggested Makana drive with him. They would make better time in a squad car with siren and lights going. It was late now and Makana gave Sindbad the rest of the night off. They would speak in the morning. As promised, the drive into the city was fast, with the police driver using lights and horn with relish. It was easy to see how the power to get other vehicles to veer aside might become addictive. The road opened up the way the Red Sea might have parted for Moses. Well, perhaps a sluggish, reluctant sea. Although it was almost midnight the city was still wide awake.

'You're sure you want me to come along?'

Okasha waved the question aside. 'Don't tell me, you have something better to do with your time.'

While two young men was not an epidemic, Makana wondered if Okasha thought this might be the start of a trend. All the two deaths had in common was the fact that the victims were male and from South Sudan, and also that someone had taken the trouble to try and displace the bodies in some way. Different method in each case. Perhaps the killer was fond of variety.

Despite the late hour they found Omar Shaddad still at work when they arrived. The ground floor of the gently crumbling modern building was occupied by a row of shops. On one side of the entrance were chintzy places selling shoes and shirts arrayed on mirrored pedestals. The other side of the building's main door was taken up by a large all-night pharmacy. Within the brightly lit interior staff rushed to and fro serving lines of customers. Sickness was a profitable business.

Shaddad greeted them in the doorway of his office on the first floor. A tall, fleshy man in his forties, he had a large gut, long, rather unkempt wavy hair and reading glasses that were twisted out of shape. His shirt was crumpled and a button was undone. A cigarette dangled in one hand.

'Sorry to bother you at this hour,' Okasha, on his best behaviour, apologised. 'I felt it best that no time be wasted.'

'No trouble at all. I understand completely. Please, come in.' Shaddad looked weary, his eyes bloodshot, but he stepped aside to usher them in. The office was dark but for a desk lamp. Stacked along the corridor and around the walls of the room were cardboard boxes and stacks of brochures and medical journals. Okasha was distracted by his telephone.

'We were worried you might not be awake,' Makana said.

'Oh, I tend not to sleep more than four hours a night. I usually work until about two.' Omar Shaddad glanced at his wristwatch before stubbing out his cigarette in an over-flowing ashtray on his desk and gesturing for them to take a seat.

'Please, tell me what this is about. I understand there has been an accident.'

Okasha snapped his phone shut with a decisive click. 'A van registered to your company was involved in an incident just off the Cairo–Ismailia road, close to 10th Ramadan City.'

'Was anyone hurt?' Shaddad turned from one to the other in bewilderment.

Okasha ignored the question. 'Can you tell us what your van was doing out on that road?'

'No idea.' Omar Shaddad held his hands up towards heaven. 'I can check.'

'The van was registered to your company, but we haven't been able to identify either of the men in the car.' Okasha's eyes met Makana's.

'The driver would have been carrying papers.'

'Nothing was found on his body. There may have been a second man in the car, but he seems to have disappeared.'

'Disappeared? This makes no sense.' Shaddad stopped himself. He glanced at Makana, who had remained quiet through all of this. 'What exactly is this all about?'

Makana glanced at Okasha, who nodded his consent. 'In the back of the van there is a metal chest, fitted to the floor.'

'All our vans have them. Sometimes we have to carry expensive items or equipment. The drivers often leave the vans to make a delivery. It makes sense to have a special compartment for valuable goods.'

'In this case it was carrying a body.'

'A what?'

'A young man, perhaps sixteen years old. He was dead.'

Shaddad removed his glasses and rubbed his eyes. 'How can that be?'

'That's why we came straight to you, Mr Shaddad,' said Okasha. 'I'm sure you'll agree that it is best to sort out these irregularities as soon as possible.'

'Are you telling me that they were up to something illegal, in my van?' Shaddad looked back and forth from one to the other.

'You keep a record of all of your vehicles, I suppose?' asked Okasha.

'Naturally. Everything is above board, I can assure you of that.' Shaddad was reaching for the telephone. 'We monitor all our vans carefully. We have to.' He dialled a number, and fished his cigarettes from a jacket slung over the back of the chair. 'How exactly did this happen?'

While Okasha explained about the tanker and the fire, Makana took a moment to examine the room. One wall was covered in bookshelves, heavy tomes that appeared to be medical journals, leather-bound volumes in sequence that stretched along entire shelves. In frames hanging behind the desk were certificates, starting with Ain Shams medical school and progressing through to institutions further afield – the University of Fribourg in Germany, and Buffalo, New York. Clearly Omar Shaddad was a highly qualified man. A number of pictures showed Shaddad in the company of distinguished-looking men from the world of business and high finance. Makana spotted at least one government minister. Shaddad was tapping the telephone receiver urgently with his fingers.

'Did you say there were two men in our van?'

'We believe there was a passenger also,' Okasha confirmed.

Shaddad put down the phone. 'There appears to be no one there. Maybe they're asleep.' He slumped back with a perplexed look on his face. 'None of this makes any sense. Are you quite sure the van is one of ours?'

Okasha produced his notebook with the registration number and description of the minivan. Shaddad sat up and began clicking at the computer that took up one side of his desk.

'It's definitely our van.' Omar Shaddad's eyes were fixed on the screen in front of him. The light illuminated his face with a blue glow.

'Does it say who the van was assigned to?' Makana asked.

'I'm afraid we're not that organised. These things tend to be arranged on a day-to-day basis.'

'So how do you keep track of your vans?'

'There's only one person with that information.' Shaddad clicked off the screen. 'Abu Gomaa. He's the caretaker of the car pool.'

'And where do we find this Abu Gomaa?' demanded Okasha.

'Well, that's who I was trying to call.' Shaddad made a show of examining his watch. 'At this time of night he might be asleep. I mean, he is a little deaf. He's rather an old man.'

'Then we can save him a trip to the station by interviewing him now, don't you think?'

Shaddad glanced at Okasha and got to his feet. 'You are right.' A smell of stale sweat came with him as he brushed past Makana. 'Why don't we go down and see him right away?'

They took the stairs down past the entrance lobby and down to the first level of the basement. The stairs continued downwards, vanishing into shadow. A badly fitting metal door brought them out into the underground car park. Neon strip lights glowed white and faint at the far end, blinding them and throwing shadows around the cavernous space. The watery glow barely penetrated the gloom. Beyond the lights a ramp rose up towards the street. On both sides darkness thickened into impenetrable blackness. A row of cars was parked along the wall, some of them clearly abandoned. A couple were covered by dusty canvas tarpaulins that gave the place the air of a forgotten tomb. Dogs were barking somewhere.

Shaddad called out again and again until a dishevelled man in his seventies shuffled out from behind a wall, rubbing his eyes.

'Abu Gomaa, where have you been? Were you asleep?'

'No, I was just watching the television.' He waved a hand in the vague direction of where he had come from as if expecting the apparatus to step up and confirm his statement. A white flicker echoed from a corner that had been fenced off by uneven rows of breeze blocks.

'These men are from the police,' said Shaddad. 'They have some questions for you.'

'Questions? What kind of questions?' He turned to snap at the two dogs. They whined and settled down. The garage was rich with the smell of them. Abu Gomaa was unshaven and missing several teeth. He wore a dark blue gellabiya that was almost as decrepit as he was. Okasha motioned him into a pool of dim light and held up his notebook with the number of the van written on it.

'You know this van?'

Abu Gomaa barely glanced at the page. 'Of course, I know all of them.' Rheumy eyes flickered towards Shaddad. 'That's my job.'

'You remember the numbers of all the vans?' Makana asked.

'Nothing wrong with my memory.' Abu Gomaa sounded irritated.

'You know where they all are at any given time?'

The old man squinted at him. 'I know who's driving them and when they will be back.'

'So where is this one?'

Reluctantly Abu Gomaa consented to glance at the paper Okasha held out.

'That's easy. It's here.'

'Here, where?' Okasha looked around.

'I'll show you.' The old man straightened up and the three men followed him around the side of the building to where a row of vehicles was stationed. The three of them spent five minutes looking, but the number was clearly not there.

'I don't see it,' said Okasha, irritated. 'Try again. Maybe you're confusing it with another.'

Abu Gomaa took offence. 'Are you saying I don't remember?'

'This is a waste of time,' declared Okasha, turning to Shaddad. 'Are you telling me that with all of your valuable instruments and pharmaceuticals, this is the most secure system you have to register your vans?'

With a pained look on his face, Shaddad led Okasha and Makana off to one side. He lowered his voice.

'Abu Gomaa started here as a child in the days of my grandfather. He's practically family. We'd be lost without him.'

'The way I see it, you're lost with him,' Okasha grunted and turned to Makana. 'You have anything to say?'

'Maybe we need to proceed more slowly.' Makana returned to address the watchman. 'How many vans do you have?'

'How many?' Abu Gomaa stared at his feet for a moment. 'Eight usually. One of them's got a broken clutch. The garage is waiting for a spare part.'

'Okay,' said Makana slowly. 'That leaves seven. How many have you got here?'

Abu Gomaa wandered up and down in the gloom, counting on his fingers. Okasha, who was muttering curses under his breath, finally lost patience.

'We're wasting our time.' He slapped the notebook into his hand. 'The van is not here. You know why? Because what's left of it is out on the road to Ramadan City.'

'Anyone can make a mistake.' Abu Gomaa appealed to Makana for understanding.

'Can you remember the last time you saw this particular van?' Makana watched the old man's face register loss and confusion. It was clearly hopeless.

'It's all right, Abu Gomaa,' Shaddad said. 'We'll deal with this. You go back to your television.' As the old man shuffled off to one side, his employer whispered, 'My apologies. He's fine for the day-to-day things. You know, not much happens around here. Drivers come and go. He knows them all and they know him.'

Makana pointed towards the exit ramp. 'Can anyone just walk in here from the street?'

Shaddad gave a light shrug. 'Between Abu Gomaa and his dogs they wouldn't get far.' As if in response the two dogs began to bark and howl once more. They were tethered to long chains wrapped around a pillar surrounded by a scattering of bones. After a time they grew bored and sat down to start gnawing away again.

'What about keys?' Makana asked. 'Who keeps them?'

Shaddad turned to Abu Gomaa again, who was staring at the ceiling.

'I keep all the keys safe,' he said, thrusting his chest out with pride.

'Show us,' said Makana.

Abu Gomaa led the way across to a door set into the far wall. His manner suggested he had taken offence at their treatment of him. Using a key that hung on a string around his neck, Abu Gomaa unlocked the door. It swung inwards on creaking hinges to reveal a gloomy cell. The floor was strewn with crushed cardboard boxes, the walls scarred with nails and holes where cupboards or shelves had once been mounted. There wasn't room for all four men at the same time. Okasha and Shaddad stood in the doorway. A single light bulb hung from the ceiling. Beyond its glow Makana could make out a hatch high up in the wall.

'It's the bottom of the lift shaft. They never finished it.'

Each building in this city seemed to have its own tale to tell. There was a clutter of broken office furniture, dusty plastic crates, cracked display cases. Things that someone had decided to store away rather than dispose of.

'Where did all of this come from?' Shaddad looked like a man who'd never set foot in the place in his life.

'It's been like this for years,' Abu Gomaa shrugged. 'People put things here and never come back for them.'

A white metal medicine cabinet with a faded red crescent painted on it was fixed to the wall next to the door. Another key on the string opened it to reveal a row of hooks on which presumably keys were hung. Abu Gomaa stepped back, a conjuror who has performed his last trick. Shaddad leant through the doorway and ran his hand along them. Some bore tags, others scraps of brown card, yet others had no identifying marks on them at all. Shaddad seemed shocked.

'What is all this?' he asked.

'Looks like a museum,' said Okasha.

'Some of these are for cars we don't use any longer,' said Shaddad as he examined the keys.

'It's not here.' He turned to the old man. 'Look, one of our vans has been involved in an accident and we need to know who took the key out.'

Abu Gomaa looked from his boss to the two others but said nothing.

'Do you remember who last used this van?' Makana asked. Abu Gomaa stared at the ground and shuffled his feet. 'Abu Gomaa, please, this is a serious matter.'

'*Ya, sidi*, please, it is shameful enough to admit this matter. I'm not young any longer. Your father, may Allah have mercy on his soul, was always good to me.'

'Okay, okay.' Shaddad looked exasperated. 'We're not going to get any further here, but rest assured that I shall get to the bottom of this matter.'

'I hope so,' said Okasha.

'I'll get on to it right away. As soon as it's light. I can make some calls. Don't worry, Inspector, we'll soon sort this out.'

'We'll need a list of all your drivers.' Abu Gomaa had retreated into the background, silently dissolving into shadow. 'Also any of your drivers who don't show up for work. As soon as we get a proper picture of the man in the trunk my officers will be paying your company a visit.'

'We will cooperate in any way,' Shaddad stuttered. 'We have a reputation to think of.'

'Well, at least that means something to you,' said Okasha.

Makana glanced at Abu Gomaa as they walked out. The old man met his gaze with something that looked very much like contempt.

Chapter Thirteen

The moon was almost full, listing in a cold, clear sky as Makana made his way down the narrow path to the awama. He had no need of lights to find his way, nor to climb the stairs to the upper deck. Sleep was an appealing idea, but he knew it wouldn't get further than a thought. His mind was preoccupied. Somehow the image of the young man lying out by the roadside had stuck with him. Events seemed to be conspiring to draw him back in time, to the world he had left behind all those years ago. Settling himself into the big wooden chair, he wrapped a blanket around his shoulders and sat back.

Directly in front of him the table that ran the width of the room constituted his office. It was reassuringly solid and quite large, an anchor to cling to. And although he rarely sat at it pondering his fate, it did serve to accommodate any amount of paper he threw at it. As a result it tended to be forever on the point of collapsing beneath the weight of books and paper that washed up there. At one end was a heap of blank scrolls that he purchased cheaply from a printer nearby. The paper was quite rough quality but there was plenty of it and it often served when he felt a need to try and make sense of a case. He would draw up the lines rather like a general planning for a battle. In the end it often resembled the ramblings of a demented mind, and served perhaps a more therapeutic purpose rather than providing useful insight. Scraps from some of these were taped to the wall behind the desk, along with clippings from newspapers, photographs, diagrams, cuttings from maps. Altogether it added up to a kaleidoscopic chart of his life over the last decade and more.

From time to time his eye would fall on some object and it would bring back the past. A papyrus painting, given to him by an old forger, showed the Hall of Judgement where the heart of the dead king is weighed against an ostrich feather. Anubis, the jackal-headed god, presided over the golden scales. Further along was a photograph of Daud Bolad, a very dangerous man whose path Makana would be glad never to cross again.

There were other things, too: a street plan of Siwa and alongside a larger map of Egypt, the Western Desert and the Nile as it traced its way south, snaking back into the continent and his past.

Whenever a face from his former life surfaced in Cairo, it would amaze him that people still sought him out, that he hadn't simply been consigned to forgotten memory. They were invariably disappointed, dismayed at how he could have cut all ties to his homeland. There was never any satisfactory answer to give them. The theory was that he was here because it was too dangerous to return. He still had enemies inside the halls of the *Jihaz*, the National Intelligence and Security Service back in Khartoum. But that wasn't the only reason. A country was little enough reason to return. He no longer believed that there was a single place he could ever feel completely at home, and so this was as good as anywhere.

At the centre of the wall was a creased and faded snapshot of a woman and small child: a girl nearly three years old at the time. His wife Muna and daughter Nasra. It was no coincidence that it was placed there, at the middle of everything, because it seemed to him that this was where it all began and this, too, was what it was all returning to.

As he sat there smoking and looking out over the river, Makana forced his mind back to what he had seen earlier that evening, the dead boy lying by the side of the metal locker. Who was he and how had he died, and why? The autopsy would, he was sure, show that he had been dead before the accident. What had he been doing inside that locker? What was the motive? Not money. If you have your eyes set on a fat ransom you might kidnap a wealthy actress, a businessman's son, or maybe his wife, but not a boy from

South Sudan who, by the look of his clothes, had little to his name. So what was the motive? Sexual, perhaps? Usually it was women who prostituted themselves, but it wasn't unheard of for men to follow that path. So then what, a fight of some kind? An accident? Someone had been taking him out of town to get rid of the evidence. It wouldn't be hard. Find a spot, dig a hole in the sand. The body would vanish for ever, or at least until someone had the bright idea of building another factory out there.

The night passed slowly. Makana's thoughts kept drifting as they often did in these mournful hours, back to the time when he had a family and a home. When he was whole. When the car they were fleeing in plunged over the side of a bridge, Muna and Nasra had perished. Makana had escaped with his life, something he had never really forgiven himself for. And so the one great mystery in his life was fated to remain unsolved, because there could never be closure for him, not now, after all these years. He had never seen them after their death, never had a chance to bury them, and that somehow made their absence all the more difficult to accept.

Over the years there had been persistent rumours that his daughter had survived, rumours that he had found unbearable. A form of never-ending torture. At one point he had even considered taking the risk of going back to Khartoum to find out for certain, a course of action that would almost certainly have led to his arrest and possibly death. He still had enemies back there, that much he knew.

Still, imprisonment, torture, death, all of these seemed like a small price to pay for the peace of mind of knowing his daughter's fate. All of his inquiries had led to nothing. The years had gone by and yet he had never been able to fully give up on the idea that somehow she might still be alive, that there was still hope that one day he might find her.

As he finally, gratefully, fell into a brief but deep sleep, he heard the sound of loudspeakers crackling to life in the distance as the muezzins began calling the faithful to prayer.

Munir Abaza's offices were in Dokki. A broad modern building in a sidestreet with a view of the Sheraton Hotel in all its glory. Turn your head to the left and one of the more elegant stretches of the river came into view, complete with two members of the rowing club out early aboard a narrow skiff. Munir Abaza's office had the buzz of a busy hub with some wealthy clients. Sharply dressed people moved with urgent purpose through the soft cloud of ringing telephones and the asthmatic wheeze of photocopier machines. The walls were splashed with colourful images of coral reefs on the Red Sea, drilling rigs in the desert, holiday resorts inhabited by happy people. It seemed an unlikely choice for a legal firm representing a small family restaurant, no matter how good the food.

'Excuse me for asking, but how did the Hafiz family come to be your clients? They don't seem to fit in with all of this.' Makana gestured at the walls.

'You're right. I was doing a favour for someone.' Abaza moved with the stiff-legged gait of a man itching to get somewhere in a hurry. He was around fifty years old, dressed in expensive clothes, a light blue shirt with matching tie held in place with a gold pin and oozing expensive eau de cologne that he appeared to have bathed in. Makana found himself in a glass-walled conference room with a view. There was no shortage of chairs around the heavy oval table that stretched the length of the room, but no seat was offered. Instead Abaza planted himself, arms folded, contemplating the river.

'My daughter is friends with Sahar Hafiz. They went to school together. She came to me and told me that Sahar's brother was missing and begged me to help. What can I do?'

Makana wasn't sure he believed him. Even a connection through their daughters sounded like a stretch. Compared with Abaza, Mr and Mrs Hafiz looked as though they had been living in a cave.

'Do you row?'

'Sorry?'

Abaza indicated the river. He was watching the rowers with the keen eye of a professional. No doubt he kept himself in shape dragging a boat up and down the river for hours.

'I rarely find the time these days,' said Makana quietly.

'It's a great way to relax, to free the mind. We Egyptians think of exercise as something we do when we are children, after that it's eat and eat. This country needs to become leaner, stronger, more confident about its own abilities.'

'A lack of self-confidence isn't something I've noticed a lot of.'

'You mistake our national pride for confidence. It isn't. We are a nation in doubt, that's why we keep harking back to Nasser, as if he was the solution to everything. We pick on people, like your fellow countrymen squatting in that square.' Abaza turned his gaze on Makana. 'Do you even consider them to be countrymen? You are so different, North and South. Physically, racially, culturally.'

'A little diversity is not a bad thing, surely?'

'A little, perhaps, but unless I am mistaken you have had a civil war for almost half a century.'

'Now we are at peace. War is over.'

'And yet you remain here.' Abaza smiled. 'That should tell us something, no?'

'Is this why you summoned me here?'

'I wanted to see who I was recommending.'

'A little late for that, don't you think?'

Abaza pushed his hands into his pockets and strolled along by the window, still admiring the view.

'Your friend Amir Medani is a colleague of mine. We do not share the same political perspective, but I believe there is mutual professional respect. He believes in working to make the world a better place and I . . .' He stretched his arms wide. 'Well, we have different priorities. Not so surprising. Anyway, I have operatives that I use for this

132

kind of work, but in this particular case I felt I needed someone different.'

'A little more downmarket?'

The lawyer smiled. 'You are a direct man, I like that. In recommending someone one should always take into careful consideration the needs and the means of the client.'

'How well do you know the Hafiz family?'

'Not that well, to be honest. I used to eat at their restaurant with my aunt, when I was a child. The place was run by Mourad's grandfather in those days.'

'They came to you for help?'

'As I said, it was through my daughter.'

'Do you know the Hafiz boy?'

'Mourad? No. The girl I've met a few times, through my own daughter, but that's about it.'

'What can you tell me about her?'

'Sahar? Well, she's a smart girl. Ambitious, but completely wasted so long as she remains tied to her parents and their business. Her best hope is meeting a man who will make a good husband.'

Not the most charitable assessment, but Munir Abaza clearly had more important things on his mind. In his view the explanation for Mourad's disappearance was simple.

'He's probably met a young woman and is off somewhere enjoying himself. Who wouldn't want to be twenty again!' The laugh was clumsy and self-conscious.

'So you don't find it odd that he hasn't contacted his family?'

'If he's anything like me he won't want anything to do with them.' More laughter. Abaza had the laugh of a man with no sense of humour.

'I still need to find him.'

'That's why they hired you.' Abaza rapped his hand on the table. The meeting was over. 'Look, don't take this the wrong way. See it as an opportunity. Play your cards right and you can make good money out of this. The Hafiz family have a lot of old clients, people with money and problems. And I am always on the lookout for new operatives. This could be very good for you.'

There was something reptilian about Abaza's smooth manners. The kind of person to whom nothing nasty or foul-smelling ever seemed to stick.

As he waited for the lift to arrive Makana found himself staring at a poster for yet another client of Abaza's. The picture showed a view of the Giza pyramids with a square building in the foreground. The juxtaposition of the two images was intended to suggest a link of some sort. *The Hesira Institute*, the caption read. *Where modern technology meets the wisdom of Ancient Egypt.* A line of hieroglyphics ran down one side of the poster, topped by a cartouche containing a figure bearing a stick. The physician himself presumably. Hesira. Yet another example of putting the ancient world to profitable use, thought Makana as the lift announced its arrival.

Sahar had promised to connect him with a couple of Mourad's friends. A rare breed if he had understood correctly. Fadihah and Ihab were waiting for him at a café by the Nile, next to the Fish Gardens. Both were dressed in typical student attire, jeans and sweatshirts. They sat huddled together, whispering and smoking as he approached.

'We're not sure how much we can help,' the boy began, almost before Makana had pulled up a chair. He could barely bring himself to sit still. He smoked nervously, his knee jogging up and down. Makana waved the waiter over. Both declined anything so he ordered a coffee for himself.

'Why don't you tell me a little about yourselves to begin with?'

'There's not that much to tell,' said Fadihah, glancing at her companion. 'We're all studying the same thing. We met Mourad in our first year.'

'So you share Mourad's interests in, what is it, city planning?'

'Something like that.'

The boy gave a derisive snort.

The girl said, 'We found we had certain things in common.'

'What kind of things?'

'Politics. The way this city is being driven into the ground by speculators.'

'Idiots who think only of lining their pockets,' added Ihab.

'What did Mourad think of that?' asked Makana.

'He thought it should all change.' The boy's eyes narrowed. This was something he cared about too much to make wisecracks.

'So he saw himself as something of a rebel?'

'How is any of this of use?' The girl was wringing her hands. 'Sahar said you were trying to find Mourad.'

'I am, but to do that I need to understand him, learn how he thinks, know the things he cares about.' They were looking at one another. 'What's the problem?'

'Nothing,' shrugged Ihab. 'We're just not sure, about you. I mean we know nothing about you.'

'I have nothing to do with the security services, if that's what you're worried about.' Makana looked from one to the other. 'The family asked me to look into this. Sahar told you that, right?'

'Sure, that's why we're here, because she asked us to help,' Ihab said. 'That doesn't mean we trust you.'

They fell silent as the waiter approached and set Makana's coffee down. He lit a cigarette.

'This is a private matter. I have no duty to report anything to the police. All I care about is helping the family to find Mourad. Whatever he may have been up to, whatever any of you are up to, it doesn't matter to me.'

'Now why would you say something like that?' Ihab was biting his nails. 'What makes you think we are up to something?'

'I didn't say you were,' said Makana, holding his gaze. 'Are you?'

136

'What kind of idiots do you take us for? We know what you're after.'

Fadihah put out a hand to restrain Ihab, which he shook off. He stared off at the river, smoking furiously. Makana addressed the girl.

'Anything I turn up remains between us. His parents want him back, that's all. You can understand that, right?'

'You mean, you don't report to the police?'

'I don't report to anyone.'

None of this seemed to do the trick of calming their fears. Makana stirred his coffee. He was in no hurry. He didn't want to rush them. Let them get used to him.

'When was the last time you saw Mourad?'

'Maybe two weeks ago.' The girl flicked ash from her cigarette towards the river.

'No, it's more like three,' the boy corrected her.

'Whatever,' she said dismissively.

'Would that have been at the university?'

The girl nodded, but Ihab immediately contradicted her.

'No, it was at the place he worked. A fast-food place.'

'Westies?'

Ihab nodded. 'You know about that?'

'I know Mourad worked there for a while. I also know he hasn't been back there for over ten days.'

Fadihah and Ihab exchanged a glance.

'Has Mourad dropped out of university? Is that what this is all about?'

'Even if he has, so what? I mean, what's the point, right? You're not going to get a job unless your father knows somebody in a ministry or something.' Ihab broke off to light another cigarette. 'Unemployment among university graduates is around eighty per cent. It's not what you know, it's who you know.' It sounded like a rehearsed speech, but he was angry. Most of their friends, Makana guessed, were in agreement. Those that weren't were not friends.

'Mourad had the courage to admit it was a waste of time,' said Fadihah.

'Just not to his father.'

Ihab came back in. 'His father is dreaming if he thinks Mourad would ever take over that restaurant.'

'What's wrong with the restaurant?'

'Are you kidding? It's a dead end. You think he should spend his life serving pasta to the ageing population of a decadent elite?'

'What do you think he should be doing?'

'He wants to change the world,' Fadihah interjected, gaining confidence. 'We all do.'

'Change it how?'

'Make it a better place, for everybody.'

'Justice, equality, that sort of thing?'

The girl nodded, but Ihab gave a sardonic laugh. 'Revolution. Kill them all. The ones who have poisoned everything.' He leaned across the table, suddenly intense and intimidating. 'There can be no revolution without violence.'

Makana wondered if he had underestimated the gravity of Mourad's situation. He stirred sugar into the thick black coffee. They made an odd couple. Beneath the boy's swagger he detected a well-brought-up son of the middle class looking to pick a fight. Did Mourad have that level of arrogance? That wasn't the impression he had formed so far, but impressions could deceive. The girl's resentment showed itself in a slight sneer. She wore loose baggy clothes that disguised her femininity, giving her a shapeless look. Her hair, which hung past her shoulders, had a lacklustre sheen to it. She tugged nervously at her sleeves.

'I want to go.'

Ihab leaned forward to stub out his cigarette. 'You won't find him, you know, not unless he wants you to.'

'Do you know where he is?'

'Mourad is his own man. If he wants to contact his family he knows how to find them. He doesn't need you.'

'Mourad had a new computer. Do you know where it is?'

'Ask that idiot he shares a room with.'

'Abdelhadi, you mean?'

The girl was on her feet now. Ihab followed suit.

'One last thing. Was Mourad involved with anyone – I mean a girl?'

Ihab levelled the same lopsided grin at Makana. 'Is that what his old man is worried about? Tell him to sleep easy, Mourad would never be foolish enough to bring her to meet the family.'

'Estrella, that's her name, right? Do you know where I can find her?' But they were already gone. Ihab's nervous energy propelling him forward. Breaking free of Fadihah's grip he raced towards the stone steps leading up to the road. The girl jogged behind. As he went, Ihab tripped from side to side, upturning chairs and even a table as he went. The waiter yelled but it was too late, the two were already almost out of sight.

'These kids today are crazy,' he muttered loudly as he went about setting things back in place. Makana felt sorry for the man and left a large tip underneath the ashtray. When he came upstairs, he found Sindbad sitting in the Datsun across the street.

'Did you see them?'

'The boy and the girl, yes, *ya basha.*'

'And you'd be able to recognise them again?'

'As easily as my own mother.'

Which was good enough for Makana.

Chapter Fourteen

The small, slight figure who emerged from the university mosque after afternoon prayers was undoubtedly the same person in the photograph Makana had borrowed from the wall of Mourad's hostel room.

'Abdelhadi?' The slightly built young man jumped at the sound of his name. He spun round to take in Makana and the rather imposing figure of Sindbad standing just behind him. For a moment it looked as though he was trying to decide whether to make a run for it. In the end, this resulted only in an involuntary step backwards, after which he froze in his tracks. Makana held up the photograph. 'This is you, isn't it?'

'Am I in some kind of trouble?'

'That depends on whether you cooperate.'

It was a constant revelation to Makana how people always assumed they were the innocent victim of a misunderstanding.

'I haven't done anything. I just came down for sunset prayers. Can you tell me what this is about?'

'It's about your roommate, Mourad Hafiz. I believe you have something of his.'

'Something of his?' Abdelhadi was becoming uncomfortable with the attention they were drawing. People were slowing down to whisper as they went by.

'Why don't we go up to your room and take a look.'

With a quick glance at Sindbad, Abdelhadi turned and led the way to the student hostel. There was music playing on the upper floor. A procession of people came and went. One carried a large ghettoblaster, the cable dragging along the floor behind him, another was holding a saucepan filled with some blackened mass. Heads turned as they made their way along.

'What have you been up to now?' called one young man, leaning in a doorway. The comment drew a chorus of catcalls and laughter down the hall. The door was jammed and Abdelhadi fumbled with the lock. In his panic he threw his shoulder at it and then fell inwards when it flew open.

Makana followed him in. Sindbad hung back in the doorway, holding onlookers at bay. People slowing down kept on walking when they caught his glare. Abdelhadi was fussing around, talking nervously as he went.

'It's really quite all right, you know. Mourad and I are friends. He said I was free to borrow it whenever he wasn't around.'

Abdelhadi was rummaging through his keys until he found one that fitted the cheap padlock on the metal trunk underneath his bed.

'You weren't too worried when he went missing?'

'Not really. I mean, he always keeps odd hours. He often disappears for days with no explanation.'

'Disappears where to?'

'I don't know. He never says.'

'You're friends, you say?'

'Well, you know how it is. We both have our own circles, but obviously, sharing a room brings you together.'

'Sure, I can see that.'

Abdelhadi bent down to reach into the trunk. He rummaged underneath a messy heap of clothes to produce a slim laptop from underneath.

'I don't like to take chances. There are people on this corridor who are . . . mischievous.'

'I see. You don't mind me taking this, do you?'

'It's to help find him, isn't it?'

'I hope so.'

After considering the situation, Abdelhadi handed over the laptop. Makana weighed it up.

'You weren't really that close, were you?'

The slight young man rubbed a hand over the back of his head. 'The truth is he made fun of me. He and his friends. I was amusing to them.'

143

'Because of your beliefs?'

'Because of who I am. I take my faith seriously, and they, well, they live frivolous existences. That's all I can say.'

'Well, you've been most helpful.'

Abdelhadi hesitated. 'Can I just say that I didn't put those pictures on it. I found them there.'

'Pictures?'

'You know, of women?' He stood awkwardly in the middle of the room, eyes roaming from side to side. A bird longing for a way out of his cage.

'I'll bear that in mind,' said Makana.

Sami was alone in the Bab al-Luq office. The place was deserted apart from him. Makana knew from experience that journalists were not given to normal daylight working hours. No doubt it was still too early for most of them. Sunlight filtered through gaps in the surrounding buildings, lighting up the grubby windows with a soft flame. The Masry Info Media Collective – MIMIC they called it – comprised a loose affiliation of like-minded individuals who shared basic amenities in exchange for a minimal rent. Still, there was a rapid turnover and you could never be quite sure who you might meet. The exceptions to that rule were Sami and his wife Rania, the unofficial godparents of the project.

The familiar woolly-haired figure peered round the side of the computer monitor. Sami Barakat looked as though he had seen better days.

'So where did you sleep last night?'

144

Sami took off his glasses and peered myopically around him. 'Here, actually.'

'Aren't you a bit past that kind of thing?'

'I would understand that coming from anyone else, but you live on a houseboat with less to your name than a hermit in a cave.'

'I take it that means you and Rania haven't sorted things out yet.'

'Ah, no, not exactly.'

'I've brought you something.' Makana set Mourad's laptop on the table and explained where it came from. Sami gave a whistle as he opened it up to take a look.

'Well, it's a good machine. Must have cost him some money.'

'Really? Are they expensive?'

Sami gave Makana a despairing look. 'Apple PowerBook. These things are not cheap.'

Which begged the question of where Mourad had got the money.

'He had a job in a fast-food place by the Hunting Club.'

'You'd have to burn a lot of hamburgers to afford one of these.' Sami ran an appreciative hand over the smooth cover. Makana dislodged a heap of folders and printed sheets to sit down in a nearby chair.

'So maybe he had something else going for him.'

'How did you come by it anyway?'

'His roommate.' Makana hooked a metal wastebin with his foot and drew it towards him as he reached for his cigarettes. 'I'm not sure what he was using it for but you might find some interesting material on it. Anything that's more recent than say ten days ago is not going to be of interest. Can you go back that far?'

'Sure, assuming there's no problem getting through the security wall. Our friend didn't happen to give you a password, did he?'

Makana stopped, lit match in hand. 'Is that important?'

'One of these days you're going to wake up and realise you're living in the twenty-first century, and believe me it's going to come as a terrible shock.'

'I'll take your word on that.'

'Any idea what we're looking for?'

'Could be anything at all. Political meetings, activism of any kind.' Makana raised his hands in a gesture of helplessness.

'Okay, so anything unusual. Let's give this a try anyway.' Sami flipped open the laptop and began clicking keys. It didn't take long for him to give up. 'It's password-protected. I don't want to lock it. I'll let Ubay take a look.' He put the laptop to one side and picked up a pencil which he started flipping round his fingers. 'I see your friend Mek Nimr is in the news again.'

Makana felt a prickle on the back of his neck. 'What did you hear?'

'He was in Washington recently. Apparently, he's a rising star, head of some new intelligence unit, counter-insurgency, something like that.'

'Why Washington?'

'The Americans are probably interested in taking a look at his address book. Khartoum was like the Club Med of terror suspects for about a decade.'

It came as a jolt to realise that the man who had once tried to have him killed had just grown more powerful. Once upon a time, Mek Nimr had been his adjutant. They had been friends, of a kind. Colleagues, in any case. Mek Nimr had not done well enough at the police academy to become a detective like Makana. Instead he had remained in uniform, until regime change came in 1989. After that his star had risen fast, and by all accounts showed no sign of slowing.

'I must have missed that.'

'Well, you should watch out.' Sami wagged a warning finger. 'With all this rendition going on they might decide to trade you in for some of our Islamists. You could find yourself on your way home with a hood over your head.'

It was a novel thought. 'They must have more important things to do with their time.'

'Never underestimate the security services. They can always think of some reason to make life miserable for someone. Just look at us.' Sami tilted back his chair to balance on the rear legs and clasp his hands behind his head. 'In February, the president announced multi-party elections. The problem being that he needed to hold a referendum to change the constitution. The only people who swallowed that little story were the Americans, which is who it was meant for.'

Protests were met by riot police and pro-Mubarak supporters – the *bultagia*, gangs of paid thugs. Naturally, the news was not reported by the state media, but other sources were emerging.

'The media is diversifying. It's no longer possible to keep everyone in the dark all the time. Things have changed.' Sami reached over to help himself to one of Makana's Cleopatras. The sun had gone now and shadows swam through the long room.

'People came together. An amazing sight. For the first time communists and Islamists were united. The younger generations are starting to realise that it's about changing the system, not just about improving things for yourself.'

Makana was put in mind of Mourad's friends. Fadihah and Ihab. They seemed to be working towards some kind of idea of change, but what form exactly did that take? The state was a huge and ponderous machine. Engineering elections made as much sense as anything. Nobody on the inside wanted change, not really, they were doing too well the way things were. And as for the world at large, well, they too seemed just fine with the current status quo. When the elections results came in and the president duly won, albeit by a margin of only eighty-eight per cent, everyone had applauded him, including the Americans, confirming what everyone in this part of the world already knew, that Western leaders were a bunch of fawning

148

hypocrites who were content to watch people suffer under a repressive dictatorship while lauding the benefits of democracy.

'Between the president's cronies running the country like it was their own private country club, and the Salafists who want to drag us back into the Middle Ages, we're struggling just to stay afloat. What's amazing is that, despite all the evidence to the contrary, there are still those who believe that given a real chance, democracy might just work.'

'Admit it,' said Makana. 'Underneath all that cynicism there is an optimist trying to get out.'

'Listen, this will come as a surprise to you, as you persist in believing we're still in the Stone Age.' Sami tapped the screen in front of him. 'Forty years ago people couldn't read. That's changed. Across the region, illiteracy rates have been inverted. From seventy-five per cent we now have thirty per cent. The world has been turned upside down. It's no longer that easy to pull the wool over people's eyes.'

'There's a difference between knowing what's wrong and being able to change it.'

'We know what's needed. The problem is that I don't think we understand what it's going to take to get it.'

'There can be no revolution without violence?' Makana recalled Ihab's words.

'And to think that sometimes I have the feeling you don't listen to a word I say.'

'I spoke to a couple of Mourad's friends.' Makana flicked ash at the wastebin. 'I'm not sure what they believe in.' He

149

got up to leave, but paused at the door. 'I don't have to tell you that if you ever need a place to stay . . .'

Sami grinned. 'What you're really saying is it would be better if I sorted things out with Rania.'

'I'm glad we understand each other.'

'Sometimes we all need someone to tell us what we know is right.'

Makana left him with his thoughts. Sindbad was waiting by the old Datsun outside the building. About to start tucking into a large pot of koshary, he looked up guiltily as Makana appeared.

'I wasn't sure how long you'd be,' he said, nodding at a smaller pot on the dashboard.

'That's thoughtful of you,' said Makana. 'But I had thought we might try something else.'

Sindbad stared mournfully at the steaming heap of lentils and pasta in his lap and sniffed.

'What did you have in mind?'

Chapter Fifteen

Westies was just getting into its early evening stride.
Already cars were nudging by, hooting their horns
for attention. More than a fast-food restaurant, it seemed
to be a place where young people could meet. They leaned
on their cars under the deep shadows of the banyan trees
having important conversations about who knows what. In
the doorway, Makana managed to avoid being flattened by
a large man emerging weighed down by a stack of paper
bags and boxes around which he could barely see, all of
which gave off the same warm, sickly sweet odour.

'Busy tonight?'

Ruby seemed happy to take a break from whatever she
was doing, ticking numbers off a form. She smiled a greeting and checked the counter where her staff were busy
running around, all in different directions at once. She

seemed in complete control of what, to Makana, was organised chaos.

'Oh, this is nothing. It doesn't start to get busy for another couple of hours.' Makana made a mental note not to try coming here late in the evening. 'Did you find Mourad?'

'Not yet, I'm afraid. That's partly why I came back to see you.'

'Sure.' Either Ruby was excited to be part of an investigation, or she was actually concerned about Mourad's welfare.

'There was a girl here last time. She was mopping the floor over there.' Makana pointed and Ruby turned her head to look. 'Small, possibly from South Sudan? I think her name is Estrella.'

Ruby rolled her head and Makana followed her across the room. Sindbad was gazing at the menu with the concentration of a man with a renewed interest in his education. One of the boys came running up to ask about something but Ruby sent him away with a curt remark. She led Makana to an empty table in the corner.

'Look, I know Estrella, but I'd rather this stayed between us.'

'You mean she's working here illegally?'

'People tell us the papers are on the way, so we give them the benefit of the doubt.'

'The owners don't mind?'

'Are you kidding? They positively encourage it. It means we pay them less. She's not officially on the payroll, so I'd appreciate it if you kept it to yourself.'

'That's not a problem, but I would like to speak to her. Is she here today?'

'No.' Ruby tilted her head to one side. 'You get used to the fact that the only reason people keep coming in to work is because they haven't found anything better yet. Sooner or later they all find something.'

'So when was the last time you saw her?'

'Two days ago, the day you were in here.'

'She hasn't been back since then?'

'I don't even have a telephone number.'

'Isn't that unusual?'

'Like I said, people come and go. I never know who I'm going to find when I come in. Why the interest?'

'I saw her somewhere else, a church.'

Ruby frowned. 'Makes you sound more like some kind of Sufi visionary rather than an investigator.'

She might have a point, Makana conceded. Wasn't that how things often went, feeling his way in the dark?

'Only I thought you were interested in her because she was close to Mourad.'

'They were close?' Makana waited.

'It was all a bit weird, but who can tell why a guy is attracted to one girl and not another, right? Anyway, I never understood why he was always hanging around her, talking to her when he thought nobody was watching.'

Ruby seemed disappointed, which suggested that perhaps she had imagined something might develop

153

between herself and Mourad. That might have explained her concern.

'Are you saying there was some kind of romantic connection between them?'

'What else? I mean, he was discreet about it. Maybe he was embarrassed.' Her gaze held Makana's to make sure he followed her meaning.

'You mean, because of the colour of her skin?'

'That and the fact that she's a Christian.'

'Was that a problem?'

'Some people teased her. You know, the usual jungle noises and so forth.' Ruby rolled her eyes. 'The kind of people working here are one step up from apes, and I mean that in the kindest possible way.'

'How did she take that?'

'Well. She's tough. And she had her defenders.'

'Mourad?'

'Mourad.' Ruby studied her hands for a moment. 'Most people just kept quiet. If I was there I would tell them to shut up, but that didn't mean anything – they'd just wait until I was out of range. Mourad always came to her defence. He was genuinely outraged by such behaviour and would lecture them on how they were a disgrace to their country.' Ruby chuckled at the memory. 'He could be pretty intense.'

'How serious was this romance?'

'Oh, I'm not even sure there was an actual romance between them.' She hesitated. 'I got the feeling she represented something to him.'

'Like what?'

'I'm not sure.' Ruby paused. 'He would talk about things. Africa. He had a thing about Africa. It would annoy him that we in this country think of ourselves as something different, superior, when we're on the same continent. We should forget about the Middle East and think about making Africa great. You know he started out studying agriculture?'

'Before he switched to engineering.'

'Exactly. He told me he once dreamed of going up the Nile and building huge farms to feed the continent.'

Mourad the idealist, Mourad the dreamer? Was he drawn to Estrella because of what she represented rather than who she was? How did all this connect to his disappearance? Had his dreams collided with the harsh wall of reality?

'Did Mourad take a lot of interest in girls generally?'

'Not really.' Ruby's tone was dismissive. 'I mean he's handsome, lots of girls liked him, but you know, he's that sort of person who are just not aware of the effect they have.'

'He talked to you?'

'Sometimes. If he was on late we would talk after we'd finished closing down.'

'Did he ever talk about politics?'

'Politics didn't interest him. It was all corrupt in his view. You had to change things from within, from beneath. I'm not sure what he really meant by that.' Ruby gave a shrug. 'I can't see it myself, but people believe what they want to believe.' She was smiling to herself now. 'He was funny, the way he talked. He said we're all prisoners of this world. Just like this city. We just take it for granted that it can't be changed.' Ruby rolled her eyes and giggled. 'Crazy. Nobody ever says things like that.' She glanced around her as if to remind herself of her surroundings. 'Nobody.'

Sindbad had decided to give the fast-food revolution a chance. Armfuls of paper bags now rested on the back seat, filling the car with an overpowering, sweet odour. Makana waved him on.

'Why don't you go home, feed your children. I'll make my own way.'

Sindbad protested, but Makana insisted. He felt relief as the Datsun puttered away and then he turned and found another taxi in less time than it took to raise his hand.

Of course it was a risk, driving all that way across town without an appointment and this late in the day, but a reck-lessness had somehow entered proceedings. Something told him that Doctora Siham would be working late. He wasn't disappointed. A crack of light at the far end of the long subterranean corridor told him he was not wrong. When he pushed through the swingdoors, however, he found the forensics lab deserted. All he could detect was a faint scent of perfume floating over the usual mix of formaldehyde and cleaning fluids. When had he started noticing what kind of perfume she wore?

There were no lights on in the office, and at first Makana assumed it was empty. The main area of the lab was taken up by six large steel dissection tables that faced one another in rows of three. All of these were empty now and meticulously washed down, scrubbed clean to be ready for the next day. The glass jars containing human organs suspended in yellowing fluids looked more tired than usual. In one a complete foetus floated upright. In another a human brain, elsewhere a spleen, a pair of blackened lungs. The laboratory was primarily intended as a teaching facility. Charts on the walls and a long blackboard added to the educational atmosphere.

It took him a second to realise there was actually somebody there. A figure sitting in darkness – Doctora Siham. She had her face buried in her hands. Makana, suddenly confused as to how to proceed, stood for a moment before tapping on the doorframe. Startled, she jerked back and for a brief second he glimpsed the depths of something like despair in her eyes. Then she sat up and composed herself.

'Sorry for turning up unannounced,' he began, but she was already on her feet and moving past him, leaving another, stronger trail of perfume behind her.

'An apology only counts if it is sincere.'

'Why would you doubt my sincerity?'

He watched her moving about the lab, gathering up her things, getting ready to leave. She spoke over her shoulder:

157

'You came here for information.'

Makana reached for his cigarettes and considered offering them, but Doctora Siham even had that covered. She produced a gold packet of Benson and Hedges from her lab coat. Makana struck a match and held it towards her like a peace offering, mildly surprised when she didn't shy away.

'You are interested in knowing whether I have made any progress with your severed head and if there is a connection with the car-crash victims.' She blew smoke briskly into the air and looked him in the eye. 'You don't need to apologise for seeking answers.'

An adequate response was not forthcoming. Hopelessly, Makana gestured towards the darkened office. 'I didn't mean to intrude.'

'Your friendly Inspector called to ask me to be accommodating. He wants me to keep you informed on an informal basis. Congratulations, you're moving up in the world.'

'It's a temporary arrangement.'

'But you're working for the police now.' Doctora Siham arched an eyebrow. 'Doesn't that compromise your independence?'

'I don't answer to Okasha.'

'Well, be that as it may, officially you have no right to be here. I would be quite justified in calling security to show you out.'

'But you're not going to do that.'

She shook her head. 'Let me be clear, my interest in this case is motivated by injustice. The police are going to do little to find out who murdered these young men.'

'We can agree on that.'

'I assume that's why Okasha is involving you.'

'Okasha is a policeman at the end of the day. He knows that he has no backing to follow a case like this.'

'So what is your motivation? Do you think finding out who killed these boys will compensate for centuries of slavery and general abuse?'

Makana sighed. On the wall behind her was a poster from the Egyptian Museum: a scene taken from one of the wall paintings from a tomb in the Valley of the Kings. In it, Anubis, the jackal-headed god, was bowed over a corpse, attending to the embalming process.

'I'm not sure we should read too much into my motives. At the moment I'm interested to know if there is any connection between the brutal murder and dismemberment of a young man who turned up on my doorstep and the body found in the back of the van.'

'Fair enough.' Doctora Siham stubbed out her cigarette in the big aluminium ashtray. She moved off, melting into the shadows at the far end of the room where the refrigerated lockers stood. With a high buzz a single bar of neon fluttered into life. It flickered a couple of times and then grew steady. The other lights remained dark. The pathologist pulled open a battered steel door, the handle hanging lopsidedly in its socket. A single stretcher

159

stood inside the tiled chamber. She pulled this out half-way, and Makana stepped closer as she drew back the white sheet.

'Okay, so we have two bodies of young men found within days of one another. Coincidence? Perhaps not. Rough estimates of the number of Southern Sudanese living in this city vary but could easily be counted in tens of thousands, perhaps even hundreds of thousands. Two dead in two days is not remarkable.'

'It's the manner in which they died that concerns me.'

'Agreed.' She allowed herself a fleeting smile. He couldn't help thinking that her mind was elsewhere. In that brief moment when he had caught sight of her sitting alone in her office, she had appeared to be crying.

'Let's begin with the most recent. The young man who turned up in the locker of the van.'

'Was he dead before the accident?'

'It appears so. Body temperature would put the moment of death at between twenty and thirty hours before the accident. Rigor mortis had already worn off but decay of the internal organs had barely begun.'

The dead man seemed to hover between them like an absent friend. Makana looked down at the face and wondered who he was and what his life had been that it should lead him to such an end.

'He didn't die in the accident, you say. So how did he die?'

'A heart attack.' Doctora Siham scanned his face for a reaction, but Makana said nothing. 'I'm still waiting for some tests to come back, but from my preliminary examination I'm pretty sure that's what happened.'

'Isn't he a bit young for that?' Despite the darkness of his skin, death lent the young man a greyness. One eye was half shut, the mouth slack. He looked as though he had been strong and sure of himself in life. Now he was a nameless cadaver in a refrigerated vault. No afterlives, no second chances. No sign of Anubis either.

'A birth defect. Something in his heart that he probably didn't even know about.' She clicked her fingers. 'One day it goes off and that's it.'

'How rare is something like that?'

'Rare, but not unknown.'

'So he dropped dead at an inconvenient moment and someone decided to get rid of him by driving him out into the desert somewhere, only fate intervened and there was an accident.'

'Case solved. We can all go back to our lives?' She looked at him for a moment and then gave a sigh. 'No, I somehow didn't think so.'

'Did you find any signs of sexual activity?'

'No contusions or torn tissue to indicate he was violated. No traces of fluids of any kind to indicate sexual activity, no semen for example, although it's possible that it might have been removed.'

'Removed, how?'

'He was clean, scrubbed all over with an iodine-based antiseptic solution. I suppose the question is why go to all that trouble.'

A cleanly scrubbed corpse was a novelty in this day and age.

'I suppose it all depends on where he was when heart failure occurred.' Makana lit another cigarette. The smell of iodine and other chemicals coming off the body in front of him was seeping through his nostrils, through his pores, into his skin. The hint of perfume he had detected earlier was no longer anything but a faint memory.

'What else can you tell me about him?'

Doctora Siham gave a light shrug. She readjusted the sheet around the dead man's shoulders.

'Young, still in his teens. Bone structure is not fully developed. The marks on the forehead indicate he was a Dinka, more accurately from the area of Bor.'

'I'm impressed. You're sure of that?'

'I told you about my friend Professor Asfour?'

'The anthropologist.'

'Perhaps you'd like to talk to him yourself? It might help. You never know.'

Makana nodded his consent.

'Good. I'll arrange for you to meet him. How about tomorrow?'

'Tomorrow is fine.'

There was a brusqueness to her this evening that suggested she had other things on her mind. She pulled the sheet back, replacing it over the face before wheeling the stretcher back into place. The door took a few tries before the latch held. Makana followed her back into the main area of the lab.

'It still makes no sense. If he died of natural causes, why go to all the trouble of cleaning up the body and then driving it out of town?'

'Perhaps he died in an inconvenient place.' Doctora Siham lit another cigarette. 'They had no plan. The young man dies. They clean him up to get rid of the evidence and then they decide to get rid of the body.'

'Could this heart defect be provoked by some kind of ill-treatment, or even a shock? Would that show up in the tests?'

'Possibly.'

'So it could be induced?'

'Possibly, if he was under stress of some kind.'

'And the body showed no signs of torture, physical abuse of any kind?'

Doctora Siham shook her head. 'Nothing that would suggest torture. Of course, it wouldn't need to be physical necessarily. Fear could do it.'

'He could have been scared to death?'

'Anybody can be scared to death. It just takes the right situation.' She smiled, but he wasn't sure what exactly it was that amused her. There was something strange and detached about the pathologist, he decided. He wondered why he had never noticed this before. In the past Makana had speculated just how old she might be. She dressed like an older woman. A precaution, no doubt. In an environment dominated by police officers and lawyers, being often in the public eye, it was no doubt imperative that she play down her femininity, which explained the heavy trousers, long jackets, lab coats and the drab headscarf she wore when she went out on call. She held this in her hands now, delaying the moment when she would don it again. She didn't seem too bothered about being seen by him without it. What did that mean exactly?

'If I were you . . .' she said. She was moving around the room, tidying things away, preparing to leave. '. . . And I'm not trying to tell you how to do your job, I would look at how he got into that van. Where were they taking him from, where to and why?' She hesitated again and looked up. 'But you're already working on that, right?'

'Among other things. Is there anything to link the two deaths?'

'There's quite a gap between heart failure and decapitation, don't you think?'

'Sure, but maybe they simply didn't get that far. Maybe he died before they could get started.'

She frowned. 'You're talking about a ritual of some kind? Witch doctors, something like that?'

'I was just thinking out loud.'

Before she could respond the door to the corridor creaked open and a heavy-set man holding a flashlight appeared.

'Ah, it's you, *ya doctora*.' He squinted at Makana as he spoke, as if trying to assess what exactly his game was. 'I was just locking up.'

'That's fine, Ahmed, we were just leaving.'

With a sense of propriety, and more than a touch of general nosiness, the nightwatchman remained in the doorway waiting for the doctor to finish gathering up her things. When they came out he followed along behind, his scuffed shoes scraping down the long corridor. Now that they were no longer alone, a certain formality had crept into their conversation.

'I can get you photographs of the victims. That might help your investigation.'

'Yes, thank you.'

'She's a good person.' The nightwatchman lingered after the doctor had driven off. Makana was lost in his thoughts, thinking vaguely that he needed to find a taxi to take him home. The air was strangely warm and the sky heavy with clouds, their swollen undersides softened by the halogen glow of streetlights. In the distance the never-ending rumble of an inland sea was the sound of late-night traffic, beeping and grunting, sighing over the high arc of an overpass. Makana sensed in the nightwatchman an old-fashioned scandalmonger looking for an audience.

'She works too much, teaching and running the laboratory.'

'What happened to her husband?'

'He's gone. He got sick and died. Something like that. She's still a handsome woman. She should marry again, have children.'

Makana couldn't quite see it, but murmured his assent to confirm his place in the fraternity of men everywhere, in whose interests it was that all women should be safely held in the institution of marriage.

'I'm surprised she was working tonight. I thought she was going out with her colleague.'

'Professor Asfour?'

'That's the one.'

The watchman seemed to have taken it upon himself to walk him to the front gate. The prospect of a long night alone probably encouraged talkativeness. Makana was inclined to speed up the pace a little, but he was curious.

'Maybe she's found a possible suitor in this Professor Asfour?'

'That's none of my business, but he's not her type, if you ask me.'

Makana found himself wondering what Doctora Siham's type might be. He should have asked Ahmed, who seemed to know everything about her, but he didn't want to encourage him, or appear too interested. He wondered if this business with Professor Asfour explained her sadness earlier, when he had seen her alone. At the gate, Makana thanked the nightwatchman for his help and took himself off before he was snared by another long story.

Chapter Sixteen

Makana opened his eyes to the sound of raindrops pattering lightly on the roof. It had been there all night, he realised, gently drumming away at his thoughts. Perhaps it was a consequence of visiting the morgue last thing at night. Somehow the image of the dead young man pulled from the twisted wreckage had remained lodged in his mind's eye. How young he had seemed, laid out on that stretcher. No more than a child. He was unable to shake off the terrible sense of how peaceful he had looked.

He climbed out of bed to gaze at the river's surface. Overnight it had become a confused puzzle of geometry and light. The city seemed to heave a deep sigh of relief when rain came, as if it were still a blessing from heaven when in fact it caused all kinds of chaos. Tyres worn smooth as silk didn't adhere too well to wet roads.

Windscreen wipers that had long forgotten they had a purpose whined in protest as they dragged themselves back and forth across scratched windscreens. Drains revealed themselves to have been blocked for ages, potholes dissolved into bottomless wells. Roads sank without trace, and everywhere people were to be seen hopping and skipping to avoid muddy shoes and wet trousers.

Aziza came running up the stairs bearing the morning papers on her head, a child again, laughing with excitement. Bare feet didn't mind the mud.

'I love it when it rains,' she said excitedly. 'It's like the whole world's on holiday!'

Makana took the papers from her and glanced through them while she made tea on the small petrol stove. He was quite capable of making his own tea, but Aziza had taken it upon herself as one of her duties as his unofficial assistant and it seemed cruel to deny her the pleasure.

The state-run papers were thick with words of praise from the American leader. President Bush was quoted at length on the subject of freedom in the world. Egypt was singled out as 'a great and proud nation', lighting the road towards peace in the Middle East. It would show the way towards democracy in the Middle East. It was a spirited defence of President Mubarak, their staunchest ally in the region, apart from Israel.

'How does one become a doctor?' Aziza asked as she tended the kettle.

'A doctor?'

'*Ya mualim*, isn't that what I just said?'

'I'm sorry, I have trouble keeping track of your plans. Didn't you tell me you were thinking of dropping out of school?'

'That's my mother talking. She thinks learning is not something for girls.'

'But where did the idea of becoming a doctor come from?'

'Well, remember the lady who was here the other day, the one who took that head?'

Makana put down the paper he was trying to read.

'What about her?'

'Didn't you see how everyone was looking at her?' Aziz grew wistful. Makana considered her. Why not? Why shouldn't she become a doctor? She was probably as smart as anyone.

'You have to study, I mean for many years.'

'I don't have a problem with that. Do I have to pay?'

'No.' Better, he thought, to spare her the truth just yet. In theory the education was free, but the sheer number of students meant that you were condemned to attending pointless lectures in enormous, overcrowded auditoriums. Unless you could afford private lessons you had no chance of scoring high enough to graduate. Still, as a plan it showed initiative and ambition. Makana couldn't fault her for that. Naturally, her mother would not appreciate his encouraging such thoughts. She already saw Makana as a bad influence, and the girl was getting older. At Umm Ali's

169

insistence a bell had been recently installed, an old-fashioned brass maritime thing with a knocker that hung on the lower deck of the awama. In Umm Ali's view it was unfitting for a girl of her age to go charging into a man's living quarters without warning. Not that it gave Makana much notice. Aziza moved so fast he barely had time to register the sound before she was standing in front of him.

'You're as smart as any of them, Aziza. If you set your mind to it, I don't see why you shouldn't make it.'

'My mother would never let me go to university.'

'Why not? You'll be able to take care of her. She won't have to work in the garden and all that, when she's old.'

'She's already old,' Aziza grinned. 'But she'd kill me if she heard me say that.'

'Then we'd better not tell her.'

Aziza brought the tea over, still brimming with excitement. He couldn't help thinking she was only a couple of years youngers than Nasra would be now. 'She was just so cool. You could see how all the men *listened* to her.'

Was that so unusual? Makana had to conclude that she had a point. If Doctora Siham commanded respect it was not because she was usually smarter than anyone in the room, although that was often the case. It was because she was also as hard as nails. It took a particular kind of stupidity to go up against her, but Makana had witnessed it once or twice and it wasn't a pretty sight. Nobody got near her. The police force was a herd of old men and their antiquated ideas. It wasn't that old-fashioned attitudes still prevailed, more that they had never evolved beyond them. If Doctora Siham managed to keep them all at bay it was because she never let her guard down. To Makana's mind she was, or had been until recently, quite terrifying in her own way. Quite why his image of her was changing he could not say.

Getting to his feet, he nudged a saucepan slightly across the floor to better catch the drops coming in through the roof. There were a couple of soft spots where successive years of sun and rain had warped and weakened the thin-nish wood. What it really needed was proper repair, a new layer of tar paper, and that wasn't going to happen until he arranged and paid for it himself.

Makana returned to his chair and resumed his scan of the newspapers for what he was really looking for: any word of Mek Nimr. Sami's mention of his old adversary had dug a hook into his skin. It was a subject he usually tried not to think about, but now he wanted to know what he was up to. Finally, he came across an article in the recently revived *al-Dustour* on the controversy surrounding Sudan's links with Iran: 'Khartoum's chief of the shadowy Counter-Insurgency and Intelligence Corps travelled to Tehran for talks rumoured to concern Iranian military and surveillance assistance in fighting rebel forces in Darfur.' There he was, a shadow moving through the world. Makana could not shake off the feeling that their fates were intertwined, now and for ever. It would only end when they came face to face once more. Disappointed, relieved,

Makana wasn't sure what he felt. He folded the paper and dropped it by the side of his chair.

On his way back to the distant neighbourhood of Arbaa-wa-Nuss, Makana checked in with Okasha on whether anything had been turned up on the Shaddad van. The answer was disappointing. Nothing further had been found in the vehicle to identify either the driver or his possible passenger.

Sindbad navigated the flooded streets with all the care of a man driving over eggs, as if he expected a hole to open up at any moment and suck his precious Datsun down into a watery grave. The roads got worse the further they went. This part of town seemed to have received an unfair share of the overnight rain. Or perhaps the explanation lay in the fact that the drains around here were inadequate, or non-existent. Children hopped gleefully through puddles, thrilled with the freshness in the air that clearly wouldn't last.

'No sign of our friends from security today?'

'Those two?' Sindbad snorted. 'In this kind of weather they probably don't dare go outside.'

Cornelius the gatekeeper was too busy trying to clear away a lagoon of water outside the church gates to give much attention to Makana. He offered a grudging nod inside when asked about Father Saturnius's whereabouts.

'Estrella?' the priest blinked. 'Why do you ask about her?' He broke off to chastise a young man who was crouched down on the far side of his office. Water stretched languidly across one corner where a gap in the roofing had allowed the rain in. The ground was uneven and a group of people were helping to try and clear it up, with more enthusiasm than was needed.

'Careful with the plaster. Oh my, we're going to have to repaint the whole thing. This is a Christmas to remember.' As he stepped out of the way, Makana's attention was drawn to the large noticeboard on one wall, where a number of photographs had been pinned with tin tacks and sticky tape. One of these had come free, no doubt due to the damp in the air, and Makana knelt to pick it up from the pool it floated in. Shaking the water off he squinted at a picture of a young man wearing a broad gap-toothed smile and an American-style cap bearing a logo that read *Buffalo Bills*. The smile of someone whose prayers had been answered.

'I'm sorry, I'm afraid you have called at a bad time.'

'Please, don't apologise.'

'You were asking about Estrella.'

'I believe that's her name. I saw her the last time I was here. I think she knows Mourad, the person I am looking for.'

Father Saturnius was distracted, trying to supervise the repair work. In the far corner the slap of heavy rags on the concrete floor was followed by the drip of water being squeezed into a bucket.

'You say she knows him? Where from, I wonder.'

'Aside from helping out here, I believe she works at a place in town, a fast-food restaurant.'

'If it's the same person, I know that she often helps out in the kitchen.' The priest scratched his round head. 'I confess I haven't seen her today. I can ask. Give me a moment.'

He disappeared out through the door, lifting the hem of his soutane to step over a threatening lagoon trapped by the sill. The two men who were crouched on the floor trying to mop up the mess regarded Makana warily. Father Saturnius was soon back with news that Estrella had not been seen today but that the kitchen staff would be sure to tell him when she turned up.

'I'd appreciate it if you let me know as soon as you hear something. Might I ask . . .' Makana held out the picture he had fished out of the water. 'I noticed these the last time I was here.'

'Oh, yes, of course. Those are, as I like to think of them, our graduates.'

'Graduates, in what sense?'

'They have left us and gone to a better place.' Father Saturnius held up a broad hand. 'I know, it's a little imper- tinence of mine. All of them have made it to the United States, where they have a new life.' He allowed himself a moment to survey the wall, the flooding forgotten. 'It's a small achievement, I know, a tiny fraction of those in need, but it signifies so much to our congregation. They see these pictures and they know there is hope, and maybe for them one day, or perhaps their children.'

Makana studied the noticeboard again. There were maybe thirty of them. Individual pictures, studio portraits, blurred amateur snapshots taken in gardens, public places, amusement parks. Blowing out candles on a birthday cake, sitting on a funfair ride, floating in a fairy-tale boat that looked like a swan. Pictures of young men and women. A lot of crosses and churches in sight. Saving their souls for God. Unfair, perhaps. What did it matter who helped them? Invariably the subjects were smiling, laughing, happy to have escaped their destiny as stateless people.

'How does it actually work? I mean, is this something you arrange?'

'Oh no.' Father Saturnius indicated a colourful strip pinned to the top of the board. It was a bright fluorescent-blue colour with gold lettering that read *The Homehavens Project*. The logo showed a crucifix with wings attached. Having faith would help you to fly? 'If you're interested, you should talk to Reverend Corbis.'

'Is he the one who runs this?'

'That's the main reason he and his sister come here every year, to conduct the interviews.' Father Saturnius wagged his head gravely. 'They interview hundreds. They are very careful about selecting the right people. If you want to know more, I can arrange for you to talk to the Reverend.'

'Thank you, Father, but right now I'm more concerned about speaking to Estrella. Do you have any idea how I could contact her?'

'I'm afraid I don't. I simply can't keep track of all our volunteers, and people often move about quite regularly. I tell you what, let me make some inquiries. I'll call you when I know something.' With a flourish he whipped a small phone out from underneath his soutane. 'Wonderful, isn't it, the way we can communicate all the time?'

'A miracle, some would say.'

Although he had no reason to doubt Father Saturnius's sincerity, Makana rather suspected that the priest had enough of his own worries to deal with. Back in the car he called Fantômas and told him who he was trying to find.

'You think she's important?'

'She might be.'

'If she's connected to the church in some way Aljuka will know how to find her.'

'Aljuka?' Makana recalled the last time he had met the flamboyant and headstrong character known as The Joker. 'I'm not sure he's going to be too thrilled about the idea of helping me.'

'He's not as bad as he looks,' laughed Fantômas. 'Don't worry, he'll do it as a favour to me.'

The rain had started again and added its own ingredient to the chaotic mix. Figures leaned under bonnets trying to coax stalled engines back to life. Passengers slid and slipped behind microbuses, urging them to move. A man hopped on one foot, his sandal swallowed up while trying to cross a deep pool. People moved cautiously, as if the rain was a warning from on high to watch their step.

Allah could be many things, but on a wet day he was particularly unforgiving.

It took over an hour to clear the traffic and get onto the highway to Ramadan City. The exit to Geneva Road was blocked by a heavy lorry whose trailer had jackknifed and was hanging lopsided over the side of the road. Wet sacks skidded from its back like happy turtles diving into the sand. They edged past and carried on. The rain had eased to a trickle, though the sky remained overcast and dark. The lone remaining wiper screeched across the Datsun windscreen to its own discordant tempo.

The accident site already resembled an ancient memory, warranting barely a glance from the flow of traffic rushing by. The remains of the two vehicles had been shunted to one side. Sindbad stayed in the taxi with the engine running. The headlights picked out the crumpled frame of the van. Makana peered inside the cab. There were brown blood-stains splattered all over the upholstery. Stuck to one corner of the splintered windscreen was an adhesive transparency from the Quran. Most of the passage was torn away. All that remained was the last line: 'To our lord we shall all return.' Consolation indeed.

Makana wandered around the vehicle. From the damage the van had suffered it seemed clear that it had rolled several times. The huge dent in the front cab seemed consistent with a frontal collision with the tanker. All in all it seemed to fit with the theory that the young driver of the tanker had simply fallen asleep. Yet something caused him to stop. What looked like a scratch in the side was actually a line of paint. In the poor light and the rain it was hard to make out the colour, but he would have guessed beige or perhaps yellow. It was fresh. Where had it come from? The tanker was blue and white. A previous mishap, then? The rain was quickening and his clothes were wet and sticking to his skin. Returning to the Datsun, Makana leaned inside to light a cigarette. Sindbad recognised the distracted look on his face.

'Not much to see out here.'

Makana wasn't going to debate the point. He resisted the temptation to get back into the car and instead he straightened up and squinted into the distance. Heavy black clouds were draped across the flat horizon. The real question was what were they doing out here with a body hidden in a steel locker? Where were they going? As if in response to his thoughts he caught the flare of a fire in the distance that seemed to flicker and beckon.

'Let's drive on a bit more,' he said, climbing back into the car.

Sindbad straightened up in his seat and a spring twanged in protest. 'It's not that I'm refusing to comply,' he grumbled, 'but I did promise my wife I would drive her to the doctor's.'

'Don't tell me she's expecting another child.'

Sindbad was taken aback. 'You say that as if it was a curse to be a father, when in fact it's a blessing.' His words remained suspended in the air. Makana stared at him, surprised at the conviction in the big man's voice, which then began to waver – 'Well, actually, I'm not sure blessing is the word I'm looking for. An honour, maybe?'

'You're the expert.'

'Look, the truth is I rarely get a full night's sleep. I can hardly get into the flat for all the toys and clothes and the rest of the junk that clutters up the place. And don't let me start talking about bills for schoolbooks and doctors.'

'You're the one who brought it up.'

'A man carries his family on his back like a camel.'

There seemed to be no adequate response to Sindbad's philosophical musings and for a time there was no sound but the light patter of rain on the sheet metal over their heads and the contented grumble of the engine. Then the moment passed and Sindbad levered the gearstick into position.

'A thousand apologies, *ya basha*. Please excuse my insolence. Which way?'

Makana pointed. They drove for another five minutes during which the glow that Makana had seen drew slowly nearer. It was off to one side of the road. There wasn't much else to look at. The road ran through flat, grey, sandy ground. Every now and then a turn-off marked the way to an industrial complex, a factory or a building site.

'Slow down here.'

The Datsun eased to a halt. Veering away from the main road a well-used strip of tarmac cut a crumbling line through the sand to the south-east.

'What is that?'

Sindbad leaned over the wheel, squinting into the distance.

'It looks like a fire, but it's inside a building.'

'Let's take a look.'

The road was a couple of kilometres long and was clearly well used by heavy lorries and poorly maintained. The Datsun bumped along over cracks and potholes that had Sindbad wincing every time they hit something a little too hard. Finally they reached a wire perimeter fence and a large sign that read Algorabi Industries. One side of the gate was left swinging in the wind. A man in khaki overalls wearing a headcloth over his face to protect him from the dust was struggling to fix it in place with a clump of breeze blocks and a tattered length of nylon rope. He straightened up as the car rolled to a halt and stared from the car to the road and back again, as if not sure where they had come from.

'There's nothing down this way.'

'I think we're lost. We need to go back to the main road.'

'Then you need to turn around.'

Makana turned to look back the way they had come.

'Sure. What is this place anyway?'

'Can't you see the sign?' The man pointed.

'I can see it, I just wondered what they do here.'

The wind whipped the gate out of the man's hand and Makana got out to help wrestle it back into place.

'What's that fire in there?'

The gatekeeper spoke through the tail of the headcloth that he gripped between tobacco-stained teeth.

'It's a foundry. They run the furnace twenty-four hours a day. Too expensive to shut down.'

The building was nothing more than a gigantic, open-sided shed, its walls and roof covered by overlapping corrugated sheets that flapped in the high wind. Time and dust had rendered it all the same colour as the surrounding landscape, almost invisible, a gigantic beetle with armoured sides and a sloping roof spiked with chimney stacks. The opening was big enough to make the trucks parked there look like toys. A deep orange glow could be glimpsed far within the shadows of the interior.

The gatekeeper pulled him out of the way as an articulated lorry approached at high speed, dust flying out from under its sides. A deafening blast on a two-tone horn shrilled as it went roaring by, whipping the gate hard and blanketing them with dust. Makana caught a glimpse of long iron rebars tied to the flatbed trailer, their ends bouncing like soft reeds.

'Is that what they make?'

'Sure. It's the iron supports they use in buildings.' They watched the lorry shrinking into the distance, then the gatekeeper turned and wandered off towards a solitary shipping container that was his guard post.

'Go back the way you came,' he called over his shoulder. 'There's nothing for you here.'

Makana took one last look at the foundry. Through the opening he glimpsed sparks flying up, rising into the air in spurts, turning over gracefully before darkness extinguished them.

Chapter Seventeen

Progress back to Cairo was slowed to a crawl when they ran into long tailbacks on the outskirts. On the dashboard a spinning wheel of coloured lights announced an incoming call on Sindbad's mobile. He stared at the device with repulsion.

'Now my life is not going to be worth living.'

Makana would have offered his condolences but for the fact that he had his own explaining to do. Hossam Hafiz rang at that moment to ask what progress he was making.

'These things take time, Mr Hafiz. It's difficult to explain how the process works.'

'I'm beginning to wonder if this is worth it.'

'I don't follow.'

'I mean . . .' There followed a lengthy pause. Makana could hear whispers in the background. He knew what was coming. 'I mean, don't take this the wrong way, but this wouldn't be a way of making more money out of us, would it?'

'I can assure you, Mr Hafiz, it is in my interests to find Mourad as soon as possible. I have a reputation to keep.'

Hafiz sounded crestfallen. 'I understand, forgive me . . .'

'There's no need to apologise. Now that I have you, do you mind if I ask you a question? Did Mourad ever mention any girls? I mean, a young man like that. Was there anyone special?'

'Girls?' There was a pause as he consulted his wife. 'No . . . no, he never mentioned anything like that.' There was a lengthy pause. 'Is this important?'

'Anything might be important at this stage. It's just one of a number of leads I'm following up on. Try not to worry too much. I'll be in touch as soon as I have anything.'

Makana rang off to find Sindbad still assuring his wife that short of sprouting wings there was no way for him to reach her any faster. He took the opportunity to make another call and discovered that Omar Shaddad answered his own telephone.

'Mr Shaddad, I visited your offices with Inspector Okasha the other night. I'm calling to find out if you have managed to get anywhere with the matter of the driver.'

Omar Shaddad laughed. 'What is it, don't you people communicate?'

'I'm sorry?'

184

'I already passed the information to your colleague. One of our drivers failed to report back. He is now officially missing, so it is possible that this is the man you are looking for. I went over all of this with your colleagues. Never mind. Look, I have it here. Do you have something to write with?'

The driver's name was Mustafa Alwan. He lived in Ramsis, off Shubra Street, and had not turned up for work yesterday and today.

'Look, Mr Shaddad, you may feel you have already answered these questions but we need to verify every fact. The memory can play tricks and asking the same question can produce different answers at different times.'

'Very well.' Omar Shaddad sounded resigned. 'Go ahead, ask your questions.'

'Thank you. I understand you own around twenty pharmacies around town. Is that correct?'

'Eighteen, yes. We opened a new one just recently in Zamalek.'

'It's a good business to be in.'

'My family have been in the business for three generations.' Omar Shaddad's tone suggested this was a story he had told countless times before. 'I have been able to expand in the last few years. Hard work and efficiency, something this country could do with more of.'

'I'm sure you're correct, but let me ask you about your drivers. How many are on your payroll?'

'It varies, but I think we have about seven or eight regulars and then a number of assistants. I couldn't tell you for sure. I have a manager who takes care of that kind of thing. There are times when we can barely keep our supplies moving fast enough. On the other hand it makes no sense keeping on staff when there is no work for them.'

'The responsibilities of an employer. I understand. It must take a lot of coordination to keep all of the pharmacies supplied.'

'And our other clients. Don't forget that we supply a number of private clinics, as well.'

There was, Makana decided, something rather simple-minded about Shaddad. It made it seem all the more plausible that someone in his employ might have decided to use his van for their own purposes.

'Very impressive. So, roughly speaking how many places do your drivers visit?'

'Altogether we supply around twenty to thirty locations on a daily basis and perhaps twice that when you take in occasional orders. Clinics tend to order from different suppliers according to prices. It's a very competitive market.'

'I'll take your word for it. We would appreciate a full list of all the clients you supply.'

'That's not a problem, I can have my secretary fax it through, but listen here, I don't want you annoying any of them.'

'We try to be discreet,' said Makana. Not being in possession of a fax machine, Makana gave him the number of the unreliable fax machine that lay under the cracked glass counter of the Komombo Kiosk down the road from the awama, sending a silent prayer as he did so in the hope that it was working.

'One other thing, Mr Shaddad. Do you have any dealings with a firm called Algorabi Industries?'

'Algorabi? No, that name doesn't ring a bell.'

'They produce steel reinforcement bars for construction.'

'No, Inspector, we have nothing to do with anything like that . . .' Shaddad's voice tailed off as he addressed somebody in the room with him. 'I can check for you, but before I do, can you tell me what the connection is?'

'I'm trying to work out what your van was doing on that road.'

'I've told you I can't help you with that. It's a mystery to me. All I can do is speculate that the driver, this Mustafa Alwan, was using the van for some kind of personal use.'

'You mean that might explain why there was a body in the locker?'

There was a long silence followed by a sigh.

'I hope you appreciate the delicate position I am in. If one of our drivers was involved in something illegal, then it's important to separate his actions from those of our company. I hope you understand what I mean.'

'I'm afraid I don't. You might have to spell it out for me. Are you asking me to cover this up in some way?'

'No, of course not.' Makana heard the nervous click of a lighter. 'All I'm saying is that the two things do not necessarily have to be linked, in my view.'

'You do accept that the van is one of yours.'

'Naturally, but I mean, right now we don't even know if one of our drivers was in it or if it was stolen.'

'And you think that absolves your company of any wrongdoing?'

There was a long sigh. 'Perhaps I'm speaking to the wrong person. Inspector Okasha is the senior investigating officer, is that correct?'

'That is correct, yes.'

'Look, I'm not trying to cause problems for anyone, but I have my company to think of.'

'Naturally.'

'Surely you agree that it's a little unfair for our reputation to suffer because of actions beyond our control.'

'With all due respect, Mr Shaddad, the full story could swing either way. If you know more than we do, perhaps this is the time to share it.'

'I didn't say I knew more than you do. Not at all. Look, I want to get to the bottom of this just as much as you do, perhaps more so.'

'I don't doubt that.'

'Look, I don't mind telling you I have plenty of good friends in government, in the Ministry of the Interior.'

'The world wouldn't be what it is if you didn't,' said Makana.

'What is that supposed to mean?' Shaddad demanded, but Makana had already rung off. Still, it took an impressively short time for word to get back to Okasha, who called Makana as they were sliding in slow motion along the overpass beside the main railway station. Down below, Ramses stood to attention, his granite face impassive to the waves of traffic flowing by it on all sides.

'Maybe you should check with me before you start going off on your own tangent.' Okasha didn't sound happy.

'I'm not sure I know what you're talking about.'

'Omar Shaddad is a big man. He has a successful business, which means he has connections.'

'What kind of connections?'

'The kind with lots of money attached.'

'And you don't want to tread on anybody's toes.'

'I just don't want you charging around with your usual disregard for tact.'

'Maybe you should have thought of that before you brought me in on this.'

'You're not in on anything.'

'Then what am I doing?'

'You're helping our inquiry in an informal sense.'

'Remind me never to ask you for a reference.'

'Just don't make me regret my decision.'

Sindbad dropped him off at the MIMIC offices. He was hoping that Sami might have made some progress with Mourad's laptop, but Sami was nowhere to be found.

'He's not here,' Rania said, when she caught sight of him. In contrast to the last time he had been there, the place was buzzing with activity. It was a reminder that the collective had been set up not by Sami, who was generally too busy with his own work to spare much time on organisational matters, but by his wife, Rania. A small, energetic figure, she had changed her hairstyle and now her wavy black hair was cut short in a rather bold, modern fashion.

'Strange, I thought you would know more about his whereabouts than me,' she said.

'He stayed with me for one night, Rania. After that I really don't know what he's been up to.'

'It's okay, I know you two are friends. I wouldn't expect you to give him up.'

'If I knew I would tell you,' said Makana, fairly sure that this wasn't entirely true. She seemed to read his thoughts, because she gave a dismissive shrug and turned back to her work.

'I asked him to help me with a laptop.'

'Try talking to Ubay. If it's anything technical he will have dropped it on him.'

They were interrupted as someone ran up with something that needed looking at urgently and another with a reminder that there was a call waiting for her. Seeing her coordinate what appeared to be total chaos was a reminder that she was more than capable of handling herself without her husband around, if proof was ever needed. Perhaps independence from Sami was not a bad thing for her. In the beginning Makana knew she had looked up to him tremendously. Sami had been the more experienced of the two. He had already established himself as a hard-hitting investigative journalist. Rania was finishing a graduate course in literature and politics. Like any marriage between career-minded people, their relationship had proved hard work. Eventually, the collective had emerged and they had started working together as partners, trying to tie the strands together in one neat little bundle. Now Sami appeared to have gone rogue, and by the looks of things Rania was learning to live with his absence.

Across the busy studio Makana spotted the lanky figure wearing a good-sized Afro that looked like a throwback to the 1970s and the days of the Jackson Five. At a corner table Ubay sat motionless, staring at a spot on the wall. He gave a start when he found Makana standing over him.

'Hey, I didn't see you.' He sat up with a start, embarrassed at being caught. 'You know how it is. Sometimes, there's just so much to process.'

Although he wouldn't have put it quite like that Makana imagined that he did know how that feeling went.

'I brought in a laptop the other day for Sami. He said he'd ask if you could get into it.'

'Oh, yes, the Apple PowerBook with the pictures on it.' Ubay chortled to himself. 'The password was no problem.'

'What pictures?'

'Let's just say he has an interesting taste in women.'

'I have a feeling that might have been his roommate. You can ignore any activity in the last couple of weeks.'

'Well, that would take care of that issue. Having said that, he's cautious.'

'Why do you say that?'

'Well, despite being password-protected and everything, he went to a lot of trouble to cover his tracks, almost as if he knew someone might come looking. Erasing his browser history, caches, that kind of thing.' Makana let him continue. Ubay talked as if all this made perfect sense; there was no point in bursting his bubble.

'What was he trying to hide?'

'I'm not sure, but I did recover a lot of stuff.' Ubay looked up as his name was called from the other side of the room. Someone else had need of his skills. He got to his feet. 'Got to go, sorry, but talk to Sami, I gave him a break-down of everything.'

'I would, except he seems to have disappeared.'

'Oh, yes.' Ubay glanced over his shoulder in Rania's direction before motioning for Makana to draw near. 'There are a couple of places you might try, but don't tell anyone I said so.'

Normally, Sami was the kind of drinker who simply got swept away with whatever company he was keeping and carried on into the early hours. He didn't have the serious dedication of a hardened alcoholic. Nevertheless Makana found himself wandering up and down the nearby streets looking into small dark spaces. Bars were not called bars any more, since the word had been banished, so instead they were 'cafeterias'. There was the Hurraya, the Honololo, the Stella, all of them frequented on a more or less regular basis by Sami, whose taste in seediness was dictated by the mood he was in. Makana tried them all, without luck. Nobody had seen him, or if they had they weren't letting on. At the Café Riche, the old waiter stared at Makana with the timeless gaze of a veteran who has seen everything.

'He was here. He's gone now.' The eyes roved the length and breadth of the room, taking in the mostly deserted tables as if to make certain. 'He'll be back.'

It was the most promising lead Makana had had all day. He decided to put the time to good use and walked for fifteen minutes before reaching a narrow street of low, lopsided buildings near Ramses station. The door to the first-floor flat opened to reveal a boy wearing a striped gellabiya.

'Is your mother home?'

'Who wants to know?'

'It's about your father.'

The door was wrenched open to reveal a woman in her twenties, cradling a baby on her hip. She tugged the boy back out of the way. Her hair was covered by a loosely tied scarf. She might have been considered pretty except for the flat hardness in her eyes that spelled out a bitter and irreversible disappointment in the world. She certainly didn't seem to regard Makana's appearance on her doorstep as an improvement.

'Go and see to your sister!' she yelled at the boy before turning back to Makana. 'What do you want?'

'It's about your husband, Mustafa Alwan.' Behind her, the boy stood his ground. He stared at Makana. His face was jaundiced and puffy. He had unusually large eyes, like dark pools in which the light barely registered.

'What about him?'

A door clicked open at the opposite end of the corridor and a wizened face squeezed itself into the crack.

'Something I can help you with?' the young woman leaned out and snapped. It was enough to send wolves howling back to the hillsides. In this case the door closed over a quiet whimper. Makana had stepped back out of her way. The door of the flat swung open behind her, affording him a glimpse of a living room that had recently been refurbished. The walls were painted a garish ruby red that would have been more at home in some of the dives Makana had just visited. In the middle of the room sat a bulbous white sofa, as incongruous as a walrus. The carved frame and feet were ornate and gilded. At least some poor local artisan was being kept in work. Alongside a lacquered wooden table there was a standing lamp with brass fittings and, to crown it all, a glass chandelier suspended in the middle of the air like a golden tree in a fairy tale. The woman resumed her defensive position in the doorway.

'What do you want?' she repeated.

'It's about your husband. He hasn't been in to work yesterday and today.'

'I told them, they should check again. He's working.'

'His boss says he hasn't come in.'

'Well, he's wrong. What can I tell you?' She shifted the child higher up her hip.

'There was an accident with a van. Did they tell you about that?'

The woman was shaking her head before he had finished speaking. 'It wasn't him. I told them they were wasting their time.'

'They took you to the morgue to identify the body?'

'I just said that.'

'You're sure it wasn't him?'

'Are you deaf? I just told you. I don't know who he is but he's not my Mustafa. Is that a problem?' Her eyes ran up and down him in a dismissive way. Whatever he was selling she wanted none of it.

'Not at all.' Perhaps Mustafa Alwan had simply run away from home. 'So where is your husband?'

'Away on business, like he always is. I don't care what they say, if he tells me he's working then he's working.'

'Sure, and when did you last speak to Mustafa?'

'I don't know. He doesn't like me calling him when he's at work. He's a very busy man, you know. Wait a minute, why are you asking me all this? I told your colleagues everything already.'

'Well, it's quite important that we find him. You can appreciate that, right?'

'It's always the same with him. He disappears for days and then he comes back. He's like that. He always says, *al haraka baraka*; staying busy brings its own blessings.'

'This must be a difficult time for you, with the police and everything.'

'You're a bunch of fools. If he'd been in an accident, they would have found his telephone. Mustafa never goes anywhere without his phone.'

It was hard to argue with such conviction. No telephones had been found at the scene, which was strange, or could simply be explained by whoever was sitting in the passenger seat.

'So you haven't heard from him?'

The woman shook her head. The child on her hip was eating a biscuit that had painted her face in chocolate. She stared at Makana with mild curiosity. The little boy had come back into view. He stared at Makana. He looked about seven years old, but there was something other-worldly about him, as if he wasn't really there at all.

'How are you managing?'

'We don't need anything,' she shrugged.

'Does he ever talk about his work?'

'To me, why would he do that?' She pulled the child more tightly to her. Now, for the first time, Makana saw uncertainty in her eyes.

'So he never talks about extra work, outside of his usual hours? You know, driving the van. Sometimes he brought home a little extra, right?' Makana nodded at the room behind her. She glanced back.

'Hey, what are you trying to say?'

'I'm just asking if he did a little extra work for anyone.'

'Look, the moment he walks out this door, I don't know where he goes, or what he does. It's another world out there. For all I know he has a whole other family somewhere, but if that's the case he'd better stay there. You can tell him that from me, when you find him. I'd sooner cut out his heart. You don't need to worry about us. Mustafa will be back soon.'

While Makana was wondering if she really believed what she was saying, the door slammed in his face.

In a taxi that stalled at every junction they came to, Makana crossed back over the river to Mohandiseen. Coasting the final few metres in the dark, he paid the apologetic driver and made his way down the ramp. Abu Gomaa, the old watchman, shuffled out of the shadows, the walls behind him illuminated by the strange flickering blue light of a television set. They were showing one of the old 1950s black and white films with Ahmed Ramzy and Soad Hosny. The Golden Age of Egyptian cinema. In the gloom the basement was a time capsule, the old man a relic from another age, surrounded by debris and dusty cars, dreaming of a time when the streets were wide and neat and the modern world seemed new. He looked up grumpily as Makana appeared. The dogs leapt up, their chains snapping taut as they began barking wildly. They bared their teeth and reared up on their hind legs. They weren't that big, but they were furious and had sharp teeth. Abu Gomaa got slowly to his feet.

'What do you want?'

Webs of sodium light filtered in from the street to brush at the glow from the screen. Seeing who it was, Abu Gomaa lowered himself unsteadily back onto his rickety chair, yelling at the dogs to keep quiet. He didn't seem happy to have his little idyll disturbed.

Makana had nothing to offer but his cigarettes, which the old man was happy to help himself to. He tucked one behind his ear and lit up another for now.

'The nights are long and cold this time of year. A man needs something to keep him company.' The grey eyes followed Makana as he circled away, glancing at the little corner where Abu Gomaa had his bed against the wall. The air was thick with a fetid, animal smell.

'What kind of dogs are those?'

'Fighting dogs.'

'Fighting dogs?'

'It's a special breed. They're almost wild, mixed with Egyptian jackals.' His eyes gleamed as a glint of light penetrated the dark. 'I raise them myself. They bring a good price, if you're interested.'

'In dogs? No, thank you. How long have you lived down here?'

Abu Gomaa's eyes narrowed cautiously, as if expecting a trap. 'I came as a boy from Upper Egypt. You know that part of the world? Nothing there but darkness. I saw the lights here and I thought I was in heaven. After a week I never wanted to go back.'

'So you've been living here ever since?'

'You ask strange questions for a police inspector.' Twin plumes of blue smoke streamed from Abu Gomaa's nostrils. The doddery old man of their first encounter seemed to have been replaced by a keener, sharper model.

'Tell me about Mustafa Alwan.'

'What is there to tell?' Cardboard boxes stacked along the wall appeared to act as a wardrobe. Something scuttled away in the shadows. No telling what life forms this living space might appeal to.

'Well, you keep track of the vans, you must know the drivers.'

'They come and go. They don't have time to talk to an old man.'

'What do you think Mustafa was doing on the Ismailia road?'

'Who said it was him in that van, anyway?' Abu Gomaa's tone had hardened. 'Did they identify the body?'

'It looks like there were two men in that van. The driver was killed but it seems possible there was a second man who has vanished.'

'I don't know anything about that.' The eyes roved around the room, stopping anywhere that was not Makana's direction. 'Someone might have stolen the van. It happens.'

'Then where is Mustafa Alwan? He is the one who signed it out, right?'

'I'll be honest with you.' The old man's eyes came to a halt on a spot on the floor. 'He has a problem.'

'What kind of problem?'

'He drinks. May Allah show him compassion. He drinks and then he forgets.'

'Why would Shaddad hire a man like that?'

'Nobody in this world is perfect. You think a man should forfeit the chance to feed his family because he has a weakness? Everyone has weaknesses, even you, I would imagine.'

'I'm not saying you're wrong.' The honeyed mewl of violins drew the old man's attention back to the television. Makana stepped in to block his view but Abu Gomaa leaned over to one side to see around him. 'I get the impression Alwan was making a bit of extra money on the side.'

'I wouldn't know anything about that.'

'I'm not asking you to squeal on him. I'm just asking if that sort of thing happens. I mean, he has the van in his possession and someone asks to borrow it.' Makana glanced back at the row of parked vehicles before smiling. 'You're not telling me the drivers never try making a little extra on the side?'

'I wouldn't say it never happens.' Abu Gomaa examined the tip of his cigarette as if it were an ancient artefact.

'And you don't think it's odd he hasn't shown up for work?'

'Like I said, he drinks. He'll disappear for a few days and then he'll come back and everything will go back to normal.'

'When did the drinking start?'

'A few years ago. Right after the thing with his son.'

'What thing with his son?'

'The boy was born with a problem. The doctors said he couldn't be saved.' The watchman sat back, giving up the idea of watching his film. 'We're all in the hands of our Lord.'

Chapter Eighteen

The walls of the Café Riche were adorned with photographs of writers, journalists, playwrights, novelists and, above all, poets. Men and women, now long gone, who had devoted their lives to the task of trying to capture the nation in words, to paint its dreams and aspirations, to put its spirit into rhyme and reason. The black and white images floated through the low lighting as if from across the foggy sea of time. Not so much another era as another world. Once this had been the place where intellectuals gathered to argue and plot their dissent. There was said to be a secret door that allowed them to escape in the event of a police raid. Nowadays it catered mostly to tourists seeking to commune with the old spirit. A séance might have been more helpful, thought Makana.

Sami sat alone down at the far end of the room, bowed beneath the disapproving gaze of his idols. His forehead rested on the tablecloth and it remained there as Makana approached. The furry white eyebrows of the impassive waiter rose imperceptibly as he went by – a faint concession to the expression of an opinion.

As Makana sat down, scraping the chair back noisily, Sami lifted his head.

'You look better with your eyes closed.'

'Ah, our intrepid investigator. Have a drink with me.'

'I'm not sure, I suspect you may have drunk the place dry.'

'Nonsense. The day this place runs dry is the day I start swimming to Europe.' He snapped his fingers in the air several times to no avail. The waiter appeared to have discovered a corner of the bar counter that needed determined polishing. 'So, what brings you here?'

'I've been looking for you.'

'Well, *mabrouk*, you found me!' Sami beamed, then his face grew serious. 'You remember the old days? We were a team. Whatever you needed I got it for you. Am I right?'

'I thought you were still helping me.'

'Sure, but it's different now.' Sami squinted at the bar, pushing his spectacles up his nose. 'Where's he gone now?'

Makana looked over his shoulder. The waiter had indeed vanished into thin air. A conjuror's trick, or then again perhaps rumours of a secret door were not unfounded.

'Look, I understand, you and Rania are going through a difficult time. Every marriage has its ups and downs.'

'This is not a marital dispute.' Sami stabbed his index finger into the table. 'This is about principles. We no longer want the same thing. Isn't that sad?'

'What do you want?'

'I want this country to come to its senses. I want the people to wake up.' Sami struggled to light a cigarette, snapping his lighter ineffectively. 'I can't do that if I'm trying to raise a family. And what about Rania, what becomes of her work? If she gives that up you know who she's going to blame, right? Maybe not today, maybe not tomorrow, but some day.'

'Maybe she's old enough to make that decision herself. Maybe she thinks you both are.'

'Come on, I can barely manage my life as it is.' Sami upended the bottle of beer into his mouth and sucked at the dregs, peering over at the bar. 'I can't understand where he got to.'

'Talking of work . . .'

'Oh, yes. Sure.' Sami juggled a cigarette between hands and mouth while fishing a notebook from his satchel. 'I don't know if I told you, but Ubay made short work of the password.'

'Ubay told me himself.'

'He did?' Sami blinked. 'Of course, he told you how to find me.'

'He made me swear not to reveal my source.'

'He's a good kid. So talented. That's what gets to me.' Sami screwed his eyes tightly shut. 'There's so much talent in this country, and it's all going to waste. Imagine what this country could be. It's just like this guy.' Sami tapped the notebook.

'Mourad.'

'I mean, I look at him and I can feel his pain. I can see the way he's thinking, how he's trying to find a way out of this mess. That's it. Everyone dreaming in their little niches.'

Makana couldn't tell if this was the booze talking, or whether he was witnessing a man on the edge of a nervous breakdown. Either way, it wasn't good. Then again maybe it was a symptom, the national malady: melancholia interrupted by flights of fantasy.

'So what exactly is he involved in?'

'Hard to say. He's thinking outside the lines. He's smart enough to try and erase his tracks, not good enough to fool us, of course. I thought maybe drugs, but this is the wrong mix, too much idealism and not enough wacky abstraction.'

'What about political material?'

'He's not planning a revolution, if that's what you're thinking. Ah, finally.' Sami waved the empty Stella bottle at the wayward waiter. 'Suleiman, please, we're dying of thirst.'

'Maybe you've had enough for one night,' said the white-haired waiter.

'You're worried about me? May Allah show you compassion. Bring us two.'

Suleiman's face remained as impassive as the Sphinx. Silently he took himself back to the bar to fetch the beer.

'Okay, where was I? Oh, yes, it's all pretty vague, but he's clearly up to something.' Sami seemed to have sobered up in a matter of seconds. 'As I was saying, drugs don't really fit with the profile. He's on all kinds of websites and blogs, under a number of assumed names, most commonly something called *Che_4Masr*. Not that original, but a play on the revolutionary poster-boy's name that locates it specifically in Egypt. He's also dabbled on 4chan and various other networking sites. He seems to connect to others in a group. They go into a room and the material there is cryptic. There are dates and times and nicknames. It's some kind of operation, but I can't figure out what.' Sami swivelled the notebook around as the waiter arrived with the beer. 'Thanks, Amm Suleiman.'

'The night is long,' said the waiter. 'Tomorrow brings another day as fresh as an apricot.'

'Another frustrated poet,' muttered Sami. 'Suleiman the Magnificent, we call him. What more could you ask for?' He returned to the notebook. 'Take this for example; new transport ready – fourteen.' Sami looked up. 'Fourteen what, it doesn't say. Kilos, boxes, sacks? Another one talks of having to change the route, but doesn't specify where to. Then there are references to people with funny names.' Sami flicked up and down. 'Like this, for example: Lasciac. No idea who that is.'

'How about dates? Can you fix when these messages were sent?'

'Well, they aren't actually sent. They don't go from one person to another. They are posted on a board. Only people with access can read them. They presumably know what all of this means.'

'And the messages stop around the time he disappeared?'

'You said he disappeared around the thirteenth, right? Messages were posted for the next ten days.'

'By Mourad?'

'It's not clear who is posting them. Until we figure out which codename is who, we won't know.'

'Can you make me a printout of all the messages you found?'

'Already done.' Sami slapped a large envelope on the table. 'What more could you ask for?' The smile on his face froze as he poured his beer and Makana got to his feet.

'That's it? You've got what you came for and now you're off? How about lending a sympathetic ear?'

'I'm not going to sit here and watch you drink yourself under the table.'

'Nobody asked you to.'

The waiter's mournful gaze followed Makana to the door. A condemned man watching his last hope of salvation turn to dust.

Makana was so lost in his thoughts on the way home that the taxi driver had to nudge him.

'*Yallah, ya basha*, they're calling you.'

He pulled the telephone from his pocket and heard a voice he couldn't place at first.

'I had a word with Aljuka about that girl.'

'And?' It came to him that Fantômas was in the middle of a crowd somewhere.

'Let's just say you're not his favourite person right now.'

'That's what I thought.'

'Yeah, but I don't think that's the end of the story. I just think he needs time. He'll come round to it.'

'Can we try without him? I mean, she must be living near the church somewhere.'

'It's a possibility. Look, let's give him a day and if he doesn't come through I'll take you there myself.'

'As long as it's not going to create problems for you.'

'You're trying to help us, right? When no one else cares? That's enough for me.'

To Aljuka, Makana represented all that was bad with the world. Guilt by association. He was a Northerner and therefore he was one of *them*. In the old days they would hunt and trade Southerners as slaves. The current regime in Khartoum was the modern face of that same sentiment. The ones who bombed and razed villages, ran militias to do their dirty work for them, to murder old men and children, to rape their women. It was strange to be associated with the same people Makana had come here to get away from, but understandable perhaps, under the circumstances.

'The brother is a long way from home,' said the driver as he rang off. His eyes never left the road.

'You could say that.' Makana was suddenly weary of the world and all its petty problems.

'Those are your compatriots, aren't they, all those people sleeping in the maidan there by the Mustafa Mahmoud mosque? People are saying the Israelis are behind it, but they say that about everything, right?'

'Why the Israelis?'

'You know, to make themselves look good, saving Christians from the evils of Islam.' The driver glanced across to see if Makana was following him. 'They take them in as refugees. It makes us look like savages.'

'I didn't know that.'

'Oh, yes. They're all trying to get into Israel. I wouldn't mind going myself, except of course for the Israelis. Still, it wouldn't be a bad life, eh?'

'I wouldn't know.'

'No, I don't know myself. Actually, to tell you the truth, I don't understand what all the fuss is about. There's room for everyone, I always say.'

Chapter Nineteen

The meeting with Professor Asfour was at the Manial Palace on Roda Island. Makana wasn't sure why. When he asked Doctora Siham she had simply said, 'He likes to walk.' The palace had been home to Prince Mahmoud Ali Tewfik, uncle to the deposed King Farouk, but was now open to the public, for a small fee. Once upon a time the island had been a botanical paradise thick with rubber trees, banyans, majestic cedars and royal palms. The prince had dreamed of a 'garden of a thousand delights', throwing architectural folly into the blend in the shape of an orientalist fantasy of a Turkish castle. The buildings displayed a bizarre mix of variations on Ottoman, Syrian and Moroccan styles.

'Have you never been here before?' Doctora Siham was waiting outside the gates. Makana had to admit that he hadn't. 'This you have to see.'

She was dressed in trousers and a long jacket. Her hair was loose. This had a disconcerting effect on him, which was bad enough. Then, as they strolled beside a low building stretching along the perimeter wall, she seized hold of his arm and impulsively dragged him inside a dark and gloomy room. The air was aflutter with small wings as birds flew in and out through the barred windows. They perched hesitantly on the old iron, as if uncertain whether it was safe to enter, and it wasn't hard to see why. The furniture was painted in gold and stood on carpets the colour of blood or wine, though it was probably safe to say neither substance had flowed here in a while. The dusty atmosphere was stirred by a faint breeze from the river that grazed the heavy crystal lobes of the chandeliers, the tarnished candelabras, the tassels of the threadbare carpet. Very little light seemed to get in. Above a tray of glass eyes a poorly printed sign declared there were a hundred and eighty-two mounted gazelle heads, as shot by the king himself or his entourage. Some were no more than kids. One stared stubbornly off to the right, defiant in death.

'I used to come here as a child, with my father. He was a professor of veterinary studies,' she offered, which was more than Makana had learned about her in years. 'Amazing, isn't it?' There was something uncharacteristically bubbly about Doctora Siham today. She seemed radiant. Unsurprising perhaps, Makana reasoned, given the presence of so many stuffed animals. Or did it have something to do with Professor Asfour's imminent arrival? If ever one asked for a definition of decadence, Makana thought, this room would come close. A table made from an elephant's ear, tusks and feet propped alongside. A tiny tortoise only thirty-six days old. A gold necklace adorned with heavy pendants, each made of the head of a baby bird, their beaks recast in gold. There was a cobra skin and a stuffed hermaphrodite goat from the island of Qumran which, according to the poorly typewritten card alongside, had apparently impregnated itself. Crocodile heads on ivory letter-openers. A cigar-cutter fashioned from rhinoceros horn. Stuffed monitor lizards, falcons, eagles, rats, even chameleons, along with lions, wart hogs, wild asses, scorpions. Gifts from visiting dignitaries. German medals from *Jagdausstellung* meetings in Berlin, along with hunting knives and sprung traps. A scarab beetle in a glass lens. Luminous, brightly coloured butterflies.

They emerged from the darkness to find a round, sprightly man in his sixties wearing a navy-blue tracksuit and a beaming smile. His eyes crinkled with delight as he grasped Doctora Siham's hands in his.

'Ah, Jehan, how lovely to see you!'

Makana had never heard her first name being used before. Professor Asfour hailed from Luxor and was delighted to meet someone from Sudan, a country he knew well, he claimed, having once studied there. All of this was blurted out within minutes of meeting. Through the thickened lenses of the professor's spectacles Makana imagined he looked as interesting as a new specimen.

'So, how did you find our bizarre trophy room?'

They were moving through the gardens now, following the winding paths, trying to keep up with the fast-moving professor.

'This is my daily routine. My doctor tells me I have to lose ten kilos. I ask you, where would you find ten kilos on me?' He slapped his hands against his sides in energetic denial before moving on. 'We have a long tradition of extracting the internal organs. As I'm sure you know, the Ancient Egyptians mummified not only human beings, but a wide range of animals also. They turned the living creature into an icon, a divine representative of the power of life.' Just following the track of the professor's thoughts was a demanding business.

'Those bizarre objects have less to do with divinity than with asserting male authority,' Doctora Siham said, managing to get a word in.

'Of course, it is a perversion of the original concept. Mummification was intended as a form of adoration, preserving life for all eternity. In the act of removing the inner organs, Anubis was performing a labour of love.' If Jehan was unconvinced by this she kept it to herself. Perhaps she had heard it all before. Asfour carried on. 'Here, on the other hand, we have a vulgar display of the arrogance of the ruling classes. Glory in life rather than in death. This palace tells us much about the way such absolutists

213

dominate our history. Men who never questioned their superiority. The prince was eventually buried in Switzerland. His mausoleum was taken apart and the marble used by Gamal Abdel Nasser for his own tomb.' The professor chuckled to himself. 'Nothing much has changed. Erasing the existence of previous rulers from history is something of a tradition. The pharaohs did it all the time.'

'Only they are no longer mummified,' said Makana.

'Some would argue they have already been mummified, they just don't know it.' Professor Asfour whinnied like a horse at his own humour. Doctora Siham's smile was set like concrete. The professor turned a corner and, finally, slowed. 'Jehan has told me something of your case and she kindly consented to allow me to look at the two bodies, even though I think she was bending the rules a bit.' The professor flashed a conspiratorial wink at the pathologist.

'In the interests of science,' Jehan shrugged dismissively. 'Officially, I can call in anyone I think might help me to complete my report.'

'Naturally, I am honoured.' Professor Asfour gave a little bow. The conversation seemed in constant danger of veering off the road.

'What can you tell us, Professor?' Makana asked.

'Well, I'm afraid there is really very little to link the two men, apart from the fact that they clearly suffered unusual deaths. Both hail from different ethnic groups. The severed head shows the distinctive markings on the forehead of the Mundari, while the young man was a Bor Dinka.'

214

'Are these tribes ever hostile to one another, traditionally speaking?'

Professor Asfour flashed a wan smile. 'We try not to use the word tribe in this day and age. It rings of imperialist notions of racial superiority.'

The distinction did not strike Makana as being particularly helpful – but it seemed wise to humour the professor. 'The Dinka and Mundari, then.'

'Two ethnic groups that are traditionally adversaries. They occupy the same territory in the South Jonglei area. The Mundari are sedentary farmers while the Dinka are cattle herders. This competing use of the land, especially during migration, can create tension.'

'Is it possible that each was a victim of the other group?'

'It's possible, of course. The uninformed view of your country's problems is of a simplistic split between Christians in the South, united against an intolerant Muslim regime in the North. Four decades of civil war testify to the gravity of that conflict. But we often forget the existence of deep rifts within the South itself.' The professor grew stern. 'Two thousand perished in the Bor massacre of 1991, for example, hundreds of thousands made homeless.'

'Do you think it is possible we are witnessing a bout of intertribal warfare?'

Professor Asfour winced at the term but Makana ignored it. People were killing one another. Fussing over the terminology seemed a luxury he couldn't afford.

'It's possible. People carry their traditions and prejudices with them.'

'And being refugees together in a foreign land? Doesn't that make them put their differences aside?' Doctora Siham asked.

'I'm afraid the evidence shows not.'

Makana pressed on. 'Does either group have a tradition of ritual dismemberment?'

'Not so far as I know.' Professor Asfour checked himself. 'Look, perhaps we should stop thinking of them as representatives of a particular ethnic group. Maybe we should think of them as people. Lost and abroad in a foreign society that despises them. The ethnic element may be just a part of a more complex grievance. Young people often have little understanding of their own traditions and practices.'

'How do they deal with that?'

'They make things up. They improvise. Of course, one might argue that all traditions are improvisations in some way, variations on what has survived in living memory. At the end of the day they grew up here, in the slums on the outskirts of the city. They know nothing else.'

'But the old allegiances can still apply?'

'To some extent, yes, but often they are adapted. When you uproot members of these groups and place them in a hostile, unfamiliar environment such as this city, new communities are formed, not always in a positive way.'

'You're talking about gangs?'

Professor Asfour nodded. 'The thing to remember is that often these young people feel as if they have nowhere they belong to. They try to make what they have their own. They reject the values of the society they find themselves in. They invent their own norms. The key is empowerment. Sometimes that can lead to crime.'

As the professor and the pathologist moved on to matters of a more personal nature, Makana turned away, lighting a cigarette.

'I was so sorry that you could not make it. The film was excellent. Next week there is a film festival at the French cultural centre. Perhaps I could send you the programme?'

'Well, I'm rather busy at the moment, as you can see,' said Jehan. If it was an excuse the professor took it gracefully.

'I understand perfectly,' he said, with another little bow, which seemed appropriate considering their setting. He returned to Makana and held out his hand. He had to be off.

'I shall never lose weight unless I stick to my exercise routine and then I will be ready for embalming.' He gave a hoot of laughter. They watched him jog off along the path, then Jehan, as he was beginning to think of her, suggested they move on. Families were streaming in as lunchtime approached. Crowds of children, women clutching bags bulging with enough food to sustain an expedition to Xanadu.

'Let's get out of here,' she said. 'You do have time, don't you?'

Ignoring a chorus of taxi drivers offering to take them wherever they were going, they cut a line through to the riverside, negotiating high pavements and speeding vehicles to arrive at a bay of relative calm. The sky had cleared up, leaving a chill breeze that seemed to sweep the city clean. The crowns of the palm trees swelled majestically overhead as Makana followed along beside Doctora Siham. Jehan. He wasn't sure how to address her now. The informality of using her first name felt extravagantly reckless. If she felt the same way the doctor gave no indication of a similar concern. She was in a relaxed mood, hair blowing freely in the wind.

'Do you have a cigarette?'

Which he did, naturally, and a few minutes passed in lighting up and savouring the bitter flavour of the tobacco. She held the Cleopatra away from her and grimaced.

'How do you smoke these things?'

'It's an acquired habit.'

'Yes, but why acquire it?' Too late, Makana realised she was smiling. A pathologist with a sense of humour. Who would have guessed? She turned and wandered off, taking long, purposeful strides, not waiting for him. He caught up with her when she paused to lean on a railing and gaze at the water.

'I always associate the river with romantic dreams. You probably find that strange.'

'Why should I find it strange?'

'Well, you don't seem like the kind of man who has much time for romance.'

Makana was having trouble understanding where this conversation was leading. She turned away to stare moodily at the river.

'Nobody excels in self-delusion like we do. We like to think we are still at the centre of the Arab world, when in fact we have little real influence. Cairo provides a playground for wealthy Arabs, produces trivial films that pale in comparison with what we made half a century ago. We boast of winning the October War when we were almost wiped out. We like to think we are descended from the pharaohs, but if they turned up today we would frown disapprovingly at their way of life.' She turned her back to the river and faced him. 'We dwell in a twilight world of nostalgia and unrealised hopes for the future.'

'The professor seems quite fond of you.'

She threw him a sharp look. 'We're colleagues, that's all.'

'I didn't mean to imply otherwise.'

He wondered if he had offended her as she pushed herself off the railings and they resumed walking. This was odd. He felt like a college student again. Where did that come from?

'He knows a lot. Unfortunately he also has some rather old-fashioned ideas about romance.'

'Another dreamer?'

'You could say that. The poor man is convinced he's in love with me.'

'I can see how that might complicate matters.' Makana recalled the gatekeeper at the university telling him that her husband had died. It didn't seem like the moment to pry.

'He's a theorist. To him the world is nothing but a test case for his ideas.'

'He's studying you.'

'It feels like that sometimes.' She sighed while the wind blew her hair around her face. 'He has convinced himself there is a bond between us. Both of us lost our respective spouses. His wife and my husband. To him that makes us twinned souls, like Isis and Osiris.'

'I thought he was a sociologist.'

'To him it's the same thing. All societies go back to them. The Bible, the Old Testament, the Torah. It's all rooted here in Ancient Egypt.'

'A fascinating man.'

'He has his moments, but he's not for me.'

'But he thinks otherwise.'

'Hence the invitations to dinner, the cinema. It all becomes very complicated.'

Makana was beginning to think the same thing. He cleared his throat and offered another cigarette. This time she declined, which was a shame. Something about the sight of her smoking with the wind blowing in her hair seemed to unbalance him, as if gravity had been temporarily suspended.

'I'm having trouble subscribing to this idea of a war between rival gangs,' Makana admitted.

'The methods are different.'

'Perhaps we are seeing something that is not there.'

'You mean, simply because the two victims are young males from South Sudan doesn't mean they have to be linked?'

It was his turn to sigh. When you put it like that there wasn't a lot to tie them together at all. What was it then that made him think there was a connection?

'So, we need to find something that ties the two bodies together,' she said. It sounded like a concession.

'Is that possible, I mean in the forensic work?'

'We still haven't had the tissue samples back from chemical analysis. Maybe there's something there.'

It seemed like a slim straw to be clutching at. He caught her smiling at him.

'What?'

'Nothing. It's just that this isn't even your case, officially. I mean, you're not actually working for anyone on this. You have other things to do, I assume. So why pursue it?'

'Someone has to, don't you think?'

'Sure, but why you? I mean, maybe you should be asking why you feel the need to help people you have no obligation to.'

'I'm not sure I'd like the answers.'

They both fell silent for a time, following the flight of an ibis that drifted like a sheet of newsprint from the sky.

Was he the only factor the two deaths had in common? It wasn't a helpful thought. Jehan leaned over towards him, plucking the cigarette from his fingers to puff on it herself.

'You might be surprised.'

Chapter Twenty

Fantômas was waiting under the statue of Simon Bolivar, a stone's throw from Tahrir Square. What could be more appropriate for a revolutionary artist than the liberator of Latin America? With his dreadlocks and dressed in a ripped T-shirt and some kind of overalls daubed in a multitude of paint, he resembled an exotic bird that had stopped off on its annual migration. Cars tooted in salute and young men hanging from the doorways of lopsided buses yelled witticisms that floated off on a toxic slipstream. Fantômas himself was unconcerned, leaning up against the *revolucionario*'s pedestal with the bemused and distant look on his face of a man immune to anything this city had to throw at him. The inner confidence of one preoccupied with the amount of work to be done and the lack of time to do it in. When Makana appeared, emerging from the crowd of strangers like an apparition, he straightened up and dropped his cigarette butt to the ground before wordlessly leading the way back to the choking line of minibuses shuttling and hooting their way forward. Jockeys called out a litany of destinations near and mostly far, while hordes of impatient passengers jostled for space. Fantômas steered Makana towards a garish purple minibus dashed with yellow inscriptions. *These Wheels are on Fire,* one read. Another was dubbed *The Tarmac Gazelle,* along with the more common sprinkling of mundane religious invocations, seeking protection from on high.

'I know you usually travel in your own car,' said Fantômas, as they squeezed into the rear seat alongside a large woman who remained as immobile as a bulging sphinx. 'I thought you should have a taste of what it is like for ordinary people.'

The price of the ticket. Makana was content to go along if it made his guide happy. 'How well do you know Father Saturnius?' Makana asked when they began to move. The woman next to him filled the air with a pungent blend of fierce perfume and perspiration. He longed for a cigarette to clear the air.

'I met him when I first arrived in this city with nowhere to stay, no money. I was young and I had nothing. If it wasn't for him, I don't know what would have become of me.'

They were shuffling slowly up an overpass, one metre at a time. It wasn't perfume, he decided, coming from the woman next to him, but industrial-grade insecticide that made his skin itch. The windows of the minibus were jammed halfway open, or closed.

'What about the American, Reverend Corbis?'

'He's a strange one. His wife is an angel. Really. She has helped so many people, gives her services for free.'

'They've been coming here for a few years now?'

'Sure. What can I tell you? They have a mission. Their God-given task to save us.'

Fantômas gave a flick of the hair, less a necessity than part of his style. The dreadlocks had a life of their own. An oasis of rubbery palms. Looking at him was like trying to get a fix on a mirage.

The conductor, hanging out of the doorway, reeled off a list of destinations to an indifferent crowd on a corner in Heliopolis. No takers.

'As if it would kill them to say no thank you,' he muttered, consoling himself by rustling through the fistful of bank-notes in his hand. 'The same faces every day, nobody ever says hello.'

'Helping people is what justifies their existence,' continu-ed Fantômas.

'This adoption programme of theirs, how does it work?'

'The Homehavens Project?' Fantômas rolled his eyes. 'They only pick the best. They interview everyone they can find, go through the whole routine. Questions and more questions. Then tests and more tests. In the end they only take a select few. A lot of people are frustrated by that.'

'Sounds like you don't approve.'

'Look, taking a handful of people and giving them a new life in America is fine, but it doesn't solve the problem. There are thousands who need help, who have a right to go home to their country. They all want a chance to start a new life.' He shook his head. 'To me, this is all about making Americans feel better about themselves.'

'How often does it happen?'

'Oh, they take a handful, a couple of times a year.'

'Do you know people who have started a new life in America?'

'Sure.' Fantômas scratched his head as he grew vague, nodding in his usual slow, steady fashion. 'You hear about cases, you know.'

'Okay, so let me ask you about something else. Aljuka and his boys there.'

Fantômas looked out of the window. 'I thought it might come to this.'

'Is there a war going on? I mean, between different factions, or whatever you call them?'

'A gang war?' The expression on his face sank. 'You mean an urban reinvention of tribal warfare?'

Makana gave an apologetic shrug. 'Is it that far-fetched?'

'It's a projection. Come on. Aljuka is a soldier. I mean he was killing people when he was nine years old. He walked out of South Sudan. The Lost Boys, they were called. He led a group of them. Some of them drowned. Others were killed by wild animals, lions, pythons, crocodiles.

There are wild stories he can tell. In the end he reached Kenya and one of those nice humanitarian organisations. One thing led to another and he wound up here.'

'He's a friend of yours.'

'I like the guy, yes. Look, I spend my life with arty types. People who see something in my work that maybe I never intended. They have money to pay for my canvases. Who knows why? Maybe it's the painting, maybe they want some excitement in their lives. I don't know, I just paint. What I'm saying is that most of the people I meet are phonies. Aljuka is genuine. He doesn't have a lot of affection for Northerners. He's capable of hurting people he thinks might be a threat.'

'Is he capable of cutting someone's head off?'

Fantômas cast him a wary eye. 'Now you're talking crazy.'

'Supposing someone was threatening him. Could he do something like that, to send a message?'

'You're talking about the head found on the riverbank.'

'Could Aljuka or his men be responsible?'

'Why? It makes no sense. Why go to all that trouble?' Fantômas chuckled to himself. 'Or is it that you think we still run around waving spears at each other?'

Makana decided that perhaps he had exhausted this particular line of inquiry.

Estrella's mother lived in a single room that was no more than a fenced-off partition in a basement off an alleyway narrow enough to take the shoulders off your shirt. None of the five small children running in and out were hers, she assured them, but the offspring of various relatives, neighbours, friends, who were earning money in the city. A woman in her late thirties, she could have passed for twenty years older. Stray wires of grey twisted out from her braids and she seemed distracted in a way that implied she was having trouble sticking to the narrative of the present.

'We've come here because we're trying to find Estrella. Nobody has seen her.'

'She's a good girl,' she smiled. It was the third or fourth time she had repeated herself. Makana had given up counting. 'She works hard. Always ready to take care of the small ones.' She lapsed into silence, her eyes seeking a corner of the room where nothing was moving. Fantômas cleared his throat.

The woman's jaw churned idly, as if chewing something that wasn't there.

'She's not in any trouble. Estrella is a good girl. She stays away from the troublemakers. She has no time for them. Work is all she cares about. She takes everything she can find.'

Around her neck she wore a small silver cross, similar to the one he had seen Estrella wearing. The woman herself seemed lost. Asking about the whereabouts of the girl seemed to be taking absurdity to new heights. Asking the day of the week would have presented a challenge.

'I was taken to Cuba as a small child.' Distant memories seemed to flow more easily than the narrative of the present. 'That's where I learned Spanish. *¿Sabes?* That's where Estrella comes from. It means star. Lucky star. I always thought it was a good name. In those days we represented something. We were orphans of an African revolution that never came.'

No mention was made of the men of the family. Brothers, husbands, fathers, siblings. All of them somehow lost in the matrix of transition. A mattress on the floor was covered in a pink sheet. The youngest of the children, a baby of no more than three months, lay drooling in blissful slumber, unaware of the world it was about to wake up in. The woman brushed flies away from its open mouth with an absent flick of the hand. She put a hand to the cross around her neck.

'Estrella has one like that, doesn't she?'

'It's from Ethiopia,' she said. 'She's a good girl, always goes to church. She gave it to me.'

'Do you have any idea where she might be?'

A spark of clarity glowed in the woman's eyes.

'America.'

Fantômas glanced back at Makana. 'America? Why do you say that, mother?'

'I know it. If she is not here, it is because her time has come. She is always talking about her chances of getting across there. We are patient.' Her head rocked up and down. 'When she is settled and all is well, she will send

229

for us. Everything will be all right. I believe this is what our Lord intends for us.'

She reached under the mattress to produce something that she passed to Fantômas. He glanced at it and handed it across to Makana. A brochure for the Homehavens Project.

'Her best friend is already there.'

'Her friend, mother? Which friend?'

'Beatrice. And her brother Jonah.' She nods with conviction. 'They have already crossed. Now it is Estrella's turn. Then it will be the turn of the young ones.' Her eyes found Makana, perched on the edge of her field of vision. He caught a flicker of wariness there which made him hold back. Throughout the conversation Estrella's mother had barely registered his presence. Now, for some reason, she seemed to seek him out. Who could say what was going through her mind? There was something she wanted him to hear.

'I prayed for them, for the young ones like my daughter, who have known only hardship. I prayed for Beatrice and Jonah and my prayers were heard. Then I prayed for Estrella, and now she too has been taken up. Hallelujah, praise the Lord.'

'Isn't it strange that you haven't heard from her?'

Her eyes bored into him. Makana the Unbeliever.

'I prayed for them and they reached safety. Then I prayed for my daughter, and He has answered. She will get in touch when she can.'

'Praise the Lord, sister.' Fantômas bowed his head in supplication and Makana felt strangely out of place, as he always did when religion made its awkward entrance.

'You wouldn't happen to have a photograph of Estrella, would you?'

'Of course.' She smiled warmly at him and reached underneath her pillow. 'I keep her safe here.' Estrella was dressed in a smart white dress. 'She's in the choir,' her mother explained. She had the faraway look of one who is no longer sure of the ground beneath their feet.

'Who are these people she was talking about, Beatrice and Jonah?'

They were walking back towards the church, turning through narrow gaps between grubby, broken walls, the air rich with the smell of ash and burning wood. It was a maze that seemed to have no order to it. Everywhere the stench of the world breaking down, rotting vegetation, stale piss. The white jawbone of what might have been a sheep, or perhaps a dog, lay in the dirt like a skeleton key to the gates of heaven, just waiting for someone to find.

'Friends of Estrella's. Brother and sister. I think I know them.'

'Why doesn't she think it strange she hasn't heard from her daughter?'

'People cling to hope where they find it. She wants to believe that God intervened and took her daughter to America. The alternative is that her daughter is engaged in some other kind of work that she doesn't want to know about. People disappear all the time. They wind up as house slaves for some wealthy family, here or abroad, in the Gulf, say.' Fantômas pushed back his dreadlocks. 'Sometimes it's better for a mother not to know.'

'We should speak to Father Saturnius.' The church was the link between Estrella and the magical ticket out of here to America. If the mother was right and Estrella was on the Homehavens Project, Makana wondered why the priest had failed to mention it. Perhaps he thought it wasn't relevant, or it had simply slipped his mind.

They were almost there when they ran into Aljuka and his boys. They fanned out with long loping strides, all of them tall and thin, moving with the surefooted grace of experienced predators. Aljuka's tracksuit top was so white it seemed to glow. He must have had a stock of them. Either that or a small army to do his laundry.

'So, what do we have here?' The heavy gold crucifix swayed across his chest like a pendulum. 'Why are you coming where you don't belong?'

'We're not looking for trouble,' Fantômas began. Aljuka ignored him, his eyes on Makana.

'I don't trust this one. He smells like government.'

'He's not government. He's like the rest of us.'

Aljuka's face tightened in a fierce grin. 'No, he's not like us.'

'Is there a reason you don't want me looking into these deaths?' Makana asked, receiving a hard shove in the chest for his pains. He staggered back until his shoulders struck the wall.

'Hold on.' Fantômas tried to step between them but found himself shunted aside by a couple of the boys. A large knife had appeared in Aljuka's hand. He pressed the tip into the wall, close enough for Makana to feel the steel against his neck, and brought his face closer.

'Why should you care about us?'

'I would have thought you'd care about someone killing Southerners, unless you have something to do with it.'

Aljuka's face was electric with fury. Makana considered the wisdom of provoking a man carrying a knife.

'We are capable of taking care of our own.'

'Who exactly do you consider your own? Dinka, Nuer, Mundari? Are you the protector of all, or only the sacred few?' Makana considered the faces of the men around him. They all seemed so incredibly young. Aljuka grunted. The knife twisted roughly. Makana felt the blade nick his skin.

'You're a long way from home, my friend. When you leave here, don't think about coming back. Next time you might not be so lucky.'

It was hard to decide if there was some part of Aljuka he could reach. How do you appeal to someone whose life has taught him that violence is the only thing he can trust? One of his men stepped up to whisper something in his ear. Aljuka nodded and then stepped back, the knife dropping to his side. He took one last look at Makana and then he smiled.

'Your kind look at us and see wild beasts who belong in the jungle. Well, take a good look, because now we've brought the jungle to you.'

With that, he pivoted and walked away. His men followed. Not a bad exit, Makana thought, rubbing his neck.

Chapter Twenty-one

Father Saturnius was eating alone when they were shown into his office. He seemed embarrassed as he scrambled to his feet, as if it were unbecoming for a priest to be seen eating. As if he was expected to live by spiritual nourishment alone.

'The remains from our Christmas feast. Won't you join me?'

'Thank you, Father.' Fantômas dipped his head in a quick bow.

The offer was a reflex, a courtesy that neither side had any real interest in taking further. Makana caught a glimpse of an enamel bowl with a thick red sauce out of which an island of steamed sorghum rose. Throwing his tablecloth, a sheet of newspaper, over his supper to keep it warm, the priest led the way outside to a standing tap in the middle of the compound where he washed his hands and face.

'To what do I owe this honour?' he asked when he had finished, running a damp finger around his ear to wipe off the excess water. Makana explained that they had come from talking to Estrella's mother.

'She mentioned a couple of friends, Beatrice and Jonah. I'm wondering if there is a connection. Her mother has the idea that her daughter was planning to follow them to America.'

'Strange,' the priest frowned. 'I don't remember seeing Estrella's name on the list.'

'Could she have been mistaken, Father?' Fantômas suggested.

'I hardly think that's possible. There is always a celebration when someone is chosen. Nobody keeps it a secret.'

'What about her friends?' Makana asked.

'Yes, definitely. Beatrice and Jonah were outstanding candidates.' The priest's face glowed. 'Both of them excelled at school. They helped out in church. Beatrice taught the younger ones to read. Jonah did odd jobs. Painting, carpentry, even installing lights. There was nothing that boy wouldn't turn his hand to, and never a word of complaint from either of them.'

'Is there a picture of them on the noticeboard?'

Father Saturnius took a moment to check but returned shaking his head. 'Perhaps in the application files.'

'Once they move to America you no longer have contact with them?'

'That is correct.'

'It's one of the rules of the project, right Father?' Fantômas said.

Father Saturnius tilted his head to one side. 'If this is important, perhaps you would like to speak to Reverend Corbis or his sister?'

He led the way along the front of the building. They found Doctor Corbis in her infirmary. She was training an assistant, a tall adolescent with bright eyes who followed her intently as she showed him how to operate the machine for sterilising instruments. She looked up when they came in and smiled at Makana.

'You're back. I suppose that means you didn't find what you were looking for.'

'I don't seem to have much luck.'

'We were hoping to run into your brother,' added Fantômas.

'What is this about?'

'I'm trying to find someone. I believe she was on your Homehavens Project,' said Makana.

'My brother is really in charge of all that.' She lifted the lid of the machine, releasing a cloud of vapour into the air.

'Well, perhaps you could just tell me a little more about the selection process.'

'I can try,' she smiled.

'I understand you do medical examinations for all the candidates?'

'Oh, yes. Our checks are quite thorough.' Liz Corbis grew solemn.

'I'm sure, and that would mean you have records of all of them.'

'That's correct, but we don't keep them here.'

'Then where?'

'At the clinic?' She made a statement sound like question.

'The clinic?' Makana gestured at their surroundings. 'I thought this . . .'

'Oh no,' she said, shaking her head. 'Not here. This is fine, but for the kind of tests we're talking about we need a proper laboratory. The Hesira Institute allows us to use their facilities.'

'The Hesira Institute?' Makana recalled seeing the poster on the wall of the Munir Abaza's office.

'It's private, a very exclusive place that caters to a special kind of patient.'

'I see, so you use their laboratories.'

'It's a collaboration.' She paused. 'The thing is, this material is personal, for use within the organisation. We have to be very strict about how we deal with that information.'

'What information?'

They turned to find the doorway blocked by the bulky figure of Preston Corbis. He wore the same baseball cap with the Homehavens Project logo on the front that Makana recalled the priest had been wearing the first time they met. The arms of the crucifix were replaced by feathered wings. The top of the cross was adorned with eyes and a smile. His black trousers and shirt showed signs of fatigue, as did his face, which was flushed and drawn. He lumbered inside to lean against the counter, his fingers splayed out. 'I apologise for my sister, who can be a little overzealous when it comes to protecting our angels, that's how we think of our charges.' He stepped over to put his arm around his sister and give her a squeeze. 'The fact is that we came here to make friends and we'd like to help wherever possible. So what's all this about?'

'Preston, this is Mr Makana. You remember we met him the other day?'

'Indeed I do.' Makana's hand was swallowed up by the reverend's huge, meaty paw. 'How can I be of assistance, sir?'

Doctor Corbis intervened. 'Preston, Mr Makana is trying to help someone. He believes she may have been a candidate for our programme. I was just explaining that the profiles we draw up are confidential.'

'Absolutely. Have to be. I mean, our charges trust us with their personal details. That carries a certain responsibility.'

'I don't doubt that for a minute. I'm really not interested in the details, all I would like to know is whether or not Estrella was part of your programme, and if she has recently travelled to the United States.'

'Well, now, even that is, in principle, confidential. People have a right to change their lives, to make a new start. That's really what Homehavens is all about. A fresh start.' Reverend Corbis beamed around the room. A confident

239

man. For the moment in any case, he held all the cards. 'We believe that it is their right to decide who to share that information with.'

'Really, and does that apply to her mother?'

'Her mother?' Reverend Corbis furrowed his brow. 'I'm not sure what . . .'

'I just spoke to her mother. She is convinced that Estrella has gone to America. She's worried, understandably.' Only a slight exaggeration. The mother hadn't struck Makana as being acutely concerned with what planet she was on, let alone anything else.

'Unfortunately that doesn't change the principle of the matter. Our candidates are over the age of sixteen, which we consider to be the age of legal consent. It's their choice how much they tell anyone.' An apologetic smile played upon the reverend's lips. There was an air of mischief about him. A man who liked to be at the centre of things. The life and soul of the party. Alongside her brother, Liz Corbis appeared to shrink.

'Having said that, I don't believe the name rings any bells.' He glanced at his sister, who shook her head in agreement. He turned back to Makana. 'Now, I assume that since you are a friend of Joseph's you are on the side of the good. I'm sure you can sympathise with our caution. We live in dark times. Nobody knows that better than the boys and girls who come to this church seeking shelter.' He addressed Makana with exaggerated sincerity, resting a hand on Father Saturnius's shoulder. 'This man is a hero, and in another time and place his country's president would be pinning medals on his chest.'

'Preston, please,' Father Saturnius protested, wriggling with delight or embarrassment, it wasn't clear which.

'Nonsense. With his help we have set up a network that gives young men and women real hope. A chance to make something of themselves in a new life, and . . .' He raised a finger towards heaven. 'In doing just that we also bring joy to good Christian families, all over the United States, who have prayed for another child to raise. Everyone's a winner!'

He'd missed his calling as a game-show host on television. In another setting he might have become one of those hellfire evangelists who enjoyed nothing more than setting a Quran ablaze. 'Estrella had a couple of friends, Beatrice and Jonah.'

'They were definitely on the programme,' Father Saturnius piped up, encouraged perhaps by Reverend Corbis's obvious confidence in him. The reverend flashed him a withering glance.

'I would have to check our records.'

'It's possible they might know where Estrella is.'

'Do you mind if I ask you the reason for your interest? I'm not sure you fully appreciate the kind of resistance we face in this country. People are not overly enthusiastic about the idea of Christians trying to help other Christians to leave.'

'I think I understand.'

'One false move and the authorities will be overjoyed to show us the door. We do not come here to evangelise, to convert people of the Muslim faith, but there are those who would claim that that is the purpose of our mission.'

Makana glanced around at the others. Fantômas had pulled himself into a corner and was following the conversation with his eyes on the floor. Liz Corbis also held herself in the background, silent, observant. Unconsciously she wrapped and unwrapped a stethoscope, wound about her hand like an asp. When she noticed Makana watching her she cleared her throat.

'Preston, I believe that Mr Makana would not be here if he did not feel there was an urgent need to find this girl. I think we should help him.'

'And there was me thinking you were being too rigid.' Reverend Corbis looked at his sister and then he beamed. 'My sister is invariably wiser than I am, and so consider us at your service. Come to the Hesira Institute. We'll get out all the files and you can look to your heart's content.'

'Thank you,' said Makana. 'I appreciate it.'

'We all have to help each other in this life. Heaven knows those kids have seen little of that.'

'Amen,' said Father Saturnius.

'Amen,' whispered the others. Makana thought it was time to take himself off.

Chapter Twenty-two

Makana climbed out of a taxi to find Aziza waiting under the big eucalyptus tree. How long she had been sitting there it was impossible to say. She didn't waste time with greetings, but quickly fell in step beside him. There was a missed call on his phone from Okasha. He pushed redial and got an engaged tone.

'When are you going to buy me a telephone?'

'What do you need a telephone for?'

'So I can call you when I need to tell you something urgent.' Head down, she strode along with purpose. Makana pulled up, turning to her.

'Are you in some kind of trouble?'

Her eyes widened. The picture of innocence. 'Why do you assume that it should be trouble, and that I could not deal with it myself?'

'So what exactly is it?'

'You have a guest.'

'Aziza, there's nothing unusual about that. It happens all the time.'

'This one is different.'

'Different how?'

'He's crying.' Her mouth twisted in disapproval. 'I don't know what to do with men who are crying.'

Not a hopeful sign for the men who might come into her life in the future. At the top of the embankment, he paused to gaze down at the awama in all her ramshackle glory. A crumbling relic of past glory. A ghost ship from a forgotten age.

'How long have you been waiting up here for me?'

'Every since he turned up.'

Her face had begun to resemble that of her mother, Umm Ali. For a fleeting moment, Makana imagined all that was remarkable about the girl being extinguished by time, leaving a ponderous woman, weary with age and confused by the world around her. It was a depressing thought, and not to be further entertained. Aziza was not her mother. She would become a doctor and go on to do great things.

'I showed him up to your office and asked him if he wanted tea or coffee. He didn't.'

'He didn't want anything?'

'He just sits there wiping his eyes. I went up three times. In the end I just couldn't bear it any longer, so I came up here to wait. You see now how I need a telephone? Then I could tell you about these things.'

'You're right. I'll think about it.'

'You won't regret it. Any news on the head we found?'

'The victim was a Mundari. That's a tribe from South Sudan. Not a tribe,' he corrected himself. 'A group of people. Something like that. Anyway, that's all we know so far.'

'Sad to end up like that, don't you think? I mean, it must be awful not having all your parts buried in one place.'

An interesting thought. Was this something the dead were concerned with? In Egyptian mythology Isis searched the length and breadth of the land to gather the scattered parts of Osiris.

'Does this mystery visitor have a name?'

'Mr Hafiz. You mean that about the telephone?'

'I wouldn't say it if I didn't mean it.' Makana reached into his pocket for his money and counted a few notes into her hand. 'Can you run over to the Komombo Kiosk and see if they received a fax for me?'

'This is too much for a fax and too little for a phone.'

Makana plucked a note out of the bundle. 'This is for the fax. The rest is for you. I know somebody who can help with the phone.'

'Okay, but watch out, because some of them are defective. People sell anything nowadays if they think they can get away with it. Like that idiot who sells *taamiya* under the bridge, he bought one and I swear he holds it to his head to pretend he's speaking when he can only hear his own voice.'

245

As she went on her way, Makana moved down the path towards the river. Over the years it had been improved. It was wider now, more stable, and had acquired bricks here and there, which meant that when it rained, as it had done now, you weren't slipping and sliding on muddy inclines as you tried to negotiate the descent.

Hossam Hafiz leapt to his feet as Makana appeared.

'Did you find him?'

'Mr Hafiz, I told you I would be in touch if I had any news.'

'I know. I know. It's just that my wife is suffering. Her nerves were never strong.' His eyes were bloodshot and his face swollen.

'All the more reason for you to remain by her side.' Makana checked the electric heater was on, which it was, of course. Aziza wouldn't leave a guest to freeze in the cold.

'I know. I just . . .' Hafiz paced over to the window to look through the slats at the river. He stared down for a long moment. 'I feel so helpless. I wish there was something I could do, something I could tell her, just to raise her spirits.'

'I understand,' said Makana. He felt a twinge of guilt. No more. Four days had gone by, and although this might have felt like a long time to the Hafiz family, a missing person's case could take weeks.

Hafiz seemed hardly to register his words. His mind was elsewhere. 'It's hard to explain. She suffers so. I don't know

246

what it is, a mother and her first-born son. She spoilt him. Pampered him, kept him close to her skirts.' A bitterness had entered Hafiz's voice. 'She wouldn't let him play in the street with other kids. Always afraid he would have an accident. Too soft on him. In the end you're not helping them.'

Makana lit a cigarette and inhaled. 'I asked you if Mourad was involved with a girl.'

'I remember, but like I said, he never talked about anyone.'

'How about a girl from South Sudan? Did he ever mention someone called Estrella?'

'Not that I can recall.' Hafiz looked worried. 'Why would he do something like that and not tell us?'

'Perhaps he was worried what you would think.'

'It makes no sense. South Sudan, you say? Impossible. Where would he meet such a girl?'

'He was working in a fast-food restaurant.'

'A what?' Hafiz's face seemed to age in an instant, eyebrows drooping to both sides.

'A hamburger place. Fried chicken, that kind of thing. Popular with youngsters.'

Hafiz's face was a picture of bewilderment. 'But I don't understand. He's supposed to be studying. If he has time to work he can help us at the restaurant.'

'Maybe this was something he needed to do for himself. Would your wife have known?'

'My wife? You mean, without telling me?' The look of incomprehension was complete. He saw conspiracies on all sides.

'It's possible his interest in the girl was political.'

'Political, how?'

'He may have been trying to help her.'

'Help her how?' Hafiz was growing more desperate with every word.

'That's what I'm not sure about.'

The bell rang downstairs. Aziza moved so quickly that she was already at the top of the gangway before the bell chimes had faded away.

'Excuse me, *ya basha*.' She held up the sheets faxed over by Shaddad and gave a small bow. Hossam Hafiz made to leave. 'I won't take up more of your time. I can see you are a busy man. Is there anything you can give me, anything to give my wife hope?'

'Soon, I hope. Believe me, when I have some firm news you'll be the first to know.'

When he had gone, Aziza said, 'I'm not sure I like that man.'

'He's a client. We don't have to like him. And besides, there are few enough of them about as it is.'

'Okay, what is this?' She held out a sheaf of papers.

'A list of drivers working for Shaddad. They deliver instruments and medical supplies.' He threw himself down into the big chair and read through the names. Mustafa Alwan was third on the list.

'Now that's a business where they have a licence to print money,' said Aziza. Makana grunted and she went on, 'When was the last time you bought some aspirin? It's all

248

so expensive. The thing about pharmacies is that people are always ill.'

'I can't argue with that.'

'Is this connected to that man's son?'

'No, this is something else.'

'The severed head?' she asked excitedly. She seemed to take some proprietorial pride in the object.

'A body was found in a van.'

Aziza whistled. 'No wonder he's in tears.'

Makana looked up but she had already disappeared down to the lower deck. The list of drivers was more extensive than he had expected, which suggested that not all of them worked full-time. This was borne out by the first ten calls he made; three confirmed that a number of the names on the list had not had anything to do with Shaddad Pharmacies for many years. Two others said they had found something better. The turnover of drivers working for Shaddad seemed high. Perhaps that was normal. Disconnected numbers indicated telephones that no longer existed. In the age of the free market people changed telephone companies and numbers as often as they did their shirts. He called Okasha back, and this time it rang. It took a while for him to answer, and when he did pick up the phone he was curt.

'Is this a bad time?' In the background Makana could hear voices.

'We're eating,' said Okasha.

'I can call later.'

'No, you don't understand. My wife's family are here. Wait, let me go into the next room.' Makana heard more voices and the sound of a hand being placed over the phone. Then a door slammed, bringing silence. Okasha kept his voice low.

'Thank God you called. These people are driving me crazy. My wife's mother and her brother, along with his wife and their four children. It's unbearable. All they talk about is eating and their poor dying relatives. I find myself praying for someone to be murdered.'

'I'm sorry to tear you away from all of that.'

'No, believe me, every moment I'm out of their reach is a blessing.'

'I'm looking at a list of Shaddad's drivers.'

'Why don't I have that?'

'Maybe he thought you had more important things to do with your time.'

'Don't start, or I'm going back to the madhouse in the next room.'

'I think Mustafa Alwan was running some kind of oper- ation of his own.'

'What makes you say that?'

'From this list I can see that drivers come and go, but he has stayed on. My feeling is that Shaddad is not generous when it comes to paying his drivers. Those who stay on do so for a reason. And Alwan's home seems to be very well furnished.'

Okasha sounded sceptical. 'Maybe he has a wealthy uncle.'

'Maybe.' Makana remembered the look in the boy's eyes. 'Also, he has a son.'

'There's no crime against that, so far as I know.'

'The son has some kind of health problem. He doesn't look well.'

'And all of this adds up to what?'

'I'm not sure, but Alwan is running some scheme, and the old man there, Abu Gomaa, I think he's in on it too.'

'Maybe that explains Shaddad's behaviour,' Okasha said. 'I got a call from someone high up. It doesn't matter who. It seems that our friend Shaddad is unhappy with our investigation. He thinks that we're trying to implicate him in something. Time wasting. Incompetence. All of these words were mentioned.'

'I don't think Shaddad is aware of what's going on. He's not the quickest boy in the class. He inherited the business and he's had some luck, but all manner of things could be going on right under his nose and he wouldn't have a clue.'

'The point is that it's only a matter of time before I am officially told to drop this case.' Okasha sounded bitter. 'If there's one thing I really resent, it's when people start telling me how to do my job. So I've decided to order a full forensic examination of Shaddad's basement. See how he likes that.'

'That might shake things up a bit.' Makana took a moment to light a cigarette. 'Has it occurred to you that maybe you're taking this a bit too personally?'

'I don't like to be told my job. They can pull me off the case as a favour to their friend, but at least let me do things as I see fit. Otherwise, what's the point?'

'Your pride is wounded.'

'Call it what you will. Our pathologist is on board and will bring a team of her students. We'll make it into a little outing and Mr Shaddad will realise that going over my head is not the way things work.'

'Sounds like you'll have a lot of fun.'

'That might well be, but don't think you're getting out of this. I think you should be there too.'

'You're forgetting something. I don't work for you, remember?'

'If you worked for me I wouldn't even bother explaining why you need to be there.'

Chapter Twenty-three

Makana's mind was not on Shaddad's basement next morning. He was thinking about Mourad and where he might be. Hafiz's visit the previous evening had been a reminder of the emotional cost of his absence. That basement was something of a distraction, which perhaps explained why Makana found himself in a pensive mood as Sindbad drove up the dual carriageway of the Dowal al-Arabiya. Everything seemed to be conspiring to direct him away from the search for Mourad. Deep down inside him was the feeling it was not going to end well for the Hafiz family. The image of Mourad's friend Ihab cheerfully upturning tables as he skipped away from the riverside café returned to him. Makana was convinced that Ihab knew more than he'd let on. He was protecting Mourad and it was very possible that he knew where his friend was. What really intrigued Makana was what they were all up to. What was this revolution they were all so taken with? What form did their rebellion take? Whatever it was he doubted the answers would be found by a forensic sweep of Shaddad's basement.

They had reached the roundabout by the Mustafa Mahmoud mosque and the commotion on the other side of the street wrenched Makana from his thoughts.

'Go around again,' he told Sindbad.

The refugee camp had grown in a matter of days. The police presence had swelled in reply. At the far end of the square a line of police trucks reached out nose to tail. Among them featured a number of high-sided blue prison vans. Bored-looking conscripts holding long batons and riot shields stood around like actors waiting for their cue. Makana spotted a group of officers in the black uniforms of the Central Security Forces. One of them he recognised. Then Sindbad swung the wheel and the Datsun lurched alarmingly before shooting off into Syria Street at a sharp angle.

'I have something for you to do after you drop me off,' said Makana.

'At your service.'

There were times when Sindbad sounded like a military cadet trying to impress. Still, Makana knew he couldn't complain. He would never find anyone else even half as devoted as Sindbad. Makana explained about Mourad's friend Ihab.

'I need you to be discreet. Don't let him see you, but follow him, find out where he goes.'

'Follow him?' Sindbad's chest swelled with responsibility. 'No problem, *ya basha*.'

The thing about Sindbad was that he required precise directions for everything you asked him to do. Allowing him to improvise was inviting trouble.

'I want you to find out where he goes, who he's with, what he does. As much as you can. You have the pen and notebook I gave you?' Sindbad tapped the dashboard. The two items were tucked safely under the strip of acrylic zebra-skin that ran along the top. 'Good. Note down any details. Addresses. Anything that might be important.'

'*Hadir, ya basha.*'

Doctora Siham had her team lined up in the street outside Shaddad Pharmacies. There were a dozen or so of them, all looking excited at this outing, all clad in light blue nylon jumpsuits with hoods and gloves. A collection of amused bystanders looked on. The funniest thing they had seen in years. Doctora Siham – Jehan, as he was starting to think of her – acknowledged Makana with barely a glance as she led her team down the ramp into the car park.

'She's not in the sweetest of moods today,' murmured Okasha as he came over.

'Why, what happened?'

'My fault, I suppose. When we arrived I said to Shaddad that this was really just a training exercise.' Okasha sniffed. 'She didn't like that.'

255

'Why would you do that?'

'I got cold feet.' Okasha looked pained. 'Supposing we go to all this trouble and nothing turns up?'

'She's a senior forensic officer.'

'Of course you're right. But it's easy for you, you don't have to answer to anyone.'

'And you're the senior investigating officer. Maybe you don't need to explain your decisions.'

'I know.' Okasha swatted the air to dismiss the subject. 'Anyway, I need to go back in there now and try to make peace with Shaddad. You want to come?'

'You think that's a good idea?'

'He seems to like you.' Okasha heaved a sigh. 'Keeps asking about the other officer. He can't even remember your name.'

Out of the corner of his eye Makana caught a glimpse of a dirty yellow Mazda parked at the end of the sidestreet with two men leaning on it. He held Okasha back.

'Do you know who those two are?'

Okasha glanced over his shoulder. 'Yes, I've seen them before. They're from Giza section. I'm not sure what they're doing here. How do you know them?'

'I've seen them around.' Makana wondered what connection there was between their interest in the church and Shaddad, or had they just heard something amusing was going to happen?

Makana followed Okasha in through the front of the building to the pharmacy. Omar Shaddad was wearing a white lab coat and consulting a sheet of printouts with a similarly dressed woman wearing a headscarf. He looked up and took off his glasses.

'There he is. Now, tell me your name again because I was trying to explain to your colleague.'

'Makana.'

'That's it. I knew it was something odd. Now look, I don't know which of you is the senior and I don't much care, but I think you need to coordinate things a little better.'

'Perhaps I should explain that Mr Makana is here in his capacity as an independent investigator.'

'Independent? You mean he's not a police officer?'

Okasha sniffed and shook his head apologetically. 'He has helped us on a number of occasions, with some quite important cases.'

'Since when has the police force needed to hire investigators from the private sector?'

'Oh, we often consult specialists. Their work can corroborate our findings.' Okasha tied himself in knots trying to get the words out. He coughed before falling silent. Omar Shaddad turned to Makana.

'And you let me go on believing you were a police officer.'

'A simple misunderstanding, I assure you.'

'Perhaps you can explain what your interest in this matter is?'

'The course of an investigation can be difficult for laymen to understand,' Okasha weighed ponderously in. Shaddad gave him a wary look.

257

'I still don't understand why you have to search my garage.'

'As I tried to explain on the phone, this exercise simply gives us an opportunity to offer trainees experience in conducting a proper forensic sweep. Doctora Siham is a senior forensic officer. She also lectures at the university.'

'I see, and you believe you'll find something that connects this dead man to my basement?'

'We like to approach these things with an open mind.'

'Do we even know that the people driving the van worked for me?' Shaddad's gaze bounced back and forth before settling on Makana. Consultant specialist or not, he seemed to sense he would get more answers from him. 'Certainly there is no evidence they were carrying out my orders at the time?'

'The driver who went missing is yours – Mustafa Alwan. How well do you know him?'

'Only vaguely. I mean, I know all of them more or less.' Shaddad released a long sigh. 'I don't really know anything about him.'

'Is it possible that Alwan was using your facilities, your vans, to run some private enterprise of his own?'

Shaddad stared at Makana. 'What kind of enterprise?'

'I don't know, you tell me.'

'You mean that he was selling things on the side?'

'Is that possible?'

'No, of course not. We have everything under control.' Shaddad caught the sceptical look on Okasha's face. 'All

258

right, I admit, some of our methods are a little short of perfect, but overall the system works.'

'We'll take your word for that, shall we?' said Okasha.

'I'm not sure, Inspector. Perhaps I should call some of my friends in the Ministry of the Interior?'

'I'm sure that won't be necessary.' Okasha sniffed and looked at Makana, throwing the ball back as it were.

'Alwan's wife insists that the dead man they pulled from the van is not her husband. It is very possible that someone else was driving the van. The driver remains unidentified.'

'Then you have nothing to tie our drivers to the van and the body you found?'

'That would be correct,' admitted Okasha.

'That's what all this is about, isn't it? Finding something to connect me to that body.'

'Your van does that,' Makana pointed out.

Shaddad was losing patience. 'Look, Inspector, you need to clean this mess up as soon as possible. I can't have my business disrupted by people scouring my basement for who knows what.'

'The team is led by Doctora Siham, one of our country's most eminent scientific investigators.'

'I don't care,' blustered Shaddad. 'I want this over and done with. What are people going to say? Imagine the damage to my reputation, my business.'

'I assure you, we will be out of your way before you know it.'

'Yes, yes,' said Shaddad impatiently. 'Just make sure you are.' With that he stamped away.

From the ramp the basement looked like a bizarre theatrical production. Figures moved back and forth in their disposable blue suits. With their goggles and hoods it couldn't have been more absurd if they had been playing saxophones, or juggling pineapples. There was an air of festivity to the proceedings. For the students it was a day out, a picnic almost. Conversations went back and forth. Advice was called for and given. Humorous remarks, muffled by the face masks they wore, were also exchanged.

'They're having a party,' muttered a rumpled grey-haired police officer on the ramp.

'It's the only way this could have happened,' Okasha muttered. 'A nameless boy like that. Who cares? I'd never have got permission for a proper forensic examination. Shaddad's too well connected. Where are you going?'

'I'm not much help here,' Makana said. 'I think I'll try and catch up with a couple of the other drivers.'

As he was about to turn away, Makana heard a shout from below that might have been his name. He saw a shapeless figure in nylon that he realised was Doctora Siham. They made their way down to her side.

'You've found something already?' Okasha asked.

'Put your hands in your pockets.' She gestured to the small utility room at the far end of the building where the keys were kept. The students lined up to one side, like a welcome committee. The interior of the room was lined with bare walls.

'Shut the door behind you.'

Hands firmly in his pockets, Makana used his foot to nudge the door closed, so as not to touch anything. He didn't want to be the one to contaminate the crime scene, especially one under the control of this particular pathologist. With the door closed hardly any light got in. With a click a handheld ultraviolet light came on. Jehan held the lamp high until they could both see it plainly. A handprint on the wall.

'Is that blood?'

'Somebody tried to wash it off.' She moved the light to the left. 'There's another fainter one here. It's like they were standing with their hands on the wall.' The three of them stared at the prints. Makana looked around the small space.

'Somebody was held in here.'

'Maybe more than one person.' Jehan pointed upward towards a hatch fitted into the wall. 'Could one have helped another to climb up there? We should find out where it leads.'

Okasha swore under his breath. He gave orders and a few minutes later a couple of uniformed officers appeared with a ladder. Orders about not touching anything were now duly cast to the wind. The rest stood back as one of them climbed up and disappeared through the hatch. As they waited, Doctora Siham spoke Okasha's thoughts aloud for him:

261

'Now you're going to have to ask for a search warrant.'

Okasha muttered something, then turned his wrath on the policeman who was above them.

'Are you coming back, or have you decided to live up there?'

The officer reappeared, his uniform now covered in grey dust and pigeon droppings.

'There's a vent of some kind. It looks like it opens onto the street.'

'Satisfied?' Okasha asked Makana, then he spun on his heels and stormed out.

'Does he always blame you?' said Jehan, tugging her mask down.

'Only when things don't seem to go his way,' said Makana. 'Is there a way of checking if that print matches our dead body?'

'There was no blood, or an open wound of any kind. The blood would have to have come from someone else.' She looked at Makana and then spoke their thoughts aloud. 'I can check the DNA against the severed head. See if there's a match.'

'That might serve as a link between the two cases,' said Makana.

'Oh, but we already have a link.'

'We do?'

'Sorry, I was going to tell you, but with all this going on . . .' Jehan nodded at the students eagerly crowding outside the door. 'The lab tests came back. They show that both victims carried traces of sodium thiopental in them.'

'Sodium thiopental?'

'It's a quick-acting barbiturate used in operations. Usually it is administered before a general anaesthetic. If injected it will render the patient unconscious in about thirty seconds. It's probably better known as a truth drug.'

'You found traces in both bodies?'

'It sits in the fatty tissue. I found some stored in the back of the neck.'

'Why would anyone be injected with a tranquilliser if they were going to cut his head off?'

'Maybe they were trying to be gentle. In small doses it would weaken your resolve, lower your inhibitions, but in higher doses it knocks you straight out.'

Now that there was a link between them, Makana was wondering what else the two victims might have had in common.

Chapter Twenty-four

Of the drivers Makana had spoken to on the phone there was only one who seemed even remotely interested in talking to him. His name was Abdou and he was to be found, he said, most mornings between ten and eleven, having breakfast on Ahmed Orabi Street. An old-fashioned place named Zouzou's. To confirm the man's presence, a Shaddad Pharmacies van was parked outside. The interior was dreary and uninviting – walls the colour of dirty smoke, the air laden with a hint of butane gas from a low heater that hissed away at the centre of the room. Despite this, Zouzou's clearly had a reputation that carried far and wide, for the place was crowded with what looked like low-grade office workers, public service employees, messengers, clerks, along with taxi drivers, casual workers, doormen and the like, all tucking into heavily laden dishes. A burly man was leaning on the counter adding up numbers with a pencil stub on a sheet of newspaper spotted with oil stains. Makana asked for Abdou and the man raised his voice without looking up.

'Abdou, somebody wants you.'

A thin man over in the corner called out, 'Who wants me?'

'We spoke on the phone,' said Makana. Not the best of introductions. The table was littered with dirty plates and discarded scraps of flat bread. The five men who sat around it regarded Makana with a mixture of curiosity and contempt. The far end of the table was occupied by a large man whose neck appeared to have vanished into the collar of his checkered shirt. He sat with his back against the wall, smoking a sheesha and picking his teeth.

'That was you? Well, here I am, what do you want?' Abdou kicked the chair next to him. The long-faced, mournful-looking man sitting on it gave a start. 'Where are your manners? Give the man a seat.' Grudgingly the man got to his feet and moved away. Makana remained standing.

'It's about Mustafa Alwan.'

'What about him?'

'Well, I wanted to talk to him about something.'

'You mean, something like business?' Abdou's eyes were red and bloodshot. He seemed to be speaking in a particularly loud voice.

'Sure, you said on the phone you might be able to help me. He's a friend of yours, I understand.'

'I know him.' Abdou raised his head from the waterpipe and narrowed his eyes against the smoke. 'We all know him.'

'So, have you seen him recently?'

'Not for a few days now.'

'Not since the accident,' someone else added.

Abdou's eyes lifted to find Makana above the heads of the others. 'You heard about the accident?'

'I talked to his wife,' said Makana.

'Which one?' somebody else at the table asked, breaking into laughter.

'He has more than one wife?' Makana recalled the remark Alwan's wife had made. Had she suspected something of the kind?

Abdou, the man of the moment, blew a long stream of smoke at the ceiling. 'Mustafa is a man of the world, if you know what I mean. He has women stashed all over the place.'

The long-faced man who had given up his chair stood to one side staring at Makana. He had dog-like features and hair oiled back from his forehead. He didn't join in the laughter and his eyes never left Makana's face.

'So no one has seen him since the accident?'

'Maybe this isn't about business,' mused Abdou. 'Is this about his wife? I can understand your concern. She's a pretty one.' Abdou pondered the matter for a moment. 'Someone is going to have to take care of her, I suppose, if he doesn't come back.'

'She has two children,' one of the others pointed out.

'Sure, but a woman has needs, just like all of us.' He grinned to a chorus of cackles. 'I'd say she could easily bear another two, or three for that matter.'

They all clutched their sides. The only one not laughing was the grim-faced man opposite, who kept up his unwavering stare.

'What did you say your business with Mustafa was?' he asked.

'I didn't,' replied Makana. The man got to his feet and there was a general move to follow him. Makana knew he wasn't going to get anything more out of them. So it was a surprise to come out and discover the dog-faced man standing by the corner of the building with his shoulders hunched. He had a lean, hungry look to him. Without looking up he waited for Makana to go by.

'Keep moving,' he muttered. 'Round the back.'

A narrow alleyway strewn with jagged oil-can lids and flattened cardboard boxes advertising Snowy Mountain Apples and Varentia oranges led away from the main street. The flare of a match lit the man's gaunt face as he sucked in his cheeks around a cigarette.

'You're interested in doing business?'

'I was interested in doing business with Mustafa Alwan.'

'Well, he's not around right now and he won't be for some time.'

'So what are you saying?' Makana wondered what he was being offered.

'I'm saying, Mustafa may not be here but business goes on.'

'Okay, so what have you got to offer?'

'Whatever you need. The inventory is exactly the same. If Mustafa got it for you, so can I.'

'What kind of rates do you offer?'

'Whatever arrangement you had with Mustafa should be fine.' He grinned, showing a row of yellowed, sharpened teeth. 'I'm not greedy.'

'How about sodium thiopental?'

The other man froze. 'What would you want that for? Most people are after Viagra, Prozac, codeine . . . slimming pills are popular.'

'Mustafa did well out of this. His place was pretty nicely furnished.'

'He was tight about letting people in. Now that he's not around that shouldn't be a problem. Look, we can negotiate the prices if that's what you're worried about.'

'I'm just a bit nervous with all this going on, after the accident.'

'Sure.' The man sucked more smoke into his lungs.

'I mean, what were they doing out on that road?'

'Who knows? I mean, Mustafa has his hand in all kinds of things.'

'You mean he was in the van?'

'Of course.'

'So where is he now?'

'Who knows?' The man shrugged his shoulders. If he knew he wasn't saying. 'If he's smart he'll wait till this all blows over.'

'It would just reassure me to talk it over with him.'

This drew a harsh laugh. 'That's not going to happen. Like I said, you don't need him. I can get you whatever you need.'

'I need to think about it.'

'Suit yourself. You know what they found in that van? A dead body. Nobody is going to see Mustafa for a while.' He looked up and down the road, suddenly unhappy about being here. 'Look, if you want to reach me, you can call this number, but otherwise don't come back here in person. That was stupid.'

'Sure. I understand.' Makana took the slip of paper. 'Listen, one thing I never understood.'

'What?'

'What's with his son?'

'His son? How should I know?' The man was backing away now. He didn't like questions.

'I was just wondering. I mean, I heard he was ill.'

'A man's family is his own business.'

'That's funny, I got the impression you didn't much care for him.'

'He's arrogant, thinks he's smarter than all the rest.' The hustler reflected for a moment. 'The boy is sick, some defect he was born with. He needs an operation.'

'What kind of operation?'

'Something pretty big, like his heart maybe. Anyway, I don't really recall. All I remember is that he found a clinic that would do it as soon as he had the money. That's what he always said. It was all for his son.'

269

'You remember the name of this clinic?'

'Sure, something strange, Hazara, Hashara?'

'Hesira?'

'Yeah,' nodded the man, pleased with himself. 'That was it.'

Chapter Twenty-five

There was a desolate air about Aswani's restaurant at that dead hour of the afternoon. People were still hard at work. Later on the place would begin to fill up when the shops began to close down and things started to tail off towards sunset prayers. Now the place was dull, lifeless and dark. To spare expense, the lights still hadn't been turned on.

'I see you've brought your radical friend with you,' muttered Aswani as he wandered over, one hand tugging at the waxed ends of his long moustache. The big cook kept one fierce eye fixed on Sami. 'Why is it that when I see your name in the paper I know there's going to be trouble?'

'The problem with you, old man, is that you'll never be satisfied until we bring the Ottomans back to rule this country.'

'What's the trouble with what we've got? Even Laura Bush, wife of the American president, says we have democracy. That's good enough for me. What do you have to complain about?'

'What do you call an eighty-eight-per-cent win, a miracle, a gift from the gods?' Sami was shaking his head. 'What you call democracy is a farce.'

'Try to talk some sense into him, will you?' Aswani appealed to Makana. In all the years he had been coming here to eat there had always been tension between these two. They just seemed to rub each other the wrong way, an insoluble conflict. 'All I know is that if you open up this country we'll all be wearing beards and cutting off people's hands. You know that. Tell him what it's like being ruled by fanatics.'

'I'd rather eat, if that's all right with both of you.' Makana glanced longingly towards the grill area behind the counter where one of Aswani's kitchen hands was stoking the flames. Aswani wasn't going to be rushed.

'All I'm saying is that once you start messing with the way things are, there's no telling where it will end.'

'That is exactly the kind of attitude that is holding us back,' Sami called at Aswani's retreating back.

'It's what most people think.'

'It's what they want you to think. If not us then the flood. The president and his jackals have the whole nation trussed up like one fat sheep awaiting the butcher's knife. Everyone lives in fear. Foreign conspiracies, Israeli agents poisoning the water and, above all, our bearded brethren.'

Sami was enjoying himself too much. It seemed like a good time to change the subject.

'How are you getting on with Mourad's computer?'

'Interesting. Whatever that boy was involved with it wasn't urban planning.'

'You found something?'

'You could call it that.' Sami flipped open the laptop and spun the screen round for Makana to see. 'Like I told you before, he's into some pretty specialised stuff, web chatrooms. Not many people get in there, and I'm guessing that our fabled State Security and Investigations wouldn't be able to find their way in with a sledgehammer.'

'This means that he and his friends were able to communicate safely, without anyone seeing what they were up to?'

'Exactly,' Sami nodded. 'If you know what you're doing there are loopholes in the internet, dark corners that are safer even than talking on the telephone. Mobile phones are particularly prone to eavesdropping. They can hear what you're saying, pinpoint where you are, listen to your messages.'

Makana regarded the object lying on the table with more contempt than usual.

'Mourad hasn't answered his phone since he disappeared.'

'That suggests he's hiding. If he's smart, he'll get himself another untraceable one that has no connection to him.'

'These message boards, or what did you call them, chatrooms? Is there any sign Mourad has been on there in the last week?'

Sami winced. 'Well, that's the problem. They don't sign on under their own names. They use aliases. So we have.' He paused to scrutinise the screen. 'Doctor Octavius. Clark Kent. Pecos Bill.'

'I saw those names on the printout of the messages you gave me.'

'They seem to have a weakness for comic-book characters.'

'There was another name you mentioned last time, Lassie something?'

'Antonio Lasciac. Not a cartoon character, but a real-life Italian architect who was here in Cairo in the nineteenth century. He built that old palace near Talaat Harb Square.'

Makana knew it. A crumbling, majestic building in the centre of town that had been uninhabited for years.

'The place where Champollion lived.'

'That's just a rumour,' said Sami, unfolding a sheet of paper. Jean-François Champollion, gifted scholar to some, barefaced looter to others, had never actually resided in the palace while deciphering the Rosetta Stone, although the street alongside was named after him. 'These are references and dates, numbers. I can't make sense of any of it.'

Makana took the paper. 'Any idea how many there are in the group?'

'It seems to vary, but altogether I've counted six. Some of them could be the same person with a different online handle. It's likely that they'd change the names they use from time to time, for security.'

It seemed to Makana that every time it felt like he was getting a grip on something, it would wriggle out of his grasp.

'So we still have no idea who they are.'

Sami rocked his head from side to side. 'A small group, young. Rebellious by the nature of the comments. Given the references and the university connection, the most likely scenario is that they're all at Ain Shams.'

'Any clue as to what they are up to?'

'Well, that's the big mystery. I thought at first it was something political. Then I ditched that and I started thinking about what sort of things interest people at that stage in life, students. I told you I considered the idea that they were into some kind of drug-smuggling scheme?'

'You said it didn't fit the profile.'

Makana was thinking about Mourad's friend Ihab, and his odd behaviour. Could he be on drugs?

'Right, and it doesn't, not really. And besides, these messages refer to transport and cargo leaving the city, not coming in.' Sami shook his head. 'We don't have drugs to export. Not unless they're coming in over the border from the south and going out north, or east. But that's serious business that could lead to the death penalty. It's not the sort of thing that this lot would be involved in.'

'I get the impression Mourad runs on idealism, not greed. He wants to make the world a better place. That doesn't square with smuggling drugs.'

Their talk broke off with the entrance of Barazil, who poked his head around the door and then sauntered straight over with the off-centre limp of someone who had suffered polio as a child. Barazil was something of a local character. Everyone knew him, while he in turn viewed them all as nothing less than potential customers. Barazil never let an opportunity slip by him. Versatility was his trump card. He could sell anything to anyone, even if they had no idea they had ever needed it before meeting him. As always, he was dressed in his own inimitable style. A checkered two-piece brown suit over a canary-yellow polo-neck sweater, the price tag still dangling from its sleeve. A walking mannequin, advertising his wares.

'I thought I spotted you.'

'You have the eyes of a hawk,' said Makana, causing Barazil to beam with delight. Mere recognition was greeting enough for him.

'Nothing escapes me. Believe me, before they print it in *Al Ahram*, it has passed my ears.'

'I don't doubt it for a second.'

'Another of your disreputable friends, I see,' muttered Aswani as he arrived to set plates on the table. Barazil had an uncanny ability to time his arrival with the food. His small eyes widened as they roamed the table, feasting on dishes of Aswani's special pickles, baba ghanoush, humous, glistening slivers of fried aubergine sprinkled with sesame seeds, an assortment of olives and fermented

276

cheese, a mountain of golden discs of warm bread heaped in the basket.

'I was hoping you might stop by,' Makana said, ignoring Barazil's mournful eyes. 'I might be in need of a telephone.'

'A new one? Why didn't you say so? Today you're in luck. I have something special.' He delved through his pockets: the oversized jacket doubled as display case and storage cupboard all in one. With the dexterity of a magician doing card tricks he set six devices on the table in a row.

'It's not for me. I just want something simple.'

'I have just the thing.' Barazil picked one up and turned it over deftly. 'Good quality. Reliable and handy. Excellent value for money.'

'How much do you want for it?'

'Oh, you know me,' Barazil grinned. 'I hate putting a price on things. I'll tell you what, why don't you just take it and then give me what you feel like.'

Makana was used to this routine. If he took it away he would be in debt. The price would rise exponentially, with no relationship to its real value. Barazil had missed his calling. In another life he would have been advising states-men and brokering world trade agreements. As it was he was an itinerant pedlar hawking household items around the bazaar and trying to avoid trouble with shopkeepers and police officers.

'I'll think about it,' said Makana, casually reaching for the bread. With someone like Barazil you had to bring your own tactics. Eating in front of him was tantamount to torture. The sooner business was concluded the sooner Barazil knew Makana might invite him for a bite to eat. A gout of flame burst from the grill on the other side of the room and the smell of roasting meat filled the place. Barazil named his price. Already low, Makana halved it and they settled somewhere in-between. Business over, Makana offered him a piece of bread until the main course arrived. Sami was eager to get back to the matter of Mourad.

'So, if it's not drugs and it's not political agitation, what is our friend up to?'

'I wish I knew. Mourad was trying to help the girl, Estrella. I have a feeling she plays a part in this, but I've no idea what.' Makana was thinking of the good Reverend Corbis and his Homehavens Project. Well-meaning Americans spreading kindness through the world, or something else? 'Estrella wanted to follow her friends Beatrice and Jonah to America. And now she's disappeared.'

'How about them, can't you ask them?'

'They appear to have already gone. I'm going to try and contact them, if it's possible.'

Estrella, Beatrice, Jonah. Somewhere in among that group somebody had to know something. Makana felt as though he was seeing with only one eye. He lacked perspective. Right on cue his phone began to buzz in his pocket. An unhappy Sindbad explained that he had lost his quarry.

'Sorry, *ya basha*, I followed him into town and then I lost him.'

'Do you think Ihab saw you?'

Sindbad's unhappiness deepened. 'It's possible. He was in a snack bar in Talaat Harb. The owner there knows me and made a big fuss, inviting me and making a lot of noise. I noticed the boy looking back at me when that happened. Right after that he disappeared.'

The moral of the story being, send Sindbad into a snack bar at your own peril. Makana sighed and stretched. He'd lost his appetite. He ought to have a serious conversation with Ihab. Drop the easygoing manner and get Sindbad to lean on him. With some people coercion was the only way to get cooperation. He sat back and watched Barazil tuck in with the gusto of a man for whom food never lost an element of novelty. He lit a cigarette as Aswani waddled over with a platter piled high with lamb chops. Skewers of his famous kofta and kebab. Barazil's smile lit up the room.

'Did you say this girl, Estrella, was trying to get to America?' Sami asked.

'Everyone wants to go to America,' offered Barazil with his mouth full. His eyes lurked over to the meat and Makana nodded his permission. Taking food from under his nose would be like kicking a stray dog.

'Try and find out what you can about something called the Hesira Institute,' Makana said, getting to his feet.

'Are you leaving me here with him?' Sami asked, watching Barazil tucking in with an alarmed expression on his face.

'Don't worry,' Makana said. 'He won't turn on you. There's enough to eat on the table.'

279

Chapter Twenty-six

Bar Kadesh was set in a narrow, blistered sidestreet behind Nasser Metro Station that appeared to have never known pavements. The ground rose and fell in uneven waves in the gloom. From the entrance a gentle incline sloped down like a soft riverbank. In the winter they hung doors across the opening. Badly neglected, the wood had been in need of attention for decades, centuries even. The faded paint was like a watermark that harked back to long-forgotten days, other regimes, other rulers. Time had a habit of smoothing out the wrinkles. Nobody could believe that things were ever quite as bad as they were now, or as good as they had once been.

Through a grubby pane of cracked glass past a torn white star advertising Stella Beer, Makana glimpsed a half-empty room. It was early. Empty tables and a desolate air that looked as though it would never recover. Marwan was sitting with a small group of men playing dominoes.

'Well, well, well,' he said, as Makana pulled up a chair. 'I thought you might turn up. That was you who rolled by the other day wasn't it, in that taxi?'

'I thought I'd look in on my compatriots.'

'In word only. Those people live a life as different from yours as night and day.' Marwan was a large, untidy presence, his Central Security Forces tunic unbuttoned at the neck, his belt unbuckled to allow room for the beer belly he was cultivating. Getting to his feet, Marwan indicated a more secluded table further over in an empty corner. He waggled two fingers at the short, scruffy figure almost hidden behind the counter.

'So, to what do I owe this honour?'

'No reason. I saw you and wondered what you were up to.'

'A social visit? Nice try.' Marwan nodded as the barman set two cold bottles of beer on the table. The glasses bore grimy testimony to years of service, like the faded painting of a victorious Ramses riding into battle on a chariot that appeared on the wall behind the bar. Everything in here looked like a sacrifice to a long forgotten god. Even Marwan. A hero from a bygone age when heroes made some kind of sense.

'You forget that I know you. If you turn up here, it's for a reason. Let's not kid ourselves that we are friends.' Marwan gulped beer. It was always hard to tell where you

281

stood with him. He seemed to bear a grudge against everyone. It wasn't personal, it was just the way he was. If you stayed on the right side of him he could be useful, generous even, but he was unpredictable and surprisingly touchy for a man with such a tough hide.

'What's going to happen with the protest?'

'It's not going to last much longer. One of these days they're going to give us the order to clear the square, and it won't be pretty.'

'Why not just leave them?'

Marwan looked aghast. 'You can't just leave people. That's an invitation to chaos. The whole country would be on the streets, thinking that sooner or later they'll get what they want.' He leaned his bulky shoulders back against the wall. 'The thing is, they don't really know what they want. Most of them don't want to be in this country to begin with, but here they are. They aren't refugees because we're neighbours and we have an open-border agreement, even if it is temporarily suspended. We're all people of the Nile Valley. They can't apply to another country for refugee status because it's the first country you land in that counts. So they're stuck.'

'And you don't think the UN will change its mind?'

'Why? If they wait long enough these people will crawl back into the hole they came from.'

A key to any exchange with Marwan was to keep your temper. He liked to think of himself as a provocateur, a convenient alibi for a bully. Nothing he liked more than to shove people around a bit and see how they responded. Makana was used to it by now. He didn't take the bait.

'What choice do they have?'

'Plenty, according to what I hear.'

'What do you hear?' Makana asked the question while pouring more beer into his glass.

Appearing to be drinking took a certain amount of technical skill, especially when you were alongside a dedicated drinker like Marwan, who was already eyeing the dregs in his glass and contemplating ordering another one.

'Israel. I hear they're all running to Israel for safety.'

'I'm surprised to hear that kind of rumour coming from you.'

'No smoke without fire. The Jews will take anyone in if they think it will improve their case. They want the world to believe they're the front line between Muslim terrorists and the civilised world.'

'I thought that was your job.'

'Careful.' Marwan waggled another two fingers at the barman. Makana didn't object. Whatever he left behind on the table would be hoovered up by his companion after he had gone. 'Essentially we're on the same side on this one. The only thing is, we deal with our fundamentalists quietly, the way we've always done. We don't go crying to the world about how wonderful we are.'

'You should tell that to the president.'

'You laugh, but just remember that when it all goes to hell you'll be glad to have us around.'

'I don't doubt it.' Makana lit a cigarette. 'Actually, I wanted to ask you about a couple of police officers. They work out of Giza. Drive a yellow Mazda.' Marwan grunted before Makana had finished his description.

'Hakim and Karim. Nasty pair.'

'What can you tell me about them?'

'We've crossed paths a few times.' Marwan chewed his lip. 'Can't say I have much of a feel for them either way. But there are stories.'

'What kind of stories?'

'They're both ex-military. At one point they were stationed in the Sinai, charged with rooting out potential terrorists. According to the stories they gained a reputation for going into villages and executing children, holding a gun to their heads until the women told them what they wanted to know.'

'How did they end up in the police?'

'They got out of hand once too often. I'm sure they weren't happy about being posted back here. Those guys make plenty of money out there from smugglers paying kickbacks. What's your problem with those lovebirds?'

'They seem to have taken an interest in a case I'm working on.'

'Take my advice and steer well clear of them.'

'I'm not sure I have a choice.'

'They aren't the kind of people you want to cross.' Marwan leaned forward. 'They have protection. They're on the inside. Either you're with them, or you're in their way.' Marwan might be a blunt instrument, but he was old-fashioned enough to still believe in the idea of the police as a force for good, aside from the odd bribe finding its way into his pocket.

'Can you think of any reason why they would take an interest in a girl from South Sudan?'

Marwan splayed his hands out wide. 'Some men go for that kind of thing. You know, the hot-blooded exotic girl?'

'Could they be running girls?'

It wasn't the impression he had of Estrella, but who could tell? It would explain the conflict with Aljuka and his men. That would make them reluctant to have Makana nosing around. Did it explain why Hakim and Karim had shown up at Shaddad's place for the visit by the forensic team?

'Sometimes it's hard to believe what goes on in this city,' Marwan said. 'It makes me feel like my time is up.'

Makana slid a handful of notes under the almost full bottle he pushed across the table.

'You don't have to.' Marwan sounded almost offended.

'Buy some of your hard-working colleagues a drink with it.'

'You know, one of these days I just might do that,' Marwan laughed as he tucked the money away.

Chapter Twenty-seven

It took almost an hour, but walking helped to clear his head. On the bridge, courting couples huddled, doing their best to ignore the traffic flying past behind them as they gazed out over the river. What was a bridge if not a reason to dream?

Reaching for his phone, Makana leaned on the rail for a cigarette while he called Doctora Siham . . . Jehan . . . What was he supposed to call her? He was no longer sure why he was calling. Staring at the instrument in his hand, Makana was about to hang up when she answered.

'Am I disturbing you?'

'No, not at all. I was reading. Well, I was reading and then I must have fallen asleep.'

'Must have been something fascinating.'

'Don't get too excited. A biography of Alexandre Lacassagne, the father of modern forensic medicine.'

'Hard to see why that might put you to sleep.'

'Exactly.' She paused to yawn loudly and then apologise. 'He actually is interesting. He devised systems, structures to make autopsies more precise, ballistics, all the rest of it. He was a pioneer. We are all indebted.'

Makana was constantly surprised at how easy it was to talk to her about other things.

'Well, I'm sorry to have woken you.'

'No, I was thinking of calling you and then . . . I fell asleep.'

'Did you get any further this morning?' This morning? It seemed like a week had passed since they'd been in the basement underneath Shaddad's offices.

'The students are keen, but they still have a lot to learn about protecting a crime scene. And the situation wasn't helped by that bawab. He's an interfering old fool.'

'Abu Gomaa? Either that, or he's hiding something.'

'Well, he was getting in the way and generally being a nuisance. Then Shaddad came down, took one look at the blood on the wall and ordered us all out until we produced a judge's order to allow us to search.' She let out a long sigh. 'It was a mistake going in there like that. Typical Okasha, trying to get things done without ruffling any feathers and ending up making a muddle of it all.'

'Did you have any luck matching the handprint to our dead body?'

'No luck there. I mean, simple measurement tells me it was not made by the same person. I'm going to try a more

287

accurate match of the hand shape and digital traces. We're testing other material, but so far it looks like an unlikely fit.'

Which meant they had nothing to tie the body in the van to Shaddad. It felt like a setback, but there had to be some connection to that basement. Makana listened as she went on.

'There's a certain amount of blur in the print. I was thinking about what you said, and it makes sense. The angle of the fingers makes it possible that the hand rested on the wall for support. Without a ladder that hatch would be impossible to reach, but if there were two of them, then one could have escaped.'

'The one who stayed behind was bleeding.'

'The question is, why were they being held there? Somebody tried to clean those prints off.'

'The same person who held whoever was in there prisoner.'

'Doesn't this implicate Shaddad?'

'Not necessarily, but the old man knows much more than he's letting on. You've been a great help.'

'It's my job, remember.'

'I'm sure you have a lot more pressing matters to keep you busy.'

'Look, if someone is killing these people then something should be done about it, and people like Okasha are going to brush it under the carpet. Nobody cares about them, and that riles me.'

'Tell me again about that drug you found, sodium thiopental.'

'Well, it acts on the central nervous system. In the right doses it can induce unconsciousness in less than a minute.'

'How long does it take to wear off?'

'That depends on the size of the patient, their weight, etc. The half-life is anywhere between twelve and twenty-four hours, depending on body fat. Thinner people take longer to break it down.'

'So in the case of the young man in the van?'

'Probably longer. Not a lot of fat on our boy.'

'So he could have had it in his system for a full day?'

'That's possible.'

'Correct me if I'm wrong, but I thought you said sodium thiopental was used as a kind of truth serum.'

'It is. It breaks down inhibitions. In the US they use it in a series of drugs for executing prisoners on death row.'

'You can kill somebody with it?'

'In combination with other drugs. It's usually used as an anaesthetic in surgical procedures, mostly combined with a gas that is faster to wear off.'

'But you found no trace of any other drug?'

'No, but that doesn't mean they weren't planning to kill him. It may just be that he died of a heart attack first.'

Makana heard her suppressing another yawn.

'I'll let you get some rest. One last thing. Have you heard of a place called the Hesira Institute?'

289

'Yes, actually. An old colleague of mine is the director. Ihsan Qaddus. Why?'

'I have to pay them a visit. Perhaps you'd like to come along?'

'Me?' She gave a little laugh. Oddly, Makana felt his heart lift. What did that mean? 'Are you trying to recruit me as your assistant now?'

'I'm not sure you're cut out to be anyone's assistant.' That provoked more laughter. 'No, I just thought you could give me your view of the place. I'm not really sure what they do.'

'Okay, I'll come along, but only on condition that you allow me to buy you dinner.'

'I'm not sure that falls into the category of an assistant's duties.'

'You worry too much.'

The matter of dinner was deferred to an undefined point in the future. Makana clicked his phone shut and remained where he was for a moment, staring down at the shimmer of coloured lights on the water. It was difficult to know what exactly was going on with Doctora Siham. It was confusing, he couldn't decide if that was a good or a bad thing.

As he made to move on his phone chirped again. Sindbad sounded excited.

'*Effendim*,' he whispered urgently. 'I have a bad feeling about this. I think something is not right.'

'Just slow down and tell me what happened. Where are you?'

Sindbad explained that he had followed the girl, Mourad's friend Fadihah. 'She's a strange one, but then all of these young people seem to be from another world.'

'Where are you?' Makana repeated. Sindbad had an affinity for melodrama. He cried over children's films, he had confessed more than once, especially the one about a baby elephant.

'They're in the old palace on Champollion Street. I think there's something going on in there.'

'Wait for me. I'll be there in ten minutes.'

He was in luck. As he stepped to the kerb, a taxi in good mechanical shape rolled up alongside him. There were objects dangling from every corner, making it look less like a taxi cab than a sorcerer's cave. Whatever spiritual problems the driver might have had, it didn't affect his driving and they sped swiftly across Zamalek. Sindbad was standing by the Datsun parked under the trees on Champollion Street. The old building took up an entire block. Behind high walls the palace rose in darkness. He explained quickly that he had been following the girl and had seen her go in, and then had heard a scream, and she'd come running out and away.

'I thought it best to wait here for you.'

'You did the right thing. How did she get in?'

'There's a side entrance.' Sindbad pointed to an indent in the shadows. 'Someone's broken the padlock.' He handed Makana a torch. It was a cheap plastic thing bought off a cart from a street pedlar, but it was better than nothing. 'Should I come in with you?'

'No, you'd better stay here and keep watch. Call me if anyone shows up.'

The palace was set back from the road, surrounded by high walls over which the upper floor could be seen. A forgotten fragment of elegance, jettisoned by history. The windows were jagged with broken glass. Wooden shutters hung lopsided in their frames or had fallen from their hinges. It had been commissioned by Said Halim Pasha, grandson of Muhammed Ali, founder of Ottoman rule in Egypt. He grew up in Istanbul and might one day have ruled the country if history had not had more grandiose plans in store for him. He was made Grand Vizier, and as such witnessed the decline and fall of the Ottoman Empire. An assassin's bullet brought his life to an end, apparently for his part in the Armenian massacres.

During the day the area around the palace was thick with car workshops and mechanics daubed in engine oil. There were stationers, tyre outlets, coffee shops. Now all the shutters were down. No light came from within. A dark spot in the universe, a black hole into which all life was sucked. He could see why it might appeal to a group of students with romantic notions about changing the world.

The night air rustled the leaves and sent a chill down Makana's spine. He reached a narrow doorway that was barred by an improvised sheet metal panel held in place by a chain and padlock. The chain hung loosely, the padlock tucked into a couple of links like an afterthought.

Makana looked up and down the street. It was after midnight and nothing was moving. He lifted the padlock, pulled the chain aside, and the door swung inwards with a soft groan. The interior was thick with tall rhododendron bushes that stirred lightly above him as he went by. A path led round to the front of the building, where from the shadows he was able to see it clearly. Close up it was impressive. Carved stone figures loomed over the arched windows. Reclining angels gazed down as he climbed the front steps. There were three high wooden doors and four stone pillars, each adorned with the head of a lion.

The door to the right was ajar. He pushed it and stepped inside a spacious entrance hall where he paused for a moment to listen while his eyes adjusted to the gloom. He clicked on the torch and nothing happened. He had to shake it a few times before it produced a stuttering, intermittent beam that he played upwards over curving staircases and galleries. A wide staircase forked in mid-air, twisting around in a spiral, rising in tiers to left and right linking the galleries that ran around each floor. The yellow tongue of light picked out a thick carpet of dust on the floor. It was criss-crossed by footprints. Too many to count. Coming and going. A regular stream of visitors, kids curious to see what was in there. Vagrants. Homeless people. Some looked more recent.

Makana passed beneath the central landing suspended in the middle of the hall and began to climb. More footprints. They scattered in different directions, but he managed to untangle what looked like a main stream and followed that. On the first floor they led him round the gallery, then deeper inside. Now he heard squeaking coming from somewhere. A scurry of feet that made his skin crawl. He moved cautiously, aware of the sad state of disrepair in the structure. Doorframes hung off the wall. There were gaping cracks, holes where someone had removed some tiles or stripped away wooden fittings. A blackboard was a reminder that it had once been used as a school. It was still possible to imagine what it must have been like in its heyday, when pashas wandered these rooms boasting of empires and statesmen clad in fine garments attended lavish galas and feasted on sumptuous dinners. Why was it that past glory only ever served to tarnish the present?

Makana came to a halt, his train of thought cut short by an object on the ground ahead that appeared to be moving. It seemed to be alive. The light flickered and went out. He shook it again and when it came on he saw a seething mound of fur. Rats. His stomach lurched. They seemed to be devouring something. He looked around for something to throw and his eye was caught by more movement further over. Another mound, and then another. The beam of light flickered on and off, bouncing from one island of fur to the next. The floor was alive.

He stepped back to the door and looked around for a weapon. Grabbing hold of the splintered doorframe, he pulled. With a screech a long piece ripped free. Two steps more and he swung hard at the nearest heap. The result was mayhem. Several of the smaller rats hopped off and scurried away in the darkness in different directions. Some carried on eating. One outsize rat took offence and threw itself at Makana, who managed to bring up the bar quickly in defence. Undeterred, the rat sank its teeth into the wood and clung on grimly until Makana, seeing that it was actually beginning to make progress, climbing doggedly towards him, flung the bar off to his right, spinning it into darkness, which in turn sparked more squealing.

Makana cast around for another weapon and found a longer, sharper piece of wood. He thrust the point into the midst of the remaining rats, to be rewarded by a rise in the frenzy pitch. Eventually they seemed to tire. A number dropped off and scurried away, leaving Makana holding the speared remains of something gruesome. He could make out white bone and dark, rotten flesh still clinging to what looked a lot like a human thigh. By now the stench had hit him. The flesh, whatever it had once been, was in an advanced state of decay.

Further over a larger object proved to be a torso, a broken rib pointing up like a curved finger. Using his improvised weapon, Makana moved around the ballroom identifying various pieces of a body. It was a job to keep the rats at bay.

As he was about to retreat outside and leave the rats to it, Makana heard another sound. It was so faint he thought at first that he was imagining it. Above the squeaking of the rats it was unmistakably human. There was someone else in the building. Flicking off the torch, Makana walked back out onto the gallery, where he stood motionless, listening. It came again. A grunt followed by whispering. Someone was talking in a low voice. It was coming from the other side of the building. He made his way around, clicking on the torch as he went. Shadows stirred around his feet like fog, skittering away from him in ripples. The gallery was lined with high arches and stone pillars, the railings decorated with wrought-iron whorls that twisted as vines around them. He tracked round to the other side, pausing to lean over the banister and peer down into the entrance hall below.

Nothing moved. The sounds came from somewhere to his right. The torch flickered teasingly on to reveal a door hanging at a skewed angle, before the beam went out again. The lintel was decorated with indented floral patterns. Beyond he saw only pitch black. Another doorway gave onto a room overlooking the courtyard. Light filtered through a half-shuttered window. It felt damp and cold. It also smelt of people. The stench of human beings trapped in a confined space.

The moaning had stopped. He waited until it came again and shook the torch. This time the beam came on to reveal a figure propped up against the wall. Despite

296

the blood and bruising to his face, Makana recognised Ihab. He was leaning so far over he was almost lying down. He held both hands to his belly. Blood had leaked through his fingers and stained his jeans, pooling around him on the ground in a sticky patch. A small rat perched nearby, its nose twitching in anticipation. Makana kicked out and it retreated, temporarily at least, darting off into the shadows. Placing the torch on the ground, he went down on one knee and pulled the hands away to assess the damage. There was no resistance. Ihab was barely conscious. His skin was clammy to the touch, his face drained pale.

'Can you hear me?' Makana slapped his face lightly. 'You need to stay awake. You've lost a lot of blood.'

Ihab seemed to giggle. He said something Makana couldn't catch.

'Who did this to you?'

There was more murmuring. Ihab's head had risen but was now beginning to sink again. He was going to be unconscious soon.

'What was that?'

'Tom and Jerry. Remember them? Always together, like Batman and Robin, the Dynamic Duo.' He went into another fit of giggling which made Makana wonder if he was on drugs of some kind. He was not so much talking to himself as delirious. His head sagged and Makana slapped him a few times to revive him. He reached for his telephone only to discover that he didn't have a signal.

'Try to stay awake,' he said, getting up. He walked back out into the main hall and moved round to the front of the gallery. He managed to get through to Okasha and told him to alert an ambulance and also to bring men and lights.

'Lights? Why lights?'

'For the rats.'

When he got back the rat was perched triumphantly on Ihab's outstretched leg. It let out a squeak of disapproval as Makana kicked it away. He knelt down again and felt for a pulse. Already he knew the ambulance would be too late.

Chapter Twenty-eight

An hour later the old pasha's palace had come back to life. It was lit up, just like in the old days, only different. Now cables trailed up the steps and through the front doors to power spotlights set up in the entrance hall. Portable generators hummed loudly. More cables threaded upwards, hanging down over the railings into the stairwell like gigantic spider threads. Everywhere you looked there were armed policemen on the alert, shouting nervously to one another. Ihab's body went by, carried out by an ambulance crew that cursed each time the stretcher hit a wall.

He found Jehan examining the remains of the dismembered torso. Makana watched her carefully transferring the remains of the carcass into a rubber body bag. She looked up as he joined her.

'Another victim, or one we've seen before?'

'Hard to tell,' she said, straightening up. 'The fact that no head has turned up yet suggests it could be our friend from the river. The feet appear to be missing.' She looked down at the remains in the bag. 'The rats haven't left us much to go on – we'll have to wait for lab tests.'

'So it is possible?' Makana asked. Jehan nodded.

'It's possible.'

He looked around him, wondering if this could be the place where the body was cut up.

'How did you find all this?'

'One of Mourad's friends led us here. A woman, a friend of the young man they just carried out.'

'This would establish a connection between your missing person and the two Southerners we've found, right?'

A connection, but what exactly was the relationship between the dead man and Mourad and his friends? What were they up to?

'Whoever did this clearly didn't like what they were up to.'

'Whoever did this is a very dangerous person indeed,' said Jehan. He couldn't argue with that. 'You said they wanted to change the world, but how does this change anything?'

Makana looked at her. Sometimes it took someone to state the obvious.

'They were hiding people here.'

'Hiding?'

'Refugees. They were helping refugees. People who had nowhere to go, nothing to live for. They brought them here.'

'But why?'

And suddenly Makana could see where this was leading. 'To smuggle them out of the country. They gathered them, held them here until it was safe to leave.'

'Then who did this, the killing, the cutting up?'

'Somebody who wanted to stop them. Someone who thought what they were doing was wrong, or rather it went against their interests.' Makana gestured at the body bag. 'They were trying to scare them.'

'That's why Mourad is missing,' Jehan said.

'If he's not already dead.'

Makana excused himself and walked back out, and across to the side where Ihab had been lying. Along the far wall was a collection of what he had taken to be accumulated rubbish. Now he went through it more carefully. There were clothes, blankets, heaps of newspaper with traces of food on them, plastic bags, discarded water bottles. A blackened patch on the wall showed where a stove had once been placed.

A policeman appeared, saluted smartly and told him that he was wanted.

He found Okasha standing in the gallery talking on the telephone and distributing orders at the same time. He beckoned Makana to follow him.

'When you decide to ruin my evening you really do a job of it.'

'Would you rather I called one of your colleagues?'

'The kid's father is a highly respected judge. He has connections and he wants answers. He's waiting for me now. He wants to meet the man who found his son.' Okasha ran a hand through his hair. 'So, what do you think they were up to?'

'They were housing people here,' said Makana.

'What for?' Okasha wrinkled his nose at the thought.

'To keep them safe before moving them. They were getting people out of the country.'

'For money?'

Makana shook his head. 'Not for money. They are, were, idealists. They thought they were doing something radical.'

'Heaven help us. Save your explanations for the father.' Okasha tapped his watch. 'Let's go.'

'You really think this is necessary?'

'He wants to know who murdered his son and why. You're going to make me look good.'

'Don't you think he might wonder why you need my help?'

'He won't remember your name. Or maybe I won't tell him. All he'll remember is that we knew what we were talking about.' Okasha jabbed a finger. 'All the favours I've done for you over the years. Is this too much to ask?'

They waited in a salon that looked as though it was never used. Ihab's father shuffled in wearing a maroon silk gown and leather slippers. The sound of women wailing came from somewhere far off in the house.

'Are you the one who found him?' he asked, his voice cracking. Daud Sabbour was a small, hunched man with a gaunt head furrowed by worry lines.

302

Okasha explained who he was and then cleared his throat. 'Mr Makana is helping us with our investigation. He's the one who found your son.'

Words failed Sabbour for a moment. At last he said, 'How could such a thing happen? What was Ihab doing in that place?'

'That's what we're trying to ascertain, sir.'

'What were you doing there?' Sabbour ignored Okasha, turning his full attention on Makana.

'It seems Ihab and some of his friends were using the old palace.'

'Using it for what?' The frowns deepened like the drawing in of a fishing net.

'We're working on a number of theories.' Okasha gave Makana a warning glance.

'He was just a boy, a foolish boy.'

'Did he ever talk about what he was up to, outside of university, I mean?' Makana asked. The judge slumped back in his chair.

'He was dishonest. I hate to admit it, but it's true. My own son was a deceptive snake. I wouldn't have trusted him further than I could throw him. But he was my son. I loved him.'

Makana glanced at Okasha, who rolled his eyes at the ceiling. Makana went on: 'Ihab was part of a group of students that seem to have been engaged in some kind of political activity.'

'What kind of political activity?'

'Well, I'm not sure political is the right word. They saw themselves as radicals.'

'You see, that's the kind of nonsense he would be involved in. Radicals? What the hell does that mean?' His eyes narrowed. 'A group? You mean boys? Were they all boys?'

'There was a girl. Fadihah. Do you know her?'

Daud Sabbour was waving a hand. 'I couldn't deal with the scandal. He was perverted that way, you know?'

It was possible that the judge was in a state of shock that allowed him to be completely candid with two strangers. On the other hand perhaps this was his way of dealing with his son.

'His mother could never accept the truth, but I knew.' He tapped a forefinger to his temple. 'You can't hide that kind of thing from a father.'

Okasha cleared his throat. A judge, after all, could be afforded some discretion.

'We have no interest in that side of your son's life.'

'Something like that can drive a man to do strange things, wouldn't you say?' Daud Sabbour made a grandiose gesture for them to be seated. Obedient to a fault, Okasha settled himself at the far end of a long sofa with a floral pattern. Once he got there he realised that Makana had remained standing and so got to his feet again.

'Our main concern is with whoever murdered your boy,' said Makana.

'Nothing you can do or say will change them.' The judge picked absently at a stray thread on the lapel of his gown.

'Children are a delight when they are young. You forget that they will be the death of you when they get older.'

'I believe this was more related to his friends at university and their political activities.'

Sabbour sank further into the large armchair that seemed to swallow him whole. 'I find all of this hard to take in.'

'Is there anyone your son may have mentioned, anyone at all he was concerned about?'

The judge shook his head from side to side, without lifting his eyes from the floor. The breath went out of him in a long sigh. 'It's important that this matter is dealt with as quietly as possible. For the family. You know how the press can be . . .'

'You don't have to worry about that, sir,' Okasha reassured him.

'My wife has suffered enough.' Daud Sabbour looked pained. 'She loved that boy, perhaps more than was good for him. A son, after all, is special.' His voice tailed off. 'She can't take any more pain. None of us can.' He lapsed into a long silence. Then he slowly seemed to come out of his reverie. 'Ihab had his own place in town, a flat that belonged to my grandmother. He moved in after she died. I think some of his friends stayed there from time to time. I didn't ask. It seemed best to just let him get on with his life.' He got slowly to his feet and shuffled away. 'Someone will bring you a key.' In the doorway he paused. 'You ask yourself why Allah in his wisdom puts a man through something like this. What did we ever do to deserve this?'

What indeed? Makana sat in the back of the squad car with Okasha in front yelling orders at the driver, who kept shouting '*Hadir Effendi*', while driving at high speed with the lights and siren on. A recipe for disaster if ever there was one, and hardly necessary at that hour. Makana tried to distract himself by thinking about the case. What had Ihab been intending? To get away from his respectable family, his father the judge, from whatever sexual concerns were plaguing him? In Daud Sabbour he had sensed disapproval, but also some kind of acceptance. He knew he couldn't change his son. What parent would not do anything in their power to accommodate their child? In that sense Ihab had won his victory, though he had probably died without the satisfaction of knowing that. The boy found rebellion attractive. It explained his eccentricity, but also his desire to help those most marginalised in society.

Was there something more between Ihab and Mourad than mere friendship? More to the point, where was Mourad? Makana's first thought on seeing the body parts in the palace was that he had finally found his quarry, yet even so, with each passing hour he became more convinced that he would never find the young man alive.

Solitary cars wobbled uncertainly over white lines. A lopsided van veered across their path, as if the driver had fallen asleep at the wheel, or perhaps just woken up. They sped through red lights at deserted junctions until they arrived at a well-kept apartment building behind Bab al-Luq. In the darkened entrance they woke the bawab, a listless and shabby young man with rheumy eyes who was sleeping on a strip of cardboard laid out on the lobby floor. He switched on the lift with a key he carried in his gellabiya pocket and escorted them up to the fifth floor, still rubbing his eyes.

It was a large apartment with the style of the Fifties about it still. The fittings looked as though they had not been changed since Ihab's grandmother had lived here. To one side a small kitchen. Beyond, a living area with two sofas separated by a low table. A standing lamp was some kind of art deco design with a woman holding aloft a torch. A life-size plastic Batman glowered in one corner. More cartoon characters. A smaller room had been fitted with a narrow bed, to convert it into a second bedroom. This was strewn with clothing. The whole place was untidy. Maybe this too was part of Ihab's rebellion – overturn all sense of order.

They wandered through in silence, broken only by sporadic remarks. The main bedroom had a wardrobe built into the wall that was filled from top to bottom. Ihab seemed to have a taste for shopping. It was mostly casual wear. There were boxes of shoes, piles of jeans, bright pastel-coloured polo shirts, sweatshirts, along with a couple of two-piece suits for special occasions. Rebel or not, he obviously liked to dress well. A long table across the window on the far side of the room was loaded with files and folders, textbooks. One end of it was taken up with cardboard models Ihab had been working on. Glue, craft knives and fragments of plants to act as trees. A computer just like Mourad's sat on the table, which prompted the thought that perhaps here was an explanation. Had Ihab bought the Apple PowerBook for his less wealthy friend? Makana lifted it up.

'Do you mind if I take this? It might tell us something.'

'Take it, but just make sure you return it.'

The living-room shelves were dedicated to cassette tapes and compact discs. A trove of popular music flanking a stereo system. There was a large set of amplifiers, one in each corner of the room. The kitchen was bare. The cupboards revealed a few tins and a packet of coffee. Like most students Ihab seemed to have spent his time outdoors, in coffee houses, snack bars and fast-food places, judging by the quantity of pizza boxes and other packaging to be seen in the kitchen. A telephone charger sat on top of the television but no phone was in sight. Before the police arrived Makana had searched Ihab and sifted through the upper floor, but he had found no telephone at the palace either.

'We're wasting time,' Okasha yawned, his interest flagging.

'I thought you wanted to find out who killed the judge's son.'

'Look, it could have been anyone. It could even have been your lost man there. Sure, maybe they had a lovers' tiff and one thing led to another.'

'This looks rather more serious than a fight between lovers, don't you think?'

'What do I know? I'm an old man who no longer under-stands what's happening in this world.'

'Ihab wasn't acting alone. There was a group of at least three. Ihab, Fadihah and Mourad. There could be more of them. We should try to find them.'

'I leave that in your capable hands.' Seeing the look on Makana's face, Okasha raised his hands in defence. 'What can I do? I have limited resources. You heard his father. He just wants it all to go away.'

Makana turned to the porter who was loitering in the doorway. 'Apart from the owner's son, who else lived here?'

'It's not my business to keep an eye on who comes and goes.'

His manner was insolent enough to strike a spark in Okasha. He stepped up to the man, causing him to back into the wall.

'It's late and I'm tired, okay? So don't play games. Just give us a straight answer.'

The man glanced at Makana, trying to work out what all the fuss was about. He decided to change his tune:

'The truth is people came and went all the time.'

'Men, women, students? Who?' Okasha growled. 'Tell us some of the names. Ihab we know. How about Mourad? Does that ring a bell?'

The bawab shook his head. 'I only knew Ihab. The others didn't really stay long enough, or if they did they didn't speak to me.'

'Young people.'

A brief nod. He had a small face, narrow features and eyes that seemed to do anything but remain in place. The wandering eyes that suggested he had all kinds of sidelines going for him. The kind of man who could get hold of anything you wanted. Hashish, alcohol, girls, if that was what you were after.

'He was generous, was he, Ihab?'

'His father was a big man.' The bawab's mournful eyes lifted briefly before diving for the floor again. 'It's a tragedy for Sayyid Sabbour. A good man.'

'He didn't come here very often.'

'The boy is old enough to take care of himself.'

'You're wasting our time.' Okasha's smile faded. He prodded the man in the chest, pushing him back against the wall. 'I ought to run you in for questioning. This is a murder investigation. If we bring the scientific team in they'll find fingerprints, hairs, all kinds of things. We'll know exactly what went on here and what your part in it was.'

'Nobody did anything wrong. I swear.' The bawab held his hands up. 'You know how young people are today. And besides, this one wasn't interested in that sort of thing, if you take my meaning.'

'Get out of here,' Okasha said. 'And make sure you don't go far. There are still things we might want to ask.' When he had gone, Okasha removed his cap and rubbed his eyes. 'I need to get some sleep.'

Makana had a mild headache and he'd run out of cigarettes. There was a twisted pack of Marlboros lying on the

310

kitchen counter. He picked it up and managed to salvage a forgotten cigarette. A matchbook lay conveniently alongside.

'He told you something before he died?'

'Nothing that made any sense. He'd lost a great deal of blood by then. He mentioned a couple of cartoon characters. Tom and Jerry. Batman and Robin.'

'Cartoons? Now you've lost me.'

'The point is I think he recognised his killers.'

'Killers? There was more than one?'

'He only mentioned pairs. I think there were two of them.'

'You call this an investigation? I'd be better off with a reader of coffee grounds.'

The fourth match finally consented to erupt into grudging flame. Gratefully, Makana drew deeply on the smoke. Okasha was waiting.

'Why do I always get the feeling you're not telling me everything?'

'They may be policemen. The couple I told you about, from Giza.'

'I don't want to hear about this. You want to help me find out who killed that boy, then fine, but don't give me your paranoid stories about police officers being involved.'

'I didn't think you'd like it.'

'I don't like it and here's why: I deal in facts. Hard evidence. Remember that? You're losing your grip. You can't go round accusing people on the basis of the mumblings of a dying man,' Okasha spluttered. 'Cartoon characters, indeed!'

He was already heading for the door. 'I'll get some people in here to take a look around properly, for the good judge's sake, but my feeling is we're wasting our time. There's nothing to find here. What's your next move?'

'Finding the girl,' said Makana. 'She can't have gone far and she's the only one who might be able to tell us what happened.'

'Let me know when you've got something solid. I don't want to get the judge's hopes up for nothing.'

Makana remained where he was for a moment. He was turning over the matchbook in his hand. The word Sothis and a badly printed star adorned the cover. He slipped it into his pocket.

Chapter Twenty-nine

The sun was a cold grey glare, the sky overcast and dull. A loudspeaker floated by out of sight along the road above the embankment, its amplified screech announcing something in electronic garble that might just possibly have been Chinese. Whatever they were advertising, a political candidate or a new type of washing powder, it remained a mystery that eventually lost itself in the hum of the city. A motor launch puttered by, the occupants gazing up at Makana through their sunglasses with the wide-eyed curiosity of visitors to an exotic zoo.

News of another suicide bombing in Baghdad filled the papers. They had become a reliable fixture, recurring every few days, as regular as clockwork. The details varied but the outcome was the same. The photographs all blurred into one. Number of casualties. Time and location. Bleak images of charred vehicles and pools of blood. The stunned faces of the victims. The fury of others. This seemed to have been a particularly good year for suicide bombers. Musab al-Zarqawi was everyone's favourite terrorist. He posed with weapons like a modern-day Al Capone, aping it up for the cameras. If he didn't exist you'd have to invent him.

Each explosion triggered further speculation from columnists and assorted observers. Could there not have been a way to remove the mad tyrant without sparking this firestorm? In the face of violence such questions sounded redundant, as though going over the same old ground. Nobody believed the invasion had anything to do with helping the Iraqi people rather than seizing the country's assets. History was repeating itself. The Western powers were busy redrawing the map of the region, just as they had done a hundred years ago. A new report had been published by the Americans announcing they had a new strategy for victory. Tell that to tomorrow's victims.

Makana tossed the papers aside. Life was depressing enough without the horror stories. The only thing he knew for certain was that he wouldn't find any answers in there. He took his second cup of coffee out onto the open deck and lit his first cigarette of the day. That made him feel marginally better. The air seemed fractionally warmer out here. On the table was the laptop he had taken from Ihab's flat. Alongside it the matchbook. He studied the symbol of Sothis on the cover. It made him reach for his phone. Sami was not answering, which could have meant that he was lying drunk somewhere, or that he had fallen under a bus. Makana finished his coffee and made a couple of other phone calls. Firstly to Sindbad, to make sure he was clear that he was to spend the day retracing Fadihah's tracks.

'Just go wherever you went yesterday. We need to try and find her before they do.' Then he tried Sahar Hafiz in the hope she might have had some luck in tracking down Fadihah, but she had nothing to report. Finally, he called the forensics lab to find out if any progress had been made on matching the body parts found at the palace, only to be told that Doctora Siham had not arrived yet. It seemed a little early to call her private number, so he decided to wait. All in all it was a fruitless start to the day. Things could only get better, he thought, as he wandered up the path to the road. But then again, maybe not.

The Hesira Institute was a modern building with a spectacular view. Modest beside the rather more glamorous Méridien Hotel that rose up next door, but equally remarkable, in a way that made you wonder where the financial backing came from. The obligatory fountain formed the centrepiece of a circular driveway, this time adorned by a rather grand statue of a pharaonic figure holding a staff and gourd. Modern artwork always made you wonder why anyone bothered. This one at least served a purpose by representing the institute's namesake in red granite. Behind Hesira, ancient god of medical matters, stood the entrance

315

to the building. Glass doors slid smoothly aside at his approach. Inside, the lobby was cool and wide, adorned with white marble pillars so bright that it made his eyes hurt. The floor too was white. Another, smaller fountain was lost somewhere out there in the expanse of marble. On either side, seating areas were furnished with discreet, elongated low sofas arranged around one another like compact little mazes. The air was infused with soft music coming from nowhere obvious, while on one wall a large television screen played out rolling repeats of world disasters like a hit parade that never ends. Furious crowds bearing the shrouded dead on their shoulders chanted of the greatness of God, as if imploring Allah to make sense of their tragedy. A warning, perhaps, to never leave this sanctuary of well-being.

The reception desk was circular. Makana was beginning to detect an architectural theme. Circles within squares. Perhaps it was meant to draw some obscure geometric link with the pyramids clearly visible through the windows, dominating the skyline like two dirty brown teeth sticking out of the sand.

'Do you have an appointment, sir?'

'Not exactly.'

It wasn't the kind of answer the woman behind the desk was expecting. She wore the frown of a sceptic to whom wrong answers were not an option. In Makana she saw anarchy, chaos, horses running wild in the street. Behind her, a managerial type in a beige shirt and a poorly knotted

316

tie pricked up his ears. He looked Makana over with an expression of concern. Makana had assumed that asking for Reverend Corbis, or his sister, would at least get him through the door. At this rate he wasn't even going to get that far. Perhaps he should have waited, as promised, for Jehan to come with him. She at least knew Ihsan Qaddus.

'Do you or do you not have an appointment, sir?'

'I know she's very busy. Perhaps she has forgotten.' Makana's smile barely grazed the receptionist's armour, let alone left a dent in it. Her glance at the managerial type seemed to trigger some male impulse to take control. He stepped in.

'You say you have an appointment with Doctor Corbis?' The way he put it, it sounded as plausible as a dinner date with Kheops himself.

'There she is.' The receptionist waved, her desk suddenly a life raft lost at sea. Across the lobby a small, compact figure wearing a white lab coat stood waiting for a lift. Makana decided to wait no longer. By the time they called security he would at least have made contact.

'Doctor Corbis, Liz?'

In the bright light of that brilliant white stone she appeared pale and vulnerable. On previous occasions he had always seen her in the afternoons and evenings at the church. Now she seemed more out of place. The sunlight made her squint, and despite the air conditioning bright beads of perspiration dotted her upper lip.

'I thought I would take you up on your invitation.'

'Yes, of course.' For a second she seemed to have forgotten who he was or what he was talking about. 'I'm sorry, my mind was elsewhere.'

'It is I who should apologise. I just happened to be in the area and I thought . . .'

'It's quite all right, you know. No apologies necessary.' She smiled and for a moment seemed almost glad to see him.

'This is quite an operation,' said Makana, looking around. 'I didn't realise.'

'Oh, yes, it is, isn't it?' They stood for a moment side by side, staring at the lobby and the fountain, then she said, 'Look, I have a bit of time. Why don't I show you around now?'

'If it's not too much trouble?'

'No trouble at all.' A glance back at the reception desk told him they had decided to leave him alone and go back to their routine as if nothing had happened, which was fine by him.

The lift pinged open and they stepped inside to stand facing one another. Liz Corbis stared at the numbers lighting up overhead, hands in the pockets of her white coat. She was smaller than he had previously noticed and wore sensible flat-soled shoes that were elevated to give her added height. She wore no make-up and no jewellery, apart from a slim gold chain around her neck that carried a cross on the end of it.

Each floor was named after a deity. Alongside the elevators on the ground floor images of Hesira, complete with staff and medicine pouch, went marching along the wall. The first floor was dedicated to Osiris, and housed administrative offices along with consultation rooms. The second and third floors, Maat and Thoth, were taken up by guest suites. The corridors were alive with colour and motion. Painted murals depicted images taken from funerary tombs. Winged scarabs, flying ibis and yawning crocodiles fought for space beside gods and goddesses. A red sun floated by on a curved raft. There were owls, jackals and hieroglyphics, all amid an astonishing array of stars and plant life.

One symbol in particular seemed to appear more frequently than others.

'The scarab beetle symbolises the god Khephri, who pushes the sun across the sky.'

'Rebirth.'

'Yes, exactly. The sun dies every night and is reborn at dawn.'

'Is that why they come here, the patients, I mean, to be reborn?'

'In a way, I suppose you could say that. People often come here as a last resort. They know they are going to die. Western medicine has nothing to offer them other than painkillers, palliative care.' She took a deep breath. 'We give them hope.'

They were standing by a wide window that looked down over the interior compound. It extended behind the main building. A wide terrace and steps led down towards a garden area surrounded by high tamarind bushes. Hidden in there, she explained, were a gym, tennis courts, water-therapy rooms, steam baths, as well as a restaurant, cafeteria, swimming pool and poolside bar. It became clear that the Hesira Institute catered largely to an ageing, if not elderly, clientele. Makana spotted a rare exception in the form of a young girl of no more than eleven, accompanied by an attentive mother and a nursing assistant.

'Cancer of the liver,' said Liz Corbis, following his line of sight. 'Tragic to see in one so young.'

'Does she stand a chance?'

'To be honest, a liver transplant is her only hope.'

'Is that likely to happen?'

Liz Corbis smiled. 'Do you have children?'

'A daughter.' Makana didn't feel that this was the moment to go into details. In his mind Nasra was still alive, somewhere, and one day he would find her. He had no evidence for this, no real reason to believe it was true. Absurd, perhaps, but what was more absurd, and true, about the human condition than a belief in the impossible?

'Then you understand that a parent will do anything, make any sacrifice to save their child.'

It sounded as though she was trying to tell him something. He waited for her to continue, but instead she moved on and he was obliged to follow. He was put in mind of Mustafa Alwan's sickly son. What sacrifice had he been prepared to make for his boy?

'People naturally want their children to have a good life.'

Liz Corbis nodded her agreement. 'I like to think that is what we do here, we make possibilities, we allow people to give their offspring a better life than they have. Hope, opportunities, isn't that what it's all about?'

'And all of this is somehow thanks to Doctor Qaddus.'

She smiled. 'He is something of a miracle worker.' Praising the institute's director made her face slightly flushed. 'He gives people hope, offers them life where before there was only the prospect of a slow and painful death.'

'Sounds like quite a character.'

'Oh, he is. Perhaps you'd like to meet him?'

'I'm sure he's a very busy man.' Makana was curious about where Ancient Egyptian medicine and Christian benevolence intersected. 'How does this connect with the work you and your brother are doing?'

'Well, it works both ways. That's the beauty of it. We give people here a chance at a new life in America.'

'And to the Westerners who come here, what do you offer them?'

'Mostly we can bring comfort to people who are dying.' She nodded towards the window. 'They come here to spend their last days close to the pyramids. A great deal of research is being done into the impact of positive thinking in treating terminal cases of cancer.'

'And prayer helps that?'

'You sound sceptical. Spiritual comfort can be a great thing to a person facing death.'

321

Makana was in no doubt that she was right. What would bring him comfort when the time came, he wondered.

'So how does this actually work? I'm not sure I understand.'

'Instead of drugs, here they get a connection to the ancient world, to the idea of immortality which is at the heart of the old civilisation. If we think of this life as but a stage in a cycle, it can be comforting.'

'Even if not exactly true?'

She gave him a wry look. 'You pretend to be a cynic, but here you are in pursuit of young people who have nobody else to believe in them. Admit it, you're as much a believer in miracles as anyone.'

Maybe she had a point, Makana conceded. 'What happens to them when they die? Do you build them a small pyramid?'

That produced a laugh. Liz Corbis wasn't much given to laughing. It brought out a girlish impulse in her and she covered her mouth with her hand.

'Most of them have enough time to get home before the end.'

'Must be expensive, flying bodies back.'

'Ashes.' She pointed to a slim chimney at the far end. 'The clinic has its own crematorium, or had. At the moment it's undergoing repairs.'

'I didn't know cremation was permitted in this country.'

'It isn't, strictly speaking. It can only be used by foreigners.' She seemed suddenly aware that she was talking too much, or perhaps it was Makana's proximity that was making her uncomfortable. She stepped back and wheeled towards the lift area, striding away forcefully. 'Perhaps we should move on? You must see the view from upstairs. It's quite unique.'

On the top floor they were greeted by an image of a winged scarab facing the lift doors. This was where their miracle patients were recuperating.

'They need silence and rest,' Liz Corbis explained as she led the way to the south side of the building. A continuous window stretched all the way along it.

'This is the panorama. It gets people every time.' The smile was back, but it had less warmth to it. The view was as idyllic as you could hope for, so long as you kept your eyes on the horizon and ignored the stream of vehicles flowing by on the dual carriageway that ran in front of the building. Beyond, the bleached, dusty landscape was broken by the iconic shapes. The pyramids were too geometrically perfect to be anything nature had intended. It was an odd juxtaposition, the ancient lending the modern transience.

'Now, tell me again,' she said, thrusting her hands into her coat pockets, suddenly businesslike and eager to get on with her life. 'How was it we could help you?'

'Well, I was hoping to have a look at the records for your Homehavens Project.'

'As I've told you, I'm afraid our records are strictly confidential. We can't give out the personal details of our charges.'

'I can understand that, and I can't ask you to do something that would put any of your charges at risk, but I believe this girl may be in some danger. You could help me to find her before anything happens to her.'

Liz Corbis drew a long, slow breath. Her eyes studied Makana for a moment as if to decide whether she could trust him, but there was something more there. Liz Corbis was a woman with few friends. Here she was in the middle of a foreign country with the thankless task of saving lives. Unmarried. No mention of a husband and no sign of a wedding band on her finger. Above all, she wanted to help. That was why she had come here in the first place.

'I can't promise anything, but maybe we can simply confirm or deny that this girl was on our programme?'

'That sounds like something at least.'

'We should go down and see Preston.'

As they stepped into the lift, Makana pointed to the image next to the lower subterranean level. A large black jackal with long ears and a fierce stare.

'We haven't seen this one.'

'The Anubis Ward.' Liz Corbis shook her head briskly. 'God of the underworld. There's nothing much to see, I'm afraid. The mortuary. Less used than you might think.'

They found Reverend Preston Corbis outside by the pool. Stretched out on a recliner under a straw parasol, he was sipping a long, cool drink that was pink in colour and adorned with a paper umbrella and a straw. In the pool itself a frail woman in her eighties wearing a sunhat was being floated through the water by a muscular attendant. It wasn't clear what this type of therapy was good for, but the patient seemed to be enjoying herself, emitting faint giggles at regular intervals. Her Egyptian consort gave Makana the knowing look of a fellow conspirator.

'Ah, there you are,' the Reverend Preston Corbis greeted his sister. His face was flushed from the heat and possibly whatever the glass contained apart from fruit juice.

'Do you remember Mr Makana? He was at the church the other day.'

'Of course, how can we be of service?' His broad smile was a professional balm, guaranteed to smooth over all the cracks. Makana explained his business.

'You mentioned this the other evening, am I right?'

'At the Church of Our Lady.'

'I promised I would help you and I shall.' He lifted his glass and tilted his head back. His front teeth were big enough to choke a horse.

'That would be very helpful. The young man's family are worried about him.'

'Remind me again what the connection is.' Reverend Corbis smacked his lips and wiped his mouth with the back of his hand.

'The young man was friendly with a girl who used to help out at the church. Estrella. She might be able to help me, only now she seems to have disappeared herself.'

'And you think she might have gone to the States as one of our angels? Well, it's easy enough to check. I have to say

325

the name doesn't ring any bells, but a lot of these young people change their names. It's a transient population and they might use one name one place and another elsewhere. It can get quite confusing.'

The Reverend Corbis didn't strike Makana as the kind of man who was easily confused, but perhaps this wasn't the moment to contradict him.

'I'm constantly astonished at how our Homehavens Project has become a tribute to its own success. Word of mouth has spread the idea like wildfire. So many people have heard of it that we are quite overwhelmed with applicants.' He drained the dregs from his glass and waggled it at a passing waiter for a refill. 'Sure I can't get you something?' Makana declined.

'Of course you can lay some of the blame on the policies of this government. Frankly, the situation has become quite alarming.' Corbis's manner grew solemn. 'The way Christians are being treated is not encouraging people to stay.'

'I imagine that doesn't actually hurt your enterprise.'

Reverend Corbis frowned. 'I'm afraid I don't follow.'

'Well, I simply meant that nothing motivates benevolence like a little religious persecution.'

That drew a sharp response. 'It's certainly not our intention to profit from the misfortunes of our fellow believers.'

'No, of course not. Forgive me, I was thinking aloud.'

'Which of course you are free to do.' The minister's manner, rather like his smile, had taken on something of an icy tone.

'As I am sure my dear sister has explained to you again, our records are confidential. We can't go around sharing that information with anyone. Now I consider myself a good judge of character, and I am in no doubt that you are motivated by good intentions. Nonetheless, I cannot risk jeopardising the reputation of our endeavours, or our position in the country.'

'He's trying to help someone, Preston.'

Reverend Corbis threw a withering glance at his sister before turning his eyes back to the pool where the old lady was being helped out of the water by her helper. She had the wrinkled skin of a golden lizard trying to look dainty.

'My sister has the heart of a saint, Mr Makana. I can tell that she is determined to help you no matter what I say, so let me impress on you what we have built here. I like to think that we are meticulous when it comes to selecting our candidates. Our success back home depends on creating trust. The donors want to invest in the future, and that means a firm bond between the child and their new family. So we interview carefully, Lizzie does her medical tests. We screen hundreds of people and we do a thorough job of it. Only a fraction make it through.'

'As you can imagine' – Liz Corbis took up the torch – 'it's not easy for them. Moving away from the people and places they know. It's a leap into the unknown.'

'A leap of faith, I like to say,' Preston Corbis grinned, pleased with himself. He sat back in his recliner as the waiter handed him a fresh drink.

327

'Well, I understand what an undertaking this must be,' said Makana. 'And naturally, anything you tell me will remain confidential.'

'You're trying to help someone, just like we are,' Preston Corbis nodded. 'We're in the same game, saving souls, as I like to say.' With that he leaned back and closed his eyes. 'I bear no grudges.'

Liz Corbis got to her feet. 'Let me take you to the office and we can check the records.'

As they were about to move someone called her name and Makana turned to see an athletic man in his forties coming towards them. He was dressed in a swimming costume, with a towel draped over his shoulder.

'There you are!'

Liz Corbis's face turned a shade of crimson and Makana thought he detected a muttered comment from her brother. The new arrival bounded up with the energy of a man half his age. He had a winning smile that displayed perfect rows of gleaming white teeth.

'Now Liz, you promised me a chance to win back my pride.'

Liz Corbis began to stammer out an excuse. Then she dismissed the idea with a toss of her head and turned instead to introduce Makana.

'This is Doctor Ihsan Qaddus, the brains behind this wonderful enterprise.'

Unusually for an Egyptian, Ihsan Qaddus had distinctive blue eyes, which now fixed on Makana. He had the easy confidence of a man who is comfortable with the fact that he wins at most things he attempts. Easy to see how Liz Corbis might be awed by him.

'Mr Makana is an investigator. He's trying to help locate someone.'

'How intriguing! I don't think I've met an investigator before.'

There was a slightly mocking edge to his tone which Makana ignored. They shook hands. Qaddus's grip was strong. Clearly he was in good physical shape. His thick greying hair only added to the distinguished manner. He grinned as if they were old friends. Whatever had brought Makana here mattered little beside his own concerns.

'She beat me yesterday at tennis and promised me a chance to get my own back.' He spoke English fluently, with the cadence of one who has lived abroad for extended periods, and barely a trace of an accent.

'Well, I'm afraid that's my fault. Doctor Corbis was giving me a tour of the institute.'

'Ah, and how do you find it?'

'Very interesting. I'm surprised I hadn't heard of it before.'

'Not many people take an interest. In this country, as in most of the developing world, people are in thrall to modern medicine. Drugs and more drugs.' He laughed and shook his head. 'We have forgotten so much of what the ancients knew. We need to trust ourselves more.'

It sounded like a speech he had made before.

'I'm sure you're right. Speaking of the medical profession, I believe we have a mutual acquaintance.'

'Really?' By the look on his face Ihsan Qaddus was uncomfortable with surprises.

'Doctora Siham?'

'Jehan?' The tension went out of his face. Qaddus threw his neck back and laughed. 'I know her well. Haven't seen her in years. How curious that you should mention her.'

'One of your old flames, Ihsan?' Preston Corbis chuckled heartily into his drink.

'Actually, yes. We were engaged to be married at one stage.'

Now it was Makana's turn to be surprised.

'Really? You must tell us what happened,' said Liz Corbis. Ihsan Qaddus gave a boyish shrug.

'You know the kind of impulsive decisions you make when you're in your twenties.'

Liz Corbis looked as though she had never made a rash decision in her life.

'We broke it off when we came to our senses. Luckily, I must say.' It was Ihsan Qaddus's turn to laugh at his own words. 'Please give her my regards when you see her. Actually, no,' he corrected himself. 'I'm going to call her myself. Is she still at the Pathology Department?'

They shook hands again and Liz Corbis led Makana back towards the main building and the records room, which turned out to be in the basement. As they stepped out of the lift Makana found an enormous painting of the jackal-headed god facing him.

'I thought this was the mortuary.'

'Perhaps that's why they gave us an office down here.' Liz Corbis smiled at her own humour as she led the way along a corridor to the right and a small room that she opened with a key she carried on a lanyard around her neck. The lights fluttered on. It was a simple room with a desk and a set of grey metal shelves along one wall. On the shelves hung folders arranged in alphabetical order.

'So, these are all arranged according to the legal names of our angels.' She flipped on a computer console. 'We'll need to look in here.'

'What can you tell me about the medical checks?'

'We have to be quite thorough. We check for everything, from HIV to TB and hepatitis C, to a host of illnesses that can lie dormant in the body. There are things like bilharzia for example, West Nile Fever. Diseases that can be picked up in tropical regions by doctors who are familiar with them. Take that patient to Nebraska or Idaho and they will only have read about them in medical journals, never actually seen, let alone treated a case. That's why we must be careful.'

Liz Corbis produced a pair of prim reading glasses from her top pocket and clicked through the keys until she came to what she was looking for.

'Estrella, you said?' She glanced up at Makana and shifted in her seat. 'Unusual name. Spanish?'

'Her mother was trained by Cubans for a time, during the civil war.'

'Well, if this is the same one, she was on our programme.'

'That's her.'

The picture on the screen showed Estrella dressed up. Makana recalled the first time he had seen her at Westies. A young woman whose eyes conveyed a wisdom beyond her years. What could she tell him about Ihab and Mourad?

'Seventeen years old. A little old for our programme, but still. Looks like she filled out the forms and took the medical check.' Liz Corbis clicked down through the pages. 'Ah, she fell at the last hurdle. She was pregnant.'

'How long ago was this?'

'Not so long. Less than a month.' Liz Corbis removed her spectacles. 'I remember her now. Nice girl, presentable. Strong. She hadn't even known she was pregnant. It was a shock to her but she took it well when I told her. Always a tragedy when that happens. But that's a no no. We can't rule on how people live their lives. We make no moral judgements, but a pregnant girl is not going to find a family to take her. It's as simple as that.' Her eyes returned to the screen. 'I'm sorry it didn't work out. I took a shine to her. She would have made something of herself in the States, I'm sure of it.'

'And you have no idea where she might be? No way of contacting her?'

'There's a telephone number. Beyond that, nothing, I'm afraid.'

Pregnant and refused the chance to go to America to make a new life for herself. It added up to a fairly desperate situation. How had she become pregnant? A day ago he might have speculated that Mourad could be the father. Now he was not so sure. He tried the number but got a voice telling him it was not available.

'Estrella had a friend named Beatrice. I believe that she and her brother Jonah were also on your programme. There was a picture on the wall at the church. I don't have a surname.'

'It doesn't matter. We cross-reference by first name. But in this case I do remember them. Rare to get a brother and sister placed.' She flicked through the files on screen before pulling them up. There was a photograph of the siblings. Beatrice was a tall girl with a broad smile. Makana's eyes were on the young man who stood next to her. Jonah. Across his forehead ran the horizontal striations that identified him as a member of the Mundari ethnic group.

'I take it they were more successful.'

Liz Corbis nodded as she read. 'A family in Seattle was willing to take them both.'

'Clean bill of health?'

'Excellent candidates. Intelligent, charming.' Liz Corbis continued nodding as if to a tune in her head. 'You understand that I can't allow you to contact them.'

'That would mean they are already in America? You have confirmation of that?'

'I don't see a confirmation here, but it may just not have come through. This is the middle of what we call our immersion period. We leave our wards alone with their host families for a period of time. Even I don't have contact with them. It helps avoid homesickness and allows them to get used to their new lives together. Contact with family and old friends can be a distraction, especially during the difficult preliminary adjustment phase.'

Makana sat back for a time and thought. After a while he became aware that she was waiting for him to leave, so he got to his feet and thanked her.

'Don't mention it, I only hope it helps you to find who you're looking for.'

Chapter Thirty

The question of Estrella's pregnancy bothered him. What would a girl do in a situation like that? Why had she told her mother that she was going abroad when she knew that she'd been turned down by the Homehavens Project? What options did that leave her?

There was something else that bothered Makana. The two cops, Hakim and Karim. The first time he'd seen them they had been hanging around the church. Was it possible that rather than trying to scare Ihab and Mourad they were actually searching for someone? Were they looking for Estrella in the hope that she would lead them to Mourad? Makana called Fantômas but was rewarded with the voicemail service. His aversion to telephones increased with each repeated clip from a song in a language he didn't recognise but which he assumed was from Darfur. Makana had started to wonder if perhaps the artist was more involved with Estrella than he let on. The meeting with Estrella's mother had felt almost staged. And then there was the fact that he managed to conveniently disappear whenever he wanted to get hold of him.

The traffic was gridlocked and it seemed that Jehan too was in a car when she called. He could hear hooting and shouting in the background.

'We both seem to be caught in the same traffic jam. Where are you?'

'I'm stuck in Mansoura. Some microbus drivers are having an argument. What is it with men that they have to control everything?'

Makana had no answer to that. Already the conversation felt disconcertingly familiar.

'What are you doing in Mansoura?'

'I'm supposed to be teaching, but at this rate I'm going to be late.' He heard her sigh. 'Tell me something good.'

'I wish I could,' he began, but he found himself telling her all about what he had learned. It helped somehow to clarify his thoughts.

'So Estrella didn't get on to their programme?'

'It doesn't look like it.'

'That means she's still missing.'

'Both her and Mourad. After what happened to Ihab, I have to say it doesn't look good.'

'But why would anyone hurt them?'

'Maybe there is no reason,' said Makana. 'Once you get to the point where you are dismembering corpses, then perhaps reason is no longer a factor.'

'It's hard to argue with that,' she said. There was a pause and some cursing which indicated that driving was distracting her from the conversation.

'I wanted to call you this morning to find out if you'd made any progress.'

'I'm still waiting for lab reports. I'll know more this evening.'

'Perhaps we could continue this conversation later,' he heard himself say. What was he thinking? Continue it how? Where? There was a lengthy silence, during which it struck him that she might have hung up, except that he could still hear the raucous racket of tooting and swearing in the background.

'Why don't we have dinner?'

'Dinner?' he echoed. Now he recalled their earlier conversation and how he had somehow managed to avoid committing himself.

She laughed. A light, pleasant sound. 'You make it sound as if you never eat.'

'No, yes, of course. Dinner . . . Where?'

'I know a nice place. I'll arrange it and text you the details.'

'What was it you wanted to tell me?'

'Never mind,' she shouted above the noise around her. 'It'll keep until tonight.'

Which left Makana staring at the instrument in his hand, wondering how it had taken control of his life. He realised he had forgotten to ask her what he had called her to find out in the first place, but he couldn't really see how to call her back now. It would have to wait.

Sami was not at the office in Bab al-Luq. Makana found Ubay wandering down the scruffy hallway murmuring to himself. It turned out he was speaking on his telephone, through a device plugged into his ear.

'It's getting harder to distinguish the insane from the sane.'

'I find that all the time,' said Ubay, plucking the earpiece out.

'How are things going around here anyway?'

'Oh, you know. Ask anyone and they'll tell you things are hard, but the fact remains we're working.' He wagged his head. 'The truth is that so long as this problem with Sami continues, Rania doesn't give any of us a moment's rest.'

'That's too bad.'

'That's why you're here, right?'

'Our man of mystery.'

'Yeah, mystery indeed.' Ubay scratched his afro, which looked big enough to give shelter to a family of sparrows. The wall beside him was scratched and scarred by years of abuse. The window frame that gave out onto the staircase was cracked. He seemed to lose track of the conversation.

'Any idea where I might find him?'

338

'The usual. He seems to have taken up residence at the Café Riche, but don't tell Rania.' Ubay's index finger hovered in mid-air like a philosopher trapped on the spur of some major metaphysical breakthrough. Makana took the opportunity to hand over the plastic bag he was carrying. Ubay took a look inside.

'Another Apple PowerBook'

'This one belongs to Mourad's friend Ihab. Maybe you'll find something that will give us a clue as to Mourad's whereabouts.'

'I'll take a look. I was looking into that stuff you gave me.'

'Stuff?' Makana fished in his pockets for a cigarette. You had to give him time. There was no point in rushing with Ubay.

'That material you wanted looking into. Algorabi Industries? The pharmacy company?'

'Shaddad Pharmacies?'

'That's the one.' Makana waited while Ubay gathered his thoughts. 'They belong to the same people.'

Makana held the flame steady in the air. Now they were both doing it. As the match burnt his finger he dropped it.

'What do you mean, the same people?'

'Well, they both belong to some kind of consortium. Is that the word?'

'You tell me.' Makana felt as if he were being led by the hand into a dark forest by a child, with no idea where he was going.

'The Al Tawq Group, which is a collection of business-men and politicians so far as I can tell.' He waited for Makana to nod before continuing. 'You may not have heard of them, but we're talking about some big crocodiles here. People close to the president and his sons. Inner circle. Elite VIP Club.'

'I get the picture.' To go into big business you had to be connected. Nobody got the concessions for factories or land developments, construction, business franchises with foreign companies – none of that ever happened without the blessing of the ruling elite.

'Circles within circles,' said Ubay.

'Omar Shaddad is part of that?'

'Well, he's a small fish compared with some of them, but he's in there all right.'

'What kind of things are we talking about?'

'Everything. Absolutely everything. From concrete pro-duction to frozen food, to luxury car concessions, to hotel developments in the Sinai, air freight, tourism. You name it and they have some piece of it.'

'Can you get me a list of these companies and the people involved?'

'It's already done. I have it on my desk.'

While he waited, Makana stood and smoked by the cracked window, gazing down into the gloomy well of the staircase. A ghostly conversation floated up between a voice on the ground floor and another above him on the subject of sandwiches which vaguely registered as a dull ache in his stomach. Makana realised he hadn't eaten anything today, but it would have to wait.

Ubay returned carrying a sheet of paper.

'I don't know if it's going to be much help to you, but there it is.'

'Everything helps.' Makana scanned the sheet quickly, his eye drawn to a familiar name, Deputy Minister Qasim Abdel Qasim. They had crossed paths before. There was also another name, one he had only recently come to know, that of Ihsan Qaddus. Makana wasn't sure what this meant. It might be significant, but then again it might simply mean that Shaddad had a hand over him, protecting him in return for certain favours. It explained the phone calls to get Okasha off his back. Shaddad had friends in high places, but that didn't imply that he knew what Mustafa Alwan got up to in his spare time. The Al Tawq Group linked Shaddad with the Hesira Institute and big players like Qasim. He folded the paper away for later study. Ubay was peering down at him.

'So you think this is important?'

'It could be.'

'How?'

'It's possible that my missing boy stepped on someone's toes. Another organisation, somebody for whom this was a lucrative business, not just a charity, which is what Mourad and his friends were running. They were just trying to help.'

'And it got them killed. At least one of them.'

'Mourad is still missing and the girl has disappeared.'

'You think he's dead?'

'I think it's very possible.'

The two of them stood smoking in silence for a moment. Neither felt the need to speak.

'How did they actually do it?'

'Do what?' Makana asked.

'I mean, move people around. Did they have a car, a bus, what?'

Makana stared at him, wondering why something so obvious had not occurred to him. A vehicle. Where would Mourad and Ihab get a vehicle from? He slapped Ubay on the shoulder and thanked him.

'For what?' The young man looked blank, but Makana was already gone.

The Café Riche was teeming with life at this hour, the clientele of ageing intellectuals staggering in from offices in the area looking for a moment's respite before enduring the daily catastrophe of the transport system that would take them home. There was, however, no sign of Sami. The waiter was busy, moving through the tables with a skilful ease that had been absent on his last visit. He regarded Makana with the grave welcome due to an uninvited rodent.

'I'm looking for my friend.'

The dark, wrinkled face remained impassive. 'What makes you think he's here?'

'You know that you'll never be rid of him if you keep asking questions like that. You'll be stuck with him for years.'

The old waiter weighed up his options and decided he would settle for peace of mind. A jerk of his head indicated the alleyway alongside the café.

'There's a storeroom up on the roof. You take the stairs next door.'

Makana thanked him and tucked some notes into an empty glass on the bar counter as he went, ignoring the tut of disapproval. A corridor led from the rear of the café to a side entrance that opened onto the alley. A staircase rose up into the gloom. It was narrow and the walls scarred but in good shape. These old downtown buildings decayed at their own pace. An old-fashioned, stately decline, as opposed to newer buildings that collapsed in a heap of rubble overnight without warning.

As he stepped out onto the roof the late afternoon sun filled the air with mysterious promise. He pushed his way through rows of laundry hanging out to dry, startling a tiny, doll-like woman in the process, her eyes burning with the waning sunlight. She hurried off without a word, arms filled with folded sheets.

Along one side there was a row of little rooms, built over years and gradually developed from storage shacks or pigeon coops into shelters for lost souls. In this case it was identifiable by the name of the café in faded letters on the door, which stood ajar. The interior was cluttered with old crates and dusty green bottles, bundles of flyers and magazines, shredded newspapers. Along the walls a striding Johnny Walker in red coat and breeches stood alongside a smiling blonde holding up a bottle of Martell cognac and, most incongruous of all, a poster for the 1968 Winter Olympics in Grenoble. The azure glow from a laptop screen was the only source of light. Sami was perched on the bed with a blanket round his shoulders and hauled up over his head like a monk, deep in meditation.

'You ought to think about whether social isolation is really what you need right now.'

'I was wondering when you might start.'

Makana looked for a place to sit. 'Sooner or later you're going to have to give this maverick life up and go home to Rania.'

Sami cast him a withering look. 'You know, I haven't had one drink today.'

'*Mabrouk*. To most people that's considered normal.'

'I'm just saying that . . . this is not a static situation.'

'Whatever that means.'

'I'd expect you to be a little more appreciative. I have been working for you, after all.' Sami tapped the machine on his lap.

'Is that Mourad's computer?'

'Full marks for observation.'

Makana tried to move, but his head bumped into something swinging from the ceiling that turned out to be a lampshade with no light bulb in its socket. The collision released a cloud of dust and expired insect life into the air that made his nose twitch.

'By the way, you know you asked me about that clinic?'

'The Hesira Institute.'

'It seems they are one of the biggest clients of guess who?' Sami waited a beat. 'The Shaddad Pharmacies. Interesting, right? They supply all their pharmaceuticals, and that's a pretty long list.'

'That is interesting,' conceded Makana. He told Sami about the conversation he had just had with Ubay. Sami nodded before going on.

'Also, I heard from a colleague who told me he was working on a story about the institute. Very hush-hush, but a serious scandal. He said it would throw everything wide open.'

'Did he say what it was about?'

'They've built something of a reputation, abroad at least, for bringing people back from the brink. Miracle cures. It's what brings them flocking from America and Europe, especially the chronically ill, the terminal cases, the elderly.'

'Did he say anything more specific?'

'Only that he had a source on the inside.' Sami shrugged. 'But you know how journalists are. We always like to think we're on the verge of breaking Watergate.'

'When will the story come out?'

'That's the thing, his source has gone missing. It happens. Here, take a look.' Sami moved along on the bed to make room. Makana remained standing. He was uncomfortable in narrow spaces. Anything confined triggered memories of being locked up. He shivered as a cold sweat blew through him. It was something that he could never shake off – he knew that now. The years went by and his recollection faded, but it never quite went away. It remained a background noise, humming on the edge of his consciousness. Lifts were bad, constricted spaces in general. Right now he was glad the door was open, despite the chill bite to the evening air.

'So I had the idea that maybe there was a way of pinpointing Mourad's movements if we could work out where he'd been communicating from.'

'I see.' If Makana seemed underwhelmed it was because when Sami got going on technical matters the only thing you could do was wait until he reached the conclusion. It was a wonder to him that so many people became obsessed with all this information technology. At times it struck him as a kind of modern-day cult. Once you had Isis and Anubis, now you had bytes and megahertz. In desperation he clawed for his cigarettes and lit one.

'Okay, let me explain.'

'Please do.'

'Whenever you connect to the internet your computer is assigned a number which is unique to you and is linked to the service you are using and to your location.'

'Okay.' Makana inhaled the acrid, familiar taste of the Cleopatra and wondered about the Olympics poster. How had it arrived on the wall here? Had the room once been occupied by a frustrated downhill skier perhaps, dreaming of open slopes and Alpine air, losing himself in drink?

'So, with the help of a friend in one of the telephone companies I was able to find out where Mourad's computer was connected at a given time. You are following this?'

'Numbers tell you the area where the mail came from.'

'Good.' Sami straightened up, getting into his stride. 'That's the simple version. In reality it's more complicated than that. There are other elements that have to be factored in and you can get variants that throw you off. The point is that with a series of providers you can begin to see a pattern. So in this case most of the traffic was sent and received from the same locations, places where he lived and worked – around the university campus, the family business in Zamalek. But a couple of them take us outside the city, and those are the ones that are interesting.' Sami turned the screen so that Makana could see the map better. He pointed to a list of numbers in a column to one side. 'The problem is that often you only get a general area. Not a precise place. Especially if he's using a mobile device such as this.' Sami indicated the thumb drive sticking out of the side of the laptop. 'So unless the number has been connected to a specific place, it's hard to pin down.'

'And that's the case here?'

'Precisely.' Sami tapped the touchpad a few times until a map appeared. 'Here.'

'Where is that exactly?'

'Hasna. A town in the middle of nowhere.' Nowhere in this case appeared to be located in Northern Sinai. 'It's about an hour's drive from the Israeli border.'

Makana perked up. 'What's out there?' All he could see was a thin strip of road running through emptiness.

'Nothing. That's the point.'

'So you're saying Mourad was out there when he sent some of his messages?'

'Right.'

'And how would he do that? I mean, could he just switch on the computer or would he need a telephone line or something?'

'Well, that's the thing. He wasn't using this computer.'

'Then what was he using?'

'An internet café, some place that provides computers and a connection.'

'Out there, in the middle of nowhere?'

'Nowadays it's not uncommon.' Sami reached for a cigarette of his own. The tiny room was filling up with smoke.

'When was this message sent? What day?'

'The twenty-first.'

Eight days after Mourad had last reported for work at Westies. Unable to bear it any longer, Makana walked over to the door for a glimpse of sky. Across the rooftops he could see the twin obelisks of the Nile City Towers. Lit like electric gods, they rose up into the night sky like the gateway to another realm. Beyond them, in the distance, on the

348

other side of the river, lights dwindled into darkness. To the Ancient Egyptians when the sun sank in the west, the god Ra descended into the land of the dead, the Underworld. A road in the middle of the Sinai might be a good place to disappear. It might also be a route out of this world and into the next.

'I have a theory,' Sami said from behind him.

'I'm happy to hear it.'

'Well, you may not like it. But I was trying to think about what these kids might be up to, right? I mean, what possible connection could there be between a couple of rebellious students and some refugees from South Sudan? But what would they do except want to help them? I was watching the news and they were interviewing people at the camp outside the mosque. A journalist asked one of the women what she wanted, and she said, a home. A place I can live in peace and make a life for myself. That's all, a home.'

'Estrella's mother was convinced her daughter had gone to America. She told her she was going to start a new life, but her application was turned down. She was pregnant.'

'So where would she go?' Sami asked. He had put his computer to one side and was reclining against the wall, smoking. At least he was sober and thinking, which was something. 'Europe is the obvious choice, but Europe is hard. Getting across the Mediterranean is expensive and it's a tough journey.'

'Especially for a pregnant woman.'

'So, what is nearer than Europe and almost as good?' Sami pulled a crumpled newspaper from underneath him and tossed it over to Makana. It landed on the floor. He didn't even need to pick it up.

'Israel,' said Makana.

Sami looked crestfallen. 'You knew.'

Makana stooped for the paper. A picture of desert guards patrolling a wire fence and a headline about refugees. He unfolded it by the doorway to read the story, listening with half an ear as Sami continued to talk.

'If they were smuggling people across the border into Israel, this might get complicated. It says there they are shooting people trying to cross over.'

'Who is shooting them, the Israelis?'

'No, we are, the Egyptians. It's a scandal, but it would help to explain some of this. Hasna is only a few hours from the frontier.' Sami was already up and pulling on his shoes.

'What are you doing?'

'You don't think you're going out there by yourself, do you?' Sami was indignant. 'Don't look at me like that. You treat me like I'm an invalid these days.'

There was a certain amount of truth to that. Makana was more cautious about involving Sami lately. He could never meet him without noticing the scars on his hands from a previous occasion when he had enlisted his help and he had wound up being almost crucified.

'Are you sure you're ready for this? I mean . . .'

'This is just what I need. Believe me, it'll be good for me. I need to get out of this place before I go crazy.'

'Why not go home to your wife?'

Standing with the blanket around his shoulders like a cape, Sami looked more than slightly deranged.

'Either you take me along, or I'm going straight downstairs and start drinking again.'

When he put it like that there didn't seem to be much choice to the matter. Still, it was too late to set out now anyway. Makana called Sindbad to arrange for an early start in the morning.

'The thing is they would need some kind of vehicle to get out there. I don't think you mentioned that either Ihab or Mourad had a car.'

'I have an idea about that,' said Makana.

Chapter Thirty-one

By night the area around the old pasha's palace on Champollion Street was dark and lifeless. During the day it came to life, as the shutters came up along the arcades to reveal service outlets, parts shops and mechanics getting to work. Pillars of tyres stacked here, vehicles of all kinds in varied states of disarray, a disassembled lorry, with the cab raised and headlights pointed into the oil-soaked ground. Everywhere the faded glory of once bright logos beckoned like a dying age, advertising brands of spark plugs and filters, spare parts of all kinds. Now, at sunset, the workshops were closing down. Across the narrow street soft rays of amber light grazed the upper walls of the old palace. There was still a police presence: a handful of guards dozed in the back of a dark blue pickup parked in front of the main gate. It didn't take him long to find what he was looking for. The first time he'd noticed it the name had struck him as mere coincidence. Now he knew it wasn't.

The paint around the door was faded and chipped, but showed the care and skill with which the lines had originally been added to the wall. Now everything was the same uniform grey, background and lettering blending in some organic process of decay. The man who stood inside the workshop showed similar evidence of time's hand. A large, untidy figure clad in overalls that were ripped and stained with all manner of organic substances. The legs rode high and the midriff was tight as a barrel around a swollen belly. Smoking a cigarette and watching the world pass him by, the man wore a scruffy beard of grey curls that matched the poorly cut thatch on his head. The eyes that followed Makana as he ducked in through the entrance were baggy and red. One grimy hand gripped a cup of tea.

'We're closed. Come back tomorrow.'

'Are you Sabbour?'

'Who wants to know?' There was a stiffening in his shoulders, as if surprised to be addressed by his own name, when it was painted in two-foot letters across the wall outside.

'I'm sorry for your loss.'

'My loss?' The man set down his glass on the workbench alongside him and squinted through the smoke of his cigarette.

Makana nodded at the old pasha's palace across the street. 'The kid they found over there. Ihab was your nephew, wasn't he?'

The frown deepened. 'What's it to you?'

Although the entrance was the width of a simple garage, the interior of the workshop space expanded into a high, gloomy cavern. A tinny radio was playing in the background somewhere. Violins working themselves up into frenzy seemed out of place in this setting. Makana slipped past the car that was stationed near the entrance. The bonnet was up and the engine partly dismantled. He felt the man's eyes following him.

'Where do you think you're going?'

A row of vehicles blocked a narrow passageway that led further inside. Beyond that he could see more vehicles parked in the gloom. He edged his way sideways through the gap. He still hadn't seen what he was looking for. To get anything through here would have been like taking a jigsaw puzzle to pieces and putting it back together again.

'Amazing how well you make use of the space in here.'

The man had moved away from the counter, hands hanging by his sides. He followed Makana slowly.

'Is there something you want?'

Once through the bottleneck the area opened up into a wide, tin-roofed parking space filled for the most part with dusty, obsolete vehicles. There was an air of desolation in here, a catalogue of mechanical time. A forgotten museum of automobile history. A tyreless rust-coloured Volkswagen Beetle sat alongside a Ford Cortina with no seats and a Fiat Topolino, circa 1950, that was now home to a family of cats. He didn't see what he had been hoping to find. Something was missing. He found that. A space between the neatly aligned vehicles. Freshly vacated. The ground clear of dust. Broken earth darkened by engine oil.

Makana paused. Out of the corner of his eye he caught a glimpse of an arc flying towards him. A fragmented reflection in the mottled chrome of a side mirror. The wrench flew past his ear, so close he felt the air part. It slammed into the roof of the Volkswagen. Makana turned to face his attacker, only to receive the full brunt of Sabbour's weight, which sent him flying backwards. He bounced off the sloping rear of a Citroën Berliner and slid to the ground. Sabbour moved fast for a big clumsy man. He loomed over Makana.

'Did you kill him?'

'Why would I come here if I had killed him?' Makana held up a hand for a moment's respite. It wasn't needed. The fight had gone out of Sabbour. The wrench was the length of Makana's forearm. Sabbour's nostrils flared as he breathed in, but his anger was no longer aimed at Makana. The wrench smashed into the side of the Citroën, leaving a dent. It seemed a shame to treat an old car like that, but if it meant not taking his frustration out on Makana then he had no complaints.

'I found him. Call your brother if you don't believe me.'

'My brother?' Sabbour looked sceptical. The good news was that he lowered the wrench a fraction. 'What are you, police?'

Makana shook his head. 'I'm looking for a friend of his, Mourad Hafiz.'

With a long sigh, Sabbour straightened up. He tossed the wrench to the ground and stood with his hands hanging limply by his side. It wasn't that the fight had gone out of him, more that he was unsure where to direct his rage. Sabbour screwed up his face and ran a hand over the damage he'd just inflicted.

'They cut him open, I heard.'

Makana got to his feet and dusted himself off, careful to make no sudden moves. 'I'd like to find out who did it.'

The mechanic said nothing. He drew a cigarette from a pocket in his overalls with a smooth, practised movement. A lighter came out of the other side somewhere. He picked up the wrench again and swung it as if trying to decide what to hit.

'You knew what he was up to, didn't you?'

'I mind my own business.' Sabbour's shrug had the same practised ease as his cigarette skills. Makana was willing to bet he had been in prison. He had the look of a man who had lost his way at some stage and was now doing his best to claw back whatever dignity remained. Hard to believe that he was the brother of a pompous judge in his fancy gown and salon stuffed with Louis XIV furniture. The black sheep of the family. The reckless uncle. The one you might go to when you needed a sympathetic ear, someone to help with something a little chancy.

'Ihab was a good kid.'

'He was.'

'A little high-strung, a little wild.' Sabbour's grin revealed a gold tooth. 'I was like that when I was young.'

'He liked you. That's why he came to you for help.'

'Kids up to some kind of prank. I thought the whole thing was harmless.'

'How did it work?'

Sabbour nodded at the empty space. 'I kept the van here for them. When they needed it I let them take it. I thought it was something that would pass. At that age, you know. They usually tried to give me some money. I only took what I needed for repairs and so on.'

'So you didn't ask too many questions?'

The mechanic shrugged. 'You know how it is with these kids. They don't really know what they want to do with their lives.'

'You know where they were going with your van?'

'Sure. I mean, they told me some of it.' Sabbour stared at him sullenly. 'Are you really trying to find the people who killed him?'

'If I can.'

'They weren't doing anyone any harm.' The mechanic's cheeks sucked inwards as he drew smoke into his lungs. He was breathing heavily and hefted the weight of the wrench in his hand. 'If I get my hands on the sons of bitches who did this . . .'

'What they were doing was risky. You must have known that when you agreed to help them.'

The wrench thumped into his hand. Sabbour looked off to the side. 'You know how it is,' he mumbled. 'I didn't want to think too much about it. I liked that he needed my help, I just didn't think it was that serious. I didn't think.'

'They must have stepped on somebody's toes.'

'I'll tell you what I believe.' The wrench shook in Makana's face. 'I believe they forgot to pay someone off. Forgot or refused. I don't know there's much difference when it comes to paying rats like your lot.'

'My lot?'

'Whatever.' He made a throwaway gesture.

'Do you know where they would take them?'

The mechanic stubbed out his cigarette and stared at the ground for a time. Then he gave a loud sniff and turned and walked back towards the front of the workshop.

'What did you do time for?'

The weary eyes flicked up to meet Makana's. He didn't look away. A man coming to terms with his misdeeds.

'It was mostly dealing with stolen goods. Nothing too serious.' A small cubicle over by the entrance was lined with grubby glass upon which newspaper was taped in some attempt at decoration. Yellowed sheets of newsprint adorned with images of faded starlets, singers and actresses who would now be middle-aged matrons, wherever they were. He sought out a packet of Cleopatras and a lighter.

'My brother helped me to get this place when I got out.'

'How many trips did they make?'

'Two or three, maybe more. I didn't keep track.'

'Whoever did this won't stop with Ihab. They'll go after Mourad and the girl, Fadihah, as well. Ihab would want to help his friends, don't you think?'

'You're not related to those other two, are you?' Sabbour examined the tip of his cigarette.

'Which other two?' Makana looked up. He already knew what the answer was going to be.

'They said they were police. They had that dishonest look of superiority on their faces. They knew all about me.'

'Describe them.'

'One of them tall and ugly, the second short and even uglier.'

'What kind of car did they drive?'

'A Mazda the colour of horseshit.'

'Tom and Jerry.'

'They didn't give their names, but I'm pretty sure it wasn't that.'

'Hakim and Karim, they are called. If you think of anything else you'd like to tell me, just give me a call.' He handed Sabbour a card with his number on it. 'It might help. One last thing, the van they used. What was it?'

'An old Toyota Hiace. Red. About twenty years old. They wanted something inconspicuous, nothing fancy. They thought it was perfect.'

Sindbad was waiting for him outside in the street. He had spent the day looking for Fadihah with no luck. Now he

359

was tired and eager to get home. As they drove he began grumbling about there being too many cars on the streets.

'I swear, if I was the president I would impose a ban. Like, say, you could have red cars one day and blue cars another.' Sindbad punctuated his spiralling thoughts by leaning on the horn. 'But what am I thinking of, it would never work. People just do what they like.'

Makana wasn't paying much attention. He was recalling the poem on the wall of Mourad's room. *Freedom ain't freedom when a man ain't free. Get on board our Freedom Train!* That is what they had been doing, running refugees up to the Israeli border, giving them a chance at a new life in a new country. A modern-day freedom train, the kind of thing that might appeal to a bunch of wide-eyed idealistic students looking for excitement. Only something happened and things took a more serious turn. What was it that precipitated the change? Was this the point at which Tom and Jerry entered the picture?

Makana tried calling Fantômas, only to be rewarded again by the distant rhythms of drums and singers. They crossed the river back into Mohandiseen. Outside the mosque a commotion threatened to spiral out of control. Blue and red flashing lights indicated the presence of dozens of emergency vehicles – police cars, vans and ambulances. Rows of prison trucks formed a wall along the southern end of the square. Officers in riot gear, bearing shields and batons, jostled the crowd. What they

360

were trying to do wasn't clear. Sindbad cast a wary eye over the scene.

'Better come back another time, *ya basha*. This doesn't look good.'

'I'll be all right. Go up a couple of streets and wait. I'll find you when I'm done.'

'Just watch out.' Sindbad shook his head. 'I have a bad feeling about this.'

The situation had deteriorated since the last time Makana had been here. The tension was visible in the faces of the men and women on the square through the cordon of armoured shoulders and helmets, and in the tense features of the policemen. They were afraid, and that wasn't a good sign. As a rule, when the forces of law are afraid violence soon follows.

What had happened, Makana wondered as he made his way round the perimeter looking for a familiar face. The wise thing, he knew, would be to leave, come back when things had settled down, but he sensed he didn't have the luxury of waiting. Time had run out for Ihab and soon it would be the turn of others.

'They're all mad,' offered a young conscript in riot gear. His helmet was too big and had tipped forward over his eyes. He pushed it back. 'They brought this on themselves.'

'They should clear the square now,' another officer added. 'Before it gets out of hand.'

'It's already out of hand.'

Makana left them talking as he pushed his way forward, slowly drawing nearer to the south end of the grassy square. Paving stones and iron railings had been ripped up to use as weapons. The road was strewn with broken concrete, bottles, clothes, an abandoned shoe. At the centre of the conflict was a confrontation between a group of black-uniformed Central Security Forces men and angry youths. As they jostled back and forth he picked out the vivid white tracksuit and jangling gold chains of Aljuka.

'You shouldn't be here.' Makana turned to find Fantômas standing alongside him.

'I was looking for you.'

Glancing over his shoulder, Fantômas steered Makana through the crowd, away from the scuffles. They stopped to allow a phalanx of charging policemen through. Between them a boy, no more than seventeen, was dragged backwards, his feet ploughing the ground, a trail of blood glistening in his wake.

'Hey!' Makana called out, but Fantômas was dragging him away, off to the side, through the lines of police and bystanders.

'You should know better than to get involved.'

It was unusual for him, but Makana felt an emotion stirring inside him that he hadn't felt in a long time. He was angry. They reached a clearing in a tree-lined street, a faint reminder of what this residential neighbourhood looked like normally. On the balcony of an apartment building a family clutched their arms to them against the chill and watched proceedings below.

'Take a good look.' Fantômas pointed a finger over Makana's shoulder. 'Those people have been here for three months, trying to restart their lives. Put yourself in their shoes. Your fate is in the hands of some UN filing clerk who has no idea what he's doing in this country, let alone what's going on outside his door. But responsibility falls on his shoulders. He has to decide if you are a genuine asylum seeker, or a liar. If he turns you down you have one chance to appeal. After that you're finished, stuck here for ever.'

'I have trouble understanding exactly where you fit into all of this.'

'Me?' Fantômas smiled, a hard, cynical grimace. 'I came here with nothing. Rags on my back, no papers to prove who I claimed to be, that I'd been in the resistance in Darfur, that my parents, my wife, my baby were murdered by the Janjaweed militia. Nothing. Just my story. Sometimes that's not enough. Once you realise you're nobody, you can become anything.'

Makana needed a cigarette. His hands trembled as he lit one. Why now? What was it about this situation that upset him so? He knew the answer. He'd just never really asked the question. He understood the frustration. Perhaps it was guilt that had made him steer clear. Not his own guilt, but that of his fellow countrymen, the Northerners, the ones who had never reacted, who had remained silent in the face of war, persecution and injustice. Silence in the face of mass injustice was an omission of conscience. Guilt by association. It made him a part of it.

'I need to find Estrella.'

Fantômas gave a click of annoyance. 'Why don't you just drop it?'

'Why would a girl like that get pregnant?'

'Why does any woman get pregnant?'

'She knew she was being vetted for the trip to America. She must have known they would find out.' It was hard to read the other man's face in the shadows. 'You knew, didn't you? You knew that she had to find another way out.'

Fantômas gave a roll of the head. 'Desperate times, desperate measures.'

'She knew what Mourad and his friends were up to. She went to him and asked him to help. She wanted him to get her out of this country. Why did she need him? Was it because she was pregnant? Because the Americans turned her down?'

'Just leave it, Makana. Drop the whole thing. It's too big.' Fantômas was backing away, hands raised before him. 'This is not your fight. This is our fight. Go back to where you belong.'

With that Fantômas turned and strode away. Makana watched him go. Somewhere nearby a siren started up and then stopped. As he made his way towards where Sindbad was waiting in the next street, he passed by a handful of policemen who were resting against a wall. They broke into nervous laughter as he went by.

Chapter Thirty-two

An hour later found Makana standing outside the Le Pacha floating restaurant in Zamalek feeling faintly absurd. What exactly did he think he was doing? In-between he had managed to go home and do his best to make himself presentable. A freshly laundered and ironed shirt and his newest jacket had been all he could summon, and still he felt like a sheep dressed up for the butcher's knife. Even now, he hesitated at the entrance and considered one last time making up an excuse. The truth was he had been trying to think of one that would stand up to scrutiny, and found himself coming up short. His plight was not helped by the fact that the entrance lobby was lined with mirrored panels. As if he wasn't self-conscious enough already. Bright lights only added to his torture, glaring down on him as he walked in. In a passing glance at his reflection he saw his father. Aged. His face drawn. Lines around the corners of his eyes and flecks of grey in his otherwise dark hair. His courage threatened to desert him completely and he turned, thinking there was still time to escape, only to find Doctora Siham standing before him. He was stunned into silence. She looked quite unlike anything he could ever have imagined. Her hair, released from the dull scarf she wore when on duty, pinned up out of the way beneath surgical caps, now flowed down to her shoulders. It seemed to shine and move with an energy of its own. But he didn't really have time to study the hair because he was too busy trying to take in the rest of her. She was wearing a dark blue dress that elegantly accentuated her figure without flaunting it. Around her bare shoulders she had wrapped a colourful shawl to keep away the evening chill.

'I'm sorry I'm late.'

Momentarily at a loss, Makana studied his watch. They were both precisely on time. The awkwardness threatened to congeal into embarrassment, with neither one quite knowing what kind of greeting was appropriate in this situation.

'Perhaps we should go in?' she suggested, putting him out of his misery.

The restaurant she'd chosen was supposed to be French, at least that's what he understood from what she told him on the stairs. There were high-backed booths and quaint lanterns, green-painted panels and columns framed in dark wood. She chose a table over by the window. The waiter was young. He looked Makana up and down in a surly fashion that seemed to ask what a lady of this style could be doing with someone like him. It wasn't as if he had never set foot in a fancy restaurant before, just that it was not his natural habitat.

'It's years since I've been here,' she said, perhaps sensing his discomfort.

He thought it wrong to tell her he'd never been there before, that nothing struck him as more absurd than a restaurant serving French food in a city that excelled in its own cuisine. He had thought the same about the Verdi Gardens, and that set off a train of thought that led back to Mourad and everything else.

'We haven't been here five minutes and already you are thinking about work,' she declared without looking up from her menu, which was the size of a newspaper. 'Perhaps we should make a rule not to talk about work until we have ordered, or perhaps until we have eaten? Wouldn't that be better?'

The waiter was hovering somewhere behind Makana's shoulder. He had been about to ask him to move away, for the simple reason that he needed more time. Now he found himself forced to make a decision.

'How do you do this?' He pointed.

The waiter gave him a worried frown. 'Chicken Kiev, *ya basha*. They take the chicken breast and slice it open and stuff it before frying it.'

367

He glanced across the table and Jehan, as he was trying to get used to thinking of her, rather than Doctora Siham, interpreted his hesitation as a logical concern.

'They don't use pig meat, do they?' she asked the waiter.

'Oh, no, Madame.' He looked appalled that such a thought could even have occurred to her. 'They use *bastourma*, naturally.'

'There you are, it's quite safe.'

Makana nodded his thanks and ordered the dish. Better to be taken for a pious idiot than an ignorant one. When the waiter had brought glasses of hibiscus juice for them, they were left alone and an awkward silence fell.

'You don't do this very often, do you?' she said.

'Oh, no. I try to eat once a day, at least.'

'I meant . . . like this.'

'Ordering Russian chicken in a French restaurant? No, I don't do this very often.'

'You're teasing me.'

'I'm sorry. The fact is that, no, I don't do this very often. I mean, I can't actually remember the last time I had dinner alone with a woman.'

'Really?' She looked surprised at first and then slowly nodded to herself. 'You live a quiet life. I respect that. You have simple tastes. You don't like places that try to be more than they are. You'd be happy in Felfela with a *taamiya* sandwich.'

'I think we could do better than that.'

They both laughed.

'It's natural, I suppose,' she said.

'I was married,' said Makana slowly, not certain why he was embarking on this subject. 'When Muna died, well, I thought that side of my life was over.'

'If there's one thing my job teaches me it's that life is terminal and generally a lot shorter than we would like to think. We need to enjoy what we have.'

'Right now I'm having trouble just thinking of you not as Doctora Siham.'

'Really?'

'Well, to start with, you don't dress like that every day.'

'I would no doubt be locked up in chains if I did. There would be petitions to have me removed from my post. The bearded ones would have a field day.' She leaned across the table with a mischievous look in her eye. 'Can I ask you a question?'

'Of course.'

'You're not really religious, are you?'

'You mean that thing with the chicken? No, I just wasn't sure what it was exactly.'

'I didn't think so.' Jehan smiled quietly to herself. 'I'm not usually such a poor judge of character.'

'I wouldn't worry about it.'

'So, you don't mind if we order wine? Normally, I have to keep up appearances. During Ramadan I fast, but only because my relatives would look down on me and because I think it's a way of losing weight.'

'Most people put on weight during Ramadan.'

369

'Well, exactly. So it takes some discipline, but it gives you one month of the year when you can convince yourself not to eat all day. You don't seem to have that problem.'

'I like to eat, I just keep irregular hours.'

'My father was like that. He never had time to eat. Always working. Worked himself into an early grave, of course. We kids always ate with my mother or my aunt, often my grandmother.'

'Both your parents were working?'

'My mother was a pediatrician, my father a surgeon.' She held up her hands in mock despair. 'A family of doctors. Two brothers, one a psychiatrist, the other an oncologist. I'm the only one who works with the dead. The rest try to keep people alive.'

'Somebody has to, I suppose.'

The wine arrived, a bottle of Omar Khayyam rosé. It didn't taste too bad. They both lit cigarettes. Makana began to feel a little more relaxed.

'You make an odd couple, you and Inspector Okasha.' She was studying him.

'I hadn't really thought of us as a couple.'

'He's so by the regulations and you . . . well, I can't imagine such opposites. Except that you do have a moral streak.' She pointed her cigarette at him.

'I do?'

'Certainly. You believe in right and wrong.'

'Doesn't everybody, in their own way?'

'We all claim to, or most of us anyway, but the truth is often far from that.'

The food arrived and Makana discovered that Chicken Kiev wasn't too bad. He might even suggest the idea to Aswani and see what he made of it. The wine drained steadily from the bottle as they talked. When they ordered coffee Makana was surprised to watch her switch back into her professional role as pathologist. Her tone, her manner, even the way she sat in the chair and gave commands to the waiter. Her hard side resurfaced from one moment to the next.

'It's still too early for the tests, but I may have had some success in matching the scratch wounds in the neck to those on the torso.'

'I paid the Hesira Institute a visit and saw a picture of Estrella's friends, Beatrice and Jonah. Jonah's forehead shows the marks of a Mundari.'

'Interesting. You think he might be our severed head?' She frowned at him. 'Wait a minute, I thought you wanted me to go along with you?'

Makana studied his plate. 'I thought you would be busy. I didn't want to bother you.'

'You mean you couldn't summon the courage to call me.' He looked up to find she was smiling.

'I met your old friend, Ihsan Qaddus.'

A shadow seemed to pass over her face, and he was reminded suddenly of that evening in the Forensics Lab when he had caught her sitting alone.

371

'Is that how he referred to me, as an old friend?'

Makana realised he might have stumbled onto delicate ground. Whatever had once existed between her and Ihsan Qaddus still touched a nerve.

'I got the impression you were once close.'

'You could put it like that.'

'What happened?'

'People change, I suppose,' she shrugged. 'Today, he's well connected. Businessmen, politicians, television celebrities, people who are in the news. Highly placed officials, people of influence. Potential investors.'

'Why did you split up?'

'I think deep down I knew I could never compete with his ambitions. I didn't want my career to be limited to standing next to him at social functions.'

'Somehow I can't imagine you fitting into that role.'

'Well, I'm happy for him. He has done well for himself. He certainly keeps illustrious company these days,' breathed Jehan. 'Quite an empire he's built for himself.'

'And all on the mud of the Nile.'

She laughed at that, then she peered into her glass. 'When we were young his ambitions were of a different nature. He wanted to rid the world of malaria, cure polio, things like that.'

'Sometimes the material world brings more tangible benefits.'

'I suppose so, but I can't believe that he's abandoned all of that idealism. He would have made a fine surgeon.'

'So when did the interest in this kind of alternative healthcare begin?'

'I'm not sure, perhaps you should ask him next time you see him.'

Perhaps she was annoyed that he had gone to the institute without her, after promising to do so. Or it might have been the idea of him and Qaddus talking together in her absence. He couldn't make out why this should upset her, but he had come to accept there were lots of things about the pathologist that he didn't quite understand.

It was her turn to change the subject.

'I haven't been able to link the blood samples we found on the wall to the skin tissue from the head. DNA analyses are expensive and I need to go through a committee.' She sighed. 'They like to make us beg, so it might not happen. What do you think this is all about?'

'I wish I knew. At the moment there are just fragments that don't seem to connect.' Makana sat up and lit another cigarette. 'Supposing the bloodstains from the wall matched the head. Then the same person who was held in Shaddad's garage was decapitated.'

'How does that help?'

'If the head is Jonah's then how did he end up in that room? What happened to his sister Beatrice?'

'You think they were both killed, but why?'

'All I know is that they are supposed to be in America.'

'You're sure of that?'

'According to Liz Corbis they are going through some kind of transition phase, settling in with their adoptive families.'

'This Liz, is she the one you went to visit at the Hesira?'

'Yes, Doctor Corbis, I should say.' Makana wondered at the question.

'You seem to be making a lot of new friends in the medical profession.' Jehan studied her glass for the moment before brushing her own comment aside. 'I've been meaning to ask you about the adoption programme. Doesn't it strike you as odd that Americans would want to adopt such old children? I mean, sixteen is almost an adult. I thought people wanted younger children.'

It was a good point, and one that Makana hadn't given much thought to. He had assumed that the reason these benevolent Americans were adopting Sudanese refugees was that they wanted to help young Christian men and women who had fled the war. It wasn't about adopting children so much as helping to do good.

'Tell me about the drug you found,' he said. 'Sodium thiopental?'

'What are you thinking about?'

'I just wonder if this could be about the drugs.'

'You mean, because of Shaddad's involvement?'

'Not directly, but he's the head of a major pharmaceuticals supplier. His drivers are engaged in some kind of private enterprise of their own, selling off his products on the side. One of his vans was involved in a collision, perhaps an accident, or perhaps forced.'

'Forced how?'

'There were paint marks on the side of the van. It's possible someone ran the van into the path of the oncoming tanker.'

'Why would they do that?'

'To silence someone? To get the drivers out of the way? Either way, the driver was never identified. Another driver, Mustafa Alwan, is missing. It's possible he was in the van at the time of the accident. He was hurt, but instead of staying there he disappeared. Either he ran off, or he was taken.'

'Shaddad runs a respectable company. I can't see him being involved in illicit trading.'

'The other thing is the body in the locker. Where were they taking it?'

'The furnace you saw out there. They could have been taking the body to get rid of it.'

Makana agreed. 'At such high temperatures you would get rid of almost everything.'

'It's like an incinerator,' she nodded. 'All that is left are ashes.'

'Ashes,' repeated Makana. 'Could they be conducting some kind of experiments, tests, with drugs that are unstable, or have side effects?'

'It's possible. The manufacture of generic pharmaceuticals in this country generates hundreds of millions of dollars a year.'

'And these would be drugs for . . .?'

'Anything, from hypertension to painkillers to Viagra. The market for alternatives to expensive Western products is vast.' Jehan produced her own cigarettes and he lit one for her. 'It's done by a kind of reverse engineering, breaking down an existing drug to see how it's put together, then they work out how to manufacture it. Sometimes they get it wrong. Impurities get in. People can die from an allergic reaction to some minor element in the formula, or an impurity.'

'Could the heart attack have been induced by some kind of drug testing?'

'It's possible, but we found no trace of anything other than sodium thiopental.'

Another dead end. Still, it shone a new light on Shaddad. Was someone using his network to distribute generic drugs without his knowledge? The one person who might know was Mustafa Alwan, and Alwan was missing.

'Alwan has a son who suffers from some kind of medical condition. He needs an operation.'

'Describe him.'

'Swollen eyes, puffy face. Also he had a kind of yellow tinge to his skin.'

'I can't say for sure, but it sounds like it might be a liver problem.'

'Is that serious?'

'It could be. Hepatitis, possibly. If that's the case it can be treated.'

'How about something more serious?'

'Well, hepatitis can be pretty serious. It could be liver failure, which is not uncommon, though in someone so young it is unusual.'

'How is that treated?'

'Oh, there's no cure. If he doesn't respond to treatment he would have to have a transplant.'

'Can that be done?'

'In this country?' She shook her head. 'He would probably have to go abroad, and that's not cheap.'

'I'm sorry,' said Makana. 'I'm ruining the evening.'

'Not at all.' She gave him a wry look. 'And besides, I hardly thought we would get away with not discussing work.'

There was a brief tussle over the bill when Makana gallantly tried insisting on paying. Jehan refused to hear of it and they ended splitting it. And then they were walking beside the river.

'You still haven't told me why you called me earlier,' Makana said.

'You're right,' Jehan laughed, putting her hand to her forehead. 'I'm sorry. I don't know what I was thinking. The thing is, it was one of my students. When we were going through the basement, one of them bagged all the bones that were lying about.'

'Bones? What bones?' A crisp wind blew off the surface of the river and he offered his jacket, which she draped around her shoulders.

Jehan laughed again. 'It's silly, I know. The bones the dogs were eating?'

Makana remembered the aggressive dogs in the basement garage. Abu Gomaa's little hobby.

'What about them?'

'Well, it's nothing really. One of the students suggested that some of the bones resembled human digits. Fingers or perhaps toes. Sometimes it's very difficult to really tell the difference between human bones and animal bones, especially when they are broken up into fragments. It's all about the thickness of the wall, and so on.'

'Wait a minute.' Makana stopped and turned to face her. 'What are you saying?'

'I'm saying I'm not sure. Without further analysis we can't tell.'

'But it's possible those dogs were chewing on human bones?'

'That can't be right, can it?' She looked at him and realised her error. 'Can it?'

But Makana was already gone, jogging back towards the road, looking for a taxi.

Chapter Thirty-three

The air was cold and tinged with damp as Makana made his way down the ramp from the street. He called out several times but there was no reply. The basement was still and oddly silent. Nothing moved.

'Abu Gomaa!'

His voice echoed through the cavernous basement. There was nothing. Not even the sound of the dogs came back. He moved further into the shadows, wishing he had managed to bring a torch with him. Even Sindbad's unreliable flashlight would be welcome. Faint slivers of light from the street above bounced through cracks, opening up channels before him. His eyes adjusted and he moved forward from memory, remembering the general layout from the last time he had been here. He could make out the muffled shapes of the cars along one wall. Ahead of him the stairwell. To the right, the service room where the bloody handprint had been found.

He reached the area that was Abu Gomaa's living quarters. Nothing there. Cardboard boxes. The makeshift bed. The television set was faintly warm. The old man was nowhere in sight. He stumbled over something that turned out to be a long chain. He pulled it up. The dogs were not fixed to the end. Where were they? Did the old watchman have somewhere else to go at night? Had he taken them somewhere? One of his dogfights?

He felt bones cracking under his shoes as he walked on and tried to step around them, wondering where they might have come from. The wind hummed through gaps in the walls. The distant murmur of the traffic. And something else. Another sound. A faint scratching. Something moving deep down inside the building. He moved further inwards, slowly tracing his way towards where he knew the stairwell was.

He stepped through the doorway into deeper blackness. A set of stairs led upwards towards the ground floor and Shaddad's offices, and he was about to move up these when he realised the sound he was hearing came from below. Running his hand along the railing, he made his way back, testing with his feet as he moved downwards. There was a lower level to the basement.

The stairs were bare concrete. Hardly any light penetrated this far into the stairwell and he had to proceed by feel, edging down step by step. The air grew warmer, a thick, heady mixture that felt asphyxiating. He groped his way forward, hands outstretched until he reached the wall. The door was in the same position as the one above. It was unlocked. He stepped out, sensing cooler air, and open space expanding around him as he moved away from the stairwell.

Down here it was even darker than the floor above. Without the ramp there was nothing to let light in. Still he groped on, his hands extended in front of him until he bumped into something, a high wire fence that seemed to stretch away along the ground. He stood still, his eyes adjusting. Ahead of him, just beyond the fence, he became aware of movement. Something slipping through the dark, just out of reach. Something glinted in the darkness. A bright opening and closing. The animal smell of damp straw. With one hand to the fence, he moved along.

Out of the darkness shadows surged towards him. Something thumped into the fence next to him, knocking him back with a jolt. Makana pulled away. He knew what the movement was. Dogs. How many he couldn't tell. They were loping along beside him, leaping over one another, snarling. Their smell was overpowering, a thick, heady, bestial reek. They were quiet, too. Unlike the dogs Makana had seen upstairs, these animals had a keen pack instinct. They moved together like a unit, brushing up against the fence, just enough to make the links jangle, before melting back into the shadows. He glimpsed their eyes, brief yellow flares that blinked out almost at once. He sensed their constant motion and their hunger.

Careful not to get too close, Makana followed the fence along to the far corner where it met a concrete pillar. A crack of light drew his attention to the right. Someone was moving, low down, close to the floor, a torch beam illuminating a spot on the floor. Stepping quietly, he made his way over. The tiny flickers of light guiding his steps.

'Hello, Mustafa.'

The man gave a cry and scrabbled backwards, crashing into a stack of cardboard boxes.

'It's all right,' Makana said. 'I'm not here to hurt you.'

Mustafa Alwan was not in good shape. Dirty bandages were wrapped around one arm which he held close to his chest at an odd angle. There was a scarf tied around his head and right eye. His face showed lacerations.

'Who are you? What do you want?'

'I want to talk, that's all.' Makana held up his hands to reassure him. 'It's okay.'

After a moment or two the fight went out of Alwan, not so much relenting as collapsing with exhaustion. Makana crouched down in front of him. Alwan stared at him out of his one good eye.

'You should see a doctor.'

Alwan shook his head. 'No doctor.'

'Have you been hiding down here since the accident?'

'Not an accident.' He was huddled in a corner of the narrow alcove, hidden behind stacks of dusty boxes and old furniture – a desk with a broken leg, a tangle of cracked chairs. A grubby blanket had been hung from a piece of

382

clothes line strung between two pillars. The torch lay on the floor where he had dropped it, the pencil of light stretching across the ground between them. Makana jerked his head.

'The dogs out there, are those Abu Gomaa's?'

'He breeds them. Crazy old man. Dogs and jackals. He bets money on fights.'

'He's helping you.'

Alwan squinted at him. 'You're the one who's been asking questions.'

'He told you about that?'

'He said he'd got rid of you.'

'I came back.' Makana was curious. 'There was a forensic team here. Upstairs. They didn't come down here?'

'He closed off the door, told them it was a storage area, that nobody ever came down here.'

So much for thorough police work. Makana eased himself down to sit on the floor. He offered his cigarettes. There was a bad smell down here. Was it the dogs or Alwan? Between them, the place stank.

'You said it wasn't an accident.'

'They ran us off the road. They wanted to kill me.'

'Who wanted to kill you?'

'They hit us from the side, rammed us right across into the other lane. A tanker was coming. Of course they wanted to kill us. It wasn't an accident.'

'You saw who did it?'

'I saw.' Alwan cupped his cigarette and stared at the floor. For a moment his mind seemed to drift away. Perhaps the blow to the head had done serious damage. He looked up. 'You came here alone?'

Makana nodded. 'I spoke to your wife.'

'My wife?' Alwan's face crumpled. 'My family. You saw them. They're all right?'

Makana recalled the wife's confident assertion that her husband was away on business.

'She thinks you're away working. She doesn't know you're here?'

'She doesn't know anything. It's better that way.'

'Tell me about your son.'

'What about him?'

'He's ill, I understand.'

'He's dying,' Mustafa Alwan said quietly. 'He needs an operation. Qaddus promised me, but then there were delays, always delays. He wanted money, he said. Then he wanted me to drive for him, clear up his mess.' His gaze came up to find Makana. 'And every day I would watch that boy growing weaker. It was too much.' His eyes flickered away. 'I told them that if they didn't save my boy they would be reading about their precious institute in the papers.'

'And that's when they decided to get rid of you.'

Mustafa Alwan nodded glumly. 'I wouldn't have done it. Well, I don't know. He's my boy. You know, a man will do anything to save the life of his own child.' Alwan tensed. He held up a hand, dropping his voice to a whisper. 'Did you hear that?'

Makana listened. 'The dogs, maybe. What was the story you were going to tell?'

384

Alwan shook his head, motioning him to be silent. 'You must go now.' He reached for the torch and clicked it off. They were plunged into darkness. 'Go!' he hissed before scrabbling away into the shadows. Getting to his feet, Makana stepped back out of the alcove. He stopped to listen. He could still only hear the muffled sound of the dogs pattering about, whining softly, rubbing up against one another, brushing the fence. He could feel their presence like a wall of suppressed fury, a storm about to break. Makana moved along, tracing his way back along the fence towards the stairwell. He was almost there when a light clicked on and a powerful torch shone into his face.

'You really don't learn, do you?'

It took Makana a moment to place the voice. By then it was too late. He opened his mouth to speak, only for the air to be knocked out of his lungs. The heavy punch caught him in the solar plexus. He felt his knees give way as he folded in half. He retched drily as his face was pressed into the ground, where the smell of dogs and straw was overwhelming. A boot ground into the back of his neck. Hakim, Karim, he wasn't sure which one of them was on the other end of the boot. From somewhere behind him he heard Alwan scream as he was dragged out of his hiding place.

'No, no. No!'

Makana was hauled to his feet. His stomach hurt and he was fighting the urge to throw up. He was shoved back against the wire fence and held there by a hand to his throat. The torch was beamed into his eyes again. He knocked the hand away only to receive another blow to the head with the end of the heavy torch. He swayed and almost fell. This time he saw stars.

'Just be patient.' Hakim, the large one, loomed close, his breath rich with garlic and alcohol. 'Your turn is coming. First you get to watch.' He swung the beam of the torch down along the fence to where Makana could see Mustafa Alwan on his knees. Karim was kicking him methodically in the ribs, interspersing this with some hefty blows to the head. He seemed to be taking his time, trying to soften him up. Alwan had his fingers locked through the links of the fence, trying to hold on. He soon regretted it. The dogs came in a rush of fur, pummelling the fence in their haste. Small and powerful, they went for his fingers. Alwan howled and in a flash of light Makana saw him pull his hand back, clutching the bloody stump where two of his fingers had been. Next to him, Makana heard Hakim chuckle while Karim broke off from the beating to grab Alwan by the collar and drag him along the floor. Hakim pushed Makana along in the same direction.

'Come on, move. You don't want to miss this.'

They reached the pillar at the far end, Makana doing his best to keep away from the fence. On the other side he could hear the snarling as the dogs grew more frantic. The torch beam darted about as they moved. Ahead of him, Makana could see Alwan trying to resist being pulled further, only to receive a punch in the face which dampened his resistance. He was dragged on his back

386

along the floor to a point halfway along, where Karim dropped him in a heap. Hakim aimed the light at the fence where a makeshift gate was held shut by a twisted metal coat hanger.

'Crazy old man and his dogs, right?' Hakim said. 'He never knew how useful they were going to be.'

'You fed them Jonah's remains.'

'Jonah?'

'The brother and sister. The ones you held in the room upstairs.'

'The ones who escaped? They were a pain, running off like that. Sure, we gave the dogs a few pieces, as a treat. The rest we used to scare those kids off. They were getting in the way. We showed them, though, eh?' Hakim broke off and slapped Makana around the head.

'Why cut him to pieces?'

'That wasn't me.' Hakim nodded towards his companion. 'He gets carried away sometimes. He didn't like having to chase that crazy *abeed* and his sister across town. Both of them out of their minds. That's tiresome, and for what?'

'Where is she now?'

'Where is who?'

'Beatrice?'

'That's what you're going to tell me, right?' Hakim smiled. 'No, wait till you see the main event. You'll talk then.'

Ahead of them, Alwan had rolled over and was very slowly trying to crawl away, leaving a glistening trail of blood on the ground behind him. Ahead of him was a mound of bloody rags that Makana made out as the old man Abu Gomaa.

'He shouldn't have tried to hide Alwan from us.' Hakim tutted in dismay. 'That's really not fair, we're supposed to be on the same side, after all.'

'Alwan and Abu Gomaa were working together.'

'Amateurs, ripping off that fool Shaddad who doesn't know the time of day unless you tell him.'

Up ahead, Karim gave the gate a kick, forcing the dogs back, then with a growl of irritation he turned back to Alwan, who cried out, clinging onto Abu Gomaa's lifeless body. At first Karim tried to just haul him off, but then he tired of tugging at two of them and bent down to prise Alwan loose. This was a mistake. He gave a shout and staggered back. Next to him, Makana heard Hakim swear. The torch beam picked out blood streaming down Karim's white shirt.

'Son of a bitch!'

Hakim went straight for Alwan, who was trembling on the floor, frozen in place by his own actions, awaiting the inevit-able. Hakim laid into him, hitting him hard. Makana knew it was now or never. Karim had staggered back and was slumped against the wire fence, his hands around the hilt of the knife that was buried in his side. Alwan must have known that Abu Gomaa carried a knife and decided to use it.

Mustafa Alwan was unconscious. His face was a bloody pulp but he seemed to be breathing. Makana went over and dragged the gate shut. The dogs were still busy but he didn't want to risk any of them getting out. The bloody mass of ripped clothes and torn flesh told him there was nothing he could do for Karim.

Upstairs he found a signal for his phone and called Okasha, who wasn't happy to be woken up but paid attention quickly when Makana told him what was going on. There was one more surprise still to come. When he came back downstairs he found that Hakim had disappeared.

Chapter Thirty-four

It took what remained of the night to deal with the aftermath. By the time Makana made his way back up the ramp towards the world, the birds were singing in the trees and daylight was breaking overhead. He only remembered his appointment with Sindbad when his telephone began to ring.

'*Ya basha*, I'm here, as we agreed, but where are you?'

He could sleep in the car, he thought, which was fine in principle, except that with Sami in the back seat chattering away, sleep became a form of torture. Although by the sound of things Sami himself had not had a comfortable night.

'The bed is really just a few beer crates with a very thin mattress over them. It's like lying on stones. No matter which way you turn something finds one of your bones.'

Makana refrained from reply. His mind was on the events of the previous night. Okasha had not been happy to discover what awaited him in Shaddad's basement. It was a mess. Two dead and one of them a police officer. Mustafa Alwan was driven away comatose. The paramedics were worried that he might have suffered lasting brain damage from the accident and the beating he had taken. They had to call in a team of specialists to deal with the dogs, who were in a frenzy.

'I've never seen anything like it,' said the vet who took charge of the operation. 'They're less dogs than jackals.' They sedated the animals with drugged meat and then took them off to the zoo for observation. This allowed the medics to get close to Karim's body, or what was left of it. He had been torn to shreds and was unrecognisable. Part of a bloody identity card was retrieved which confirmed that he was a police officer from Giza district. Okasha was reluctant to lay the blame at the feet of fellow officers. He tried to turn the story on its head to explain their presence in the basement.

'Maybe they were here doing their job, investigating.'

'Is that what you really think?' Makana asked. 'Or is that what you'd like to think?'

'Who knows. One of them got himself killed and the other disappeared.'

'You're saying you don't believe me?'

'Look at it from my position. How am I supposed to report this? Two officers murder an old bawab and almost murder a driver. What's the explanation for that kind of behaviour?' He held up a hand to silence Makana's protests. 'You go away, you think it over, and you come in tomorrow and make an official statement.' He turned away before Makana could say more. It had been a long night and he was tired. 'And I don't need to tell you that you can't leave town.'

Which, of course, was exactly what he was doing right now. The warm air from the desert blew in through the open window, making the previous night feel like a nightmare he had just woken from. When he decided that Qaddus was just stringing him along, Mustafa Alwan had contacted a journalist and threatened to go public about the Hesira Institute. Of course, he probably wouldn't have gone through with it. Threatening to go to the press was just his way of trying to call their bluff. All he wanted was to find a cure for his son – understandable under the circumstances – but Hakim and Karim weren't the kind of people to take a threat lightly, so they dealt with him in their customary way. It was two different levels of the same game, and everything seemed to go back to the Hesira Institute.

What wasn't yet clear to him was the question of Beatrice and Jonah. Clearly they hadn't made it to America. They had wound up in Shaddad's basement room. One of them, Jonah, had been bleeding. He had helped his sister climb up through the hatch and get away. Where had she gone?

Jonah's fate was lamentably clear. He had been murdered and cut to pieces, his feet fed to the dogs and his head thrown into the river. The other pieces of his body had been arranged as a macabre display in the old palace, as a warning to Mourad and his friends. They'd been stepping on somebody's toes. How? Most likely through sheltering Beatrice. They had taken her onto their freedom train, possibly at Estrella's request. There were still a lot of questions, but Makana hoped that some of the answers would be found out here in the Sinai, at Hasna.

There was little traffic at this early hour, and once they got out past the city the roads were almost empty. It was a warm day, which made a pleasant change, and the bright light reflecting off the sand made it feel as if winter had turned a corner. Optimistic, he knew, but over the past few weeks the awama had been cold, dank and creaking with discontent. He didn't think he could take much more of that.

The warmth brought back other memories: his dinner with Jehan. He found himself drumming his fingers on the roof of the car. It was something of a surprise to him that the evening hadn't been as awkward as he had feared. She too appeared to have enjoyed herself. All of this felt alien, and at the back of his mind there was the sense that he was going against his nature, that being in the company of another woman was, in some strange, unfathomable way, being unfaithful to Muna.

His fingers ceased their drumming and with a sigh he straightened up in his seat. He checked the roadmap that was folded on the seat beside him and looked at his watch. They were making good time. There was no guarantee that they would find Mourad, but it did make sense that he might be there. Assuming that he was still alive, then this might be far enough away for him to feel safe.

Out of the barren landscape a roadsign loomed up far ahead. Five minutes later they were turning towards the north-east. In the distance soft hillsides of sand were like pencil lines scratched across the flat grey landscape. Gradually the square outline of buildings emerged, simple houses set low against the surrounding starkness. The town was quiet, hardly any movement worth reporting. A horse-drawn wooden cart trotted ahead of them, bearing a washing machine on which a little boy was perched. His eyes followed them as the car went by. They passed a row of shops selling machine parts, hardware, aluminium windows and doors. A small supermarket, a post office, clusters of yellow brooms, orange bedsheets, metal rakes, a water-pump specialist.

'Not much here,' commented Sindbad, sceptical as ever about the purpose of the excursion. Makana ignored him. He wished he knew what they were looking for.

'The address you have, where is it exactly?'

Sami laughed. 'It's an IP address – I mean, you know, it's not a real location.'

Makana glanced back at him. 'Not real?'

'No, it's a virtual location, a number, an address in cyberspace.'

Makana turned back to the street. 'I had a feeling this wasn't going to be straightforward,' he muttered.

They were almost out of town already. It was a small place. Makana signalled for Sindbad to turn around. The Datsun pulled off to the side, then swung round and back up onto the lip of the road.

'Let's go more slowly.'

This time a couple of people stopped to watch them, following them with their eyes, wondering what they were doing. A sign pointing east indicated the road to Al Qusouma. 'Take that,' said Sami.

They turned left, but a few hundred metres found them leaving the town behind. As the buildings thinned out Makana noticed what looked like a service station set on the right-hand side of the road. Two faded petrol pumps and a rusty sign stood out in the sun. Further back stood a low single-storey building with a raised veranda running along the front of it and a sign displayed along the top. The black lettering had faded to the point where it was only a few smudged lines, but there was a drawing at either end. A logo that was strangely familiar.

'This is it,' said Makana.

They pulled off the road and drove up to the building. There were no other cars in sight. When they got out Makana pointed up at the sign. The five lines radiating out of a point. A star.

'Sothis.' Makana held up the matchbook he had found in Ihab's kitchen.

There was an air of abandon about the place. Sami went up onto the veranda and sat down at one of the tables. Makana walked around the building before coming back to join him. They sat there listening to the squeak of a faded metal sign swaying in the wind. Sindbad was cleaning the windscreen with a rag. Sami sat deep in thought, smoking and staring out at the arid landscape.

'Maybe we could get some breakfast,' he suggested. 'I'm starving.'

A door creaked open and a woman appeared. She was small and dressed all in black, adjusting the scarf that covered her head. Her lower lip was tattooed blue in the manner of the Bedouin. Beside her stood a boy of about ten.

'Is there any chance of getting any breakfast around here?' Sami asked.

'Breakfast?' The woman pronounced the word as if it were alien to her.

'Sure, you know, some eggs, beans, bread, maybe some *taamiya*.' Sami was miming with his hands as he moved towards her, stopping when he saw her pull back. 'How about tea?'

She stared at them for a moment longer and then turned to the boy and began speaking quickly before retreating through the doorway she had come from.

'I'm not sure I actually got through to her. I mean, they do speak Arabic around here, right?'

After a time the little boy could be seen running across the forecourt in the direction of town. Maybe there would be a chance after all.

The air was warm and dry and there was a certain serenity to the place. Sindbad stood out by the car, leaning on the Datsun calling his wife. Traffic along the road in front of them was sparse. The occasional car or lorry swished by. A pickup with a camel sitting regally in the back.

After a time the door opened again and the woman in black reappeared. She set down a tray with three glasses of mint tea and a pink plastic bowl filled with sugar. As she turned to go, Makana asked her to wait a second. He showed her the photograph of Mourad but she shook her head wordlessly and vanished back inside. Sindbad joined them and they sipped their tea in silence.

'It's nice here,' observed Sindbad, stretching like a man of leisure. 'It's peaceful.'

Makana felt like reminding him they were here for a purpose, but he decided against it. In the distance he spotted the little boy returning from town, his young arms weighed down by plastic bags.

'Here comes breakfast,' he said.

'About time,' said Sami. 'I don't know about you, but driving makes me hungry.'

Sindbad brightened. 'It has the same effect on me. That's what's so terrible about driving all day, you're always hungry.' Makana had never known Sindbad to speak of anything with such passion as he spoke of food.

Sami disappeared inside in search of a bathroom. When he came back he gestured for Makana to join him in the doorway.

'Take a look.'

The interior was gloomy and deserted. At the far end of the room two rather old computers were set against a grubby wall. Above them an incongruous and rather tattered sign announced it as the 'Sothis Internet Café – Welcome!' The hearty greeting seemed at odds with the setting, as indeed were the computers. They returned to their seats and soon the boy reappeared bearing a tray he could barely carry. He set down plates of white cheese, flat

397

discs of bread, dried dates and finally a bowl of *ful mudames*, fava beans crushed into a paste and flooded with olive oil. Sami was eager to tuck in.

'Well, I think we might survive,' he said, smiling at the boy, who turned without a word and was gone. 'So do you really think this is the place?' he asked as he tore off some bread and began to eat.

'It's possible,' said Makana. He was thinking about the woman and how quickly she had replied, barely glancing at the photograph.

'Desolate place, though,' Sami continued. 'I mean, if they drove through here at night with a vanload of refugees nobody would notice.'

It wouldn't even have to be at night, Makana thought. You could drive a herd of elephants through here in broad daylight and no one would bat an eyelid. The *ful* was watery and the oil had a slightly rancid taste. It seemed like a comedown after last night's meal. This, he reminded himself, was how things in his life tasted normally. It made the prospect of eating Chicken Kiev in a fancy French restaurant in the company of an attractive woman seem oddly surreal.

'We live with the self-created myth that once you leave the city everything tastes much better.'

'I don't know about you,' Sindbad said. 'Personally, nothing I eat is ever as good as the food I eat at home.'

'Your wife is a good cook, then?' Sami ventured. Makana raised his eyebrows. It wasn't a good idea to get Sindbad started on the subject.

'Every man should be proud of his wife's cooking,' Sindbad beamed before launching off into a long and detailed account of every dish his wife had ever prepared for him. Sami listened but said nothing. He seemed to be deep in thought. Suddenly restless, Makana got to his feet and paced to the far end of the veranda to peer around the side of the building. The landscape stretched southward in a flat, open sweep. A side door opened and the little boy who had served them now came out to sit on the steps. He was eating a sandwich, his reward no doubt for fetching their breakfast.

'Hello,' said Makana, as he wandered over. 'Is that as good as it looks?'

The boy chewed for a bit longer and then nodded.

'What's your name?'

'Wahid.'

'You like living out here, Wahid?'

For that he got a shrug. Makana nodded his understanding. He allowed a few moments to go by in silence, then reached into his shirt pocket for the photograph and held it out for the little boy to take.

'Have you ever seen this man before?'

Wahid grinned. 'Sure, he's my friend.'

'When was the last time you saw him?'

Wahid curled up his shoulders. Time wasn't something he was too concerned about. Out here you saw people when you saw them.

'Not so long ago.'

'You remember when that was? A week? A few days? How many?'

'Three.' The boy held up as many fingers.

Three days? Could they really be that close? Makana tucked the picture into his shirt pocket. 'Tell me, the last time you saw him, was he alone?'

'No.' The boy shook his head. 'He had his friends with him. They were going on a trip.'

'Do you know where they went?'

'Where he always goes.' The boy took another bite of his sandwich and then pointed off into the distance.

'Out there? But there's no road.'

'It's a track. Not everyone knows about it.'

'Can you show me?'

The boy looked thoughtful. He studied his sandwich and took another bite. Then he glanced over his shoulder at the kitchen.

'My mother doesn't like me going off by myself.'

'It won't be for long. Just show me where it starts.' Makana considered the wisdom of offering money to a child – was this how the seeds of corruption were sown? 'I'll tell you what, you show me the place and I'll buy you an ice cream.'

'Any kind?'

'Whatever you like.'

The boy was already on his feet. Makana followed him out across the sand towards a large grey rock. It was further than it looked and the day was getting warmer. By the time they reached it Makana was sweating. If the boy was right, three days would mean Mourad had left Cairo the day before Ihab was killed. The boy skipped along happily, picking up sticks and throwing stones to amuse himself. On the far side of the grey boulder, which was the size of a small house, a track twisted off through the sand in a south-easterly direction. The boy pointed into the distance. Makana handed him a couple of notes.

'You think that's enough?' Makana asked. 'I need you to go back and tell my friends to come and pick me up in the car. Can you do that?'

'Do I get another ice cream for that?'

Makana added another note to the pile and then watched the boy skip off back in the direction they had just come from. So much for the innocence of youth.

It took another ten minutes before Sami and Sindbad appeared in the Datsun. Makana waved them down and climbed into the back.

'This is starting to feel like an adventure,' Sami laughed into the wind.

After they had followed the track for half an hour Makana was beginning to wonder if perhaps the boy had truly taken him for a ride. It was Sindbad who had the sharpest eyes.

'There,' he pointed. There was something there. Another ten minutes brought it into focus. A red Toyota Hiace. It was lying on its side.

'Slow down,' said Makana.

As they approached a brown smudge broke away and trotted away from the overturned minivan.

'What is that, some kind of dog?' Sami asked.

'A jackal,' said Makana. 'Stop the car here.'

He got out and made his way over on foot. The stench hit him before he had gone five paces. Approaching the vehicle from the rear he could see shadows through the glass. Bending down he picked up a hefty stone and threw it. The stone clattered against the side of the car and brought an ungainly pair of vultures hobbling out. They flapped their wings and took themselves off a short distance, where they settled to watch him.

The heat had done its work. The bodies were swollen and the skin blackened and taut as a drum in places, burst in others to reveal the suppuration beneath. Three bodies sprawled in the rear of the minibus. They were fresh, no more than a few days old. Two of them he guessed were Beatrice and Estrella, the third he could not identify any further than that it was male. Makana moved around and squatted down to look through the side window at the driver. Mourad's family would not recognise their son. Reaching through, Makana rummaged through his pockets until he found what he was looking for: a wallet with an identity card in it. It seemed a sad end to the young man's dreams of changing the world for the better. It was a dismal task and the stench drove Makana back a couple of paces. He reached for a cigarette to fight the nausea crawling in his gullet.

'Isn't it facing the wrong way?' Sami asked. 'I mean, if they were going towards the border, they should be facing in the other direction.'

Makana looked from the crushed minibus to the sandy track. A set of wide tyre tracks cut across. A heavy jeep had turned around here.

'They were trying to escape. My guess is they ran into an army patrol and tried to get away. The soldiers chased after them. They were driving too fast. They lost control.'

The rest was obvious. The light minibus had slammed into a rock and then rolled. The driver and both passengers must have been killed at once. Makana moved back to the vehicle. There was a bullet hole in the side, which might have sparked the accident. Certainly it proved that the soldiers had fired at them. Through a cracked window he saw that Estrella still wore the silver Ethiopian cross like her mother's, the one she had been wearing when he had first seen her. He reached in to remove it.

'Is that Mourad?' Sami nodded at the driver.

'I'm afraid so.'

'I don't get it. Why leave them out here?'

'A warning perhaps, to others thinking of trying the same route.' Makana straightened up and looked at the horizon. It was one explanation, but out here it was anyone's guess. Shooting unarmed civilians was surely not an official policy. More than likely it was a group of trigger-happy kids, soldiers who got carried away with a chase. It was that easy, and that pointless.

Chapter Thirty-five

Heavy traffic turned the journey back into an ordeal, but all tedium was overshadowed by what they had just witnessed. There was almost no conversation between them, each trapped in his own thoughts. The search for Mourad had come to an end. All that remained was to break the news to his family. There seemed no point in prolonging their agony.

As they progressed in fits and starts, Makana called Okasha and filled him in about their day. Sami had fixed the spot where they had found the Toyota using his telephone.

'I'll text you the grid reference.'

'That would be helpful. I'll make some inquiries, find out exactly what happened.' Makana didn't believe anything would come of it, but there was nothing wrong with letting him try. At least that way the army would know they couldn't just do what they liked. Sami was going to write about the matter too, he was willing to bet, and that might change things.

'There's one other thing you can do for me.'

'As if I haven't done enough for you already. I can just give up my position and devote my time to assisting you.'

'Mustafa Alwan has a son. The boy has something wrong with him.'

'Why is this of any importance?'

'The boy needed an operation. Alwan, despite what he was earning on the side, could never afford to pay for something like that. The Hesira Institute promised to perform the operation, but then delayed. Alwan got fed up. He thought they were stringing him along, so he threatened to go to the press.'

'The press? This makes no sense. What was he going to tell them?'

'We didn't get that far.'

'Well, he's still in a coma.'

'Is his wife at the hospital with him? Maybe you can ask one of your men to check with her. I'd like to confirm what kind of treatment the boy requires.'

Okasha promised to do his best. Makana rang off and told Sindbad to take him to the Verdi Gardens. On the way through town they dropped Sami off.

'Are you sure you don't want me to come along?' he asked as he climbed out.

'And do what?'

'You're right. It was just a thought.'

Makana watched him pick his way through the lanes of traffic, the crushed, tilted metal, the wheezing engines and thick gusts of foul black smoke. This city could swallow a man whole, but he still hoped Sami would do the right thing and repair things with Rania.

The Hafiz family seemed to sense bad news. Perhaps it was written too clearly on Makana's face, but Mrs Hafiz burst into tears and had to be led away by her daughter. Mr Hafiz gestured at the large round table in the centre of the room and asked him to be seated.

'It's not good news, I'm afraid.'

'No matter how much you try to prepare yourself, it's never enough.' Hassan Hafiz sniffed. He took a napkin from the next table and wiped his eyes. 'Tell me what happened.'

So Makana told him, as much as he had managed to piece together. Mourad and his friends had been running a freedom train, helping people less fortunate than themselves to escape this country in the hope that they might start a new life elsewhere.

'He was a brave boy,' nodded the father.

'I think so.'

'Never turned his back, always went straight on with his head held high.'

It was certainly a risky undertaking, and a credit to the young man's conviction that he went through with it.

The only person who could tell them how many people they had helped over the border was Fadihah, and with Hakim still on the loose, it was important they tried to find her.

'I have passed the details to a contact in the police force who will make sure that the remains are recovered and brought back here.'

'That is kind of you.' Hafiz looked down at his hands. 'I owe you some money, I'm sorry, my mind.'

'Don't worry about it. We can settle that another day.' Makana was uncomfortable taking money from a man he had just informed of his son's death. It would have to wait.

'Thank you, for being so understanding, and for all you have done.'

'I'm only sorry it couldn't have ended in a better way.'

Hafiz nodded, more to himself than to Makana, and shuffled away down the room. Makana sat for a time in the empty restaurant and then decided that perhaps it was time to take himself off. Okasha called back as he was getting into the Datsun.

'I heard back from the officer at the hospital. It seems that Mustafa Alwan's son has a chronic condition. His liver is failing. He'll die unless he gets a transplant, which pretty much means he's done for. Unless he gets a new liver, of course.'

'That's what Alwan was promised.'

This confirmed what he had been told. It also went along with Jehan's analysis of the boy's condition from

Makana's description. Was this what Liz Corbis had been hinting about when she talked about sacrifice? She didn't mean the parents literally sacrificed themselves, but that they benefited from somebody else's sacrifice. To perform a transplant you needed a donor, and as far as Makana knew, a liver donor didn't walk away from the operation. The Hesira Institute was saving the lives of rich Westerners by the sacrifice of the less privileged.

'That's what they're doing. That's what Beatrice was running away from.' Makana rang off and tried to think of his next move. They had stopped at a roadside shack for something to eat. When he looked up Sindbad was holding out a sandwich.

'What is this?'

'Liver. They do it the Alexandrian way with lots of chilli.'

'Not tonight,' Makana handed it back.

'I thought you liked liver. You want kidneys instead?'

'Just eat your sandwich and then take me up to the mosque.'

It was close to midnight. The maidan in front of the Mustafa Mahmoud mosque was flooded with light from the lamps that illuminated the white walls. In the harsh glow the makeshift camp looked more wretched than ever. The police presence had swollen overnight. There were now thousands of policemen and security officers milling around. A wall of vans and buses had been brought in. It looked as though they were getting ready to clear the camp. The atmosphere was a lot more tense than it had been the last time he was here. Off to one side he glimpsed officers mounted on horses jostling with protesters, pushing them back, as if trying to provoke a reaction.

In all the confusion, it was somehow easier for Makana to push his way through. Within the cordon there was an air of rising panic. Children were crying. Men and women stood holding younger ones, clutching babies in their arms. The tense expressions on their faces reflected the uncertainty. Some rushed about trying to find a safe spot to shelter, but there was nowhere left to go. Everybody seemed to be on the move. Indeed, the whole camp seemed to be trying to lift and transform itself. Everywhere tents were collapsing, shelters trampled and tripped over. They came apart producing a layer of debris that flowed underfoot. Over the heads of the crowd Makana glimpsed the blunt snout of a high-sided armoured vehicle with a water cannon mounted on the roof. He pushed his way through. You had to be aggressive or you would be swept aside. Just to stay upright was a challenge, never mind actually finding someone. By some miracle he caught sight of Aljuka, an image of stillness amidst the mayhem, issuing orders to his men. He saw Makana but ignored him until he was standing in front of him.

'You chose the wrong time to come back, brother,' he snarled.

'They're going to clear you out. You should comply.'

'And go where?' Aljuka was breathing hard. 'What do you think they will do? Imprison us, take us to the border, dump us in the desert? We know all their tricks.'

'People are going to get hurt.'

'They are already hurting,' Aljuka yelled. 'We didn't ask for this battle but they refuse to treat us like human beings. We have no choice.' He shook his head in incomprehension. 'You don't have to be here. Did you come to watch us die?'

'I found Beatrice and Estrella.'

Aljuka's face darkened. 'You found them where?'

'In the desert. They're not coming back.'

Aljuka said nothing. He looked down at the ground for a moment before his eyes returned to Makana.

'She's dead?'

'Estrella? Yes, she's dead.' Somebody crashed into Makana and he stepped aside, moving closer to Aljuka. The noise around them was increasing. 'Are you the father of her child? Is that why you were trying to protect her?'

Aljuka snorted. 'She wasn't pregnant. That was just a story she told that crazy preacher and his sister. She faked the sample.'

'You mean Preston and Liz Corbis.'

Aljuka nodded. 'Beatrice and her brother escaped. Jonah never made it, but Beatrice managed to get here. She wanted to see Estrella. Still, it wasn't safe. Those two policemen were looking for her. I promised to help them, but

Estrella refused to listen. She was headstrong.' He allowed himself a smile, and for the first time Makana saw a gentleness to him.

'She had found a way out of her own. Mourad had promised to get them both to Israel.'

Aljuka nodded. 'She wanted to do things her own way.'

'You knew what was going on at that clinic, yet you let Corbis and his sister still work among your people?'

'They provide useful medical services. But don't worry. When the time comes they will pay.' He drew a hand across his throat.

'You cared about her.'

'Estrella? I would have done anything for her. I've known her since she was a kid. We grew up in the same streets.'

'Tell me about Beatrice. What happened to her?'

'She showed up one night, scared out of her mind. Nobody knew where she'd come from. She was supposed to be on her way to America.'

'With her brother Jonah.'

'Exactly, only there was no America. No happy family waiting for them. It was all a lie.'

'What did she say?'

'It was crazy. Unbelievable. Like something out of a film. She said they were drugged. When they woke up they were in this place, underground. There were bodies all around, like in a hospital. All unconscious or dead, she didn't know. Jonah was there. He helped her up. She could hardly walk. They managed to escape, I don't know how.

411

Then they were running down the road, she said, just running and running.'

'Where were they, did she say?'

'No.' Aljuka was growing impatient, his attention drawn to the battle building up around him. His men were imploring him to move. There were things to be done, preparations.

'Wait,' Makana said. 'What else? What else did she say?'

'She said they wanted to cut her open and take her heart. She was hysterical. It didn't make a lot of sense. I told you, it's crazy. They were caught and taken to a small room. They were locked up, but Jonah helped her to climb up the wall and get out. She never saw him again.'

The clamour of the clash was growing. Aljuka was in a hurry to get back to the battle.

As he went to turn away, Makana grabbed Aljuka's arm to stop him. He felt himself seized from behind and lifted into the air, immobilised, his feet off the ground. Aljuka stepped closer.

'This isn't your battle. Go back to your Egyptian friends.'

There was a roar from somewhere off to the right. Makana saw batons rising in the air like branches in a storm. The water cannon opened up. A solid jet of water shot out over the heads of the crowd, provoking wails and screams. Aljuka was issuing orders. His men went left and right. Makana was forgotten. He turned and began struggling out of the mayhem. Nobody paid him any attention now. People had other concerns. The riot-police batons were being met by makeshift weapons. The cries and screams multiplied, grew more intense. Over the top of everything the powerful jets of water hissed, sending protesters flying backwards, sprawling to the ground. Already the CSF were breaking through, dragging people away – a woman, a young child – picking off the weaker ones the way a predator attacks a herd.

Makana stumbled on, the crowd thickening about him. It seemed to harden towards the edges as it met resistance. The police were fencing them in from the outside. Rows of men in riot gear were advancing, shields and batons held aloft. He could see people being loaded into buses on one of the sidestreets. Sirens were going off in every direction. A man clutching a bloody rag to his head stumbled into him before careening off into the turmoil. Fighting a rising sense of panic, Makana roughly pushed his way back and in the opposite direction until a gap opened up and he managed to slip through the police lines. He reached the line of lock-up vans and commandeered buses where people were being shepherded into cowering huddles.

'Where are they taking them?'

'Back to where they belong,' replied one policeman leaning on his baton.

The violence kept pushing him along. Even if he had wanted to get back to the centre he couldn't have. He had no idea if Fantômas was in there somewhere. Looking back he could see the stream of water playing over the heads of the crowd. It slowed to a trickle, allowing a moment of respite before launching another powerful spurt that knocked people onto their backs. Four CSF men dragged a man backwards up the road past him. They paused to turn and pummel him with their boots and shields. Makana stepped towards them but an officer blocked his path.

'Don't get involved,' he said with a smile. 'Just go on your way. Just keep walking.'

Flashing symbols on his phone told him that someone had tried to call and left a voice message for him. Makana fiddled with the instrument, trying to figure out how to retrieve it. After several attempts, he finally managed to hit the right combination of buttons and was rewarded with the sound of Jehan's voice.

'Where are you?' she asked immediately. 'I hate leaving messages, but I have no choice. I wanted to ask you about something. I have a feeling I know what they are up to at the Hesira Institute. I'm going to go over there and talk to Ihsan. After this you'll have to officially promote me to your assistant.' The sound of her laughter echoed in his ear long after the message had ended. He tried to call her back but only got the annoyingly tinny voice of a woman telling him that the number was unavailable.

Chapter Thirty-six

The Hesira Institute was dark at that hour. The statue of the clinic's namesake that stood in the forecourt was lit up by spotlights. He appeared to hover in the dark air like an ethereal presence. Liz Corbis had been asleep when he called. He explained that he needed her help.

'Now? But it's almost two in the morning.'

'I'm afraid things are moving quickly and I'm worried that one of my friends might be in danger.'

'And you think I can help?'

'I hope so. I need to get into the Institute.'

'Tonight?' She sounded incredulous, but at the same time he thought he detected a tremor of excitement in her voice. She directed him to a side entrance that avoided the main lobby and accessed the grounds through a door set into the high surrounding wall.

'This is the way we come in usually, so we don't have to use the front entrance all the time. It's more discreet.'

She was talking quickly in a low voice and seemed nervous, struggling with the key to lock the door again. Dr Corbis was wearing some kind of tracksuit that she seemed to have pulled on over her nightclothes. The collar of a pyjama top stuck up awkwardly at the back of her neck.

'I'm not sure I should be doing this.'

'I appreciate it.'

Liz Corbis looked at him. They stood in the garden, between high rhododendron bushes that stirred gently in the night air. To the right the main building was lost in shadows, except for minimal security lighting here and there in the darkened lobby and by the stairwell.

'What exactly is it that you think is going on here?'

'I'm not sure it's going to make much sense, but before I tell you any more I need to access the files again.'

'You mean *our* files?' He could see her beginning to shy away.

'Please, bear with me. You may not want to hear this, but I think you need to listen to what I have to say.'

'I'm listening.' Her voice had gone slack, her eyes were flat.

'Tell me, how much contact do you have with your angels, as you call them, once they are placed with a family?'

'Me personally, almost none. Preston takes care of the follow-up. I don't really have the time. Why do you ask?'

'I mean, if you have no contact with them, how do you know if the match has been a success?'

'Oh, if it wasn't we would hear about it. And like I said, Preston is in contact with the families. It's entirely up to them, but their feedback is useful, especially for fund-raising purposes. We want to show that the project is a success.'

'But it's your brother who deals with all of that.'

Tight-lipped, Liz Corbis gave a brief nod.

'Many don't want to. I understand that. They want to work on building a solid relationship.'

'So you have no actual proof that they are safely with their adoptive families?'

'In some cases we do, but often it's nothing more than a thank-you letter. Sometimes they send pictures, you know, like the ones in the church.'

'Of course, but it's quite irregular. Isn't it odd that there is no administrative check?' Makana said. 'I mean, otherwise they could almost disappear off the face of the earth.'

Liz Corbis grew still. 'I'm not sure I see what you're getting at.'

'The girl I was looking for, Beatrice? She and her brother Jonah were on your programme.'

'Right. We talked about them.'

'Well, according to your records they should be in America by now. Only they're not. Both of them are in this country still, and both of them are dead.'

'That can't be. There must be some mistake.'

'What percentage of the candidates would you say have sent firm proof of their new life?'

417

'I'd have to check, but off the top of my head I'd say fifteen, twenty per cent.'

'So, for the other eighty per cent you have nothing.'

'Like I say, I'd have to check.'

'Can we do that?'

'Now?' Liz Corbis glanced around her as if suddenly unsure of where she was. She swallowed. 'Okay, let's do it. I won't be able to sleep after this anyway.'

'Thank you,' he said.

Without another word she led the way towards the main building. Through the glass the lobby was dark and deserted. Makana was trying to think where Jehan might be. He felt sure she was somewhere in the building.

'Usually there's a nightwatchman, but he goes off to sleep for a few hours when he knows he won't be disturbed.'

She struggled with a key, and then the door opened and they slipped inside. In darkness, the cavernous space of the lobby seemed to rise up above them with the weight and depth of a temple. Another key unlocked the door to the stairwell, where emergency lighting illuminated the way. She looked back at him as they descended.

'Perhaps you should tell me everything you know.'

Makana explained what he knew. The accident on the road. The dead man in the locker. The dismembered body in the palace. Someone was going to a lot of trouble to get rid of the evidence.

'But evidence of what?'

'Of what Doctor Qaddus has really been using this place for.'

418

By now they had reached the lower level. The door opened to reveal the mural that covered the opposite wall. Anubis, the jackal-headed god, leaning over the body of the king. It seemed all the more appropriate now, Anubis removing the pharaoh's vital organs. Not a mortuary at all, but something much more.

'I asked myself, why go to the trouble of having a crematorium, of burning bodies in a furnace? Why not just bury them somewhere?'

'Why do you think that is?'

'Evidence. Concealing the fact that they'd been tampered with, that vital organs had been harvested from them.'

Liz Corbis stopped dead. 'You can't mean that? But how?'

'Let's check your records first, and then I need to find Ihsan Qaddus.'

'You'd better be sure of your case, because he's not the kind of guy who will take an accusation like that lying down. You'll find yourself up to your neck in lawsuits. You're going to need a good lawyer.'

'A lawyer is going to be the least of my worries,' said Makana.

'This woman, the doctor, what is your relationship to her?'

Makana looked at her. It wasn't a question he had anticipated. They were by the door to the office now, and Liz Corbis was trying to find the right key. She seemed to be taking her time, waiting for an answer. He thought about answering the question. What was his relationship to Jehan? It seemed hardly fair to even use the word relationship, and yet Makana was aware of something quickening out of the ether of the void in which he had lived for almost fifteen years.

419

'We're colleagues,' he said quickly. The nod he received in return was as convincing as his answer. Thankfully the door opened and in a moment they were seated at the desk with the computer blinking into life.

'Now, let's see.' She clicked buttons and tapped her fingers impatiently. Makana longed for a cigarette, but it had been a long day and he had none. 'You do understand the implications of what you are saying? If what you say is true then it would destroy our Homehavens Project. My brother and I would be implicated.'

'You can prove that you were unaware. Ihsan Qaddus has been exploiting you.'

'He has powerful friends in this country.'

'They're not going to be able to help him. This is going to be an international scandal. His friends will wash their hands of him.' Makana dragged his eyes from the screen to look sideways at her. 'It could be bad for you and your brother, though.'

She gave him a brave smile. 'If what you say is true and I don't do something about it, how do you suppose I shall live with myself?'

He couldn't really argue with that. The computer was busy going through its start-up sequence. Impatient, she got to her feet and began pacing the room behind him.

'I really can't take in what you are telling me. I mean, I need to see proof.'

'And you think you can find that in here?' Makana nodded at the screen. It was now running through some kind of virus scan. He looked at his watch. Wherever she was, Jehan could be in danger, but he couldn't risk confronting Ihsan Qaddus unless he had proof.

'I've just had a terrible thought. Do you think my brother could be involved in this?'

Makana sighed. 'I don't know, but it would be hard to explain this happening without him having some knowledge, don't you think?'

'That's what I was afraid you would say.'

There was something wrong about the tone of her voice. And something else. Something he should have noticed earlier. A detail, nothing more, but it had slipped by because he had been distracted.

'I never said that the person I was concerned about was a woman. How did you know?'

He caught a glimpse of something, a flicker of movement in the glass of the computer screen as it darkened briefly before turning bright again. Nothing more than a shadow, but it was enough. Even as he began to turn, he knew it was too late. He felt the needle go in as he threw himself backwards. The chair skittered back to hit the wall. She had stepped neatly out of the way. He tried to stand, tried to reach round to grasp the syringe, but couldn't do it. Liz Corbis was pressed into the corner, as far away from him as possible. He felt the blackness surging through his veins, felt his legs go numb, then his spine. The room spun away and the floor came up to meet him. Then he was lying there staring up at the cold white lights.

Chapter Thirty-seven

Although he could not move, Makana was aware of things going on around him. He had the sense that he was moving, sliding smoothly over the tiled floor. He seemed to be floating. Lights above him flickered by in quick succession. Then darkness again. A long corridor, followed by a door opening and more space filled with bright light and the hum of air conditioning, machinery. A highly modern room, or series of anterooms. The sound of voices. The smell. Antiseptic. Cleaning fluids. Plastic. Steel. He was left alone at intervals, in a dimmed alcove where the light was low. More voices nearby. Faces floated in, peering down at him. Some wore masks. A needle was slipped into his arm. He could not move anything, not even turn his head. He wasn't even blinking. He couldn't seem to close his eyes. Voices grew muffled. There was more movement nearby. The sound of another stretcher rolling by. A woman came into his field of vision. She leaned over and began stripping off his jacket and shirt, cutting the clothes off him with a pair of scissors. This struck him as a terrible shame. He liked that jacket. Scissors snipped. Compressed air hissed through a tube just behind him and the electronic beep of machinery came from somewhere. His hearing seemed to be enhanced. He was inside a large steel machine that hummed around him. Red and green eyes flashed off to his left. More movement. More voices. How long had passed? Then he was rolling again, being transferred to another room. The single eye of a powerful white light glared down at him from above. Ra, the Sun God, flying majestically across the heavens. He was on his way down, down into the Underworld. In this room he felt cold. The harsh reek of antiseptic cleaning fluids filled his nostrils, a nauseating smell that he associated with mortuaries and death. Oddly, he felt no panic. Where was Jehan? She was in danger, but he couldn't see how to help her. Failure, yet again, to protect those he cared about.

Although his eyes were open he felt strangely helpless, as if pinned down by a huge hand. When he tried to move he found that he had difficulty even feeling his limbs. He couldn't sense any restraints on him, only a tingling sensation all over his body. With some effort he managed to turn his head slightly, and then his eyes could pick out something lying under a green sheet on a table alongside him. At the top end of this emerged the head of a woman.

Strands of dyed blonde hair, grey at the roots, protruded from underneath the cap pulled down over her skull. A woman he had seen before. The old lady he had seen being helped around the swimming pool.

There were muffled voices coming from somewhere close at hand. Beyond the woman, through an open doorway he saw people moving in some kind of adjacent space. They were visible through a couple of glass panels on a pair of doors. They looked as though they were preparing for something. At last it occurred to him where he was. This was an operating theatre. They were doctors and nurses. How long had he been out. An hour? More? Less? More important, how much time did he have?

Out of the blur a face appeared above him. Upside down. A man wearing a green cloth-cap and green clothes. He pulled down the mask to reveal his face.

'Can you hear me, Mr Makana?' Ihsan Qaddus asked. It was a rhetorical question. He nodded gently before going on. 'Well, clearly it's a shame to meet again under these circumstances, but there you have it. Actually, more of a shame for you than for me, and as for Mrs Hollister here, she is delighted you could make it, also that you could spare a couple of kidneys for her failing one. Her body is basically shutting down, one organ at a time, but Mr Hollister left her enough money to replace them as they go. So, a very important client. And that is what this is all about, keeping the clients satisfied.' A muffled voice said something and Qaddus broke off to issue orders to an assistant, also wearing a surgical mask.

'You are persistent, I give you that. But if you had not forced her hand, Liz would perhaps not have felt compelled to act. She doesn't like violence as a rule, prefers to see herself as somewhat removed from the sacrifices that must be made.

'Speaking for myself, I find it hard to understand what motivates a man like yourself. If it's money then clearly you have not been very successful. A matter of principle, then? Perhaps, but who really cares about such things in this day and age? People have a hard enough time getting from day to day. And our patients have a right to a better quality of life, don't they? Think of it as something like an extension of natural selection. I'm a man of science, as you can imagine. Darwin, surely, would understand that wealth is now a factor in our survival.'

Makana became aware of the other person moving around behind Qaddus. A woman dressed in green surgical scrubs and a mask, preparing instruments. Qaddus was still talking.

'In a world of diminishing resources we live on because we can afford to do so. Even more telling is the question of how the rich became rich and the poor remained poor, don't you think? Do you really believe that nameless, forgotten refugees, people without a home, or a family, at the bottom of the food chain, as it were, that they really deserve a better fate? Their sacrifice goes to the greater good of the human race. Can you not follow the argument that I am simply an instrument of Darwinism?'

Ihsan Qaddus smiled to himself. Again, the handsome face and the perfect teeth. Makana was reminded of Jehan. And where was she? He had made a mistake and once more it seemed somebody else was going to pay for that. The anger fizzed inside him like a tonic, striving against the despair. He would have liked to hit Ihsan Qaddus hard enough to rearrange those perfect teeth, but something told him it wasn't going to happen any time soon.

'Doctor,' Qaddus addressed his assistant. 'Perhaps you'd care to observe.' He leaned forward over Makana. 'I have one last surprise for you, an acquaintance of yours. I think you will be amused, and don't worry, this isn't going to hurt. If it makes you feel any better, think of it as your sacrifice for the greater good.'

Makana felt his heart lurch as the assistant pulled down her mask to reveal herself as Jehan.

'I thought you'd like that. How poor we are at judging even people we feel we know well.'

A mixture of anger and disbelief coursed through Makana's veins. Whatever might have happened next was interrupted by the sound of an alarm somewhere. Ihsan Qaddus yelled out:

'Somebody see to that please!'

'It's the fire alarm,' one of the nurses said.

'Well, switch it off before it brings the fire brigade. That's all we need.' With a tut of annoyance Qaddus pulled off his gloves and headed for the door. 'Why do I have to take care of everything myself?'

There was a long silence. The alarm was still ringing. It was loud and insistent and helped to arouse Makana. He thought about trying to make a move. If he could tip himself off the stretcher, that might jolt him awake. It might also kill him, but that was a chance he had to take. The masked face of the assistant floated into view. Makana tried to wriggle away, without much success. He had never felt so helpless. Jehan leaned over him.

He watched as she held a syringe up, squirting fluid into the air before bending over to insert it into his arm. Now he could smell her cologne. She straightened up.

'It'll take a few moments. You should try to sit up. The more you move the faster it will start to work.' She leaned over and put her arms around him. It struck Makana that this was a strange sort of embrace upon which to embark on a relationship. She managed somehow to bring him upright.

'Stay there.' Jehan smiled at him. 'You've looked better, but let's deal with that later. Can you stand?'

Could he? His bones seemed to have dissolved. He slipped and crashed into the next stretcher, knocking Mrs Hollister sideways. She sighed, as if in the midst of a pleasant dream, but otherwise did not stir. Jehan draped an arm around his shoulders and together they started to walk, taking tiny steps. There was an emergency staircase to the left of the operating theatre. They managed to get through that. Then the alarm cut out and there was silence. It wouldn't be long before they were caught. Makana tried to will his feet to move. He was shuffling like a geriatric and had trouble controlling his movements. One foot crashed into the railing and he felt a jolt, which had to be good news. Feeling was coming back.

'I thought . . .'

'Don't talk. Try to conserve your energy.'

'How?' he managed to say. 'Fire alarm?'

'I lit one of your precious Cleopatras and attached it to a smoke alarm. Now, save your energy for walking.' She looked at him and then relented as they started to climb the stairs.

'I thought about everything you'd told me and I figured out that something was very wrong and that it was centred here. So I went to see Ihsan. I told him that I had worked out what he was up to and that I was interested in working for him. He was flattered. He's so vain he probably thought I was still chasing after him, though God knows we're not twenty-five any longer.' She stopped talking as Makana lost his grip and started to swing backwards. He felt like an old man trying to climb a mountain. Ridiculous. Helped by a woman, not even wearing a shirt. He had no pride left to be wounded. They resumed their upward movement. By now the sounds of shouts could be heard from below. How long before somebody thought to look at the emergency stairs? By some miracle they reached the floor above and pushed open the bar. Jehan looked out cautiously, Makana swaying, one hand flat against the wall. He was capable of moving, but overestimated the speed of his recovery. When Jehan beckoned he moved, took two steps and sprawled at her feet. She bent over him and was struggling with his full weight, trying to turn him over, when the sound of laughter came from behind them. Jehan stopped struggling. Ihsan Qaddus appeared from the stairwell behind them. He wasn't even breathing hard. He was, however, carrying a gun. A neat silver automatic that looked modern and highly efficient.

'This is really not something I would have imagined of you, Jehan.'

'I'm sorry to be such a disappointment.'

'Not at all, it shows that my instincts were right, all those years ago.' The smile on his face was that of a man who is in no doubt of his superiority. 'You were not destined for great things. You lack courage and vision, far too conventional. Your mind is stuck in the past. That's why your husband killed himself, isn't it? He couldn't stand living with you.' Ihsan Qaddus shook his head. 'Who can blame him? I might have had the same crisis of faith if I had stayed with you.'

'That's generous of you to say,' Jehan muttered. Makana managed to roll himself into an upright position. With a look of derision Qaddus wagged the gun.

'Still, I thought we might have some fun before that high and mighty moral code of yours began to assert itself.'

'You were always too in love with yourself to ever care about anyone else.'

'Well, I'm sorry you feel that way.'

'What happens now?' Makana said, the words coming slowly. He sounded drunk.

'Ah, look, it speaks. What am I going to do, did you say? I'm going to finish what I started. Mrs Hollister gets her kidneys and then we will see. You'll be glad to hear that our incinerator has been repaired, so now the cremation process can continue as before. I think it's safe to say that nobody will miss you.'

'What are you going to do with them?' A voice spoke in English.

The three of them turned to see Liz Corbis. She stood in the middle of the darkened lobby. She was dressed to travel it seemed. A little way behind her the large figure of the priest stood oddly bowed, fidgeting, a suitcase in each hand weighing him down. Ihsan Qaddus smiled.

'Don't worry yourself about that, my dear, just run along and catch your plane. By the time you are enjoying your glass of champagne the whole matter will be behind us.'

'Listen to what he says, Liz,' Makana gasped. 'He won't hesitate to kill you if he has to.'

'I don't believe it. You wouldn't hurt me, would you?' She faced Qaddus, shaking her head as if trying to convince herself of her words. 'There's always been a complicity between us, Ihsan. You understand why I can't let you kill them. Helping people to a better life is one thing. I can see the logic of it, but this . . . killing them for no reason. That's wrong.'

430

'Listen to yourself.' Ihsan smiled slowly. 'How naïve you sound. What do you think you've been involved with all this time? Some kind of mission of mercy?'

'I'm not leaving until you let them go.'

'Come on, Elizabeth, for God's sake!' Preston Corbis urged.

'Listen to your brother, Liz. He's urging you to walk away from this. There's too much at stake, for all of us.'

'I didn't sign up for this.' She stood upright and steady but a flutter in her voice betrayed her.

'Perhaps not, but you are part of it. You can't just change your mind now, you're in too deep. Think of all that money you have tucked away. A life of luxury in any part of the world you care to choose.'

'I'm not running away. I won't let you hurt him.'

'Him, really, is this about him?' Ihsan Qaddus wagged his head in wonder. 'There must be something about you, Makana, to have all these women fighting over you.'

'I mean it, Ihsan. There's a line, and this is it.'

Qaddus tilted his head to one side. 'And what are you going to do, if I refuse?'

'Lizzy, come on. We have to go. Now.'

Liz Corbis didn't even look back at her brother. Instead she took a step towards Qaddus. 'I'm not proud of what I've done, but we did it for a reason. We were saving lives, remember? It was about quality of life.'

'And you saw some noble purpose to your life. I understand. The idea of profit disgusts you. Fine. Then go, leave, walk away.' Ihsan Qaddus lowered the gun slightly and wagged it at the priest. 'Take your sister away, Preston, before it's too late. Get her in the car and get her out of the country. I never want to see her here again.'

Preston Corbis finally managed to stir himself. He set down the suitcases and moved towards his sister.

'Come along, Lizzy. There's nothing more for us here. It's over.'

'Yes, run along, Lizzy,' Ihsan Qaddus sneered. 'See if you can make a life for yourself.'

Preston Corbis went to grab his sister's arm, but she tore free. She continued to advance on Ihsan Qaddus. Makana rolled his feet underneath him. He couldn't get his legs to obey him. Qaddus wasn't paying him any attention. His eyes were on Liz Corbis. He took a step backwards. His voice hardened.

'I'm warning you, Liz. Don't make me hurt you.'

'You could never hurt me,' she said, throwing herself forward. She went for his gun hand, which was probably a mistake. Makana got his feet under him as they struggled. He didn't exactly sprint but rather shuffled towards them. He was halfway there when the gun went off. He heard Preston Corbis give a cry of disbelief as his sister slid to the floor.

'Lizzy!' Preston Corbis knelt beside his sister. Her eyes fluttered towards the ceiling and then she was still. Blood pooled underneath her across the smooth marble.

'Stupid woman!' shouted Ihsan Qaddus. 'Why couldn't you just listen to me?'

He was still shouting when Makana hit him with all his weight. It wasn't much of a blow, but it knocked him off balance and the gun skittered away across the floor. Preston Corbis rose up and started to back away. The look on his face was that of a man whose faith had deserted him. He ran for the door. Makana, catching sight of the battered Datsun and the large figure climbing out of the driver's seat, signalled to Sindbad to stop the fleeing priest. For his part, Reverend Corbis did try to throw a punch, but Sindbad caught it easily in one hand and twisted the American over the car bonnet. There were already sirens in the distance.

Ihsan Qaddus was scrabbling towards the door. Jehan picked up the gun and followed him.

'There's nowhere left for you to run,' she said. 'Don't tempt me.'

Qaddus slid round on the floor and lifted his hands in a gesture of despair.

Chapter Thirty-eight

Sami was waiting for him in the El Horreya. He sat in the back, close to the wall. Makana was encouraged to see that he was drinking tea rather than beer, since this was one of his old haunts. At the table next to them two old men were arguing over a chessboard. One of them, white-haired and wearing an eyepatch, appeared to be trying to teach his opponent how to play. Every time he made a move he would tell him it was a mistake. The other man frowned at the board in confusion. Makana knew the feeling well.

'Where did you stay last night?'

'A friend lent me his apartment. He's gone to Amman for a holiday. Who has time for holidays anyway, and why Amman?'

The boy who was serving passed by. He paused, tray on one shoulder, rapping his knuckles on the table. Makana ordered coffee, strong and no sugar.

'You heard about last night?' Sami asked, folding his newspaper. 'They're trying to keep the number of casualties down, but it's not going to work.'

The battle outside the Mustafa Mahmoud mosque had dominated the day's news. The number of casualties reported varied from twenty to almost thirty. Nobody knew for sure. What was clear was that a number of those killed had been children.

'This is a turning point. I can feel it.'

At the next table the aspiring player announced checkmate. His white-haired opponent chuckled to himself.

'They've crossed a line.' Sami lowered his voice, glancing over at the nearby table, and got a glare from the man in the eyepatch. 'It shows how desperate they are.'

They being the regime. Images of the camp in tatters had flashed around the world. It gave the impression of the regime as an ugly bully, picking on those who were incapable of defending themselves. Not that anyone was going to be brought to task. The Americans and Europeans would remain silent. Nobody wanted to risk upsetting their most important ally in the region.

'Twenty-seven dead. Eleven children. Nothing like this has ever happened before. The human rights organisations are up in arms.'

'It's a bit late for that, isn't it?' said Makana. His coffee arrived and he sipped it too quickly, scalding his mouth.

'This thing makes me so angry, I need to write about it.'

'Sounds like the old Sami.'

Sami sat back. 'Yes, maybe it is.'

Makana considered the case of Aljuka and his men. The bulk of the protesters had been dumped at a camp somewhere in the sand to the east of Cairo. According to Fantômas, Aljuka was leading a group of them back to the city, which summoned the image of Moses.

They left the café and walked for some time in silence. The city surged around them, jostling, finding its form as if changing its shape with the light. The markets behind the Ghouriyya were choked with merchants and customers, brushing past one another. Hefty women balancing crates of bread on their heads, young men with arms like taut cables, hauling sacks of goodness knows what to who knew where. Trolleys, bicycles, the smell of spices, sweat and rotting fruit. As if life was a feast that no one had the time to stop and enjoy.

It would be fair to say that Aswani had not quite embraced the concept of Chicken Kiev. He pulled a face, his moustaches curling downwards in disapproval. It wasn't that he was averse to the idea of new things. He actually considered himself something of a dab hand at throwing things together in his own inimitable fashion. Perhaps it was the name, or the idea of something coming from abroad. It

436

might simply have been the way Makana explained it. And although he claimed not to like pretentious food, but preferred good honest dishes, as he put it, he had put a remarkable amount of effort into a dish he had modestly dubbed Chicken Aswani.

'What's in it?' Makana asked when a hefty platter was set before him.

Aswani hissed, as touchy as a ballerina. 'You ask that? You think they pepper the chef with questions in those fancy French places you have been frequenting? Naturally, they do not. They eat, they enjoy.' The rotund cook folded his arms and waited for Makana to give his verdict.

Chicken Aswani was served on skewers. Rolls of chicken had been coated in crushed almonds and a heady blend of spices including cardamom and cloves and a dozen other things Makana could not readily identify. It was then further wrapped in sheets of salty *bastourma*. A spectacular sight, and Aswani, never a man to avoid the limelight, took a bow.

'Seems like a lot of trouble to dress up a piece of chicken, but never let it be said that I do not try to meet the tastes of my more classy customers, which would be you.'

He retired behind the counter, leaving the group staring at the table of starters and salads set before them. Aswani had clearly outdone himself. Everyone was there. Well, almost everyone. Fantômas had joined them. Rania and Sami were actually sitting next to each other, which seemed like a good sign. Makana had even managed to bring Aziza along this time, under the pretext that she was accompanying him into

437

town to help choose the material to make new covers for his divan, which was starting to look rather threadbare. Sindbad was holding forth about the terrible deeds of Hakim and Karim and how justice had finally caught up with them, as it always does with crooks like that. Hakim had been arrested trying to board a plane to Jeddah. He was charged with the murder of Abu Gomaa and Jonah, and that was just the beginning. Tom and Jerry had made a lot of enemies over the years, and new witnesses were coming forward every day. More charges related to corruption, fraud and extortion were pending. Okasha was pursuing the case with remarkable zeal, perhaps due to the fact that the rotten apples were in another department's barrel.

On the other hand, it looked as though no charges would be brought against Omar Shaddad, who had pleaded ignorance of all that went on in his basement. His powerful friends included Munir Abaza, whose legal firm was defending him. Amir Medani was preparing a case against the border guards for unlawful killing and the case was drawing a lot of attention in the international press. An investigation was under way. As for Mustafa Alwan, he was still in a coma. His prospects did not look good, but Jehan was looking into the possibility of helping his son get treatment abroad, which was something. Fadihah had come forward when she heard about Mourad's death from his sister Sahar. She had been living rough on the streets. After what she witnessed in the old palace she had been too scared to go back home or anywhere she was known. There was something unfair, it seemed to Makana, about the fact that the three young people had paid such a high price for their courage and conviction. However misguided they might have been, they had wanted to change the world for the better, and surely that counted for something.

Liz Corbis was recovering from her injuries at the American embassy where she and her brother were being held. A team from the FBI had flown in to question them and they would be repatriated to face charges in the United States as soon as she was fit to travel. Makana felt sorry for her in a way, despite everything. She had been a victim of her own misguided principles. That and being unable to stand up to her brother and Ihsan Qaddus.

Aswani's boys appeared at regular intervals, bearing huge platters of rice and roast meats, vegetables from the grill, and more of the Chicken Aswani; stuffed peppers and one of his pastries, the dough fine enough to dress a bride on her wedding night, as he liked to put it, inside was a succulent mix of quail meat and dried apricots.

While everyone was tucking into the food and commenting on the case and the way things had turned out, Aswani leaned over and whispered in Makana's ear,

'I believe there is a lady outside who wishes to speak to you.' He twirled his moustaches and raised an eyebrow with all the theatricality of a seasoned actor. The others did not seem to notice.

439

Makana slipped as discreetly as possible from the room. Outside he found Jehan waiting. She was dressed in rather sensible clothes, but still looked uncharacteristically glamorous, her hair loosely wrapped in a colourful and expensive-looking silk scarf.

'You should come in and eat something. Aswani has outdone himself.'

She smiled. 'No, I don't think so. This is where you are most at home.'

Makana hesitated. 'It's something of a tradition. I've been coming here for years.'

'And you should continue to do so.' There was a long pause. 'We don't have to like the same things, or even do everything together,' she said. 'I mean, I hate those couples who are never apart. Have no kind of life of their own.'

'Yes,' said Makana.

'We don't have to do that.'

'No.'

'You can enjoy your time with your friends, and at other times we can do other things.'

'That sounds reasonable.'

'I'm glad we see eye to eye,' she smiled.

He watched her walk away, still wondering what exactly he'd just agreed to. Then he turned and went back inside, to be met by a hearty cheer from the others.

Read on for a preview of the first Makana Investigation . . .

The Golden Scales

Prologue

Cairo, 1981

The bright light struck her full in the eyes and for an instant she was blinded, as if struck by some ancient curse. Liz Markham reared back, completely stalled by the human mass that confronted her. Her heart racing, she began to run. Her child was somewhere out there, lost in this madness.

She stumbled. Behind her she heard someone make a remark that she couldn't understand. Several other people laughed. Darting away from the eyes that seemed fixed on her, closing in from every angle, she ran on. Glancing back, certain that someone was behind her, she moved away from the hotel, pushing impatiently through the crowd of tourists and tea boys, pushing at everything, knocking over tables, sending glasses and trays flying, hearing cries of astonishment and curses. But she didn't care. All she cared about at this moment was Alice.

Where had it all gone wrong? Her life, this trip? Everything that had happened since she had arrived in Cairo had turned out differently from the way she had expected. From the moment she'd stepped off the plane and been hit by the oppressive heat, the clothes instantly sticking to her back. It was supposed to be the end of September, for Christ's sake, and it felt like the middle of July in sunny Spain. It had seemed such a good idea at the time: get away from London, with all its weary habits and old accomplices. A chance to get clean, to start a new life. But what did she know about him, really? When she first met Alice's father he was just another of those listless young men hanging round the bazaar shops selling trinkets, or so it seemed. He and his friend had trailed behind them, her and Sylvia, calling out to them. It was irritating at first, and then it became a game, a challenge. Sylvia was always up for a challenge. And where was she now? Gone. Swept away in the urgent blue clamour of an ambulance that led to the dead end of a cold, impersonal corridor in the Accident and Emergency unit. Liz knew she didn't want to end like that.

He had been so charming, so confident. For three weeks they had been inseparable. That should have been the end of it, only it wasn't. Liz had been careless. When had she not been? The entire course of her life was marked by reckless impulses. She remembered how he had led her round the city and doors fell open before them. She liked that. As if she was somebody, as if they were important.

They walked into a crowded café or restaurant and a table would be cleared for them in an instant. People bobbed their heads in respect. He had drugs too, in easy supply, and in those days that was something to consider. It wasn't meant to last. That was five years ago. It wasn't meant to change her life, but it did.

When she got back to England and discovered she was pregnant, Liz had straightened herself out for the first time in years. No booze, no smack. Clean living. She had seen enough horrors – children born without fingers – to know that she didn't want to run the risk. It didn't last, but it was something. A start, proof that she could do it if she wanted to. Alice was the best thing that had happened to her. Liz knew that it was worth it, that despite the difficulties of taking care of a small child – the tantrums, the constant demands – despite all of that, Alice made her mother want to be a better person. But she couldn't manage it in London. Too many temptations, too many open doors. Then it came to her, like a window opening in the darkness. Cairo. A new life. Why not? 'Any time you need anything, Liz, you come to me,' he had told her.

All around her the little figures spun. Monkey kings and gods shaped like dogs, baboons, crocodiles and birds, all carved from green stone, or obsidian. A window stuffed with jewellery, silver crosses   ankh, the symbol of life. Miniature pyramids; some so big you couldn't lift them with both hands and others small enough to dangle from your ears. Turquoise scarabs. A window full of chessboards. Silvery blue mother-of-pearl, shooting arrows of sparkling light. A mad funfair.

'Alice!'

Liz rushed on, her mind reeling. She turned, crashing into the arms of a woman balancing a tower of tin jugs on her head. Liz wheeled round. Nothing was as she recalled it. The streets, the noise, the leering men. It felt like a different country. Had she been so blind five years ago? So off her head that it didn't register? The bazaar she had recalled as an Aladdin's cave of glittering wonders. Now all she saw was row after row of cheap trinkets, clumsily fashioned artefacts designed to seduce the eye. To dupe rather than to satisfy the soul. The place made her sick, literally. At first she'd thought she must have eaten something that disagreed with her because she'd spent the first night crouched over the toilet bowl. Only it wasn't the food, of course, it was the drugs, or lack of them. Withdrawal symptoms. This was the first time she had really been clean since Alice was born. She'd lain in bed, feverish and weak but determined to carry on, the child tugging at her arm.

The only kindness she'd experienced here was in the warm reception given to her little girl. It was as if they recognised something in her, as if they knew Alice belonged here. Everywhere they went people smiled at the little golden-haired girl. Women, old and young, clucked and pinched her cheeks, tugged her pigtails. Men made swooping motions with their hands like birds darting around her head, making her squeal with delight. She was something of a novelty. Those were the moments when Liz had told herself everything was going to be all right. But there were other moments: when anxiety made her pace the room sleeplessly, scratching her arms, clawing at her throat, struggling to breathe in the oppressive air as the wail of yet another call to prayer echoed over the square. Moments when she thought her mission hopeless. She would never find him, or even if she did, what then? Liz was beginning to get the feeling that there was a limit to how long she could keep this up. Alice was impatient with her. As if she sensed her mother was out on a limb. Always asking questions, refusing to move, asking to be carried, clinging to her, dragging her down like a dead weight.

Then, yesterday afternoon, a man had walked straight up to Liz. No hesitation. Had he been following her? 'I help you.' He led her to a narrow doorway opening into a shadowy interior. Narrow darts of light cut through slits set high in the walls, bouncing off the polished brass and tarnished mirrors. The place was deserted but for a man sitting against the far wall. His thick, lumpy features put her in mind of a bullfrog she had once dissected in the school biology lab years ago. His eyes were like hard black rivets, almost lost in the swollen face. His hair was smoothed straight back with scented oil. His whole body gave off an aromatic air, like an ancient eastern king. On the table in front of him stood a heap of tangerines on a huge round tray of beaten bronze, like the disc of Ra the Sun God as it travels westwards across the sky.

It couldn't have been that big a place, but to her mind the distance between the door and the far corner where he sat, waiting, stretched before her into infinity, as if she was shrinking and the room growing longer even as she walked. There was movement flitting through the shadows behind him. A couple of louts hung round by a counter on the left. Nasty-looking, but Liz knew the type and wasn't particularly afraid. She caught sight of herself in the mirror above his head, and despite the dim light could see that she looked terrible. Her hair was lank and lifeless, her face filmed with sweat and the sooty grime of the streets, which turned the towels in her hotel room black every night. Her eyes were ringed with red and swollen like eggs. He gestured for her to sit and so she did. Alice pressed herself to her side. The man's ugly face creased in a smile that made her blood churn.

'Hello, little girl,' he said in English, stretching out a hand towards her daughter, fingers like plump dates. Alice shied away, pulling back, pressing herself in towards her mother. The smile waned. The fingers withdrew. The black eyes turned to Liz.

'Tell me, why do you want to find this man so badly?'

'Do you know him?'

'Yes, of course. He is . . . an associate.'

His English was not bad. In itself, this was not surprising. Everyone in the Khan al-Khalili had at least one foreign language. It was a veritable Tower of Babel.

'Associate?' Liz repeated, thinking it an odd word to use. 'Where can I find him?'

'He works for me. Or rather, he used to. Now he has . . . gone into business for himself.'

He bared his teeth in what might otherwise have been a smile and Liz felt a cold shiver run through her. Holding her gaze as the smile faded, he plucked a tangerine from the pile in front of him and handed it to the child. As she began to eat, sucking the little lobes of fruit contentedly, Liz felt uncomfortable that her daughter could so easily trust a stranger they had only just met.

'This is not your first time in Egypt?'

Liz shook her head, feeling his eyes scrutinise her, lingering on her fingernails, bitten to the quick. The raw hunger in her stare, the desperation she was unable to hide. She was reaching the end of her meagre funds. Her patience was running out. She was climbing the walls. And then there was Alice, with her constant demands for attention, for reassurances that Liz couldn't give her. The only thing that would make sense of any of this was finding him. She didn't care who helped her find him, so long as somebody did. The dark, sunken eyes met hers.

'Is he the father of this child?'

Liz hesitated, sensing that any information she gave this man would place her further in his power, but she had no choice. If she wanted to enlist his help, she had to trust him. She nodded.

'Ah.' He sat back. 'Then she is a valuable child indeed.'

'Valuable?' Liz placed an arm protectively around Alice's shoulders. 'I don't understand.'

'You don't trust me,' he smiled. It wasn't a question, and she detected the steel underlying his voice.

'I don't know you.' She didn't want to offend him, but by now Liz could hardly breathe. She was beginning to sense that this had been a big mistake.

'What is there to know? I am a man of simple tastes. Ask anyone.' He reached for another tangerine and broke it into segments. She watched him, helpless to stop him feeding her child; wanting, more than anything, to leave, but finding herself unable to.

'What is it you really came for?' The deep-set eyes flickered upward, catching her off balance. 'If you need money, all you have to do is tell me.' Again the toothy grin. 'People come to me all the time because they know I will help them.'

'It's not money.'

'No? Something else then?'

Without warning he seized her wrist and held it firmly, almost without effort. She struggled to pull back, but couldn't move. With ease he tugged up the long sleeve of her blouse, past the elbow. Relentless eyes searched for the telltale tracks. She wriggled helplessly. When he was satisfied, he let go. Liz pulled her arm back, massaging her painful wrist. A segment of tangerine fell from Alice's mouth as she watched in silence, eyes wide. She crawled on to her mother's lap.

'You have no right . . .' Liz began, struggling to control her voice. It was futile, but he tilted his head understandingly.

'This is Cairo. Everyone's business is common knowledge.' He gestured with a wide sweep of the hand that encompassed their entire surroundings. It was true. Life was lived on the streets here. Hadn't she once admired the carved wooden *mashrabiyya* screens over the old windows, and wondered at the veils covering the faces of some of the women on the street, feeling their eyes sear through her flimsy clothes like hot pokers? She understood now this obsession with secrecy, the value of preserving a private space.

'She's my daughter,' Liz whispered hoarsely.

'But of course.'

'I want the best for her.'

'That's only natural.' He inclined his head.

Then Liz had managed to make her excuses, pull Alice into her arms and flee. Later that evening there was a knock at the door of the hotel room. It was late; she had been dozing, and rose from the bed half asleep. She opened the door a crack to peer round it. In the hallway stood a young boy, no more than twelve years old. He had a keen intelligent gaze despite his grimy appearance and an ear that was swollen and misshapen. They stared at one another for what felt like hours but was really only a matter of seconds.

'Yes? What do you want?' asked Liz.

Without a word he thrust forward an envelope. It was thick and heavy and she turned it over in her hands. There was nothing written on it. No name or address. Nothing. When she looked up the boy was gone.

Alice slept on blissfully, her damp hair stuck to her forehead with perspiration. Liz sat on the bed and opened the envelope. Inside was a bundle of banknotes. Dollars. A lot of them. So many she couldn't count. She rifled through quickly – fifties, hundreds, tens, twenties, no sense of order to them at all. And there was something else, something that shifted around at the bottom of the envelope. Throwing the money on to the bed, she tipped the rest of the contents out into her hand. A simple twist of paper. Liz stared at it. She knew what it was. She could feel her heart start to beat. It was fear, excitement, or both mixed up together, that coursed through her veins then. She knew what this was. It was what she had come here to get away from. Or had she really? Her first instinct was to throw it away. Don't even think about it, Liz. Just flush it down the toilet. And with that intention she got up and headed for the bathroom. She locked the door behind her and leaned against it, the wrap clenched between her fingers. All she had to do was take it one day at a time . . . But she was tired. Tired of the pain in her limbs, the dull ache behind her eyes. Tired of sleeplessness and weariness.

Lowering the toilet cover, she sat down and unfolded the wrap. She stared at the contents, feeling her pulse accelerate. She dipped in a finger and touched it to her tongue.

Still there was a moment's hesitation, in which she saw the road to ruin laid out before her in that single brown thread tapering across her hand. Then the despair rolled back over her like a thick carpet of cloud blotting out the sun, and there was no alternative. Kneeling on the floor, she tipped the heroin on to the seat cover and used the edge of the paper to divide it into narrow lines. She rolled the wrap into a tight tube, pushed it into her left nostril and leaned over. It was like sinking into a warm bath. She felt weightless and free, sliding back to the floor and slumping against the wall. Time stopped. Someone cut the safety line and she watched the blue world floating off into the dark void.

When she opened her eyes she realised it was light outside. Her head felt fuzzy and unclear. She struggled to her feet, her eyes going to the empty wrap on the floor beside her. She threw it aside as she wrestled with the door latch. The first thing she noticed was the money lying on the bed where she had left it. The second thing was that Alice was nowhere to be seen.

She checked the windows, the wardrobe, under the bed. Each option offered a fleeting, absurd ray of hope before the inevitable realisation. Then she was running. Along hallways, down stairwells, through the narrow arteries of the bazaar. She ran in disbelief, in shock, numbed, crying the name of her child. Alice. She walked until she was ready to drop. She was lost herself by then, delirious, finding herself reflected back in pieces, divided into strips by shards of mirrored glass, slivers of shiny metal. The men hanging around, leaning in doorways, called out as she went by, again and again, like a game.

'Hello, welcome!'

'Where you from?'

A gust of cold air wafted from a dark passage, making the hairs on the back of her neck stand up. She spun round, seized by the strange sensation that somebody was watching her, and found herself staring into the fierce gaze of Anubis the jackal, guardian of the Underworld. Or rather, an ebony carving decorated in gold leaf, of exactly the same height as her.

Alice was hidden somewhere in this nightmare . . . but where? Turning a corner and then another, not stopping, Liz ran left, right, left again. She paused for breath, looking back, only now she was not sure which way she had come. It all looked the same; the stalls, the narrow streets, the vegetable peelings on the ground, the discarded newspapers. Another corner brought her to a shop filled with junk no one would ever want: old rusty copper trays, wooden tables, strange tablets covered with letters that looked like no language she had ever seen before. Clusters of oil lamps dangled from the rafters. Centuries old. The kind a genie might fly out of if you rubbed them. A man shuffled out of the shadows. Liz looked at his wizened face, the wrinkles inscribed like hieroglyphics. Eyes filled with a very old light, in which she seemed to see her fate written. He smiled, revealing a row of stained yellow teeth. She closed her eyes tightly, then opened her mouth and screamed, 'Alice!'

THE GHOST RUNNER

A MAKANA INVESTIGATION

A question of honour. An eye for eye. The truth cannot stay buried for ever

It is 2002 and as tanks roll into the West Bank and the reverberations of 9/11 echo across the globe, tensions are running high on Cairo's streets when a routine surveillance job leads Private Investigator Makana to the horrific murder of a teenage girl. Seeking answers, he travels to Siwa, an oasis town on the edge of the great Sahara desert, where the law seems disturbingly far away. As violence follows him through the twisting, sand-blown streets, Makana discovers that the truth can be as deadly and as changeable as the desert beneath his feet.

'Bilal whisks the reader straight to the dark heart of Cairo ...
His prose has a subtlety that is rarely found in crime novels'
ECONOMIST

THE BURNING GATES

A MAKANA INVESTIGATION

**A war criminal on the run. A mercenary hunting him down.
A man caught in the crossfire**

Private Investigator Makana has a new client, the powerful art dealer Aram Kasabian. Kasabian wants him to track down a priceless painting that went missing from Baghdad during the US invasion. All the dealer can tell Makana is that the piece was smuggled into Egypt by an Iraqi war criminal who doesn't want to be found. Soon Makana finds himself caught between dangerous enemies on a trail that leads him into the darkness of war and threatens to send the new life he has built for himself up in flames.

'Government ministers mingle with gangsters in a superb
crime novel set in corrupt Cairo'
SUNDAY TIMES MUST READS

ORDER YOUR COPY:

BY PHONE: +44 (0) 1256 302 699; BY EMAIL: DIRECT@MACMILLAN.CO.UK

DELIVERY IS USUALLY 3–5 WORKING DAYS. FREE POSTAGE AND PACKAGING FOR ORDERS OVER £20.

ONLINE: WWW.BLOOMSBURY.COM/BOOKSHOP

PRICES AND AVAILABILITY SUBJECT TO CHANGE WITHOUT NOTICE.

B L O O M S B U R Y